The Life of Arseniev

The Life of Arseniev

YOUTH

Ivan Bunin

Books 1–4 translated by Gleb Struve and Hamish Miles
Book 5 translated by Heidi Hillis, Susan McKean, and Sven A. Wolf

Edited, Annotated, and with an Introduction by
Andrew Baruch Wachtel

NORTHWESTERN UNIVERSITY PRESS / EVANSTON, ILLINOIS

Northwestern University Press
Evanston, Illinois 60208-4210

Printed in the United States of America

ISBN   CLOTH 0-8101-1187-X
       PAPER 0-8101-1172-1

Library of Congress Cataloging-in-Publication Data

Bunin, Ivan Alekseevich, 1870–1953.
    [Zhizn´ Arsen´eva. English]
    The life of Arseniev : youth / Ivan Bunin ; books 1–4 translated
by Gleb Struve and Hamish Miles, book 5 translated by Heidi Hillis,
Susan McKean, and Sven A. Wolf ; edited, annotated, and with an
introduction by Andrew Baruch Wachtel.
        p.   cm. — (Studies in Russian literature and theory)
    English translation of books 1–4 published by Knopf in 1933 as The
well of days. Book 5 never before published in English.
    ISBN 0-8101-1187-X (cloth). — ISBN 0-8101-1172-1 (pbk.)
    1. Bunin, Ivan Alekseevich, 1870–1953—Fiction. I. Struve, Gleb.
II. Wachtel, Andrew. III. Title. IV. Series.
PG3453.B9Z213   1994   94-24869
891.73'3—dc20   CIP

The paper used in this publication meets the minimum requirements of the American National Standard for Information Sciences—Permanence of Paper for Printed Library Materials, ANSI Z39.48-1984.

Contents

Acknowledgments

First, I would like to thank my three former students, Heidi Hillis, Susan McKean, and Sven A. Wolf, who wanted a challenge and worked hard to meet it. Brenda Tunnock, director of the Multi-Media Learning Center at Northwestern University, agreed to scan the text of the first four books, and her assistant Tony Matthes did a fabulous job with the actual scanning. Thomas Marullo read the whole manuscript and made a number of helpful suggestions. Finally, I would like to express my appreciation for my editor, Susan Harris, and the rest of the Northwestern University Press staff for sticking with the project despite many complications in getting the rights to the novel.

The Life of Arseniev: Editor's Introduction

LITERATURE AND EXILE have gone hand in hand in Russian culture for most of the modern period. For example, in the nineteenth century, exile, either governmentally or self-imposed, was a prominent factor in the lives of such major writers as Alexander Pushkin, Nikolay Gogol, Ivan Turgenev, and Fedor Dostoevsky. The history of Pushkin's exile offers perhaps the paradigmatic case for this period; in 1820, by order of Tsar Alexander I, the twenty-one-year-old Pushkin was banished from St. Petersburg to the southern reaches of the Russian Empire. Ultimately, Pushkin was to spend six years away from the literary and cultural centers of the empire, at first filling trivial quasi-governmental posts in Kishinev and Odessa, and for the final two years holed up at his family estate under loose police surveillance. According to one scholar, "Exile made problematic for the rest of Pushkin's rather short life an entire set of attitudes toward what it meant for him to be a Russian and to be a writer in Russia."[1] The same could be said for all of the authors mentioned above: Gogol firmly believed that only the distance of self-imposed exile in Rome allowed him the perspective to write his masterpiece, *Dead Souls;* Turgenev's most trenchant analysis of the Russian condition of his day is expressed in the novel *Fathers and Children,* most of which was written in self-imposed European exile; finally, it was during his stint in a Siberian prison that Dostoevsky underwent the spiritual conversion which allowed him to produce his major novels after his return from exile.

By the twentieth century, therefore, the experience of exile and its potential as a spur to creativity was well ingrained in Russian culture. However, the situation in which a whole generation of exiled Russian writers found themselves after the 1917 Bolshevik revolution was, in many respects, completely unprecedented. For nineteenth-century Russian authors, exile was strictly personal: their friends and relatives went on living much as before; literary and cultural life continued uninterrupted in St. Petersburg and Moscow. What is more, except for Dostoevsky, these writers were able to communicate freely with the centers of Russian culture, and even to publish while in exile. That is to say, the material practices and forms of cultural life did not change radically, although the authors were removed from them. Exile was perceived as a phase that would conceivably come to an end with the return of the writer to the center of his land.

After 1917, however, previous assumptions regarding exile did not obtain. The writer was not merely separated from his homeland, but the homeland itself and everything it stood for had been destroyed. Exile became a permanent condition. It also became a mass phenomenon. While it is hard to say precisely what percentage of major prerevolutionary writers ended up leaving their country after the Bolshevik takeover, the numbers were quite considerable, and they included many luminaries of Russian culture: Dmitry Merezhkovsky, Zinaida Hippius, Konstantin Balmont, Vyacheslav Ivanov, Aleksey Remizov, Marina Tsvetaeva, and Alexander Kuprin were among the most illustrious. These authors, along with talented critics, philosophers, and historians, created an independent émigré culture in the interwar years, centered in Paris and Berlin. Although established writers tended to be in the forefront of things, a younger generation made its mark as well—for instance, it is from this milieu that Vladimir Nabokov emerged.

Perhaps the single most famous writer among the exiles, however, was Ivan Alexeevich Bunin (1870–1953). Born to an old impoverished gentry family and bred on an estate in the center of Russia's agricultural breadbasket, Bunin first appeared on the Russian literary scene in the late 1880s as a poet and then as a short-story writer. By the turn of the century he had been recognized as one of Russia's leading writers, and his status was confirmed by his being awarded the Russian Academy's highest literary prize (the Pushkin Prize) in 1903. He was intimate with most of the major Russian prerevolutionary writers, and particularly close to Anton Chekhov. A second Pushkin Prize was conferred in 1909, and the accolades for his work continued to pour in. Maxim Gorky, for example, proclaimed in 1911 that "the best contemporary writer is Ivan Bunin; soon this will become clear to all who sincerely love literature and the Russian language."[2] In the first decades of the twentieth century, Bunin turned more and more to prose rather than poetry. It was, however, a supremely lyrical, evocative prose, quite different from the more precise and terse style of contemporaries like Chekhov and Gorky. In the last years before the Revolution, Bunin produced a number of masterful novellas, including explorations of the decay and destruction of the patriarchal ways of life in the Russian countryside like *The Village* (*Derevnia*, 1909–10) and *Dry Valley* (*Sukhodol*, 1911).

After the Revolution, Bunin and his wife moved first to Kiev and then to Odessa. The latter city was fiercely contested during the civil war, and the Bunins did not leave until just before its final fall to the Red forces in 1920. Eventually, the Bunins made their way to France, where the writer was to spend most of the rest of his life. In 1923, they moved to a villa near Grasse in the south of France, where Bunin wrote most of his major émigré-period works, including *The Life of Arseniev*. It was there, too, that Bunin received the news that he had become the first Russian author to be awarded the world's most prestigious literary award, the Nobel Prize in literature for 1933.

The Life of Arseniev is unquestionably Bunin's major work from his émigré period and, along with some of the novels of Vladimir Nabokov, the most significant exploration of the émigré experience in twentieth-century Russian literature. The novel itself has had a strange publishing history. Bunin wrote and published the first four books serially from 1927 through 1929, and it was this version of the novel that was translated into English by Hamish Miles and Gleb Struve under the title *The Well of Days* (New York: Knopf, 1934). Bunin, however, was an inveterate reviser of his work, and *The Life of Arseniev* was no exception. In 1933 he began writing and publishing serially what was eventually to become Book Five of the novel but was called "Lika" at the time. Probably because "Lika" was not officially part of Bunin's novel, this section was never added to the existing English translation. However, according to his wife and biographer, "Ivan Alekseevich published 'Lika' separately only because *The Life of Arseniev* had already been published, but at the first opportunity he added 'Lika' as the fifth chapter of *The Life of Arseniev*." This opportunity did not arise for quite some time, and it was not until 1952 that the Chekhov publishing house in New York brought out a complete edition of Bunin's novel. Bunin made substantial cuts in the first four books and added the "Lika" chapter to create the final version of the novel.

The Life of Arseniev was the crowning achievement of Bunin's illustrious career. It is also the culminating work of a specific tradition of Russian writing: the pseudo-autobiographical novel devoted to childhood. Earlier examples of this tradition include Lev Tolstoy's trilogy, *Childhood* (1852), *Boyhood* (1854), *Youth* (1857), and Sergey Aksakov's *The Childhood Years of Bagrov's Grandson* (1858). In turn, these pseudo-autobiographical novels spawned an entire mythology of Russian childhood, particularly among Russia's gentry class. Childhood was seen as a happy, carefree time, spent in the countryside in the bosom of a loving family that normally consisted of an emotional, serious, loving mother and a spendthrift, pleasantly disorganized father. Memories of this type of childhood sustained many a Russian through darker adult days. In fact, this childhood mythology became thoroughly ingrained in Russian culture and was eventually challenged by a new set of pseudo-autobiographical works, including Maxim Gorky's *Childhood* (1913) and Andrei Belyi's *Kotik Letaev* (1916).[3]

The pseudo-autobiography is an autobiographically based work that imitates the autobiography in all respects but one: its author and narrator are not the same person. Although the formal distinction might seem trivial

3

(after all, lacking the title page, it can be impossible to tell a "real" autobiography from a pseudo-autobiography), it is not. For both author and reader, the lack of identification between author and narrator means that the work is to be treated as fiction, read and judged by a set of criteria different from those applied to nonfiction. Although the pseudo-autobiography often sticks quite closely to the facts of its author's life (and must include substantial amounts of autobiographical material), it cannot simply be considered a subset of the autobiography proper. In a recent influential book on autobiography, Philippe Lejeune defines the genre as follows: "A retrospective prose narrative that a real person writes about his own existence. The emphasis is on his personal life, in particular on the development of his personality."[4] According to Lejeune, if the author hides behind the mask of an independent narrator, he breaks the unspoken "autobiographical pact" that exists between himself and his reader. Once this pact is broken, the reader perceives the work as fiction, no matter how much autobiographical material it contains.

I believe that Lejeune is only partially correct here. It is true that the author loses some of the immediacy of autobiography when he chooses a fictional narrator. On the other hand, if the fiction produced is in the form of an autobiography, and if it contains autobiographical material, certain narrative advantages that would be lost in a third-person text are retained. Thus, the pseudo-autobiography frees the novelist from a too close association with his text, while partially maintaining the special bond that links the reader of an autobiographical text and its narrator.[5] In effect, the pseudo-autobiography denies the identification of the author with the narrator while simultaneously enticing the reader into believing in its existence.

In the case of *The Life of Arseniev*, Bunin uses the pseudo-autobiographical form in order to show the ways in which Arseniev's experience was typical for that of Russia as a whole. For, if the task of a normal autobiography is to justify and explain an individual existence,[6] the writer of a pseudo-autobiography should also try to generalize, to let the fictional narrator be both an individual and a symbol for his age. One of Bunin's purposes in *The Life of Arseniev* was indeed to speak for an entire generation. Whenever asked, he was careful to insist that the novel was not an autobiography: "I definitely do not want my work to be distorted, that is described by the unfitting label autobiography, nor connected to my life; that is, discussed not as *The Life of Arseniev*, but as the life of Bunin. Perhaps there is much that is directly autobiographical in *The Life of Arseniev*. But to speak of that is not the business of *artistic* criticism."[7] Although he does not deny the use of autobiographical material (which would have been pointless), Bunin emphasizes that its presence is relatively unimportant. Arseniev's experience, the peculiar concatenation of time, space, and culture which he describes, exists independently of Bunin. The facts of Bunin's life make up only one of the novel's subtexts.[8] The others are composed of material borrowed from other pseudo-autobiographies, from Russian history and literature in general, and from Russian life in the last decades before the Revolution. The "artistry" of the novel lies in Bunin's ability to create, from these varied subtexts, a work so true to itself that readers could take it for an autobiography.

In the wake of the Bolshevik Revolution, the gentry autobiographical tradition should have been as irrelevant as the class whose myths it had once expressed. Paradoxically, however, the myths of gentry childhood thrived and even became stronger in Russian émigré culture. In their haste to depart after the Revolution, the émigrés left their most precious possessions behind. Among the few things almost all of them carried into exile were rose-colored memories of the days before the Bolshevik takeover. As the reality of prerevolutionary Russia gradually faded farther and farther into the mists of time, the myth of the happy childhood lost none of its lustre. In fact, in postrevolutionary émigré autobiographies a proper childhood became almost an article of faith, the badge of a true aristocratic background. Thus, when in *Speak, Memory* Nabokov says, "The nostalgia I have been cherishing all these years is a hypertrophied sense of lost childhood," he is merely one of the last and greatest writers in a 100-year-old tradition.[9]

Among the rich lode of émigré works, fictional and nonfictional, Bunin's novel *The Life of Arseniev* stands out both as the most persuasive attempt to keep the Russian gentry conception of childhood alive and as the crowning achievement of the traditional pseudo-autobiography. Building on the rich legacy of the nineteenth century, Bunin captured the poignancy of an individual life while at the same time continuing the cultural and historical traditions of the entire gentry line of Russian literature. The traditional characteristics of the Russian pseudo-autobiography—idealization of life on a country estate, bittersweet nostalgia for lost time and space, an idealized mother figure, an eccentric father, and the sensitive central figure of the experiencing child—all are present and receive an unprecedentedly satisfying treatment in *The Life of Arseniev*.[10]

In part Bunin succeeded in summarizing the results of more than a century of cultural, literary, and social development because he quite consciously built on the work of those who had come before him. At the same time, the new circumstances of postrevolutionary Russia and his place as an exiled writer lent Bunin's nostalgia a depth that was rarely possible for nineteenth-century writers. For Tolstoy, Aksakov, and their gentry followers, nostalgia was primarily for lost time. The innocence of youth was gone forever, but the basic surroundings (even if threatened by change) remained. In addition to the inevitable displacement in time, Bunin was fated to experience an irrevocable displacement in space; not only was youth spent, but the Russia he had known, along with the social structures that had been characteristic of it for more than a hundred and fifty years, had been destroyed. What is more, the line of Russian gentry culture that had produced Pushkin, Turgenev, Tolstoy, Aksakov, and Bunin himself had been severed by the social upheavals that accompanied the Revolution. Bunin felt himself to be the last of his race, the end of a historical line, and his literary expression of this feeling deepened the interplay between personal and general that is typical for the genre as a whole.

The extent to which Bunin felt the Tolstoyan tradition can be seen late in Arseniev's novel when the struggling young writer is searching for a theme. "So, I thought, maybe just start a story about myself? But how? Along the lines of *Childhood, Boyhood?* Or still simpler? 'I was born in a certain place at a certain time . . . '" (p. 194). In addition to emphasizing the place of the novel in the Russian literary tradition, this passage is recognizable to the reader as the embryonic draft of the novel's second paragraph, which consists of the sentence "I was born a half-century ago in Central Russia, in the country, on my father's estate" (p. 17). The device of allowing the reader to see the author (in this case, the putative author Arseniev) actually creating the work whose final result is the finished novel is common for various types of first-person narrative. As we shall see when we examine the dynamics of the novel's beginning, however, the way in which Arseniev actually starts his novel shows a great deal more sophistication than the beginning he first proposes. In the actual novel the narration is not uniformly retrospective. There is a constant and complicated overlapping of time frames, and we see events both through the eyes of the narrator looking back from his vantage point in time and from the unmediated point of view of the child. The result is that an event which happened later in life can appear to have occurred in the distant past, while events from early childhood are often seen depicted in the present.

The first chapter of the novel is one of the most evocative in Russian literature and introduces all of the work's basic themes and compositional methods. It begins with a quotation that imitates the diction of a Russian saint's life, although its provenance is not revealed: "Such things and deeds as are not written down are covered in darkness and given over to the sepulchre of oblivion, while those that are written down are like unto animate ones" (p. 17). Through the sentence's archaic form one feels the weight of the Russian literary tradition, the crucial, almost mystical importance of the act of writing itself, and the written word's ability, at least figuratively, to cheat death. While fear of death and oblivion has always been a powerful stimulus to writing, an explicit connection between writing down one's life and the literary vocation of the narrator had not been part of the Russian pseudo-autobiographical tradition. In earlier works the narrator is not a professional writer, and the question of why he chooses to write or recite his autobiography is left open. In *The Life of Arseniev*, on the other hand, we are dealing with the modernist phenomenon of the "(self-) portrait of the artist

6

as a young man." Arseniev is an artist, and what we are reading is a consciously literary work.

The next sentence, "I was born a half-century ago in Central Russia, in the country, on my father's estate" both does and does not give specific information about the writer. It places him in time and space and identifies him as a member of a certain class, but leaves much room for generalization. This is certainly a more open-ended beginning than the one proposed by the fledgling writer Arseniev later in the novel. The very vagueness of his temporal and spatial designations has a generalizing, depersonalizing effect. As he comes from the "center" of Russia, the narrator, it can be inferred, is a typical representative of his nation. The reader's desire for further autobiographical detail is, however, frustrated by a philosophical passage that delves into the realm of the abstract. It begins: "We lack a sense of our beginning and end."

Naturally, the search for beginnings (the beginning of life and the dawn of consciousness) is often important for the autobiography, particularly because the idea of beginnings is closely connected to the problem of memory. As Arseniev asks a bit later, "What do we remember—we who sometimes remember even yesterday with difficulty?" (p. 22). Despite the inherent impossibility of the task, it is the writer's duty to search for that elusive beginning. The following passages from Bunin's posthumously published "Notes" illustrate the extent to which Arseniev echoes Bunin's feelings here: "As with everyone, my life is something having neither beginning nor end, it is a book doomed to decay and oblivion. . . . Birth is in no way my beginning. My beginning is in the impenetrable darkness in which I was surrounded from conception to birth and in my father, my mother, my grandfathers, great-grandfathers, and forefathers, for they are also me."[11]

For Bunin, a partial solution to the problem of beginnings was the writing of his pseudo-autobiographical novel. He wished to pierce the veil of personal consciousness, to allow his narrator to describe the world before he was born. Arseniev constitutes his "prenatal" world through an exploration of his historical and cultural roots. The history of Russia and of Russian culture is important to him because it provides that "beginning" which personal memory is incapable of giving. His questions as to his personal origins are echoed by his lack of complete information about his family: "Of the Arseniev stock and its origin, I really know nothing. What, after all, do we know? I only know that in the Armorial our family is included among those 'whose origins are lost in the mists of time.' I know that our family is 'noble though impoverished,' and that all my life I have sensed that nobility, feeling proud and glad that I am not one of those who have neither kith nor kin" (p. 17). The narrator's story is inseparable from that of his ancestors.[12]

The next two paragraphs of the first chapter consist of a prayer for the dead and a commentary on that prayer. The use of a borrowed text (literary or ecclesiastical) followed by commentary is typical of Arseniev's narrative technique throughout the novel. The theme of death, treated on many levels from the intensely personal to the historically significant, complements the literary and personal concerns of the narrator. In particular, the loss caused by death is easily linked to the loss of a way of life and the loss of Russia, so that the personal, the historical, and the cosmic are never entirely separated. The section of the service reproduced here asks God to give peace to those of his servants, "From Adam even to those among our fathers and brethren, friends and kinsmen, who have served Thee this day in purity" (p. 17).

The narrator's commentary shows that he has grasped the historical implications of the prayer as well as the religious ones. He emphasizes the idea of community and the ability of the religious service, by virtue of its constant repetition, to escape the time frame of birth and death to which humans are subject. "Is it not a joy to feel one's connection, one's communion, with 'our fathers and brethren, friends and kinsmen' who have sometime done that service?" (p. 17). Religion was not a subject of great concern to the narrator of the nineteenth-century pseudo-autobiography. For Arseniev, however, the Orthodox liturgy, its ritual unchanged (or barely changed) by time or place, is an anchor, a last connection to a way of life that is gone forever.

The chapter ends with a paragraph that combines the themes of history and death and adds one more: that of exile. The narrator's position as an exiled writer in the south of France gives him a spatial distance from his childhood, which, together with the distance caused by time, encourages his mind to range freely over his past. Because Arseniev cannot experience Russia physically, his nostalgia for a childhood paradise takes on another dimension. This situation is, of course, typical for the exiled writer, and other exiles also make extensive use of the double nostalgic distance.[13]

One part of Arseniev's personality was forged in relation to his family: to his loving and emotional mother, his light-headed and slightly eccentric father, and his older brothers; this type of family was typical of the Russian country-dwelling gentry. There was only one other influence as strong as that of the family: the land itself. Arseniev, writing his autobiography in the south of France, feels compelled to point out the crucial importance of the physical surroundings of his childhood. "I was born and grew up, as I said, in an absolutely open country such as cannot even be imagined by a European. A vast expanse, with neither obstacles nor boundaries, surrounded me" (p. 43). In this world, time is measured in the natural rhythms of the changing seasons, birth and death. For Arseniev, recollections of the natural world form a lifelong theme. It is his ability to recall sights, smells, and sounds that transports him back into his past and allows him to compose his memoir. Looking back to early childhood, he says that the world around the cowshed had a "special look, color, smell, and taste" (p. 25). Such synesthetic associative patterns are one of the roots of his creativity. He speaks a bit later of how he fell in love with a girl whom he saw for the first time next to a fountain that was surrounded by a flower called "tobacco." After setting the scene of youthful puppy love, Arseniev says, "From time to time, throughout my life, I remembered her and the coolness of the fountain and the playing of the military band as soon as I caught that scent" (p. 65). It is the associative power of Arseniev's memory that allows him to build up his self-portrait.

If an exploration of self is one basis for the novel, another is Bunin's attempt to answer the question that Arseniev poses in very the first book: "And why, in general, did Russia meet the fate she did, destroyed before our eyes with such miraculous rapidity?" (p. 44). Before Arseniev can address this question, however, he must first explain what gives him the right to do so. He must show his connection to the Russian past, must generalize his voice so that it can speak for the country as a whole.

After listening to his father's stories of bygone days, Arseniev begins to realize that he is not simply an individual with no ties to the outside world, and to be thrilled by this knowledge. "No doubt it was on that particular evening that I first became aware of being Russian and living in Russia . . . and suddenly I felt Russia, felt her past and present, her wild, sometimes terrible yet somehow captivating peculiarities, and my own kinship, my intimate relation to her" (p. 56). This passage is typical of the poetics of *The Life of Arseniev,* with its anaphoric verbs, parallel constructions, and balance between a simultaneous personalizing and generalizing tendency. Arseniev, writing, as he tells us, from France, far from his native country, speaks for the entire Russian emigration.

At many points in the narrative Arseniev's view of a thing is conditioned by its historical significance. He is particularly fascinated by anything that can be called "ancient," an adjective which appears with amazing frequency in the novel. Both the natural and the man-made worlds are seen historically. Looking at a river, Arseniev thinks, "even in the days of the Pechenegs, it had followed the same course" (p. 82). Looking out at a barrow through the window of a train, Arseniev feels a nebulous, but nevertheless strong connection between his world and the prehistoric Russian past. "There was here, despite all its simplicity, something really extraordinary, something so ancient that it seemed infinitely alien to all living, modern things; and yet it was so familiar, so close, so intimate" (p. 146). The dialectic of ancient/modern is typical for his perception. It is not clear from these historical and geographical musings how Arseniev finds a synthesis for this dialectic. However, when he describes his feelings upon seeing two paintings on the gates of a monastery, the source of the connection becomes more obvious. The paintings depict two saints holding parchment scrolls in their hands. Arseniev muses: "How long have they been standing thus, for how many centuries have they been not of this world? Everything will pass; everything passes; the time will come when we won't be of this world either . . . and these ancient Russian saints with their holy and wise writings in their hands will still stand just as dispassionately and sadly on the gates" (p. 82).

The importance of "antiquity" in light of the novel's first sentence now becomes clear. These relics preserve the memory of a past that has otherwise died and left no record. Anything that does leave some record has, in effect, cheated death and prolonged the forces of life in the world. The saints, for example, have done so both through their painted presence on the gates (which implies the work of an unknown human artist) and through the parchments they hold, through the written word; that is, through the very medium Arseniev has chosen to cheat death and decay. The written word, by leaving a trace of the man who has written it, imparts immortality both to the writer and to the human race as a whole.

Throughout the novel Arseniev tries to orient himself in the flow of historical time. The work's original title, *The Well of Days*, reflects this concern with beginnings or origins. In addition to personal memory and to history, however, there is another, parallel though not synchronized, process in which he must find a place. Since, as opposed to the previous narrators of Russian pseudo-autobiographies, Arseniev is a professional writer, it is only natural for him to define himself in terms of the literary tradition as well. He measures his perceptions and his writing against the achievements of Russian literature, and his own autobiography is an extended dialogue with the Russian literary past.

In this respect, too, Arseniev closely resembles his creator. Bunin felt that he had a special place as the last in a great series of Russian writers linked by upbringing, shared culture, and a unique feeling for Russia in general and the Russian language in particular. He expressed this sentiment in a number of places, but perhaps most strongly in an article on Tolstoy:

> I say this too, as Tolstoy's fellow-countryman, belonging to the same background as Tolstoy . . . a wonderful place, he has many glorious fellow-countrymen! Zhukovsky and Tolstoy—from near Tula. Tiutchev, Leskov, Turgenev, Fet, the brothers Kireevsky, and the brothers Zhemchuzhnikov—from near Orel, Anna Bunin and Polonsky—from near Riazan', Koltsov, Nikitin, Garshin and Pisarev—from near Voronezh. . . . Even Pushkin and Lermontov are partially ours, since their relatives, the Voeikovs and the Arsenievs, are also from our area, from the same kvass, as they say here.[14]

In exile, after a revolution that had clearly swept away the tradition forever, it was up to Bunin and, specifically, to his creation Arseniev, to keep the flame alive, to ensure that the traditions of the "gentry" line of Russian literature were not forgotten. Arseniev thinks in more or less the same terms, although, characteristically, he merely hints at the connection without expressly making it: "Yesterday, I heard that somebody's hunt rode by along the highroad to the outlying field, together with the hunt of the young Tolstoys. Isn't it wonderful—I am *his* contemporary, and even his neighbor! After all, it is the same as if one were to live at the same time as and next to Pushkin" (p. 134). Arseniev constantly measures himself against the heritage of the "gentry" line in Russian literature. He chooses to include the visits he made to the estate of Lermontov (p. 133) and to the one that was supposed to be Turgenev's model for *A Nest of Gentry* (p. 161).

Arseniev perceives the world through the mediation of the literary tradition from his earliest childhood. As he explains: "A great impression was produced on me by Gogol's 'Old-World Landowners' and 'A Terrible Vengeance.' What unforgettable passages they are! How marvelously they still ring in my ears, having from childhood irrevocably entered my inner self, endeared to me for the rest of my life, having turned out to be among those most important things which went into the making of my 'vital substance' (to use Gogol's own expression)" (p. 41).

Arseniev creates entire chapters of his novel—that is, he characterizes entire portions of his life—through a series of poetic quotations accompanied by short explanatory commentaries. As certain religious people find quotations from the Bible or the Koran to characterize their actions and feelings, so Arseniev uses Russian literature.

He starts the chapter describing the period when he was about fifteen years old with a simple statement: "At that time Pushkin was a genuine part of my life" (p. 109). Indeed, the connection between life and poetry is so close that it is not clear whether life produces poetic situations or whether poetry allows those situations to exist.

> Here I wake up on a frosty sunny morning and feel doubly happy because I can exclaim with him, "There's frost and sun—a lovely day"—with him who described that morning so wonderfully and also gave me a wonderful image: "And still you doze, my lovely friend. . . ."[15] (P. 109)

The outside world recalls the poem to Arseniev's mind, but then the context of the poem begins to live its own life and to give him a special, poetically associative, way of seeing the world. The remainder of this short chapter continues in the same way. The narrator describes a situation from life and then borrows a Pushkin quote that allows him to express the situation in language. Pushkin teaches him to crystallize the ephemeral world through art. Bunin has discovered an entirely new way of expressing the difference between the adult's perception and the child's. While the adult Arseniev is now capable of choosing his own words to describe what he felt and saw at the time, the adolescent (although perhaps feeling the same thing) could express it only in another's words.

In addition to providing a vocabulary for describing the natural world, a world that Arseniev more or less understood by virtue of having grown up in it, the world of poetry provides details about a host of other, less directly familiar situations. In the natural world the external situation evokes its poetic representation. In the area of human emotions, on the other hand, poetry speaks first and provides a pattern for existence. Describing an early love, Arseniev says:

> My feelings for Lisa Bibikov were a result not only of my childishness but also of my fondness for our way of life, with which all Russian poetry was once so closely connected. I was in love with Lisa in an old-fashioned, poetical way, as with a being belonging entirely to our set of people. The spirit of that set, to which my imagination added a halo of romance, seemed to me the more beautiful as it was in the process of vanishing forever under my very eyes. (P. 110)

This passage illustrates the relationship between life and art characteristic of the adult Arseniev's worldview. The girl is not merely a beloved, but a symbol for a specific historical time and place and for a whole literary culture. All of Russian poetry was "once" tied to Russian life. Of course, from a position of exile it is obvious that the connection has been lost. Even so, the admission that the spirit of the gentry way of life was "vanishing forever under my very eyes" indicates that it was not simply the experience of revolution and exile that destroyed the organic unity of the Russian social and literary tradition. Indeed, Bunin had held a nostalgic view of the Russian literary tradition and had searched for the reasons for the "fall of Russian literature" well before the Revolution. He sometimes blamed it on the "raznochintsy" (that is, the nongentry writers and intellectuals), "almost completely lacking tradition, thrown off the track by the eighties and nineties and, in addition, by that which had to go along with those years, European influences."[16]

However, Bunin did not exempt his own class from a share in the blame for the Revolution. In *The Life of Arseniev* this criticism comes through in Arseniev's meditation on the course of his brother's life. Analyzing his brother's involvement with a group of populists, Arseniev wonders why he became so caught up by the personality of a local activist named Dobrokhotov. He rejects any political reasons for his brother's concern and adds:

> But what did my brother have in common with Dobrokhotov? . . . Obviously it was just a result of that everlasting light-headedness, the enthusiasm so characteristic of the Russian nobility, and which the Radishchevs, Chatskys, Rudins, Ogarevs, Herzens never gave up, even in their old age; because Dobrokhotov's qualities were deemed to be lofty, heroic; and, finally, for the simple reason that, recalling Dobrokhotov, he recalled all that happy festive atmosphere amid which his youth had been flowing. (P. 76)

This passage is noteworthy for a number of reasons. The most important, perhaps, is the realization of the historical continuum of Russian revolutionary thought and the identification of its cause, not with conditions in Russia, but with the character of a certain group of people. The fact that Arseniev does not distinguish between fictitious literary personages and actual historical figures illustrates the extent to which he perceives life and art as being intertwined. He sees the same characteristics in Radishchev (an eighteenth-century author), Herzen (author and publicist of the 1840s–60s), and literary heroes like Chatsky (from Griboedov's *Woe from Wit*, 1820s) or Rudin (the hero of Turgenev's novel of the same name, 1856). The double subtext of literary and historical roots is as important to Arseniev's explanation of his family as to his conception of the novel as a whole. The text is centered at the point where literary and historical lines of development cross.

Immediately after the description and analysis of his brother's "revolutionary" activity, the focus is broadened and the author's voice pronounces a universal judgment on Russia itself: "That everlasting Russian need of holiday! . . . wasn't it the traditional dream of rivers flowing with milk, of unfettered freedom, of holiday, that was one of the main causes, for instance, of the Russian revolutionary spirit? And what, generally speaking, *is* a Russian protester, rebel, revolutionary, always ridiculously severed from reality and despising it?" (p. 76). This is certainly not a very orthodox interpretation of the Russian revolutionary movement, but it shows Arseniev's concern to understand all the phenomena that affected his life within their historical context. Thus, in Arseniev, Bunin created a narrator for whom no situation in life or nature exists as a thing in itself. Everything is refracted through the subtexts of Russian literature and a certain type of Russian life.

Nowhere is this clearer than in the chapter that describes Arseniev's decision to travel through the Ukraine. He talks a bit about the wonders of the past and then says, *"The Tale of Igor's Campaign* drove me wild" (p. 150). This statement is followed by a series of quotations from the poem, all given as a background to and an explanation for the journey. To some extent, Arseniev becomes Igor and sees the world through the medium of the Igor tale. "I visited those very banks of the Donets where in the olden days the prince had fled from captivity, 'like an ermine into the rushes, like a white goose on the water'; then I went to the Dnieper, to the very spot where it 'pierced the rocky mountains across the Polovtsian land'" (p. 150). He enters Kiev to the sounds of the populace rejoicing at Igor's return. But, instead of ending his journey with a triumphant return from exile (as occurs in the original), he inverts the order and ends his modern-day "tale" in the steppe, to the accompaniment of Yaroslavna's heart-wrenching lament. For the adult Arseniev, despite his verbal ability to discover "temps perdu," realizes that the past has been destroyed, and that the loss commemorated by Yaroslavna's lament is more appropriate to the situation than the triumphant return from exile—a return which, for Russian culture and the way of life that Arseniev had known as a child, can never be.

For Arseniev, both history and literature, important as they are in and of themselves, are particularly crucial because they represent the poetization of loss, death, and destruction. The themes of death and decay and Arseniev's growing ability to come to terms with them, primarily through the act of writing (that is, preserving their memory so that they are not "covered in darkness and given over to the sepulchre of oblivion"), become more and more central in the course of the novel.

The theme of death is sounded on the first page: "Are we not born with the sense of death?" (p. 17). In the course of the novel's first book, Arseniev recounts his reminiscences of three deaths: that of a farm worker who drives a cart and horse over a cliff into a ravine; that of his younger sister; and that of his grandmother. Book Two closes with the death of Arseniev's brother-in-law. Book Three begins with a long description of the brother-in-law's funeral. Arseniev sees death as a type of parting and measures time by these partings. They do not always have to include a person's death to have an aura of finality about them. He starts Book Two, for example, with the line "on the day when I left Kamenka, not realizing that I was leaving it for good . . ." (p. 55). Book Four begins: "My last days at Baturino were also the last of my family's former life" (p. 125). Thus, Arseniev's life is impelled by a whole series of deaths, those of people close to him and those of an entire way of life.

There is one death in the novel, in this case not of a member of Arseniev's family, that typifies the dual nature of the pseudo-autobiographical narrative. It confirms the existence of the narrator in two places and two times joined by the act of reminiscing. In addition, the parallel deaths described, those of Grand Duke Nikolay Nikolaevich Senior (the son of Nikolay I) and his son, Nikolay Nikolaevich Junior, place the narration within the context of historical events. They provide the narrator with still another opportunity to muse on the meaning of death and to reemphasize the destruction of Russia and his exile from it. When Arseniev is working in the offices of the Orel newspaper, *The Voice*, he sees the funeral train of the grand duke on its way from the Crimea to Moscow. He watches in fascination as a gigantic young hussar (Nikolay Nikolaevich Junior, who was about six feet six) steps out of the train to salute the crowd. Everything is solemn, elegant, regal.

Up until this point the narrative has proceeded chronologically. The narrator has hinted at his position as an exile in France a number of times, but he has never described anything of his life there. Now, prodded by the reminiscences connected with this death and its symbolic implications, he moves thirty-eight years into the future, almost to the actual time of writing the novel. Both Arseniev and Nikolay are living in exile in southern France. Arseniev reads about the grand duke's death in the newspaper. He thinks: "Shall

I go there? It is inconceivably strange to have met but twice, and both times in the company of death" (p. 156). Even so, the pull is too strong for him to stay away. As always, Arseniev must test himself, must see if he can create life from death, as he has done so many times in the course of his life and his narrative. He looks at the dead man and listens to the beginning of the funeral service: "that low, harmonious chanting, the rhythmic tinkling of the censer, the sorrowfully submissive, dolefully affectionate invocations and supplications that have already sounded a million times on earth! Only the names change in these supplications, and for every name the turn comes in due time" (p. 157). The Church Slavic of the funeral service is interspersed between Arseniev's musings on death, just as in earlier chapters Pushkin's poetry filled the gaps where unquoted words could not express the requisite feeling. The universal fact of death as expressed in the Orthodox burial service is linked to the specifics of Nikolay's life and to Arseniev's own fate by the latter's associative memory. "I think about his past life, so vast and complex; and I think, too, of my own" (p. 158).

In adapting the pseudo-autobiography to the new literary and social conditions prevailing in exile after the Revolution, Bunin was an archaist and an innovator simultaneously. In matters of style he is unquestionably an archaist; many of his sentences could easily have come directly from a novel of Tolstoy or Turgenev. The family structures and childhood situation he depicts are very similar to the ones that Aksakov (describing the 1790s) and Tolstoy (describing the 1830s and 1840s) had described. This was possible, in part, because of the remarkable continuity of Russian gentry life; but, in addition, it was the result of a conscious decision by Bunin. He wished to emphasize his connection to his predecessors and therefore arranged his text to include as much traditional childhood material as he could.

On the other hand, there is much that is new in Bunin's work. He makes his central character a professional writer. This both fits with the general modernist trend of producing "a portrait of an artist" and helps to motivate the very existence of the pseudo-autobiographical text. More importantly, Bunin weaves the historical and historico-literary situation of his narrator into the text in subtle and complicated ways. Arseniev feels his connection to real events in the real world far more strongly than do the narrators of nineteenth-century pseudo-autobiographies. In part, the actuality of the historical situation in the novel is a function of Bunin's reaction to the physical dislocation caused by the Revolution. Nineteenth-century writers, while often affected by personal shocks, were spared a "world-historical event" of such sweeping consequence. Bunin felt a need to explain the Revolution, and this necessity (which directs the novel away from the more personal orientation of its precursors) is reflected in Arseniev's constant concern with the historical situation.

In addition, Arseniev's profession allows him to fashion a much more consciously literary text. Bunin's narrator weaves large portions of his text around other works of literature. This technique of subtext with commentary has a literary effect similar to the historical effect produced by Arseniev's musings on "world-historical events": it places the narrative in a tradition and, most importantly, enforces the narrator's unspoken desire to show that the literature of emigration is the true continuation of Russian literature. Similar techniques are used by other émigré writers (particularly Nabokov) in order to emphasize their rightful place in a national literature which, in their homeland, had no use for them.

Finally, the extraordinary concern with death, decay, and destruction balanced by the capacity of art (primarily verbal art) to resurrect lost time and space is a theme which had not been typical of Bunin's nineteenth-century models. This is, of course, a common theme in modernist art, but it is lent new poignancy by the tragedy through which Bunin (and his surrogate, Arseniev) lived. Even the final death in the novel (that of Lika, the woman with whom Arseniev lived for a number of years) is redeemed on the last page by two short paragraphs in the voice of the adult narrator: one describes the notebook she gave him and the words she wrote in it; the other depicts his vision of her in a dream. This final visual image, clearly resurrected in association with Lika's literary heritage (meager as that may be), is symbolic of the narrator's quest throughout the novel: to write down and thereby preserve the personal, literary, and historical world of his youth and the gentry tradition to which he belonged.

Andrew Baruch Wachtel
Evanston, Illinois
1994

Book One

Such things and deeds as are not written down are covered in darkness and given over to the sepulchre of oblivion, while those that are written down are like unto animate ones. . . .

I was born a half-century ago in Central Russia, in the country, on my father's estate.[1]

We lack a sense of our beginning and end. And it is a great pity that I was told exactly when I was born. Had I not been told, I would have no idea of my age—the more so as I do not as yet at all feel its burden—and would therefore be spared the absurd thought that I must supposedly die in ten or in twenty years' time. And had I been born and lived on a desert island, I would not have suspected even the existence of death. "What luck that would have been!" I am tempted to add. Yet who knows? Perhaps, a great misfortune. Besides, is it really true that I would not have suspected it? Are we not born with the sense of death? and if not, if I had not suspected it, would I be so fond of life as I am, and as I used to be?

Of the Arseniev stock and its origin, I really know nothing. What, after all, do we know? I only know that in the Armorial our family is included among those "whose origins are lost in the mists of time." I know that our family is "noble though impoverished," and that all my life I have sensed that nobility, feeling proud and glad that I am not one of those who have neither kith nor kin.[2] On the day dedicated to the Holy Spirit, the church invites us at mass to "do homage to the memory of all who died since time began." It offers up on that day a beautiful prayer full of deep meaning: "O Lord, let all Thy servants rest within Thy courts and in Abraham's bosom—from Adam even to those among our fathers and brethren, friends and kinsmen, who have served Thee this day in purity!"

Is it accidental that service is mentioned here? Is it not a joy to feel one's connection, one's communion, with "our fathers and brethren, friends and kinsmen" who have sometime done that service? Our remotest ancestors, too, believed in the doctrine of the "pure, continual Path of the father of all that is," handed on from mortal parents to mortal offspring through immortal "continual" life; they believed that it was commanded by the will of Agni[3] to watch over the purity, the continuity of blood and stock, in order to prevent the desecration of that Path, lest it should be interrupted; they believed that every birth must further purify the blood of those born, and enhance the closeness of their kinship with Him Who is the sole father of all that is.

Among my ancestors there were probably many bad men too. And yet from generation to generation my ancestors enjoined one another to remember and watch over their blood. And how shall I express the emotions with which I sometimes look at our family crest? A knight's armor, coat of mail, and helmet with ostrich feathers; and beneath, a shield; and on its azure field, in the middle—a ring, emblem of loyalty and eternity, toward which, from above and below, point three rapiers with cross-shaped hilts.

In the country which for me has replaced my native land, there are many towns like the one that gave me refuge, towns once glorious but now decayed, poor, living out their humdrum everyday life. And yet over that life there always reigns—and not in vain—some gray tower of the Crusaders' times, the vast mass of a cathedral with its glorious portal protected by an immemorial guard of sacred carven figures, a cock perched high up on the cross, God's exalted herald calling toward the celestial city.

2

My first recollection, something trivial and yet perplexing. I call to mind a large room lit by the sun of a late summer's day, spreading its parching glow over the sloping hill-side seen through the window facing south. . . . And that is all—only one single instant! Why was it just on that day and at that hour, at that precise moment, and on such a slight occasion, that for the first time my consciousness flamed up so brightly as to make it already possible for my memory to come into play? And why, immediately afterward, was it extinguished for a long time?

I always remember my early childhood with sadness. Every childhood is sad; barren is that quiet world in which a timid and tender soul not yet quite awakened to life is dreaming its dream of life, still alien to everybody and everything. Golden childhood, a happy time, people usually say. No, it is an unhappy, morbidly sensitive, miserable time.

Was my childhood sad for some particular reason? The fact, for instance, that I grew up amid great solitude? Lonely fields, a solitary manor in their midst. . . . In winter, a boundless snowy sea; in summer, a sea of grainfields, grass, and flowers. . . . And the eternal quietude of those fields; their enigmatic silence. . . . But, does a dormouse or a lark grow sad in quiet and seclusion? No, they ask for nothing, they marvel at nothing, they do not sense that hidden presence which the human soul always fancies in the world surrounding it; they know neither the call of spaces nor the course of time. I knew all that, even then. The depth of the summer evening sky, the melancholy vista of the fields betokened something else that seemed to exist apart from them, called forth a dream and a yearning after something I lacked, moved me with an incomprehensible love and tenderness, I knew not for whom or for what. . . .

Where were people at that time? Our estate was called Kamenka Farm;[4] our main estate was considered to be the one on the other side of the Don, where my father often used to go for long periods. At the farm the household was small, and the servants few. Still, there were people, there was some life. There were dogs, horses, sheep, cows, farmhands; there was the coachman, the elder, the cooks, the cattlewoman, the nurses, father and mother, the brothers who were at school; sister Olya still rocked in her cradle. So why has my memory retained only moments of utter solitude? Here, a fine summer day is drawing toward evening. The sun is already behind the house, behind the garden; the large deserted courtyard lies in shadow, and I (quite, quite alone in the world) am lying on its green cool grass, looking up into the bottomless blue sky, as if into someone's wonderful and intimate eyes, into my own paternal bosom. There, high up, floats a white cloud; growing rounder, it slowly changes shape and melts away in that concave blue abyss. What poignant beauty! I long to board that cloud, and sail and sail on it in those uncanny heights, in the spaces beneath the firmament, close to God, close to the white-winged angels who dwell somewhere there, in that heavenly world!—Here, I am outside the manor, in the fields. It still seems to be the same evening, only now the low sun gleams warmly. Round me, wherever the eye turns, stretch the stubbly fields of rye and oats, and in their midst, in the dense thicket of inclined stubble, the partridges live their hidden, watchful lives. At present, they are still silent, but then, everything is silent; only at times, a little russety corn-beetle, entangled in the stubble, starts humming, starts a gloomy buzz. I disentangle it and examine it eagerly, with surprise: what is it, who is it, this russety beetle? Where does it live? Whither and for what purpose was it flying? What does it think and feel? It is angry, earnest; it bustles in my fingers, making a rustling noise with its hard wing-cases from beneath which peeps out something very fine, pinkish-yellow; then suddenly the tiny shields of those wing-cases split apart and open out, the pinkish-yellow something also opens out—how gracefully!—and the beetle rises in the air, humming now with delight, with relief, and quits me forever, vanishes into the sky, enriching me with a new emotion—leaving behind in me the sadness of parting. . . .

Or else, I see myself in the house, again on a summer evening, again in solitude. The sun has vanished behind the quiet evening garden; it has abandoned the empty hall, the empty drawing room where it shone happily the whole day long; now its last lonely ray shows red in the corner on the floor, between the tall legs of a small antique table, and oh! how tantalizing is its sad, speechless beauty. Late in the evening, when the garden already stood black behind the windows, with all its mysterious nocturnal blackness, and I lay in my cot in the dark bedroom, there looked at me through the window, from on high, some tranquil star. . . . What did it want of me? What silent message did it bring me, whither did it call? And of what did it remind me?

3

Childhood began gradually to link me up with life, and in my recollections of it there are already glimpses of a few persons, of a few scenes of manor life, a few happenings. . . .

Among these happenings, the first place is held by the first journey of my life, the farthest and the most extraordinary of all my subsequent voyages. Father and mother were going to the forbidden land called "town," and they took me with them. Here for the first time I experienced the sweetness of a dream about to come true, and at the same time the fear that for some reason it might not come true. I remember even now how I stood languishing in the middle of the courtyard, exposed to the blazing sun, looking at the tarantass which had already been taken out of the coach house: when will the horses at last be harnessed, when will the preparations for departure be finished?

I further recall that we drove for an eternity, that there was no end to fields, dales, field roads, crossroads, and that by the way there was the following incident: in one of the dales—it was drawing toward evening and the place was quite deserted—there was a thick oak undergrowth, dark-green and frizzly; and on the opposite slope, stealthily making his way through the coppice, there was a "brigand" with an axe at his belt—the most mysterious and the most terrible, perhaps, of all the peasants I ever saw, not only then, but since. How we entered the town, I do not remember. But then, how well I remember the city! I was hanging over a precipice, in a narrow ravine of huge houses I had never seen before, and I was blinded by the glitter of the sun, the windowpanes, the signboards; and above me, all over the world was diffused some marvelous musical medley: the ringing and booming of the bells from the belfry of St. Michael's Church, which rose above everything in a magnificence and splendor of which St. Peter's of Rome had never dreamt, and so huge that afterward I could never be struck by the pyramid of Cheops.

But the most marvelous of all things in the town proved to be the boot polish. Never in my life have I experienced from things seen by me on earth—and I have seen many things—such rapture, such joy, as I did in the market of that town holding a box of boot polish in my hands. That round box was made of simple bast, but what bast it was! And with what incomparable artistic skill the box was made! And the polish itself! Black, tough; with a dull lustre and an intoxicating, spiritous smell. And then there were two other great joys: I was given little boots with red morocco leather edging on the uppers, about which the coachman again said something that I remembered all my life: "Boots to perfection!"—and a leather riding crop with a whistle in its handle. . . . How blissfully, how voluptuously did I finger that morocco leather and that elastic, flexible leather thong! At home, lying in my cot, I simply gasped with happiness at the thought that beside the cot stood my new boots, that under the pillow was hidden the riding crop. And the familiar star was peering from above into the window of the bedroom, saying to me: *Here, now, all is well, there can and need be nothing better in the world.*

The same trip that first disclosed to me the joys of earthly existence left me with another deep impression, which I received on the way back. We left town just before evening, driving through the long, wide street, which already struck me as quite poor in comparison with the one where stood our hotel and St. Michael's Church; we crossed a spacious square, and once more in the distance opened up before us the familiar world—the fields, their rural simplicity and freedom. Our way lay directly to the west, toward the setting sun, and here I saw, all of a sudden, that there was one more man who was staring at that sun and those fields. At the very exit from the town there rose an extraordinarily huge and extraordinarily dreary yellow house that had absolutely nothing in common with any house I had hitherto seen. It had a great many windows, and over every window was an iron grating; it was enclosed by a high stone wall, and the big gate in that wall was closed tight; and behind the grating of one of those windows stood a man in a gray cloth blouse and a cap to match, with a yellowish puffy face. On that face was written something complicated and painful, something which, again, I had never seen in my life: a mixture of the deepest longing, sorrow, blunt resignation, and at the same time some passionate and somber dream. . . . Of course, I was told what that house was, and who the man was; it was from father and mother that I learned of the existence in the world of that particular class of people called criminals, convicts, thieves, murderers. But then, the knowledge we acquire during our short personal life is too scanty—there is another, infinitely richer, that with which we are born. My parents' explanations would not have been enough to account for the feelings which the grating and that man's face called forth in me: I felt for myself, I divined for myself, with the aid of my own knowledge, his peculiar, his uncanny soul. The peasant had been terrible stealing through the oak undergrowth in the dale, with an axe at his belt. But he was a brigand—I never doubted that for a moment; it was something very terrible, but also fascinating, fairy-tale. But this convict, this grating. . . .

4

My further recollections of my first years on earth are more commonplace and definite, though no less scanty, casual, and disjointed: what, I repeat, do we know, what do we remember—we who sometimes remember even yesterday with difficulty?

My childish soul begins to get used to its new abode, to find in it a great deal of happy charm, to view the beauty of nature already without pain, to notice people and to have different, and more or less conscious, feelings toward them.

The world is still confined, in my eyes, to the estate, the house, and the human beings nearest to me. I have not only noticed and felt Father, his dear existence, but also scrutinized him: strong, high-spirited, careless, easily inflammable but cooling down very easily, kind and generous.[5] He loathed malicious and spiteful people. I began to take an interest in him, and already came to learn something about him: that he never did anything—and, in truth, he spent his days in that happy idleness which was then so characteristic not only of the life of country gentlemen, but of Russian life in general; that he was always very animated before dinner and gay at the table; that, on waking up from his after-dinner nap, he was fond of sitting by an open window and drinking some acid water with soda, delightfully fizzy, tickling one's nose, and that in those moments he would suddenly catch hold of me, put me on his knees, hugging and kissing, and then as suddenly put me down, disliking anything durable. . . . I came to feel not only a sympathy for him, but at times also a delighted tenderness; I already liked him: he satisfied my forming tastes by his courageous looks, by the straightforwardness of his changeable character, and above all, I think, by the fact that he had at some time taken part in a war in a place called Sevastopol, and was now a hunter, a wonderful shot—he could hit a twenty-kopeck coin thrown into the air—and so excellently, with so much heart, and when need be so skillfully, so captivatingly, played songs on the guitar, especially the old popular songs of Grandfather's happy days. . . .

I also at last noticed our nanny; that is to say, I realized the presence in the house, the particular nearness to our nursery of that large, stately, authoritative woman who, although she always called herself our servant, was in fact a member of our family; and if she quarreled (which she did often enough) with our mother, it was only because it was absolutely necessary to their reciprocal love and their need for tears and reconciliation shortly after the quarrel. My brothers were not my age at all and already lived a life of their own, coming to us during the vacations; but then I found that I possessed two sisters, of whom I also at last became aware, and whom I associated in different ways, but equally closely, with my own existence: I felt a tender love for the chubby, laughing, blue-eyed Nadya who took her turn in the cradle; and I imperceptibly began to share all my games and pastimes, joys and sorrows, and sometimes also my most intimate dreams and thoughts, with dark-eyed Olya, an impetuous girl who flamed up easily like Father, but who was also fundamentally very kind and sympathetic, and soon grew to be my faithful friend. As to mother, of course I noticed and understood her before all the others. Mother was to me, among all the rest, quite a special being, inseparable from my own, and I probably noticed and felt her at the same time as myself. . . .[6]

With mother is connected the bitterest love of all my life. Everything and everybody we love is our torment, albeit a sweet and joyful torment—think only of that eternal fear of losing the beloved person! And from my early childhood I bore the great burden of my immutable love for her who, having given me life, had filled my soul with torment, and filled it the more as, her soul being brimful with love, she was also sorrow incarnate. How many tears did I see in her eyes as a child, how many sad songs did I hear from her lips!

In her far-off native land, let her rest in peace, lonely, forgotten forever by all the world, and let her precious name be blessed for all time! Is it really possible that she whose eyeless skull and gray bones are lying somewhere there, in the churchyard grove of an out-of-the-way Russian town, at the bottom of a now nameless grave, is it really possible that it was she who used once to rock me in her arms?

"My ways are above your ways and My thoughts above your thoughts."

5

Thus passed away the loneliness of my childhood. Again, I remember: one autumn night something woke me up, and I saw the room filled with a mysterious twilight and in the great uncurtained window a pale, sad autumnal moon standing high, high over the empty courtyard of the manor, invested by its own sadness and loneliness with such unearthly charm that my heart also was seized by an ineffable bittersweetness that seemed to be just what suffused that pale autumnal moon. But I already knew and remembered that I was not alone in the world, that I was sleeping in Father's study—I cried, I called, I woke up Father. . . . In this way, gradually, human beings were entering into my life, and inalienably becoming part of it. . . . I already noticed that in the world, besides summer, there were autumn, winter, spring, when one could be but rarely outdoors. Yet at first I did not remember them—the childish soul is impressed above all by the bright and sunny—and so now I recall, apart from that autumn night, only two or three dark pictures, and these only because they were out of the ordinary: a certain winter evening with a terrible and fascinating snowstorm behind the walls—terrible because everybody said it was always like this on the eve of the Day of the Forty Martyrs,[7] and fascinating because the more terribly the wind shook the walls, the more one enjoyed the warmth and snugness of their protection. And again, a certain winter morning when something really remarkable happened: on waking up we saw a strange twilight in the house, we saw that from the courtyard something whitish and incredibly huge was obstructing the light, rising above the house—and we realized that a snowdrift had blocked us in the night, which it took the farmhands the whole day to clear. And finally, a certain gloomy April day when a man, dressed only in a light coat, appeared suddenly in our courtyard, tottering and bent in the icy wind that drove him along, poor bandy-legged devil, pitiably gripping the cap on his head with one hand, while the other clumsily pulled the coat over his breast. . . . Yet, on the whole, I repeat, my early childhood appears to me only as a string of summer days, the joy of which I shared almost invariably, first with Olya, and then with the peasant children from Vyselki, a village of a few homesteads over beyond the Gap, about three-quarters of a mile from us.

Poor was that joy, almost as poor as the one I had experienced from the boot polish and the little riding crop. All human joys are poor; there lives within us something which at times inspires us with a bitter self-pity.

Where was I born, where did I grow up, what did I see? Neither mountains, nor rivers, nor lakes, nor forests—only the undergrowth in the dales, copses here and there, and occasionally a sort of wood, the Zakaz, or the Dubrovka; otherwise, it was fields, fields, a boundless ocean of grainfields. It was not the south, the steppe with browsing flocks of scores of thousands of sheep, where one drives for a whole hour through some village or cossack settlement, marveling at the whiteness, cleanliness, populousness, and wealth. It was only substeppe, where the fields undulate with ravines and hills everywhere, and shallow meadows, mostly stony; where the tiny villages and their bast-shod inhabitants seem to be godforsaken—so unpretentious are they, so primevally simple, so akin to their willows and stubble. And here I am, growing up, learning to know the world and life in that deserted yet beautiful country, through its long summer days. One of the very first pictures of that time seems to be this: hot noontide, white clouds float in the blue sky, a wind blows—now warm, now quite hot—bringing the sun's heat and the odors of warmed-up grain and grass, and there, in the field, beyond our old granaries—they are so old that their thick thatched roofs look gray and solid like stone, and the beamed walls have become bluish-gray—there is the heat, the glitter and splendor of light, and, shot with dull silver, there surge and surge without end, on the hillside, the waves of an unfathomable sea of rye. They are glossy, they undulate, and run and run, enjoying their own density, their own impetuosity, and over them run the shadows of the clouds.

And then, in the middle of our courtyard, thickly overgrown with curly grass, there was a sort of ancient stone trough under which you could play hide-and-seek, taking off your shoes and running with white bare feet (their whiteness pleased even you) on that green curly grass, hot with the sun on the top and cool underneath. And by the walls of the granaries there proved to be shrubs of henbane, of which Olya and I once ate so much that we had to be given fresh milk so marvelously dizzy were our heads, while soul and body were filled with the desire, and even a sense of the absolute power, to rise in the air and fly anywhere. . . . By the granaries, too, we found countless nests of big velvety-black and golden bumblebees, whose presence underground we guessed. And how many roots did we discover, how many sweet stems and grains in the kitchen garden, round the grain barn, on the barn floor and behind the servants' cottage, the back wall of which was close to the fields and meadows!

6

Behind the servants' quarters and under the walls of the cattle yard grew enormous burdocks, tall nettles, both dead and stinging, luxurious crimson cotton-thistles with prickly little crowns, and something full-blown, pale-green, called viper's grass; and each had its own special look, color, smell, and taste. The little under-herdsman whose existence we also had at last discovered, was extremely interesting: his hempen-cloth shirt and short trousers were all rags; his feet, hands, and face were dried and burnt by the sun, and peeled off; his lips were sore, for he was always munching something—now a crust of sour rye bread, now the burdocks, now that very viper's grass, which corroded his lips to real wounds. His sharp eyes strayed stealthily: he realized very well all the criminality of our friendship with him, as also the fact that he incited us to eat goodness knows what. But how sweet was that friendship! How enthralling everything was that he told us—secretly, in snatches, constantly looking around. Besides, he could crack his long whip wonderfully as if he were firing a pistol, and he would laugh a devilish laugh when we tried to do the same, making our ears tingle with the end of the lash.

But for real abundance of all the fruits of the earth one had to go to the kitchen garden, situated between the cattle yard and the stables. Imitating the herdsboy, you could secure a salted crust of black bread and eat long green arrows of onions with their gray grainy nodules at the end, red radishes, white radishes, small cucumbers, still hairy and pimply, which gave such pleasure to seek out rustling under the endless creeping suckers covering the friable beds. . . . What did we want it all for? Were we hungry? No, of course not, but during that meal we communed unawares with the earth, with all that sensuous, material substance of which the world is made. I remember: the sun was scorching the grass and the stone trough in the courtyard hotter and hotter, the air was growing heavier and duller, the clouds were gathering ever slower and closer, until they were shot through with a sharp crimson gleam and began, somewhere in their farthest reverberating heights, to rumble, and then to thunder, to roll in resonant booming, to roar with mighty claps, growing ever heavier, ever more grandiose, ever more magnificent. . . . Oh! how I felt that divine splendor of the world, and of God who ruled over it and had created it in such fullness and force of solid substance! Then came darkness, flames, hurricane, a violent downpour with crashing hail; everywhere everything was tossed about, quaked, seemed to be perishing; all the windows in the house were closed and curtained, and a Passion-week wax candle was lighted before the black icons in their ancient silver frames; people made the sign of the cross repeating, "Holy, holy, holy Lord God of Sabaoth!" But then what a relief it was afterward, when everything grew calm and quiet, breathing freely the ineffably delightful damp freshness of the soaked fields; when the windows in the house were once more thrown open; and my father sitting by the study window and looking at the cloud that still hid the sun and stood like a black wall in the east, beyond the kitchen garden, sent me there to bring him a nice big white radish. Few moments in my life could match that one—when I ran quickly over the tall glistening weeds, got the radish, and greedily bit off its tail along with the thick blue mud that had stuck to it. . . .

And then, gradually growing bolder, we learned about the stockyard, the stables, the coach house, the farmyard, the Gap, Vyselki. The world expanded more and more, became more and more concrete; yet at first it was not men and human life but vegetable and animal life that most attracted our attention, and our favorite haunts were still those where there were no people, our favorite time of the day—the afternoon, when the adults slept. The garden was gay and green but already familiar to us; the only attractive things in it were the thickets and copses, the birds' nests (especially if inside them, in those little cups tressed with twigs and carpeted with something soft and warm, there sat, looking out with sharp black beads, something speckled), and the raspberry bushes where the berries tasted incomparably better than those we used to eat with milk and sugar after dinner. And so—the stockyard, the stables, the coach house, the grainbarn in the farmyard, the Gap. . . .

Every place had its own charm.

In the stockyard, deserted the whole day long, the gate creaked with lazy roughness when we pushed it open with all our puny might, and it smelled pungently, foully, but with an irresistible attraction, of dung and pigsties.

In the stables the horses lived their own horsey life, which consisted of standing up and noisily chewing hay and oats. How and when did they sleep? The coachman said that they, too, sometimes lay down and slept. But this was difficult and even somehow uncanny to imagine—horses are heavy and clumsy in lying down. This evidently happened during the most desolate hours of the night; as a rule the horses stood in their stalls, grinding the oats with their teeth to a milky substance all day long and worrying the hay, picking at it with their soft lips; they were all fine and powerful, with glossy croups it was a great pleasure to touch, with stiff tails reaching to the ground, and feminine manes, with large violet eyes which they sometimes squinted menacingly and wonderfully, reminding us of the terrible thing which the coachman had told us: that all horses have their special day in the year, the day of St. Flor and St. Laurus[8] when they are intent on killing man in order to avenge themselves for their enslavement, for their horsey life, which consists in the eternal expectation of being harnessed, in fulfilling their strange destiny in this world—only to carry, only to run. . . . Here, too, it smelled strongly, and also of dung, but not at all in the same way as in the stockyard; the dung was quite different here, and its smell mingled with the smell of the horses themselves, of the harness, of the rotting hay, and of something else peculiar to stables.

And in the coach house stood the droshky, the tarantass, Grandfather's old-fashioned coach. The vehicles were associated with dreams of long voyages; at the back of the tarantass was a curious and mysterious traveling box; the coach attracted one by its old-fashioned clumsiness, and by the secret presence of something left over in the world from Grandfather; it was like nothing modern. The swallows darted to and fro incessantly, like black arrows, now from the stables into the blue celestial expanse, now back again into the gate and under the roof, where they sculpted their rounded, firm, chalky nests, so extraordinarily attractive in their firmness, their shapeliness, and the skill of their sculpting. It often occurs to me now: "Well, you will die, and never again see the sky, the trees, the birds, nor many, many other things to which you are accustomed, which have grown to be part of you, and with which it will be such grief to part." As for the swallows, it will certainly be a great grief: what lovely, tender, pure beauty! And how graceful those little birds are, with their lightning flight, their pink-and-white breasts, their small blue-black heads with blue-black wings to match, pointed, long, folded crosswise, and always twittering so happily. The gate was always open—there was nothing to prevent us from dropping into the coach house whenever we liked and watching those twittering creatures for hours; from dreaming of catching one of them; from sitting astride the droshky; from getting into the tarantass, or the coach, and traveling somewhere far, far away. Why is man, from his childhood onward, allured by distance, by things wide and deep and high, by the unknown and dangerous, by the things that enable him to swing his life round or even to lose it for the sake of something or somebody? Would this have been possible if our lot were confined to "that which God has given," only to the earth, only to this one life? Obviously, God has given us much more. Recalling the fairy tales read or heard in childhood, I still feel that the most fascinating things in them were words about the unknown and the unusual. "In a certain kingdom, in an unknown land, beyond thirty-nine countries. . . . Beyond the mountains, beyond the valleys, beyond the blue seas. . . . The Maiden-King, Vasilisa the Wise. . . ."[9]

And the grain barn was fascinatingly terrifying in its gray strawy bulkiness, its sinister emptiness, vastness, the twilight inside, and in the fact that when you got inside, ducking under the gate, you could lose yourself as you listened to the wind groping and rustling and soughing; in one corner hung a holy icon board covered with dust, but people said that the devil came there at night nevertheless, and this combination of the devil and the board so dangerous to him inspired particularly frightening thoughts. And farther on, beyond the granary and the farmyard, beyond the tumbledown kiln and the millet field, was the Gap. It was a narrow but very deep dell with steep slopes and the famous "gap" at the bottom, overgrown with tall weeds. To me it was the most desolate of all the desolate spots in the world. What a blessed silence! It seemed you could sit in that dell for a lifetime, loving and pitying someone. What a lovely flower—both in aspect and in name—grew in the thick, tall grass on its slopes: the crimson Virgin's Flower, with a brown sticky stem! And how sad and tender sounded the brief song of the greenfinch in the weeds! Chirp-chirp-chirp . . . .

8

Henceforth my childish life becomes more varied. I begin more and more to notice the life of the estate, to pay more frequent visits to Vyselki. I have already been to Rozhdestvo, to Novoselki, to Grandmother's in Baturino.

On the estate, at sunrise, with the first twittering of the birds in the garden, Father wakes up. Fully convinced that everybody must wake up with him, he coughs loudly and shouts, "Dashka, the samovar!" We too wake up, full of joy at the sunny morning—the rest of them, I repeat, I still don't want to or can't notice—eager and impatient to run down to the cherry orchard, to pick our favorite cherries, bird-pecked and sun-baked.

In the stockyard at that hour the gate creaks in a new, a matutinal way, and from it, with bellowing, yelping, and whip-cracking, driven to the succulent morning pastures, there emerge cows and pigs and the gray-curled, compact, and agitated herd of sheep; horses are driven to the field pond, and the earth rings to the strong stamp of their hooves as they pass in a tight drove, while in the servants' cottage and the manor-house kitchen the ovens are already ablaze with orange flames; the eager work of the cooks begins, and the dogs gather under the windows and on the thresholds to watch and sniff, often jumping away with a yelp. . . . After the morning tea, Father sometimes takes me with him in the droshky to the field where, perhaps, according to the season, there may be plowing going on, and barefooted, hatless, unkempt peasants walk and walk with swinging strides, stumbling in the soft furrows, their bodies following the straining of the horses, and the groaning plows, whose shares turn over the moist layers of earth; or numberless young girls, whose motley colors, pertness, laughter, and songs rejoice the heart, may be harvesting millet or potatoes; or else the mowers, their backs black with sweat, their shirts unbuttoned at the neck, their heads bound with strips of cloth, are swinging their swishing scythes with a curtseying movement, straddling their legs, felling the thick wall of hot yellow rye—and behind them the rakers work, while the women, bent over and stooping, wrestle with the prickly, big-headed sheafs smelling of sun-warmed golden rye, trample them with their knees and bind them up tight. . . . What an inexpressibly fascinating sound it is—the sound of a scythe being sharpened, its glistening blade being skillfully whetted, now on one side now on the other, with a short piece of wood rough with sand and steeped in water. There is always some mower who will not fail to delight you by telling how he nearly sliced a whole nest of partridges and almost caught a partridge, or cut a snake in two. And as to women, I already know that they sometimes bind sheaves at night, if there is a moon—by day it is too dry, the ears of grain come to pieces—and I feel the poetic charm of that night toil.

Do I remember many such days? Of course, very few; the morning which I imagine now is made up of patchy pictures, flitting through my memory from various times. Of noontides I seem to see only one picture: the hot sun, the stimulating smells from the kitchen, the keen anticipation of dinner awaiting everybody returning from the fields; my father; the sunburnt, red-bearded elder riding with a broad rocking amble on a sweating nag saddled with a high cossack saddle; the farmhands, who have been mowing with the mowers and now enter the courtyard on top of a cart full of grass and flowers mown together at the field boundaries, the gleaming scythes lying beside them; and the men who have brought the horses back from the pond, their coats shining like glass, their dark tails and manes dripping with water. At one such time I saw my brother Nicholas also sitting on top of a cart, on grass and flowers, returning from the fields with Sashka, a peasant girl from Novoselki. I had already heard something about them from the servants—something I could not understand but for some reason took to heart. And now, seeing them together on the top of the cart, I was suddenly aware, with a secret rapture, of their beauty, their youth, their happiness. Tall and slender, still no more than a girl, with a delicate pretty face, she sat holding a pitcher, turning away from my brother, her bare legs swinging down from the cart, with downcast eyes; he, in a white peaked cap and a light cambric Russian shirt with unbuttoned collar—sunburnt, clean, youthful—was holding the reins; and he looked at her with shining eyes, telling her something, and smiling joyfully, lovingly. . . .

9

I remember a couple of trips to Rozhdestvo, to Mass.

Here, of course, everything was unusual and festive: the coachman, in a yellow silken shirt and corduroy sleeveless jacket, on the box of the tarantass drawn by three horses abreast; Father with a clean-shaven chin and dressed in town style, in a nobleman's peaked cap with a red band under which his hair showed, still wet and black, combed in the old-fashioned way in braids running from temples to the eyebrows; Mother in some beautiful, light dress with a multitude of flounces; myself, pomaded, in a silk shirt, with a holiday tenseness in body and soul. . . .

In the fields it was already stuffy and hot; the road between the tall, still fields of grain was narrow and dusty; with an air of noblesse oblige the coachman passed some peasants, also decked out and going to the feast. In the village I experienced the heart-sinking feeling of the descent down an extremely steep, stony slope, and the novelty and richness of impressions: in the village the peasants' homesteads were large and wealthy, with old oak trees in the farmyards, with beehives, with friendly but independent hosts—tall, robust freeholders; and under the hill, in the shadow of tall willows alive with cawing rooks, meandered a deep black stream smelling, in a peculiar cool and rivery way, of those willows, and of the dampness of the plain on which they grew. In the village, on the opposite hill that one climbed after crossing a stone bridge washed by the clear water, in the open space before the church, there was a motley crowd: young girls, women, stooping and decrepit old men in clean peasant tunics and cone-shaped hats; and in the church there was a throng of people, and one felt warm with smelly warmness because of that throng, and the blazing candles, and the sun striking through the cupola, and again there came a feeling of secret pride: we were in front of all the others, we could pray so well, so masterfully and so decorously; after mass, to us first the priest handed the cross, smelling of copper, and he bowed obsequiously. We rested after mass in the courtyard of old Danilo, a benevolent and bent wood-sprite with gray curls, with a brown neck resembling cracked cork; and we drank tea with warm cakes and honey piled up like a mountain in a wooden tureen, and all my life I remembered—I felt offended!—that once he simply took a huge piece of flowing, melting, amberlike honeycomb with his black rigid fingers and put it into my mouth. . . .

I already knew that we had become poor, that Father had "squandered" a lot during the Crimean campaign, had gambled away a lot while he lived in Tambov, that he was horribly carefree and would often say, trying in vain to frighten himself, that our last belongings would soon be under the hammer; I knew that our estate on the other side of the Don had already been auctioned off and was no longer ours; yet I have preserved from those days a feeling of contentment and prosperity. I remember the gay dinner hours in our house, the abundance of succulent and plentiful dishes, the greenness, the glitter, and the shadow of the garden beyond the open windows, numerous servants, a great number of hounds pushing their way through the open doors into the house, lots of flies and magnificent butterflies. . . . I remember how sound asleep the whole manor house was in the long after-dinner hours. I remember also my evening walks with my brothers, who had already began taking me with them, and their youthful enthusiastic talk. . . . I recall some marvelous moonlit night, and how unspeakably beautiful, light, and clear was the southern horizon under the moon, how the sparse azure stars twinkled in the moonlit vault of sky, and my brothers said that all these were worlds unknown to us and perhaps happy and beautiful, that we, too, might probably go there sometime. Sometimes, on nights like these, Father slept not in the house, but in the courtyard, in a cart under the windows: the cart was filled with hay and on the hay his bed was laid. It seemed to me that he ought to be warm with the moonlight streaming upon him, shining golden on the windowpanes, that there could be no greater happiness than to sleep like that and to feel the whole night long, through slumber, that light, the peace and the beauty of the country night, of the familiar neighboring fields, of the familiar manor. . . .

One event alone marred the happiness of those days, a terrible and majestic event. One evening the herd boys who used to bring up the working horses from the field dashed at full speed into the courtyard of the manor, shouting that Senka had tumbled with his horse at full gallop into the Gap, right to the bottom, into that terrible undergrowth where, it was said, there was something like a slimy funnel. The farmhands, my brothers, my father, all rushed there to try and save him, to drag him out, and the manor was hushed in fear and expectancy: would they save him? But the sun had set, it began to grow dark, then darkness set in—and still there was no news from "there," and when it came everybody felt still more subdued: both Senka and the horse had perished. . . . I remember those terrible words, "We must tell the police at once and send someone to guard the 'dead body.'"' . . . Why were they so terrible, those words, quite new to me?

10

People are not all equally sensitive to death. But there is a category of people who live their whole life under its sign, who have from early childhood an acute sense of death (most often by reason of possessing an equally acute sense of life). The Archpriest Avvakum, speaking of his own childhood, says, "And I saw once at a neighbor's a dead beast, and having risen that night I wept fairly long about my soul before the holy image, recalling death, since I also was to die. . . ."[10] Well, I too am one of these men.

In my early childhood I listened with particular sensitivity to tales of dark and evil forces existing in the world, and of the dead who were in a way related to these forces. I heard people talk about my "late" uncle, my "late" grandfather, I constantly heard it said that the dead were somewhere "in the other world'; and listening to this I acquired certain unpleasant and bewildering impressions, a fear of dark rooms, of the attic, of the dreary night hours, of devils and ghosts—that is, of the dead themselves resuscitated and wandering by night.

When and how did I acquire faith in God, the notion and sense of God? I think, together with the notion of death. Death was, alas, somehow associated with Him (and with the icon-lamp, with black icons in silver and gilt frames in Mother's bedroom). Likewise associated with Him, of course, was deathlessness. God is in heaven, in the inconceivable altitude and power, in that incomprehensible blue which is above us, endlessly faraway from earth. This notion had grown in me from my very first days, just as the idea that, in spite of death, every one of us has a soul and that soul is immortal, located somewhere in the breast. But nevertheless death remained death, and I already knew, and sometimes even felt with dread, that everybody on earth would die—generally speaking not very soon, but in particular at any time, and more especially on the eve of Lent. In our house, late on that evening, everybody would become suddenly meek, humbly bow to each other, ask one another for forgiveness: we all, as it were, took leave of each other, thinking that this night might indeed prove to be our last night on earth. I, too, thought so, and always went to bed with a heavy heart at the possibility of the Last Judgment on that fatal night, of the dread Second Coming, and worst of all, of the "resurrection of all the dead." Then Lent would begin—six whole weeks of renunciation of life and all its joys. And then—the Passion Week when our Savior Himself died. . . .

During Passion Week, in the bustling preparation for the festival, we all still felt sad even though anticipating the coming joy, and we redoubled our fast, preparing ourselves for the sacrament—even my father made vain efforts to feel sad and to fast—and I already knew that on Friday, in front of the altar in the Rozhdestvo church, they would place the thing called sudarium, which had been so frighteningly described to me by my mother and my nanny before I had seen it for myself. By the evening of Holy Saturday our house shone with the utmost cleanliness, both inward and outward, benign and happy, quietly awaiting in its grace the great Feast of Christ. And then the feast would come—in the night from Saturday to Sunday some marvelous transformation was accomplished in the world, and Christ vanquished and triumphed over death.

We were not taken to midnight mass, but even so we used to wake up with the sense of the beneficent transformation, so that it seemed there would be room for no more sorrow. Yet it was there, even on Easter. Toward evening, in the silent, rose-colored spring fields there was heard, at first from afar, then drawing nearer and nearer and repeated with joyous insistence, "Christ has risen from the dead"—and after a little there came into sight the "Christ-bearers," hatless young peasants with white girdles, bearing aloft a huge cross, and young girls in white kerchiefs carrying the church icons in clean towels. They walked with triumphant singing, entered the courtyard, and at last reaching the porch, paused, joyous and moved, with a sense of a task honorably accomplished; then, with brotherly equality, they kissed us all with their soft, tender, pleasant young lips, and carefully carried the cross and icons into the house, into the hall, where in the fine twilight of the spring sunset the icon-lamp gleamed in one corner; they set the icons on the tables, drawn together under the icon-lamp and covered with beautiful new tablecloths, and the cross in a sack of rye. How lovely it was! But, alas, it was also a little sorrowful and frightening. Everything was pleasing and comforting, the icon-lamp burned so tenderly, so softly, so peacefully in the greenish spring dusk. And yet it all had in it something of the church, something divine, and so again connected with the sense of death and sorrow. And more than once I saw the sorrowful rapture with which my mother would pray before that corner, remaining alone in the hall and kneeling before the icon-lamp, the cross, and the icons. . . . What was her grief? And why did she grieve all her life long, even when there seemed to be no reason, praying for hours at night, sometimes weeping even on the finest summer days, sitting by the window and gazing into the fields? Because her soul was full of love for everything and everybody, and especially for us, her own kin, and because everything passes and will pass for ever and beyond recall, because the world is a place of partings, of illnesses, of sorrows, of unfulfillable dreams and unrealizable hopes, of unutterable or unuttered and unshared feelings—and of death. . . .

I say this to explain that it was not Senka, of course, who gave me the first notion of death. Even before that I knew and to some extent felt it. But it was through Senka that I first really became aware of its actuality, of the fact that it had at last affected us too. I realized then for the first time that sometimes it actually covers the world as a cloud covers the sun, suddenly vitiating all our "deeds and things," robbing us of our interest in them, of the sense of the legitimacy and meaning of their existence, covering everything with grief and weariness. On that memorable evening it rose from behind the farmyard, from behind the barn, from the direction of the Gap. And long, long afterward I imagined that something very dark, painful, and even ghastly, existed there, and whatever I thought, whatever I saw was associated in my mind with Senka. I was tormented by futile questions. What happened to him after he was crushed to death? What is he now? And why did he perish on that precise night?

11

Days shaped themselves into weeks, and then months; autumn followed summer, and winter autumn, and spring winter. . . . But what can I tell of them? I remember only something general: the fact that I had already imperceptibly entered upon the conscious phase of my life.

I remember. Once, dashing into Mother's bedroom, I suddenly saw myself in a small mirror in an oval wooden frame that stood facing the door—and for a moment I froze: there, looking at me with astonishment and even with a certain fear, was a slender, nimble boy, already fairly tall, in a brown Russian shirt, black lustrine knickerbockers, and worn but well-fitting goatskin boots. Of course, I had often seen myself in a mirror before, but without remembering, without noticing it. Why did I notice it now? Evidently because I was surprised and even slightly frightened by the change that at some time—perhaps in the course of one summer, as often happens—had taken place in me and I had suddenly discovered at last. I don't know exactly at what time of year it happened, nor how old I was then. I believe it happened in autumn, judging by the fact that, so far as I recollect, the sunburn on the boy's face in the mirror was pale, as it is when it is going off, fading away, and that I must have been about seven; with more precision I know this—that I liked the boy for his slimness, his beautiful curly hair bleached by the sun, the lively expression of his face—and I know that there was a somewhat startled amazement. Why? Evidently because I suddenly perceived (as a stranger) my own attractiveness—in that discovery there was even, goodness knows why, something sad—my already fairly tall stature, my thinness; and my lively, intelligent expression; in fact, I suddenly saw that I was no longer a child, I felt vaguely that some change, perhaps for the worse, had come into my life. . . .

And so, in reality, it had. About this time the general tendency to recall only happy times ceased—which in itself meant a good deal, of course—and this coincided also with certain quite new and truly difficult discoveries, ideas, and feelings which I acquired on earth. Soon afterward I made the acquaintance of a rather remarkable man who came into my life and with whom I started my studies; I underwent my first grave illness; I experienced the death of Nadya and then the death of my grandmother. . . .

12

The frock-coated man who had suddenly made his appearance in our court-yard one icy and gloomy spring day, appeared once more in our house. Just when, I don't remember; but appear he did. And he turned out to be a really unhappy man, but of a quite peculiar kind, in that he was not merely unhappy but had created his unhappiness by his own will, longed for it, and bore it with almost savage cheerfulness—in a word, he turned out to belong to that dreadful species of Russians which, of course, I came to understand properly only later, in my mature years. His name was Baskakov; he came from a wealthy and noble family; he was clever and gifted, and consequently could have lived, if not better, at least not worse than many others. It was not for nothing that he was thin, stooping, hook-nosed, dark-faced, "like a devil," it was said; his temper was wild and violent: when still at the lycée he fled with curses from home after some quarrel with his father; then, after his father's death, he was so infuriated with his brother over the division of the property that he tore up the deed of partition, spat in his brother's face, shouting that if that was how things were he would divide nothing with such a scoundrel and would not accept a single penny for himself, and once more—and this time for good—he slammed behind him the door of his home. With that his wandering life began: in no place, in no house could he get along, even for a few months. Nor did he get along with us at first: soon after his first appearance in our courtyard he and my father nearly came to blows. But the second time a miracle occurred—after a certain period Baskakov declared that he would stay with us forever; and he stayed with us for three full years, until I was sent to school. He even admitted that, though in general he felt for his fellowmen nothing but contempt and hatred, he had conceived a warm affection for us all, especially for me. He became my tutor, and after a time I, in my turn, came to like him; and this was the source of many very complex and strong feelings which I experienced in my close contact with him.

A strong impressionableness, which I inherited not only from my father and mother but also from my grandfathers and great-grandfathers, men of that highly original type of which the Russian educated class was once composed, was an inborn quality in me. Baskakov contributed much to its development. As a tutor in the usual sense of the word he was completely useless. He quickly taught me to read and write with the aid of a Russian translation of *Don Quixote* that happened to have found its way into our house among other books; but what was to be done further, he knew not and did not really care to know. With my mother, toward whom, by the way, he always behaved with respect and delicacy, he usually spoke French. She advised him to teach me to read French also. This he did rapidly and very willingly, but again went no further: he ordered from town some textbooks, which I had to read for admission to the first grade in school, and simply began making me learn them by heart. But it turned out that his great influence upon me was exercised in quite a different area. In general, he led a very secluded and savage life; sometimes he would be extraordinarily gay, agreeable, affable, talkative, witty, and even brilliant—an inexhaustible and masterful storyteller; but for the most part he kept a caustic silence, always thinking something, smiling sardonically, mumbling malignantly, and endlessly pacing up and down the rooms or the courtyard with quick steps, swinging evenly and rapidly on his thin, crooked legs. At such times he would ward off any attempt to talk to him, either by a curt, stinging politeness or simply by rudeness. But even then he would be completely transfigured on seeing me. He would at once hurry toward me, put his arm round my shoulder, and either lead me into the fields or the garden, or sit with me in some quiet corner of the house, and start telling me some story, reading something aloud, kindling the most contradictory feelings and ideas within me.

He was, I repeat, an excellent storyteller, impersonating his characters with gestures and swift changes of voice. You could also lose yourself in listening to him when he read aloud—always, as was his habit, screwing up his left eye, holding the book in his left hand and at a great distance. And that clash of feelings and ideas which he kindled in me was due to the fact that the stories which he generally chose to tell, without in the least taking my age into account, were all the most bitter and biting, it seemed, among his experiences, bearing witness to human meanness and cruelty; while for his readings he chose something heroic and exalted, expressive of the fine and noble passions of the human soul; and as I listened to him I would now be burning with indignation against men and with poignant tenderness for him who had suffered so much at their hands, and now be panting and breathless with a sense of joy. He had eyes like a crayfish, short-sighted and always bloodshot, of a fiery-brown color, and the expression of his face struck one by its tenseness. Whenever he walked, or rather ran, about, his dry graying hair and the lapels of his invariable frock coat, extremely old-fashioned, floated and flapped about. "Not wishing to be a burden upon anyone"—this was a mania with him—he smoked (and continuously) only the cheapest cigarettes, slept in summer in a barn and in winter in the footmen's room (long vacant for lack of footmen), and as regards food seemed to be firmly convinced that the idea that people must eat was mere prejudice: at table he was interested only in vodka, and mustard and vinegar. In truth, everyone wondered how he kept alive. . . .

He told me about the violent collisions he had had in his life with "scoundrels"; about Moscow where he used to study; about the dense, bear-infested forests beyond the Volga where at one time he had long wandered about. He read with me *Don Quixote*, the review *The Universal Traveler*, some book called *Lands and Peoples*, *Robinson Crusoe*. . . . He painted in watercolors—and for a long time captivated me with a passionate dream to become a painter. For a long time I would tremble from head to foot at the very sight of a box of paints, daub paper from morning to night, and stand for hours looking at that marvelous blueness of the sky, bordering on mauve, which shows on a hot day facing the sun, among the treetops bathing as it were in that blueness; and I became forever imbued with a deep sense and consciousness of the truly divine meaning and significance of the colors of earth and sky. Surveying all that life has given me, I see this as one of the most important things. That rich mauve blueness, showing among branches and foliage, I shall remember even on my dying day. . . .

13

On the wall of my father's study hung an old hunting knife. Sometimes I saw him draw its white blade from the sheath and rub it idly with the flap of his loose jacket. Afterward I did the same myself. What voluptuous joy thrilled me then at the mere touch of that smooth, cold, sharp steel! I longed to kiss it, to press it to my heart—and then to stab something, to thrust it in up to the hilt. My father's razor was also of steel, and even sharper, yet I hardly paid it any heed, whereas the sight of any steel weapon excites me even to this day—and what is the source of these feelings in me? As a child I was kind and tenderhearted, and yet once I slaughtered with real delight a young rook with a broken wing. The courtyard, I remember, was deserted; indoors like-wise, for some reason, all was empty and quiet, and then suddenly I saw a large and very black bird hurrying clumsily somewhere, sideways; with its drooping wing unfolded, it hopped over the grass toward the granaries. I dashed into the study, grasped the dagger, and jumped out of the window. . . . The rook, when I overtook him, suddenly stood still; with terror in his wild gleaming eye, he flung himself to one side, pressed close to the ground; bristling up fiercely, lifting up his wide-open beak, and scowling, he hissed and croaked with anger, evidently resolved to fight me to the death. . . . The murder I then committed for the first time in my life proved for me a major event; for several days after it I was out of sorts, secretly imploring not only God but the whole world to forgive me my great and dastardly sin for the sake of my soul's great torment! But all the same, I did kill that wretched rook who had so desperately fought me and drawn blood from my hands, and I took great pleasure in the killing of him.

And how often did I climb with Baskakov to the attic where, tradition said, some saber of Grandfather or Great-grandfather was lying about! We climbed there up very steep stairs, in semidarkness, stooping. In the same manner we made our way farther, treading on beams, girders, piles of rubbish and cinders. It was warm and stuffy there, in the way proper to attics, smelling of cold smoke, ashes, stoves. In the world there was sky, sun, expanse, and here it was twilight, something stifled, tedious, somnolent. The free wind from the fields was sounding about us on the roof, and here its noise came muffled, turning into some other sound, witchlike and sinister. . . . The twilight grew gradually lighter, we turned round the flue of the chimney, and in the light coming through the dormer-window we kept wandering to and fro, peering under the beams, under the dusty rafters that lay slantwise over them, digging among the cinders, now gray, now violet, depending on the spot, on the light. . . . If only we had found that fairy saber! I think I would have choked with joy! Yet what good was it to me? Whence came my fierce, aimless love for it?

But then, everything else in the world was aimless, existed goodness knows why, and I felt this already.

Tired by the fruitless search we would rest. The queer man who shared that search with me, the man who for some reason had utterly ruined his life and was aimlessly dragging it about the world, the only person who understood my pointless dreams and passions, would sit down on the girder, roll a cigarette, and, thinking thoughts of his own, mumble something angrily while I stood looking through the dormer-window. It was now almost daylight in the attic, especially near the window, and the noise of the wind did not seem so sinister. Nevertheless, we felt somehow apart there, and the estate also was a thing apart, and I imagined it, and its peaceful flowing life, as if I were a stranger.

Straight below me, in the sunlight, billowed the gray-green and dark-green tops of the garden trees, so strange to view from above. The sparrows strewed them with lively chirruping; shadowy inside, their tops glistened with a glassy glitter under the sunlight, and as I looked at them I thought—what was it for? Probably only for the sake of its being so lovely. Beyond the garden and the adjacent fields, right on the horizon, Baturino was showing blue, like a distant forest; and there, heaven knows why, my grandmother, my mother's mother, had been living for eighty years in her old-world manor, in a house with a very high roof and colored windowpanes. To the left, everything shimmered in the hot haze; there, beyond the meadows, was Novoselki, that is, the willows, the kitchen gardens, the scant peasants' farm-yards, and a row of miserable cottages down a long and always deserted street. . . . Why did they all exist there—hens, calves, dogs, water-casks, shanties, pot-bellied babies, toothy women, beautiful young girls, shaggy, dull peasants? And why did my brother Nicholas go there almost every day to see Sashka? Only because for some reason he liked to contemplate her kind, modest face, the nice circular cut of the white calico shirt round her neck, her tall figure and bare feet. . . . That cut I also liked, and it also called forth something languorous and insoluble: I wanted to do something with it, but what in particular, or why, I could not understand.

Yes, in those days the saber hidden in the attic fascinated me most. But time and again I would also remember Sashka, for whom once, when she came to the estate and was standing by the porch with bowed head saying something shyly to my mother, I had suddenly felt a particularly sweet and pining feeling—the first flash of the most incomprehensible of all human feelings. . . .

14

Don Quixote, by which I learned to read, the illustrations in that book, and Baskakov's stories about the age of knights made my imagination run riot. I could not rid my head of castles, crenellated walls and towers, portcullises, cuirasses, vizors, swords and arquebuses, fights and tournaments. Dreaming of the stroke of the falchion on the shoulder of a kneeling youth with flowing hair, fatal like the first communion, I felt goose bumps all over my body. In the letters of Alexey Tolstoy one finds these lines: "How nice it is in Wartburg! there are even instruments of the twelfth century. And just as your heart jumps in the Asiatic world, so mine started thumping in that knights' world, and I know that I formerly belonged to it."[11] I think I also did. I have visited in my life many of the most famous castles of Europe, and strolling about them I wondered more than once how could I, a child little different from any child in Vyselki, how could I, gaping at pictures in books and listening to a half-crazy vagabond smoking cheap tobacco, feel so rightly the ancient life of those castles and so accurately imagine them? Yes, I too used to belong sometime to that world, and had even been an ardent Roman Catholic. Neither the Acropolis, nor Baalbek, nor Thebes, nor Paestum, nor Saint Sophia, nor the old churches in the Russian kremlins are, to my mind, even now comparable with Gothic cathedrals.[12] How struck I was by the organ when, in my years of adolescence, I first entered a Roman Catholic church, though it was but an ordinary Polish church in Vitebsk! It seemed to me then that there were no more wonderful sounds on earth than those menacing, loud roars, booming and thundering, amid and athwart which, in the wide-open heavens, sound vociferating, exultant angelic voices. . . .

Don Quixote and knights' castles were succeeded by seas, frigates,

Robinson Crusoe, the world of ocean and tropics. To that world I had unquestionably belonged at some time. The illustrations in *Robinson Crusoe* and *The Universal Traveler,* as well as the large yellowed map of the world with the great lacunae of the South Seas and the dots of the Polynesian islands, fascinated me for the rest of my life. Those narrow canoes, the naked men with bows and javelins, the coconut groves, the fronds of the huge leaves and a primitive hut underneath them—all this I felt to be as near and familiar as if I had just left that hut, as if only yesterday I had been sitting beside it in the heavenly quietude of a sleepy afternoon. What sweet, bright visions, what real nostalgia did I experience looking at those pictures! Pierre Loti tells of the "disturbing and miraculous" meaning which the word "Colonies" had for him in his childhood. But then he adds: "Il y avait une quantité de choses des colonies chez cette petite Antoinette: un perroquet, des oiseaux de toutes couleurs dans une volière, des collections de coquilles et d'insectes. Dans les tiroirs de sa maman, j'avais vu de bizarres colliers de graines pour parfumer; dans les greniers on trouvait des peaux de bêtes, des sacs singuliers, des caisses sur lesquelles se lisaient encore des adresses de villes des Antilles. . . ."[13] And what could there be like that in Kamenka?

In a book called *Lands and Peoples* there were colored illustrations. I remember two in particular: one represented a date-palm, a camel, and an Egyptian pyramid, and the other, a coconut palm, very slender and tall, the upward-sloping line of a tall spotted giraffe stretching forward, to its feathery top, his feminine squint-eyed little head, his fine stingerlike tongue, and a thick-maned lion springing through the air straight for the giraffe's neck. All this—the camel, the date-palm, the pyramid, the giraffe under the coconut tree, the lion—was painted against a background of two screaming colors: the glaring, rich, unrelieved blue of the sky and the bright yellow of the sands. And, heavens! what torrid parchedness, what blaze of sun did I not only see but feel with all my being, as I gazed on that blue and that yellow, and gasped with a really celestial delight! Amid those Tambov fields, under that Tambov sky, I recollected so vividly all that I had seen and absorbed once upon a time, in my former, immemorial lives, that afterward in Egypt, in Nubia, in the tropics, I could only say, "Yes, yes, this is all just as I first 'remembered' it thirty years ago!"

15

Pushkin, some of whose poetry Mother used to recite to Olya and me, struck me by his wizardly prologue to *Ruslan and Lyudmila:*[14]

A verdant oak on curvéd shore,
A golden chain upon that oak. . . .

What a trifle it may seem—a few good, let us even say sublime, uncommon-ly sublime, lines. And yet they permeated me for the rest of my life, became one of the greatest joys I knew on earth. What nonsense it would seem—some curved shore that has never existed anywhere, some "learned" cat that for no earthly reason came to be there and—heaven knows why—is chained to the oak tree, some wood-sprite, water nymphs, and "on unknown tracks the footprints of unfamiliar beasts." But then, evidently the point is in its being nonsense, an intoxicated vision, something totally absurd, unreal, not anything rational or real; its effect sprang from the poet himself having been under the spell of some irrational creature, someone intoxicated and versed in intoxications: how priceless in itself is that evocation of circling, continu-ous movements ("by day, by night, the learned cat keeps walking round upon his chain"), and these "unknown" tracks and the "footprints of unfamiliar beasts"—the footprints only, not the beasts themselves!—the simplicity, pre-ciseness, vividness of the opening (the curved shore, the verdant oak, the golden chain), and then—the dream, the spell, the variety, the confusion, something floating and changing, like the early morning mists and clouds of some hidden country of the north, of dense forests by the sea now instilled with such magic:

> There wood and dale are thronged with visions,
> At dawn the waves will break with plashing
> Against the sandy desert shore,
> And thirty knights, all fair and handsome,
> Come forth in turn from limpid waters
> Together with the ocean loud. . . .

A great impression was produced on me by Gogol's "Old-World Landown-ers" and "A Terrible Vengeance."[15] What unforgettable passages they are! How marvelously they still ring in my ears, having from childhood irrevoca-bly entered my inner self, endeared to me for the rest of my life, having turned out to be among those most important things which went into the making of my "vital substance" (to use Gogol's own expression). These "singing doors," this "lovely" summer rain which sounds "luxuriously" in the garden, these wild cats dwelling in the forest beyond the garden where "the old tree trunks, hidden by the dense hazelnut underwood, were like the feathery feet of pigeons. . . ."

And what about "A Terrible Vengeance"!

> There was a bustle and an uproar in a quarter of Kiev: the Esaul Gorobets was cel-ebrating his son's wedding. A great many people had come as guests to the wed-ding . . .
> The Esaul's adopted brother, Danilo Burulbash, came too, with his young wife

Katerina and his twelve-month-old son, from beyond the Dnieper. . . . The guests marveled at the fair face of the young wife Katerina, her eyebrows black as German velvet . . . her boots with silver heels; but they marveled still more that her old father had not come with her. . . .

And further on: "There was a soft light all over the earth: the moon had come up from behind the mountain. It covered the steep bank of the Dnieper as with a costly damask muslin, white as snow, and the shadows drew back farther into the pine forest. A boat, hollowed out of an oak tree, was floating in the Dnieper. Two lads were sitting in the bow; their black Cossack caps were cocked to one side, and the drops flew in all directions from their oars like sparks from a flint. . . . "

And here Katerina is talking to her husband; wiping with a kerchief the face of the child sleeping in her arms: "that kerchief had been embroidered with leaves and fruits in red silk" (the very same ones that I see, remember, and love all my life long!). Here, she "sat silent looking down into the slumbering river; and the wind ruffled the water into eddies and the entire Dnieper shimmered silver like a wolf's skin in the night. . . ."

Again I marvel: how could I then, in Kamenka, visualize with such precision all these pictures? More broadly, how well my child's soul already discriminated and guessed what was good and what was bad, what better and what worse, what it wanted and what it did not want! Toward some things I was cold and unmindful; others I grasped gladly, passionately, to remember and retain forever—and here, more often than not, I acted with an amazingly unerring flair and taste.

"They all go out. A thatched roof came into sight behind the mountain: it was Danilo's ancestral home. Beyond it was another mountain; and then the open plain, and there you might travel a hundred miles and not see a single cossack. . . ."

Yes, this was what I needed!

Danilo's house lay between two mountains in a narrow valley that ran down to the Dnieper. It was a low-pitched house like a humble Cossack's hut and there was only one large room in it. . . . There were oak shelves running round the walls at the top. Bowls and serving pots were piled upon them. Among them were silver goblets and drinking cups mounted in gold, gifts or booty brought from war. Lower down hung costly swords, muskets, arquebuses, spears. . . . At the base of the wall were smooth-planed oak benches; beside them, in front of the oven-step, the cradle hung on cords from a ring fixed in the ceiling. The whole floor of the room was beaten hard and plastered with clay. On the benches slept Danilo and his wife; on the oven-step the old serving-woman; the child played and was lulled to sleep in the cradle; and on the floor the serving-men slept in a row. . . .

And best of all—the epilogue: "In the days of Stepan, prince of Semigrad . . . there lived two Cossacks . . . Ivan and Petro. . . ."

"A Terrible Venegeance" awakened in my soul that lofty feeling which is inherent in every soul and will live forever—the feeling of the sacred lawfulness of vengeance, the most sacred necessity of the final triumph of good over evil, and the utter ruthlessness with which evil is punished when its time comes. This feeling is, doubtless, a craving for God, faith in Him. The moment when His triumph and His just punishment are fulfilled throws man into a sweet terror and trembling and finds its climax in a storm of ecstasy, seemingly baleful, but in reality an explosion of our supreme love both for God and for our fellow beings. . . .

16

Thus began my boyhood, during which I lived with extreme intensity, not in the real life that surrounded me, but in that into which I transformed it, and most of all in an invented life.

Real life was scant and simple.

I was born and grew up, as I said, in an absolutely open country such as cannot even be imagined by a European. A vast expanse, with neither obstacles nor boundaries, surrounded me: where, in fact, did our estate end, and where began that boundless plain into which it merged? But then I saw only the plain and the sky.

Colonies! I knew only Baev's "colonial shoppe" in Rozhdestvo. To me everything "colonial" was confined to the cinnamon with which the cheese-cake used to be spiced for Easter; to the black glistening sweet pods whose mawkish taste I experienced at the fairs in Rozhdestvo; and to the labels ("sherry," "madeira") on the bottles in fine mesh nets with which I amused myself, stretching them this way and that, and which began again to appear more and more frequently at home, because my father was again taking more and more to drink. It was in Rozhdestvo, too, that I saw the supreme splendor—in the church. To an eye accustomed only to grainfields, grass, field roads, tar-smelling carts, smoky cottages, bast shoes, hempen shirts; to an ear accustomed to quietude, to the singing of larks, the cheeping of chicks, the cackle of hens—the deep cupola with the menacing white-haired God of Sabaoth spreading his hands wide over the lilac puffs of clouds and His own undulating robes, the golden iconostasis, the icons in golden frames, the slender wax candles, crowded slantwise before the day's icon, blazing hot in a golden bonfire of light and melting together, the loud discordant chant of the deacon and the sexton, the vestments of the priest and the deacon, their invocations, the recital in an exalted, rather obscure language,[16] the genuflections and the burning of incense, its spicy smoke rising densely from the thurible adroitly swung and jingling with its silver chains—all this seemed regal and splendid, exalting one's spirit with festal solemnity. . . .

Moreover, I grew up amid that dire impoverishment of the gentry which likewise can never be grasped by a European, to whom the Russian passion for self-destruction in all its forms is utterly alien. That passion was characteristic not only of the gentry. For consider the Russian peasant, who led an impoverished existence even though, in his large expanses, he possessed riches such as a European peasant never dreamed of, and who justified his idleness, his sloth, his dreaminess, and his general fecklessness by the mere fact that the government had been loath to deprive his neighbor the squire, who was every year growing poorer, of an extra acre of land. Why did the covetousness of the grasping merchants now and again alternate with wild fits of squandering accompanied by curses on that very covetousness, by bitter drunken tears about one's own ungodliness, and with feverish dreams of deliberately becoming a Job, a vagabond, an idiot? And why, in general, did Russia meet the fate she did, destroyed before our eyes with such miraculous rapidity?

Among my relations and those who were near to me, my mother alone could perhaps be understood, with her tears, her sorrow, her fastings and prayers, her longing to stand aloof from life: her soul lived in constant and sublime religious tension, she thought God's Kingdom to be not of this world and believed with all her being that the lovely, brief, and sad life on earth was but a preparation for another, everlasting and happy. But all the others—our dissipated neighbors, relatives, my father, Baskakov? What Baskakov had done with his life I have already mentioned. And what did our father do with himself and his fortune—he, so strong, noble, magnanimous, yet carefree as a bird? And we ourselves, the young heirs of the former glory of the Arseniev family and of the miserable remnants of its past wealth? My brother Nicholas, for the sake of Sashka and the charms of country indolence, left school. My brother George spent all his days in reading Lavrovs and Chernyshevskys.[17] The auspices under which I grew up can be judged by what follows. One day Nicholas began painting my future for me. "Well, there you are," he said jokingly. "We are certainly ruined already, and when you grow up you'll take a job somewhere; you'll drudge; you'll marry; you'll have children; you'll save a bit and buy a small house . . . "—and suddenly I felt so vividly all the horror and ignominy of such a future, that I burst into bitter tears. . . .

17

The last year of our life in Kamenka I survived my first serious illness: in other words, I learned for the first time that astonishing thing which people usually just call "illness," which in reality is an unconsummated death, a crazy journey into certain realms of the beyond. I fell ill in the late autumn. What happened to me? I felt a sudden weakening of all my mental and bodily forces, a miraculous change that occurs at such moments in all of the five human senses—sight, taste, hearing, smell, touch; I felt a sudden loss of the wish to live, I mean to move, drink, eat, be merry or sad, or even to love anyone, not excluding those dearest to my heart; and then came whole days and nights of a kind of nonexistence, broken only by occasional dreams, by visions, mostly ugly and absurdly complex, seeming to focus in themselves the whole of the physical crudity of earthly life, which, in disintegration, in a fierce struggle with itself, perishes amid something feverish and flaming that has, no doubt, contributed to the human notion of hellish tortures. How well I remember when I was starting to get better and I saw my mother like a huge white ghost. Instead of the bedroom, I saw a dark and gloomy barn, where a candle set on the floor behind the head of the bed made thousands of loathsome figures, faces, beasts, plants, move tremulously in its flaming waves. My soul was filled with unearthly lucidity, with quietude, with meek joy and tenderness, long after I had returned to earth, from my descent into hell, to the simple, lovely, familiar vale of earth. For some reason, in those days I took particular delight in eating black bread, the mere smell of which enraptured me, and which through the simplicity of the country folk was hardly ever refused me. . . .

Then Nadya died—a couple of months after my illness, after Christmas.[18] For me that Christmas passed in strange joyousness. My father drank, and every day from morning till night there was reveling under our roof; the house was full of guests. My mother was happy: her supreme joy had always been when our whole family was gathered together, I mean when my brother George came for his vacation, as he did that Christmas. Then, suddenly, amid all that crude rejoicing, Nadya, who just before had been briskly stamping all over the house on her firm little feet, making everybody admire her blue eyes, her shouts and laughter, fell ill. Days passed, the holidays were over, the guests ebbed away, my brother went off, and still she lay unconscious, burning with fever, and in the nursery there was always the same thing: the windows curtained, the half-light, the lamp burning before the icon. . . . Why should God have chosen particularly Nadya, the joy of the whole house? Everybody felt depressed, dejected; and yet no one expected that this anguish would come to such a sudden climax late one evening, with the exclamation of the nanny, who suddenly opened the dining-room door with the terrible news that Nadya was "expiring." Yes, that staggering word "expiring" first struck me late one winter evening amid the desolation of dark snowy fields, in a lonely manor. At night, when the wild confusion which thereupon seized the whole house had subsided, I saw, lying still on the table in the hall, in the sepulchral light of the icon-lamp, a dainty doll with bloodless, inanimate face and black eyelashes almost shut. . . .Never in my life has there been a more terrible, a more magical night.

In the spring my grandmother died. It was wonderful May weather; my mother was sitting by an open window, in a black dress, thin and pale. Suddenly from behind the barn emerged a peasant on horseback, a stranger, gaily shouting something to her. Mother opened her eyes wide and, with a light and apparently joyous exclamation, tapped the windowsill with her palm. . . . Again the life of the manor suddenly and brusquely came to a halt. There arose on all sides a peculiar bustling—alas, already familiar to me— the farmhands rushed to harness the horses, my mother and father to dress . . . us children, thank God, they did not take with them. . . .

18

For a long time Nadya's death, the first I saw with my own eyes, deprived me of the sense of life—life which I had just come to realize! I suddenly recognized that I, too, was mortal, that to me, too, this strange and terrible thing which happened to Nadya might happen at any moment, and that, generally speaking, all earthly, living, material bodily things are unfailingly subject to death, to putrefaction, to that purplish blackness which had covered Nadya's lips by the time her body was taken from the house. And my terrified soul, with something like a deep sense of disgrace, as if somehow offended, turned to God for help and salvation. Soon all my thoughts and feelings merged into one—a secret prayer to Him, a constant unspoken request to spare me, to show me the way forth from the shadow of death which had spread over me and over all the world. My mother prayed passionately day and night. Our nanny pointed out to me the same refuge: "One must pray to God more assiduously, dearie. Look how the saints prayed, fasted, tormented themselves. It is a sin to cry about Nadenka, one must rejoice for her," she would say weeping, "she is now in heaven, with the angels. . . ."

Thus I entered into one more world, wonderful and new to me: I set about reading greedily, endlessly, penny lives of saints and martyrs, which were brought to me from town by the cobbler, Pavel of Vyselki, who often went there to buy materials for his craft. Pavel's house smelled not only of leather and sour glue but also of damp and mildew. And so the smell of mildew came always to be associated in my mind with those thin booklets printed in large characters which I read and reread with such morbid ecstasy. Even that smell became eternally dear to me, vividly reminding me of that strange winter: my half-crazy, my sweet, tormenting dreams of the early Christians' tortures, of young maidens torn by wild beasts in some place called "arena," of kings' daughters, pure and fair as God's lilies, beheaded at the hands of their own ferocious parents; of torrid, silent deserts where, covering her nakedness only with her own hair that reached to the ground, there lived, purging with prayer her lechery in the world, Mary of Egypt; of the Kiev catacombs where lie the hosts of martyrs who, for our Lord's sake, buried themselves there alive in order to pass their time in tears and constant prayer and vigil in the underground obscurity full of all kinds of nocturnal horrors, temptations, and devil's scoffings. . . .[19] I lived solely by the inward contemplation of these pictures and images, isolating myself from home life, enclosing myself in my fairy-tale holy world, intoxicating myself with my painful joys, with the craving for sufferings, for self-exhaustion, for self-mortification. I hoped fervently to be one day canonized as a martyr and would kneel secretly for hours on end in some empty room; from old pieces of string I knitted myself something like a hairshirt, drank only water, ate nothing but black bread. . . .

This lasted through the whole winter. But toward the spring it began gradually to pass, somehow by itself, I do not even remember how. Sunny March days arrived, the double windowpanes began to warm up, and between them crawled the flies who had come back to life—it was difficult not to be distracted by all this as I knelt and writhed on the ground, actions which no longer gave the former full, sincere, prayerful ecstasies! April came, and on one particularly sunny day, the storm windows sparkling in the sun began to be taken out, to be torn off with crackling sounds, and the whole house was filled with animation, with disorder, bestrewn all over with dried putty and tow; and then the summer windows were thrown open to the fresh air, to freedom, toward the new young life, and through the rooms spread the smell of the fresh and soft field air, of the earth and its soft dampness; and there came the first solemn, lazy cawing of the rooks that had arrived some time before. . . . In the evening, blue spring clouds would pile up fantastically against the scarlet, slowly fading Western sky; the frogs would start their sleepy, dreamy, soothing trilling on the field pond, in the slowly thickening darkness, promising a warm, beneficent rain in the night. . . . And again, again the ever-deceiving earth drew me tenderly and insistently into its maternal embrace.

19

By August of that year I was already wearing a blue peaked cap with a silver badge on the band. Alyesha simply ceased to exist—there was now Arseniev, Alexey, a pupil in the first grade of the boys' school.[20]

By summer no trace seemed to remain of the bodily and mental distresses which I had undergone the winter before. And I felt tranquil and cheerful—quite in harmony not only with the cheerful, dry weather which lasted throughout that summer, but also with the light mood which pervaded our house. Nadya had already—even to my mother and the nanny—become only a beautiful memory, a conception of a childishly angelic image dwelling happily somewhere up above, in the everlasting mansions of heaven; my mother and the nanny would still be sad, would often talk about her, but rather differently from before—sometimes even with smiles; they would sometimes weep, but not with the same tears as before. As for my grandmother, she was simply forgotten; indeed, her death was one reason for the light mood of our household: in the first place, Baturino now belonged to us, which had greatly improved our finances; and second, the autumn was to see our move there, which also secretly made everyone rejoice, as any change of surroundings usually does, involving hopes of betterment, or maybe unconscious recollections of distant, nomadic times.

Through my mother's stories I pictured to myself the scene that had been enacted in Baturino when my mother and father went driving there in such haste: a May day, the cozy courtyard surrounded by old outbuildings, the old wooden house with wooden columns at the porches, the dark-blue and crimson upper glass-panes in the hall windows—and underneath them, on the two tables placed together, covered with hay under a sheet, and butted askew against the icon corner, a small pale old woman in white indented bonnet, is neatly laid, with small transparent hands crossed on her breast. At her head stands a nun, a very neat elderly maid, who without raising her long eyelashes is monotonously reading aloud in a high strange admonitory voice, which my father, with a malicious smile, called seraphic. . . . That word often came to my mind, and I was vaguely aware of its uncanny, fascinating, yet rather unpleasant meaning. Unpleasant also was the whole scene I pictured to myself. But now only unpleasant—nothing more. And that unpleasantness was more than compensated for by the pleasant though sinful thought, occurring now and then, that grandmother's beautiful manor had now become ours,[21] that I would go there on my first vacation—already God willing as a second-grader—and my father would pick out for me a riding mare from among my grandmother's horses, which would grow so fond of me that she would follow me everywhere at my beck and call.

That summer there were, of course, scary things too: the anticipation of a painful parting from my mother, from Olya, from Baskakov, and from my childhood nest, the fear of a lonely unfamiliar life with strange townspeople, the fear of something called school, with its strict, stern, uniformed teachers. . . . Now and then I would feel a pang in my heart at the sight of my mother or Baskakov, who of course felt the same at seeing me, but at once I would cheer myself by saying, "It won't be for some time yet!"—and my mind would turn gladly to the pleasant, inviting things which also lay in store for me. After all, I would be a schoolboy, wearing a uniform, living in town, with comrades from whom I would choose a faithful friend. . . .The person who chiefly encouraged and allured me with pictures of that new life was my brother George, who seemed to me to be quite an extraordinary being: he was then extremely handsome in his slim, fresh youthfulness, the candor of his high forehead, his radiant eyes, the dark flush of his cheeks. He was not just an ordinary somebody, but an undergraduate of the Imperial University of Moscow, who had graduated with a gold medal from that very school which I was about to enter.[22]

At last, in the beginning of August, I was taken to the examinations. When the tarantass rumbled up to the porch, the faces of my mother, the nurse, and Baskakov altered; Olya started crying, and my father and brothers exchanged awkward smiles. "Well, let's sit down for a bit,"[23] said my father resolutely, and we all sat down hesitatingly.

"Well, God speed you," he said still more resolutely after a moment, and everybody at once started to cross themselves, and rose. My legs felt weak with fear, and I was crossing myself so zealously and hurriedly that my mother rushed toward me, her eyes full of tears, and began kissing and crossing me. But I had already recovered—while she was tearfully kissing and crossing me, I was thinking: "Who knows? Perhaps, with God's help, I'll flunk after all. . ."

But, alas, I did not. For three years I had been trained for that ominous day, and I was merely asked to multiply fifty-five by thirty, to tell who the Amalekites had been, to write a tricky sentence in a fair legible hand, and to recite "the rosy dawn colored the east."[24] They did not even let me finish the poem: I had hardly come to the awakening of the cattle "in the soft meadows," when I was stopped; probably the teacher (a red-haired man with gold spectacles and wide-open nostrils) was all too familiar with that awakening, for he hurriedly said: "That's all right—quite enough—I see you know it. . . ."

Yes, my brother had been right: there proved to be "nothing particularly dreadful." Everything turned out to be much simpler than I expected and came to a close with unexpected swiftness, ease, and uneventfulness. And yet I had crossed a really important threshold in my life.

The fairy road to the town, where I had not been since the time of my first famous journey, the town itself, once so magical—nothing was the same as before, nothing now fascinated me in any way. The hotel near St. Michael's I found rather unprepossessing; the three-storied building of the school behind a high wall at the end of a large cobbled courtyard I accepted as something already familiar, though never before had I entered such a huge, clean, echoing building. Nor did the teachers in their gold-buttoned tailcoats turn out to be either astounding or alarming—some with flaming red hair, others with tar-black, but all equally large—not even the headmaster himself, who looked like a hyena.

Immediately after the examination we were told that I had been admitted and was being given leave till the first of September. A great burden seemed to fall from my father's shoulders—for the simple reason, of course, that he had been terribly bored sitting silently in the teachers' common room where my knowledge was being tested, and still more so had I been. Everything turned out excellently: I had passed, and I had three more weeks of freedom ahead.[25] I really ought to have been terrified, I who since birth, and up to that very moment, had always enjoyed complete freedom and who had suddenly become enslaved, being given only three weeks' respite, but I felt only one thing. "Thank God! Three whole weeks!"—as if those three weeks would never end.

"Well, let's hurry to the tailor now—and then in for dinner!" said my father gaily, as we left the school.

We called on a small short-legged man who surprised me by the rapidity of his speech, with interrogative, and as it were slightly offended, pauses at the close of each sentence, and by the adroitness with which he took my measurements; then to a hatter's, where there were dusty windows warmed by the town sun, and one felt stuffy and squeezed because of the countless hatboxes lying all over the place in such disorder that the owner fumbled among them tantalizingly long, shouting angrily all the time in some incomprehensible language[26] to a woman in the next room with a mawkish, white, languid face. He, too, was a Jew, but of quite a different sort: an old man with heavy side-locks, in a long frock coat of black lustrine and a lustrine skullcap pushed back on his head, he was large, very fat round the chest and armpits, morose, discontented, with a big sooty-black beard growing from right under his eyes—altogether, a dreadful, sepulchral creature. And it was he who at last chose for me an excellent blue peaked cap with two bright white silver twigs standing out on its band. I had that cap on when I came home—to everybody's joy, even my mother's, a joy quite incomprehensible to me now, for wasn't my father quite right when he kept saying, "What the devil does he need those Amalekites for?"

20

Some time toward the end of August my father put on his top boots, girded himself with the cartridge belt, flung the game-bag over his shoulder, took his shotgun from the wall, called me, then his favorite dog, the beautiful ruddy-brown Djalma, and we went across the stubble fields along the road leading to the pond.

My father had on only a multicolored Russian shirt and a white peaked cap; I, in spite of the dry, hot weather, was of course in my school cap. My father, tall and strong, strode ahead firmly and lightly, blowing his cigarette smoke back over his shoulder, the yellow brush of stubble rustling under his feet. I hastened behind, keeping to the right, according to hunting rules, which it gave me great pleasure to observe. He whistled encouragingly, exhilaratingly, and Djalma, with sustained eagerness, in a state of controlled expectancy, wagged and shook her stiff tail at frequent short intervals; all ears, eyes, and nose, she skirted in front of us in swift zigzag, searching movements. The fields were by now deserted, spacious but summerlike, bright and gay. Now the hot breeze would subside completely, and the sun begin to be scorching, and one heard the grasshoppers croak hotly, hammering, tick-tocking like little clocks; and now it would blow with soft, arid warmth, grow stronger, fly past us, and suddenly curl up a small cloud of dust playfully, on that road that had been so well trodden during working days, lifting it up, whirling it in spirals or cones and buoyantly carrying it forward. But our eyes were focused on Djalma, who was steadily and quickly drifting away from us, imperceptibly drawing us farther and farther on. From time to time she would suddenly stiffen, straining forward and raising her right paw, and stare at something invisible to us that was in front of her. My father would say something in a low voice—she would dash at the invisible thing—and at once—ffrr!—a plump, short-tailed partridge would free itself heavily and clumsily (being fat) from under her nose, and after flying only a few yards would flop back onto the field, shot down. I would run forward, pick it up, put it into my father's game-bag. . . .

Thus we crossed the whole rye field, then the potato field, leaving aside the clayey pond, its elongated surface shining hot and dreary to our right, in a hollow amid bare downs trodden by the cattle. Here and there on these, exposed and lost in meditation, sat some rooks. My father looked at them and remarked that the rooks, too, had begun to gather in councils as was their way in autumn, to think about migrating; and for an instant I was once more overwhelmed by a sense of deep anguish, of the imminent parting, not only from the summer that was passing, but from all those fields, from all that was so dear and familiar to me in that lovely and desolate country outside which I had as yet seen nothing in the world, in that quiet abode where had blossomed, in such peace and loneliness, my infancy, my childhood, unknown and unwanted by anyone in the world. . . .

Then we bore to the left, making our way toward Zakaz, following the boundary lines across a measureless black tilled field that was under the harrow. It was still our field, and one of the harrows was dragged over the dry clods of grayish earth by a bay stallion that once, as a thin-legged foal with a silky curling turnip of a tail, had been given to me, and was now, most unfairly, without my permission being asked, set to work. A hot wind was blowing, and over the tillage shone an August sun, which still looked summery but was already somehow aimless, and the stallion, which had grown very tall— though tall in a strange, boyish way—was walking obediently along the field, dragging his rope traces, and behind him shuffled and jerked the grid of the harrow, smashing the soil with its slanting iron jags, and a lad in bast shoes, awkwardly holding the reins, also of rope, in both hands, was hobbling behind. I looked at that picture for a long time, once more with unaccountable sadness. . . .

Zakaz was a fairly big copse belonging to a half-mad landowner who, in lonely hostility toward the whole world, had shut himself up as in a fortress in his manor near Rozhdestvo, guarded by ferocious German shepherds and having endless lawsuits with the peasants from Rozhdestvo and Novoselki; he could never come to an agreement with them about wages, so that he frequently had whole acres of grain left unmown or thousands of stacks rotting in the fields far into the autumn and then perishing under the snow. So it was now. We walked toward Zakaz across unmown yellow oat fields trampled and crushed by the cattle. Here Djalma put up a few more partridges; I would again run and pick them up, and we would go farther on, circumventing Zakaz along a thick millet field that glistened silkily under the sun with its brown tassels, bent to earth, full of grain, which sounded underfoot particularly dry and sonorous, like beads. My father unbuttoned his collar, his face reddened. "It's dreadfully hot, and I am terribly thirsty," he said. "Let's go across the wood, to the pond." And jumping a ditch which separated the field from the wooded glade, we went through the wood, entering its August realm, clear and luminous, touched here and there with yellow, all gay and charming.

There were only a few birds—just blackbirds in flocks, with merry, would-be fierce screaming and sated clucking, flew hither and thither; the wood was deserted, spacious, sparse, sunny, and one could see right through it from end to end. We walked now under the old birches, now across the broad glades where stood free, strong, spreading oaks, not nearly so dark as in summer, with thinning, sere leafage. We walked in their checkered shadow, breathing their dry fragrance, on the dry slippery grass, and looked ahead where other open glades shone in the heat, and beyond them a small copse of young maple undergrowth showed canary yellow. When we entered the path through that copse to the pond, there flashed up suddenly, with a crackling from the undergrowth, from among the palmate hazel trees, from almost under our feet, an old golden-russet snipe. My father was so struck by such an early visitor that he was quite taken aback—he fired, of course, instantly, but missed. After wondering where a snipe could have come from at that time of the year, and giving vent to his vexation at the miss, he went to the pond, laid down his gun, squatted, and began to drink with cupped hands. Then, puffing with pleasure and wiping his mouth with his sleeve, he lay on the shore and lit a cigarette. The water in the pond was crystal-clear, a special woodland water, for there is in general something quite peculiar to these solitary woodland ponds almost unhaunted by anyone but birds and beasts. In its fathomless clarity, the tops of the surrounding birches and oaks were quietly reflected, and through them the wind from the fields lisped and rustled. To the sound of that rustling, lying with his head propped on one arm, my father shut his eyes and dozed off. Djalma also drank some water from the pond; then she flopped into it, swam for awhile, keeping her head warily above the water, her ears drooping like burdock leaves, and then, suddenly turning back, as if afraid of the depth, she dashed out swiftly onto the shore and shook herself vigorously, spattering us with water. Now, with her long red tongue lolling out, she was sitting next to my father, now looking at me inquiringly, now gazing about her impatiently. . . . I got up and wandered aimlessly away among the trees, in the direction from which we had approached the wood across the oat field. . . .

21

There, beyond the glade, beyond the trunks, from under the leafy awning, the expanse of fields shone yellow and dry; from it rose the caressing warmth, the light and happiness of the last days of summer. On my right, from behind the trees, floated up a large white cloud from goodness knows where, and growing irregular and marvelously rotund against the azure, slowly sailed by, changing shape as it went. After walking a few steps I also lay down, on twigs and slippery grass, amid scattered, luminous, sunny trees, which seemed to be walking about me, in the soft shade of a two-forked birch tree, two white-trunked sisters with tiny grayish leaves and catkins; I, too, propped my head on one arm, and began looking now over at the field shining bright yellow behind the trunks, now up at that cloud. A dry heat wafted softly from the field, the light-colored wood quivered and rippled, one heard its slumberous noise, which seemed to run away somewhere. At times that noise increased, grew stronger, and then the meshlike shadow would become variegated, would stir, the sunny patches would flame up and gleam on the ground and on the trees, their branches bending and opening up to show the sky. . . .

What did I think—if indeed it can be called thinking? I thought, of course, about school, about the amazing people whom I had seen there called teachers, who belonged to a peculiar species of men whose sole mission was to teach and to inspire their pupils with constant fear; and I felt terrified and bewildered—why was I being given into slavery to them, severed from home, from Kamenka, from that cheerful copse? Then I thought about the stallion I had seen harrowing the field. My vague thoughts ran, I suppose, like this: Yes, everything is really illusory in this world—I had imagined that stallion to be mine, and they disposed of him without asking me, as if he were their own property. Yes, there had once been a thin-legged, mouse-colored foal, trembling and skittish like all foals, but also gay, trustful, with clear eyes like plums, attached only to his mother who always neighed with sustained pleasure and fondness at the sight of him, but otherwise absolutely free and careless. . . . That colt one happy day had been presented to me, given into my full keeping, and for a time I rejoiced in him, dreaming of him, of my future with him, of the intimacy that not only would spring up, but already had sprung up between us because he had been given to me; and then I had begun gradually to forget him—so no wonder that everybody else forgot he was mine. After all, I had ended by forgetting him completely—just as I should probably forget Baskakov, and Olya, and perhaps even my father, whom I loved so much now, with whom it was such a joy to go shooting, and just as I would forget the whole of Kamenka, where every nook and cranny was dear and familiar to me. . . . Two years had passed—as if they had never been there!—and where was he now, that silly carefree colt? There was a three-year-old horse, a stallion—and where was his old happy freedom? There he was, trudging the fields in harness, dragging a harrow behind him. And was not the same thing happening to me as had happened to that colt?

What need had I of the Amalekites? I felt awe-struck and bewildered in turn, but what could I do? The cloud shone and whitened from behind the birch trees, changing its shape continuously. . . . Could it help changing? The luminous wood rippled, quivered, and ran away somewhere with its sleepy lisp and rustle. . . . Where, and why? Could one stop it? And closing my eyes I vaguely felt that everything was a dream, an incomprehensible dream—the town somewhere over there, beyond the wood, beyond the distant fields, whither I was bound to go, and my future there, and my past in Kamenka, and this bright late-summer day already drawing toward evening, and I myself, and my thoughts, my dreams, my feelings—all a dream! Was it sad, or painful? No, for the time being it was happy and pleasant.

As if to confirm my pleasant feeling, a shot suddenly rang out behind me, echoing through the whole wood, encircling it with its reverberation, after which my ears caught a particularly fierce screaming and clucking of the blackbirds, which had apparently flashed into the air in a huge flock, and the mad, delighted barking of Djalma: it was my father who had woken up and fired. And instantly forgetting all my meditations, I rushed off like an arrow toward him—to pick up the dead blackbirds, bleeding and still warm, smelling sweetly of game and powder.

54

Book Two

1

On the day when I left Kamenka, not realizing that I was leaving it for good, and drove off to school—by the Chernavsk road, new to me—I first became aware of the romance of the forsaken highways, of the soul of old Russia that was becoming a thing of the past, a legend. Highways were passing into oblivion; so also was the Chernavsk road. Its old ruts were grown over with grass, the ancient willows standing here and there on either side of its wide deserted track looked lonely and sad. I remember one, particularly lonely and decrepit, a hollow, storm-battered skeleton. On it, black like a black brand, sat a great raven, and my father said—and this impressed me deeply —that ravens live for several hundred years and that this particular raven may have lived under the Tatars. . . . Wherein lay the fascination of what he said and of what I then felt? In the sense of Russia and of it being my homeland? In the sense of my connection with things past, things remote, things held in common, which always gives our soul, our personal existence a reminder of our link with those common things?

He said that once upon a time Mamay[1] himself had marched through those parts on his way to Moscow from the south, and in passing had razed and sacked our town; and then that we were going to pass Stanovaya, a big village, which had quite recently been a famous brigands' den and had acquired particular notoriety through a certain Mitka, so gruesome a monster that, when at last he was caught, he was not simply hanged but quartered. I remember that between Stanovaya and us, to the left of the highway, a train passed: I had never seen one before. Evening was drawing near, behind us the sun was sinking westward and throwing a straight beam of light on something that looked like a mechanical toy and quickly outpaced us as it sped toward the town—a small, perky engine with a tail of smoke trailing backward from its large-headed funnel, and tiny green, yellow, and blue houses upon quickly spinning wheels. The engine, those little houses which made one long to live in them, their small windows glittering against the sun, that swift inanimate rolling of the wheels—it was all so quaint and amusing; but I well remember that I felt much more drawn to the other thing, to something which my imagination fancied yonder, beyond the railway line, where one could see the willows of the mysterious and terrible Stanovaya. The Tatars, Mamay, Mitka. . . . No doubt it was on that particular evening that I first became aware of being Russian and living in Russia, and not simply in Kamenka in such-and-such a district and such-and-such a parish, and suddenly I felt Russia, felt her past and present, her wild, sometimes terrible yet somehow captivating peculiarities, and my own kinship, my intimate relation to her. . . .

2

Certainly, the general setting of my early days was very Russian. Take, for instance, Stanovaya. Later on, of course, I was frequently in Stanovaya and became fully convinced that there had been no highwaymen there for a long time. Yet I could never view the place quite straightforwardly; I always felt that there was good reason for its inhabitants still being famed as born villains. And then the famous Stanovliansky ravine. The main road descended, near Stanovaya, into a fairly deep ravine, and this place invariably inspired an almost superstitious terror in any belated traveler, at any time of the year when he passed through it; and more than once in my youth I myself had felt that purely Russian terror when passing near Stanovaya. There were many other famous spots on the Chernavsk road, where once upon a time, at their fated hour, from various hidden ravines and gulleys, the "brave lads" came out onto the highway as soon as their quick ears caught the distant plaint of bells or the clatter of ordinary carts in the still night; but the Stanovliansky ravine enjoyed the greatest fame of all. At night, one's heart would always sink as one approached it, and heaven knows which was worse—to drive the horses at full speed or to lead them at a walking pace, straining one's ears for the slightest sound? One fancied all the time that in a moment they might be there—slowly crossing your path, hatchets in hand, low and tightly girdled over the loins, with caps drawn down over their keen eyes—and that they would suddenly stop and in low, exaggeratedly quiet voices give the order: "Hold on, wait a moment, merchant." . . . And which would be more dreadful—to hear that order of theirs amid the peaceful silence, the quiet semi-darkness of the nocturnal summer fields, or through the howl of a wintry wind, or a white blinding blizzard, or under the sharp, icy, autumnal stars in whose half-light one can see the dead, blackening earth spreading far around, and when one's own carriage wheels make such a terrible clatter on the stone-hard road?

After Stanovaya, the main road was crossed by another road, and here there was a barrier, a tollgate: one had to stop and wait until a soldier of the time of Nicholas I, emerging from his striped sentry box, would release a similarly striped bar; with clinking chain it would slowly rise up (for which one had to pay the government a toll of two kopecks, regarded by all travelers as out-and-out robbery). The road next ran past the Runaways' Suburb, a fathomless swamp of filth that bore an extremely obscene name, and at last along the causeway between a new prison house and an ancient monastery. The town itself boasted of its antiquity, as it was fully entitled to do:[2] it is indeed one of the most ancient Russian towns, situated amid the wide black-earth fields of the substeppe, at that fatal line beyond which there once stretched "wild, unknown lands"; and in the days of the principalities of Suzdal and Ryazan it had been one of the principal bulwarks of Russia, which, according to the chroniclers, were the first to take the impact of the storm, the dust, and the cold from the threatening Asiatic swarms that ever and anon gathered over them, the first to see the sky aflame with the terrible fires they kindled by day and night, the first to forewarn Muscovy of imminent calamity, the first also to lay down their lives for her. In its time it had, of course, lived more than once through everything you could think of: in such-and-such a century it was "razed to its foundations" by one khan, in such-and-such by another, in such-and-such by a third, in the year so-and-so it was "laid waste" by a great fire, then by famine, by plague, and so on. . . . Under such conditions it could not, of course, preserve any tangible historical relics. But the past nevertheless was very much felt in it; it was perceptible in the solid way of life of the merchants and the lower-middle-class, in the mischief and fisticuffs of its workers who lived in the Black Suburb, Riverside, and Agramacha, which lay over the river on those yellow cliffs that had struck me when I was a small child and over which some Tatar prince was said to have toppled with his horse. And what a smelly town it was! It smelled almost from the town line, whence it was already in full view, with its countless churches sparkling far off in the vast plain: first, it smelled of the swamp with the obscene name, then of the tanneries, then of the sun-warmed iron roofs, then of the square where the peasants took up their trading stances on market days, and then it smelled of something one could no longer distinguish— of everything that befits an old and well-to-do Russian town. . . .

3

While in school, I spent four years staying as boarder with the family of a certain Rostovtsev, in poor, lower-middle-class surroundings: to other surroundings I could have no access, as well-to-do citizens were in no need of boarders.

How dreadful was the beginning of that life! The mere fact of it being my first evening in town, the first after parting from my father and mother, the first in absolute solitude and, besides, in new and poverty-stricken surroundings, in two cramped rooms, among people absurdly unfamiliar and alien to me, whom I, a gentleman's son, naturally regarded as beneath me, and who had yet suddenly acquired even some power over me—that in itself was dreadful. The Rostovtsevs had another boarder, a boy of the same age and in the same grade as I, the illegitimate son of a Baturino squire, red-haired Glebochka; but on that evening we had not yet established contact: he sat sulkily in a corner like a caged cub, shyly and doggedly silent, looking at me askance with an animal mistrust; nor was I in any hurry to proffer him my friendship—because, among other reasons, he seemed to me to be a not entirely normal boy from whom one ought to keep aloof: when still in Kamenka I knew that we were going to live together, and once I heard our nanny call him a bad name referring to his bastard origin. Outside it was gloomy, as if on purpose; toward evening it had started to drizzle, the endless stony street on which I gazed from the little window was dead and deserted, and on a half-bare tree behind the fence of the opposite house, a crow sat croaking, humpbacked and taut, portending no good; on the tall belfry rising far beyond the dusty iron roofs, into the murky darkening sky, something sang and played every quarter of an hour, softly, pathetically, and hopelessly. . . . On such an evening my father would have shouted at once for someone to light the lamps, bring in the samovar, or lay the table for an early supper— "I loathe this beastly gloom!" But here lamps were not lit till it was quite dark, and people did not sit down to table at any odd time—here everything had its fixed hour. And so it was now: the lamps were lit only when it grew quite dark and the master of the house came home from town. He was a tall, stately man with regular features, a dark-complexioned face, a stiff black beard shot here and there with silvery hairs; extremely sparing of words, invariably exacting and edifying, he had firm rules in every matter, alike for himself and for others, a sort of charter for respectable life, both domestic and public, drawn up once and for all, "not by us, fools that we are, but by our fathers and their fathers before them." He was a buyer and reseller of grain and livestock, and was therefore often absent. But even when he was absent, in his house, in his family (which consisted of a comely and tranquil wife, two quiet young girls with bare rounded necks, and a son age sixteen) there invariably reigned an atmosphere established by his austere and noble spirit, one of silence, order, businesslike ways, deliberation in every action and word.[3]

. . . Now, in this sad twilight hour, the mistress of the house and the girls, all engaged in handiwork, were silently but watchfully expecting him for supper. And as soon as the gate outside banged, they all frowned slightly.

"Manya, Ksyusha, will you set the table," said the hostess in a low voice, and rising from her seat she went into the kitchen.

He came in, quietly frowning, took off his cap and overcoat in the small parlor, and was left with only a light gray jacket which, along with his embroidered Russian shirt and well-fitting calf-skin boots, emphasized his true Russianness. After saying something discreetly affable to his wife, he carefully washed his hands under a brass water container that hung over a basin in the kitchen, rinsing and shaking them vigorously. Ksyusha, the younger girl, with lowered eyes, handed him a long clean towel. He dried his hands deliberately, threw the towel onto her head with a gloomy grin—whereat she blushed joyously—and, entering the room, made several neat and beautiful signs of the cross, and bowed to the icons in the corner. . . .

My first supper with the Rostovtsevs also remained firmly embedded in my mind—and not only because it consisted of dishes very strange to me. First we were given some broth; then, on a round wooden plate, some gray, shaggy tripe the very look and smell of which set me trembling, and which the master of the house minced and cut into small bits, taking them simply with his hands; the tripe was accompanied by pickled watermelon rind, and in the end came buckwheat pudding with milk. But that was nothing. The point is that, as I ate only the broth and the watermelon rind, the host looked askance at me and dryly remarked: "One must get used to everything, young sir. We are simple Russian folk; we eat normal stuff; with us there are no delicacies."

I had the impression that he had pronounced the last words almost haughtily, with particular emphasis and gravity—and here, for the first time, I caught the savor of something which afterward I inhaled very deeply in town—pride.

4

Generally speaking, pride sounded more often than not in what Rostovtsev said. Pride in what? In the fact, of course, that the Rostovtsevs were Russians, genuine Russians, that they lived the especially simple and outwardly modest life that was the real Russian life, and than which there was and could be nothing better: for, after all, it was modest only in appearance, and in fact it was richer than anywhere else, and in general was the natural outgrowth of the traditional spirit of Russia; and Russia was wealthier, stronger, more righteous, and more glorious than any other country in the world. And was that pride characteristic only of Rostovtsev? Afterward I saw that it was present in many others, and now I see another thing too: that in a way it was a sign of the times, that it made itself particularly felt at that epoch, and not only in our town.

Where did it disappear to later on, when Russia was going to rack and ruin? Why did we not uphold everything that we so proudly called Russian, the solidity and righteousness of which we seemed to be so certain? However that may be, I know for sure that I grew up in the epoch of the greatest Russian might, and of the full consciousness of it. The scope of my boyish observations was very limited, yet what I then observed was, I repeat, typical. Yes, afterward I learned that Rostovtsev was far from being the only one to hold forth like this; time and again I heard those feignedly humble assertions—we, people said, are simple folk, even our tsar Alexander Alexandrovich wears tarred boots—and now I have no doubt that they were quite characteristic not only of our town but generally of the Russian sentiments of that time. In the manifestation of those sentiments there was, of course, a lot of showiness—thus, for example, every townsman performed at every street corner at the sight of a church at the bottom of the street, taking off his cap, crossing himself, and bowing almost to the ground. Now and again, of course, people would forget their roles; words often were not attuned to life; often enough one feeling would give place to another and opposite one. Yet what prevailed?

Rostovtsev said once, pointing to a window ledge on which he had chalked some marks: "What do we want bills for? It ain't Russian. In the good old days no one so much as heard of them, and a tradesman simply wrote down who owed him what, like this, for instance, with chalk on the ledge. The first time the debtor failed to pay on time, the tradesman reminded him of it politely. One more failure to pay and he warned him, 'See, here, don't you forget a third time, or else I'll wipe off my mark—what shame that will bring you then!'"

People like him were, of course, few. By his occupation he was a kulak, but he did not naturally regard himself as such, and had no reason to: he rightly called himself a simple tradesman, being quite unlike, not only other kulaks, but a great many of our townsmen as well. Occasionally he would look in on us, his boarders, and suddenly ask with a faint smile: "Did they give you any poetry to learn today?"

"Yes," we said.

"What poetry?"

We mumbled: "The sky in the hour of watch—traversing the moon—shines through the pattern—of the frosted window-pane. . . ."[4]

"Now, that doesn't sound good somehow," he would say. "'The sky in the hour of watch traversing the moon'—I can't quite figure that out."

Nor could we, for somehow we never paid attention to the comma after the word "traversing." Quite true, it did not sound good. And we did not know what to say when he went on to ask: "And what else?"

"And then 'Of the shade of the old tall oak tree a tuneful little bird was fond, in the storm-shattered branches it sought shelter and rest. . . .'"

"Well, that's nice, that's sweet. But read those others—about the even-song and 'Under the vast tent.'"

And I would begin confusedly: "'Come ye O suffering! Come ye O joy-ous! they ring for evensong, for gracious prayer. . . . '"[5]

He would listen and shut his eyes with a quiet smile. Then I would read Nikitin's "Under the vast tent of the azure sky I see the vista of the steppes stretching away. . . . "[6] It was a broad and enthusiastic description of the vast expanse, of the great and manifold riches, forces, and deeds of Russia. And when I came to the proud and joyous finale, to the finale of that description: "'Tis thee my potent Russia, my orthodox country!'"—Rostovtsev would clench his teeth and turn pale.

"Yes, that's a poem!" he would say, opening his eyes, trying to look com-posed, rising and making for the door. "That's a thing to learn hard. And who wrote it after all? An ordinary decent man of our class—a countryman of our own!"

The rest of the "trading men" of our town, both great and small, were not Rostovtsevs, I repeat; usually their worth lay only in their words: in their businesses they were often simply robbers "intent on stripping both living and dead"; they short-measured and short-weighted customers like down-right swindlers, lied and perjured themselves without shame and conscience, led dirty and coarse lives, slandered one another, gave themselves airs, exud-ed animosity and envy, made horribly mean and cruel fun of the idiots, crip-ples, and village fools, of whom quite a number paraded the town, looked down on the peasants with quite undisguised contempt, and swindled them with diabolical daring, adroitness, and cheerfulness. Nor were the other fel-low citizens of Rostovtsev particularly saintly—everybody knows what was and is a Russian official, a Russian boss, a Russian man-in-the-street, a Rus-sian worker. But then, they also had their merits. As for pride in Russia and everything Russian, there was, I repeat, enough and to spare of it. And it wasn't Rostovtsev alone who could, in those days, turn pale repeating Nikitin's exclamation "'Tis thee, my potent Russia!"—or talking about Sko-belev, about Chernyaev, about the Tsar-Emancipator, listening in the cathe-dral to the mention of "our most pious, most autocratic, great Sovereign Alexander Alexandrovich"[7] issuing from the thundering lips of the golden-haired and golden-robed deacon—and suddenly perceiving, almost with ter-ror, over what a really unfathomable realm of various countries, tribes, nations, over what incalculable riches of the earth and forces of life, of "peaceful and prosperous living" the Russian crown was raised. . . .

The beginning of my school life was even more dreadful than my worst expectations. My first evening in town was enough to make me think, "All is over!" But still more dreadful, perhaps, was the fact that after this I very quickly submitted myself to fate, and my existence became a rather ordinary school life, apart from my rather unusual sensitivity. The morning when Glebochka and I went to school for the first time was sunny, and that in itself was enough to cheer us. Besides, how well dressed we were! Everything was brand-new, everything solid, well-fitting; everything made us rejoice—the well-polished boots, the light gray cloth of our trousers, our blue suits with silver buttons, the bright blue caps on our close-cropped heads, our creaking book-bags smelling of leather, containing textbooks, pen-cases, pencils, notebooks bought only yesterday. . . . And then—the vivid and festive newness of the school—its clean cobbled courtyard; the windowpanes and the brass door handles shining in the sun; the spacious echoing corridors; the bright classrooms, halls, and staircases freshly painted during summer; the echoing hubbub and shouting of the thronging mob of boys invading them with an excitement redoubled after the summer break; the decorous solemnity of the first prayer before studies in the great hall; the first sorting-out into classes "in pairs and in step," preceded by a real soldier, a retired captain commanding and briskly marching ahead of us; the first disputes over taking possession of seats; and finally, the first appearance in the classroom of the teacher, his long coat with its crane's tail, his thick gleaming spectacles, the air of myopic surprise in his eyes, his uplifted beard, the briefcase under his arm. . . . In a few days it all became as habitual as if no other life had ever existed. And days, weeks, months ran by. . . .

Learning was easy for me, though I was good only in subjects that I more or less liked; in others I was mediocre, relying upon my ability to grasp everything quickly, except some particularly loathsome things like aorists.[8] Three-quarters of the things we were taught were, of course, of no earthly use to us, left no trace in us, and were taught in an obtuse, official way. Most of our teachers were ordinary, insignificant men; among them stood out a few cranks, who were, of course, "ragged on" in the classrooms, and a couple of real lunatics. One of these was remarkable: he suffered from a fear of life's dirt; he talked rarely, dreaded people's breath, touch; he always walked in the middle of the street; in school, after taking off his gloves, he would at once extract his handkerchief in order to avoid directly touching the door handle or the chair in front of the desk; he was short and thin, with splendid chestnut curls combed backward, a wonderful white brow, amazingly fine features, a pale face, and dark immobile eyes that stared sadly and quietly somewhere into emptiness and space.

What else is there to be said of my school years? During them I grew from boyhood to adolescence. But just how that transformation occurred, again, God alone knows. Outwardly my life went on, of course, in the workaday way. The same going to school, the same sad and reluctant evening preparation of lessons for the next day, the same unfailing dream of the coming vacation, the same counting of the days that remained till Christmas, till summer break—oh, if only they would flash by more swiftly!

6

Here is September, a fine, bright evening. I stroll about the town—they dare not make me learn and box my ears, as they do to Glebochka, who is becoming more and more enraged and therefore more and more obstinate and lazy. My soul is full of sadness about the past summer, which, it seemed, would be endless and promised the fulfillment of a host of wonderful plans; of sadness about my alienation from all who walk and drive in the streets, who trade in the market, who stand about the shops. . . . They all have their own business, their own conversations, all live their habitual adult life—unlike the lonely and sad schoolboy who doesn't as yet have a place in it. The town is chock-full of its own wealth and populousness: wealthy to start with, the town trades year in year out with Moscow, with the Volga, with Riga, with Reval, and now is still wealthier—from morning till night the peasants bring into it all their harvests; from morning till night grain pours out all over the town, the markets and squares are covered with veritable mountains of the fruits of the earth, of every kind. Now and again one meets peasants hurriedly walking right in the middle of the street, talking loudly, as satisfied, tranquil people do when they have at last completed their town business, have already emptied a glass, and now, walking toward their carts, are taking a snack of coarse bread. Talking with animation, there also walk on the pavements those who have spent the whole day working these peasants over—the sunburnt, dust-covered, everlastingly brisk wholesalers, who first thing in the morning go outside the town to meet the peasants, outbidding each other and then leading them to their shops and grain stores; they also are resting now, going to the taverns to drink tea.

And Long Street, straight as an arrow, leading out of town to the prison and the monastery, is drowned in dust and in the dazzling glitter of the sun, which is just setting at the end of the vista, and in that dusty gold flows a stream of people walking and driving, returning from the trotting races for which our town is likewise famous; and how many dandified clerks and shop assistants there are, how many young women decked out like birds of paradise, how many spruce gigs in which broad-beamed young merchants flaunt before the populace, seated beside their young wives and reining in their trotters! And in the cathedral the bells ring for vespers, and sedate, bearded coachmen, on heavy and comfortable coaches drawn by well-fed horses, are driving old merchants' wives holding wax candles in their hands, and striking one either by their yellow puffiness and abundance of jewels, or by their sepulchral pallor and gauntness. . . .

Here is a feast-day, a mass in the cathedral. Our captain, before taking us there, examines every one of our buttons in the school courtyard where we are all mustered. The teachers are in uniform, wearing decorations and three-cornered hats. Marching along the streets we are pleasantly aware that the passersby look upon us as upon an official semimilitary body taking a direct part in all the ceremonies which are to mark this day. Toward the cathedral converge the other "departments," which means more uniforms, decorations, three-cornered hats, rich epaulets. The nearer we approach the cathedral, the more sonorous, heavier, thicker, and more solemn is the din of the cathedral bell. But here is the parvis—"Caps off!"—and, pressing together, closing into single file, we enter the cool magnificence of the wide-open portal, and the roaring and din of the seventeen-ton bells is already somewhat muffled, right overhead, amply and mercifully yet sternly welcoming, receiving, and covering you. And what a crowd inside the cathedral, what ponderous magnificence of the iconostasis decked from top to bottom with gold, of the chapter's golden vestments, of blazing candles, of officialdom of every rank pressing close to the pulpit steps carpeted with red cloth! For a boy's heart all this was not very easy: one's head spun with the long-drawn-out pomposity of the service, with those recitations, incensings, appearances and disappearances of the priest; with the loud roaring of the bass singers and the sweet dying-out of the altos in the choir, elegantly displaying now power, now tenderness; with the hot and uncanny proximity of huge bodies pressing in upon you on all sides, with the vision of the boar's carcass of the police chief, dreadfully jammed into his short uniform and silver belt, rising just above you. . . .

At night on such occasions the town blazed with purple flames, smoked and reeked of flares placed on the pavement; the beflagged houses shone in the darkness with fiery, transparent monograms and crowns—this, among my early town impressions, is one of the most memorable. On such occasions there was always a grand parade in the town. And one day Rostovtsev's son— he was also at school, a sixth-grade boy—took Glebochka and me to one of these parades in the public garden, and I was impressed by the dense crowd moving sluggishly along the constricted line of the main avenue, smelling of dust and cheap perfume, while at the end of the avenue, on a bandstand shining with multicolored flares, a military band poured out a languorous waltz, roaring and booming out with all its brass trumpets and kettledrums. On that avenue Rostovtsev suddenly stopped face to face with a pretty young girl who was coming toward us with her girlfriends; blushing, he jokingly clicked his heels and saluted her, and she beamed all over under her waggish hat, in an openly joyous smile. Before the bandstand in the square a gushing fountain spouted forth in the middle of a large flower bed, bedewing it with cool, watery vapor, and I always remembered its coolness and the fresh, charming smell of the flowers it sprinkled, which, as I afterward learned, were just called "tobacco": I remembered them because for me that smell became linked with the feeling of being in love from which I suffered for the first time in my life for a few days after that. It is thanks to her, that provincial young girl, that I still cannot smell without emotion the fragrance of tobacco flowers, and she never even as much as knew about me and about the fact that, from time to time, throughout my life, I remembered her and the coolness of the fountain and the playing of the miltary band as soon as I caught that scent. . . .

7

And here came the first cold spells: the scant, leaden, tranquil days of late autumn. The town, grown quiet and deserted, has put in the storm windows, lit the furnaces, donned warm garments, and is stocking up on all the necessities for winter, already pleasantly aware of the winter coziness and of that ancient, hereditary way of life it has been living for centuries—of the repetition of seasons and customs.

"The geese are flying away," Rostovtsev says with pleasure, entering the house in a warm overcoat and warm cap and bringing in with him a chill, wintry air. "I just saw a whole gaggle. . . . I've bought two carts of cabbage from a peasant; take them in, Lyubov Andreevna; he'll bring them around right away. Perfect cabbage, one head identical to another. . . ."

And I feel comfortable at heart, and so sad, sad. I put aside a book by Walter Scott which I got from the school library, and grow pensive—I want to understand and express something that is going on within me. I conjure up the town, scrutinize it. There, where one enters it, stands an ancient men's monastery. . . . Everybody says that all the monks in it keep some vodka and sausage behind the icons in their cells; Glebochka is very curious to know whether the monks wear pants under their cassocks, while I, thinking of the monastery, call to mind that morbidly rapturous period when I fasted and prayed and wished to become a saint, and, furthermore, I am somehow stirred by the thought of its antiquity, of its having been more than once besieged, stormed, burnt, and looted by the Tatars: I feel some beauty in it which I crave to understand and to express in verses, in a poetical fancy. . . . Then, if one walks from the monastery in the direction of the town following Long Street, there lie on the left miserable and dirty streets sloping down toward the ravines, toward the foul-smelling tributary of our river where hides are being soaked and rotted: it is shallow, its bottom covered all over with their black layers, and on the shore lie whole mountains of something dirty-brown, stinking pungently and spicily, and there is a line of black trellised sheds where those hides are being dried, treated, where some dreadful species of men work noisily, in huge multitudes, smoking and swearing, powerful, incredibly greasy and coarse. . . . These are very old places; they are three, four hundred years old; and, thinking of them, I feel a longing to say something, to invent something wonderful about them too, about these foul places. . . . Farther on, beyond the tributary, are the Black Suburb, Agramacha, the rocky cliffs on which it stands, and the river that, for thousands of years, has been flowing beneath them, toward the remote south, toward the lower reaches of the Don, where once upon a time a young Tatar prince perished. About him, too, I'd like to invent something and to say it in verse; he is said to have been chastised by the miraculous icon of Our Lady which is still to be found in the most ancient of all our churches, standing above the river just opposite Agramacha—that ancient image before which burn undying icon-lamps, where some woman in a dark shawl is ever kneeling in prayer, pressing her thumb and first two fingers to her forehead and staring persistently and dolefully at the dusky-golden frame as it glistens dully in the warm light of the icon-lamp, showing through its holes the narrow, blackish-brown right hand, just like a strip of wood, pressed to the breast, and a little higher up the small and equally dark medieval face, humbly and sorrowfully bent toward the left shoulder, under the silver-laced, prickly little crown consisting of diamonds, pearls, and rubies sparkling minutely and variedly. . . . And beyond the river, beyond the town, stretching wide over a plain, lies Riverside: it is really a town in itself, with a whole railroad kingdom where, by day and by night, calling forth a yearning to travel far away, away where the gaggles of geese are now filing under the cold and gloomy sky, the locomotives are commandingly and appealingly, sadly and freely, echoing in the icy, resonant air. There lies the station, which also torments one with its odors—of fried meat pies, of samovars, of coffee—blended with the smell of coal smoke, that is, of the steam engines which, by day and night, are setting off for every part of Russia. . . .

I remember not a few such days, scant and short, which gave one a bittersweet torment, by the coziness of home and by dreams, now of the town's antiquity, now of the free autumnal expanses one saw from it. These days dragged endlessly amid the boredom of the classroom at school, where I had to learn all that men were supposed to know; then, in the silence of two warm commonplace rooms, their quietude heightened, not only by the sleepy tick of the alarm clock on Lyubov Andreevna's chest of drawers covered with a little knitted napkin, but also by the minute crackling of bobbins in the hands of Manya and Ksyusha, who sat all day long making lace—they dragged on slowly and monotonously, and suddenly were cut short. On some particularly sad dusky evening the gate outside would unexpectedly bang, then the door in the passage, the one in the anteroom; and suddenly on our threshold, brightening the whole house with light and joy, my father would appear in his furry earcap and unbuttoned raccoon coat, and I would run toward him full tilt and throw myself on his neck, stinging with my kisses his lovely warm lips beneath the cold and frost-moistened moustache, and feeling, with rapture: Lord, how unlike anybody else in the world he is! How quite, quite different from all the rest!

8

The street on which we lived ran the whole length of the town. Our part of it was empty and deserted, consisting of merchants' stone houses that seemed uninhabited. Its middle part, by contrast, was very animated—here it adjoined the market and had everything you could expect: taverns, arcades, high-class shops and hotels, including the one that stood at the corner of Long Street—the Noblemens' Hotel, which wasn't called that for nothing: its only guests were landowners, and through its basement windows the passersby smelled the sweet odor proper to a restaurant kitchen, saw the chefs in white caps, and, through the glass entrance door, a gently sloping and wide staircase carpeted in red.

My father, during my school years, was living through his last rise: having moved to Baturino, mortgaged it, and sold Kamenka—all this with a pretense of wise economic forethought—he once more felt himself a rich gentleman, and therefore, on his visits to town, he would again stay only at the Nobles', always occupying the best suite. Thus, when he used to come, I would be removed, for two or three days, from Rostovtsev's house into a quite different world, once more becoming for a time a little gentleman to whom everybody smiled and bowed—the cabmen before the door, the porter at the entrance, the valets, the maids, and even the clean-shaven Mikheich himself in his large tailcoat and white tie, a former serf of Prince Sheremetev who had in the course of his life tasted everything—Paris, Rome, St. Petersburg, Moscow—and now, sad and dignified, was living out his life as valet in an out-of-the-way town, in some Noblemen's Hotel where even the real gentlemen now only pretended to be such, and the rest were mere "district monschers" as he called them, people with exaggeratedly gentlemanlike manners, with suspiciously insolent exactingness, with voices that were low because of vodka rather than breeding.

"Good morning, Alexander Sergeich," the cabmen would outshout each other before the entrance to the Noblemens' Hotel. "Will you tell us to wait?—maybe you'll want to go to the circus tonight?"

And my father, who could not help feeling the falsity of his acting as wealthy as he had once been, was nevertheless pleased by these cries and gave instructions to wait, although there were always plenty of cabs near the Noblemen's and therefore no sense whatever in paying them for waiting.

Behind the glass entrance door it was very warm, unusually and excitingly bright with glowing lamps, and one was at once pleasantly enveloped in all that nice, gentlemanly atmosphere proper to old provincial hotels for the conferences and meetings of the nobility. From the ground-floor corridor which led to the restaurant came loud voices and laughter; someone shouted, "Mikheich, do tell the count, devil take you, that we're waiting for him!"

And on the staircase leading to the first floor, a giant in a huge fur wrap would meet us and suddenly stop, give a surprised exclamation, roll his cold vulture eyes with feigned joy, and kiss with courtly urbanity my mother's hand; he resembled at once a peasant and an old Russian prince, and my father would instantly emulate his society manner, firmly shaking his hand: "Please, please, do drop in, Prince. We'll be very glad!"

And in the corridor would be walking a short-legged, stocky young man in a jacket and high-collared cambric shirt, with sleek whitish hair and protruding eyes, bright-blue and always drunken-looking, who would shout from afar in a loud hoarse voice, in a hurried and extremely intimate manner (though he was no relation of ours at all): "Dear Uncle, it's been a long time! And I heard them say: 'Arseniev, Arseniev,' but I did not know whether it was you. . . . Good evening, dear Aunt," he would keep on saying, kissing my mother's hand in such an intimate way that she was compelled to kiss him back on the temple—"Good evening, Alexander," he would turn eagerly to me, calling me, as always, by the wrong name, "you look great. As for me, you see, Uncle, this is already the fifth day I've been sitting here waiting for that beast Krichevsky—he promised to lend me some money to pay the bank, and he himself, the devil knows what for, has bolted off to Warsaw and only Mordechai knows when he'll be back. . . . What about you, have you already had dinner? If not, let's go downstairs, there's a whole gathering there. . . . "

My father would kiss him heartily, and suddenly, for no good reason, unexpectedly even to himself, he would invite him to our room, take him there, and with great animation order from Mikheich an incredible quantity of hors d'oeuvres, dishes, vodkas, and wines. What a dreadful lot and how greedily our supposed relative ate and drank. How noisily and ceaselessly he talked, ejaculated, laughed, wondered. I can still hear his hoarse shouting, his ever-recurring arrogant sentence, "But do you, Uncle, really suppose me capable of such baseness?"

In the evening we sat in the vast glacial tent of the Brothers Truzzi, which smelt pungently and pleasantly of all the things a circus usually smells of. With sharp, parrotlike vociferation, wide-trousered clowns with floury faces and flaming orange hair flew out into the arena, accompanied by the spectators' guffaws and flopping flat on their bellies, with sham clumsiness, into the sand; in their wake gallumphed an old white horse on whose broad hollow back galloped a short-legged woman, erect, bestrewn with golden spangles, in pink tights, with pink taut thighs under her protruding ballet skirt. . . . The band was drumming away with unheeding élan "Willow, willow, my green one"; the handsome black-bearded ringmaster, dressed in tailcoat, spats, and top hat, standing in the middle of the arena and whirling around, was rhythmically and wonderfully cracking his long whip; the horse, stiffly and obstinately arching his neck, all curved aslant, galloped heavily around the very edge of the circle; the woman was tautening expectantly on his back, and then, all of a sudden, with a curt coquettish shout, jumped up and with a cracking noise broke through the paper hoop which the grooms in doublets had flung up before her. . . . And when, trying to look lighter than down, she at last got off the horse, back onto the trodden sand of the arena, she curtsied with the utmost grace, waved her little hands, twisting them in some peculiar way, and, accompanied by a storm of applause, vanished with an affected childishness into the wings, the music suddenly stopped short (although the clowns, prancing floppily about the arena with the air of forlorn idiots, shouted, rolling their r's, "Try again!"), and the whole circus gasped in delighted horror: the grooms ran out in a terrible flurry to the arena, dragging behind them a huge iron cage, and from the wings was suddenly heard a monstrous rolling roar, as if someone was abominably sick, and it was followed by such a powerful, kingly breathing that the whole tent of the Brothers Truzzi shook to its very pegs. . . .

9

After the departure of my father and mother, it seemed as if Lent had descended on the town. And somehow they often left on a Saturday, so that on the same evening I had to go to vespers to the church of the Elevation of the Cross, situated in one of the desolate lanes near our school.

And heavens! How well I remember those quiet sad evenings of late autumn under its low gloomy vaults! As a rule we would be brought there long before the beginning of the service and have to wait a long time in its tense stillness and twilight. There is no one but us—only the figures of a few old women kneeling in the corners, and not a sound but the whispering of their prayers and the slow crackling of the few candles and icon-lamps before the altar. The twilight steadily darkens, behind the narrow windows the dying evening turns blue and purple, ever sadder and sadder. . . . And then come the soft footsteps of the priests, in warm cassocks and high galoshes, walking through to the altar. But after that, again the stillness, the expectation, lasts for a long time; mysterious preparations go forward at the altar, behind the Tsar's Gate[9] upholstered with red silk; then, upon its opening—

which is always a little unexpected and terrifying—a long and silent incensing of the altar table, until at last the deacon comes out to the pulpit, calling out with a sustained solemnity, "Arise!"—until from the depth of the altar he is answered by the humble and sad inaugural voice, "Glory to the Holy and Consubstantial and Vivifying and Undivided Trinity," and until this voice is drowned by the still, concordant music of the choir: "Amen. . . ."

How it all moves me! I am still a boy, an adolescent, but then, I was born endowed with the sense of all this, and during the past years I have so many times passed through that expectation, that tense silence preceding the service, so many times heard those exclamations and the "amen" that unfailingly follows them and drowns them out, that the whole thing has become, as it were, part of my soul, and my soul, divining beforehand every word of the service, now gives a double response to everything, intensified by its expectation. "Glory to the Holy and Consubstantial . . ."—I hear the pleasant familiar voice coming faintly from the altar, and for the rest of the service I stand as if bewitched.

"O come, let us worship God our King! O come let us worship. . . . " "Bless the Lord, o my soul," I hear, while the priest, preceded by the deacon with a taper, quietly walks about the church, silently filling it with whiffs of the fragrance of incense, and bowing to the icons; and tears dim my eyes, for already I know with certainty that there is, and can be, nothing more beautiful or loftier on earth than all this; that even if what Glebochka said was true when he asserted, on the authority of some ill-shaven schoolboys from the upper grades, that God does not exist, all the same nothing can be better than what I feel now as I listen to these ejaculations and chants, and gaze now at the little red flames before the dull-golden wall of the old iconostasis, now at the Lord's holy warrior, the godly Prince Alexander Nevsky, painted full length in complete warrior's armor, in helmet and coat of mail, on the gilded pillar near me, one hand pressed to his heart in token of his fear of and veneration for God, and his menacing and pious eyes lifted heavenward. . . . [10]

And on and on flows the holy mystery. The Tsar's Gate is closed and opened alternately, symbolizing now our ejection from the paradise lost by us, now the new contemplation thereof; wonderful light-prayers are recited, giving vent to our sorrowful awareness of our earthly weakness, our helplessness, and our eagerness to be led along the path of God; the vaults of the church grow brighter and warmer with the light of many candles lit in token of the human expectation of the Savior's advent, symbolizing the illumination of human hearts with hope, and a firm belief in God's bounties is sounded in the earthly requests of the great liturgical prayer: "For the peace from above, and for the salvation of our souls. . . . For the peace of the whole world, and the welfare of God's holy churches. . . . " And then again that feeble, humble voice which peacefully resolves everything: "For unto Thee are due all glory, honor and worship, to the Father and to the Son and to the Holy Spirit, now and forever. . . . "

No, it is not true what I said about Gothic cathedrals, about the organs: I never wept in those cathedrals as I did in the tiny church of the Elevation of the Cross on those dark lonely evenings, after seeing off my father and mother, and entering, virtually as into my paternal home, beneath its low vaults, into its silence, warmth, and twilight, standing wearily under them in my long school uniform and listening to the sorrowfully humble "Let my prayer be fulfilled" or to the deliciously drawling "O Kindly Light—holy glory of the immortal—Heavenly Father—of holy, blesséd—Jesus Christ . . ."—mentally intoxicated by the vision of some mystical sunset which I pictured to myself when I heard recited: "Having come to the setting of the sun, having seen the evening light . . ."; or kneeling in that sad and mysterious moment when once more a profound silence enfolds the whole church for a while, the candles are once more extinguished, plunging it into the old-testamental nocturnal darkness; and then there would begin as if from afar—drawling, cautious, barely audible, portending the dawn: "Glory to God in the highest—and on earth peace—goodwill toward men . . ."—with those passionately dolorous yet blissful thrice-repeated cries in the middle: "Blessed art Thou o Lord; teach me Thy statutes!"

10

And then I remember many hard, gray, wintry days, many dark and dirty thaws, when Russian provincial life would become particularly painful, when everyone's face would turn gloomy, hostile—a Russian is primitively subject to the influence of nature!—and everything in the world, just as one's own existence, tormented one by its futility, aimlessness. . . .

I recall impenetrable Asiatic blizzards, raging sometimes for whole weeks on end through which the town belfries barely loomed. I recall the Epiphany frosts that made one think of most ancient times of Russia, of the frosts that made "the earth crackle seven feet deep": then, at night, over the snow-white town all drowned in snowdrifts, blazed menacingly in the raven-black sky the white constellation of Orion, and by day, crystalline and sinister, two dull suns shone; and in the taut and resonant immobility of the burning air the whole town was slowly and wildly besmirched with livid smoke from the chimneys and creaked and resounded all over with the footsteps of the pedestrians and the runners of sleighs. . . . During one such frost the mendicant idiot, Dunya, froze to death on the cathedral parvis; for half a century she had roamed the town, and the town, which had always mocked her with the utmost ruthlessness, suddenly gave her almost a royal funeral.

Strange as it may seem, immediately after this comes to my mind a ball at the girls' school—the first ball I went to. The weather was again very frosty. As Glebochka and I returned home after school, we intentionally took the street on which the girls' school was located; in its courtyard the snowdrifts bordering the drive that led to the main entrance were already being leveled out and planted with two rows of extremely thick and fresh fir trees. The sun was setting; everything looked clean, youthful, and rose-colored—the snowy street, the snow-laden roofs, the walls of the houses, their windowpanes shining with golden mica, and the air itself, also youthful, strong, penetrating one's breast like exhilarating ether. On the way we met schoolgirls coming from their school, dressed in fur coats and shod in high galoshes, wearing pretty hats and hoods, with long frost-silvered eyelashes and radiant eyes, and some of them said in full, clear, affable tones as they passed, "Come to the ball!"—troubling one by that full, clear tone, rousing in me the first feelings for something which lay inside those fur coats, galoshes, and hoods, in those tender excited faces, in the long frosted eyelashes and quick ardent glances—feelings that were afterward to possess me with such force. . . .

Long after the ball I felt intoxicated by recollections of it and of myself—of that well-dressed, handsome, light, deft schoolboy in a new blue uniform and white gloves who, with such a joyously brave chill in his heart, mixed with the dense and elegant girlish throng, ran about the corridors and staircases, drank many almond syrups in the refreshment room, glided among the dancers on the floor sprinkled with some glistening powder, in the big white hall flooded with the pearly light of the chandeliers and echoing from the balconies with triumphantly resonant thunders of the military band, breathing in all that fragrant ardor with which balls drug the novice, and enchanted by every tiny shoe he came across, by every white cape, every black velvet ribbon on the neck, every silk bow in the braid, by every youthful breast heaving in blissful dizziness after a waltz . . . .

11

While in third grade I once talked back to the prinicpal for which I nearly got expelled. During a Greek lesson, while the master was explaining something to us, writing it on the board, chalking it down firmly, skillfully—and feeling greatly pleased with his own skill—I, instead of listening to him, was rereading for the hundredth time one of my favorite pages in the Odyssey—about Nausicaa going with her handmaidens to the shore to wash the yarn.[11] Suddenly the headmaster entered the classroom; he was in the habit of pacing the corridors and peeping through the doors; he made straight for me, snatched the book from my hands and shouted furiously, "Go into the corner till the end of the lesson!"

I rose, turning pale, and answered, "Don't shout at me, I'm not a boy. . . . "

Indeed, I no longer felt myself a boy. I was rapidly growing up, mentally and physically. I no longer lived only by feelings; I had acquired a certain mastery over them, begun to discriminate what I saw and took in, begun to look as if from above at the things that surrounded me—and those I lived through. I had already experienced something of the kind at the transition from childhood to boyhood. Now I was living through it with redoubled force, and often, wandering on holidays about the town with Glebochka, through the suburbs and Riverside—already wandering freely, independently—I would notice that my stature was almost that of an average passerby, that only my adolescent's leanness, slenderness, and slimness, and the fineness and freshness of my beardless face, distinguished me from those passersby.

Early in September of the year I passed into the fourth grade, one of my classmates, a certain Vadim Lopukhin, suddenly expressed a desire to make friends with me. One day, during the long break, he approached me, took my arm just above the elbow, and said, looking straight and blankly into my eyes, "Look here, would you like to join our club? We have formed a club of nobles' sons, so as to not to mix any longer with all the Arkhipovs and Zausailovs. Get it?"[12]

He was in every respect older than I, for in every grade he invariably sat for two years; and he already had the tallness of a grown youth, broad-boned, fair-haired, with light-colored eyes, with a golden moustache struggling through. One had the impression that he already knew everything, had experienced everything, one felt that he was debauched, and also that he was proud of it as a sign of bon ton and his own grown-upness: during recess he strolled absently and rapidly amid the crowd with his well-bred, easy, rather springy and shuffling gait, thrusting his body forward nonchalantly and insolently, his hands in the pockets of his wide light trousers, all the time whistling and gazing around him with cold and somewhat mocking curiosity; for a chat he approached only people of his own set, and on meeting the vice principal nodded to him familiarly. . . . By that time I had already begun to take an interest in people; in watching them, my likes and dislikes began to take shape, and I divided people into certain categories, some of which forever became loathsome to me.

Lopukhin certainly belonged to the loathsome. And yet I was flattered and gave whole-hearted assent to the idea of the club, whereupon he offered to take me that same night to the municipal gardens.

"First you must get to know some of our chaps better," he said, "and second, I'll introduce you to Nalya R. She's still a schoolgirl, the daughter of very stuck-up people, but she already knows what's what, is clever as a devil, gay as a Frenchwoman, and quite able to drink a bottle of champagne without any help. She herself is small, and her feet are like a fairy's. . . . Get it?" he said, looking as usual into my eyes and thinking, or pretending to think, of something else.

And now, immediately after that talk, something quite extraordinary happened to me: for the first time in my life I suddenly felt not only that I was in love with this Nalya, whom I imagined to myself according to Lopukhin's description—this being in love no longer resembling that fleeting, light, mysterious, and beautiful thing that had once touched me at the sight of Sashka, and afterward at the meeting of young Rostovtsev with that girl in the garden on the tsar's name-day—but also something that was virile and physical. How tremblingly I awaited the evening! There it was, I fancied, at last! What "at last," and what was it, really? Some fatal and seemingly long-coveted line over which at last I, too, had to step, the uncanny threshold of some sinful paradise. . . . And already I felt as if everything was to happen, or at least to begin, that very night. I went to the hairdresser, who cut my hair *en brosse* and, after scenting me, combed it up with a round brush smelling of grease and spice; I spent nearly an hour washing, dressing, and cleaning myself at home, and as I made my way to the garden I felt my hands grow ice-cold and my ears ablaze. In the garden there was again music, the tall gushing fountain was spouting its cool powder, and it smelled, in a feminine-ly luxurious way, of flowers in the crisp icy air of the purple autumn sunset; but there were only a few people around, which made me still more ashamed of walking alone, in everybody's sight, in that select group of nobles' sons, and of keeping up with them some special noblemen's conversation—when something suddenly struck me, as it were: in the avenue was walking swiftly toward us, with minute steps, a cane in her hand, a little woman-girl, extremely well formed and very neatly and simply dressed. Rapidly she approached us and, making affable play with her agate eyes, freely and firm-ly shook our hands, her own small hand in a tight black glove, and began talk-ing and laughing fast, once or twice throwing a fleeting but curious glance at me; and I, for the first time in my life, became so vividly and sensuously aware of all that peculiar and terrible something which lurks in the lips of a laughing woman, in the childlike intonation of a woman's voice, in the round-ness of a woman's shoulders, in the slimness of a woman's waist, in that inex-pressible something which there is even in a woman's ankle—that I could not utter one word.

"Take him in hand a little, Nalya," said Lopukhin quietly and insolently nodding at me, with a smile in his inexpressive eyes, and alluding with such unabashed significance to something, that I was seized by cold shivers and my teeth nearly chattered. . . . Fortunately, in a few days Nalya left for the provincial capital—her uncle, our vice governor, died suddenly. Fortunately, too, nothing came of the club. Besides, a great event soon befell our family: my brother George was arrested.[13]

Even my father was dumbstruck by this event.

It is now impossible even to imagine how in the old days the average Russian looked upon anyone who dared to "go against the tsar," whose image, notwithstanding the continual pursuit of Alexander II ending in his murder, still remained as the image of "earthly God" and aroused a mystical reverence in people's hearts and minds. There was something mystical, too, in the way people uttered the word "socialist"—it implied deep disgrace and horror, for it was associated with the conception of every kind of villainy. When the news spread that "socialists" had appeared even in our parts—the brothers Rogachev, the Subbotin girls—this struck our family as if plague or biblical leprosy had befallen the district. Then something still more dreadful happened. It turned out that the son of our nearest neighbor had suddenly disappeared from St. Petersburg, where he was studying at the Military Medical Academy, had then made his appearance in the neighborhood of Elets at a watermill, as an ordinary laborer, in bast shoes and hempen shirt, with a long shaggy beard, and before long had been recognized, charged with "propaganda"—this word, too, had a dreadful sound—and incarcerated in the St. Peter and Paul Fortress.[14] Our father was no obscurantist, and far from timid in any way; as a child I had heard him, on more than one occasion, insolently call Nicholas I "Nicholas the Flogger" and "upstart," yet the next day I also heard him solemnly, and just as sincerely, utter something quite different: "His Majesty the Emperor Nicholas Pavlovich reposing in God. . . ."[15] With my father everything depended on his lordly mood—and which, after all, did prevail? That is why even he could merely shrug his shoulders disconcertedly when that bearded young laborer was "seized."

"Poor Feodor Mikhailovich!" he said with horror, referring to the father. "Probably this little birdie will be hanged. Most certainly he will," he would say, with his usual fondness for a striking situation. "And serve him right, serve him right! I'm sorry for the old man, but one mustn't stand on ceremony with them. Otherwise we'll bounce into something like the French Revolution! And wasn't I right when I said, 'Remember my word, that stiffnecked, morose duffer will end as a convict, a disgrace to his whole family!'"

And now the same disgrace, the same horror, had suddenly befallen our own family. How? Why? After all, my brother could by no means be called a "stiff-necked, morose duffer." His "criminal activity" sounded still more absurd, still more incredible than that of the Subbotin girls, who even though they belonged to a wealthy and good aristocratic family might simply have been led astray, in girlish folly, by people like the Rogachevs.

What my brother's "activity" consisted of, and how exactly he spent his university years, I do not really know. I only know that this activity had begun when he was still at school, under the leadership of a "remarkable personality," a seminary student called Dobrokhotov. But what did my brother have in common with Dobrokhotov? True, my brother, telling me about him afterward, still admired him, spoke about his "rigorism," his iron will, his "ruthless hatred of autocracy and self-denying love for the people";[16] but did my brother possess even a single one of these features? And where did his admiration come from? Obviously it was just a result of that everlasting light-headedness, the enthusiasm so characteristic of the Russian nobility, and which the Radishchevs, Chatskys, Rudins, Ogarevs, Herzens never gave up, even in their old age;[17] because Dobrokhotov's qualities were deemed to be lofty, heroic; and, finally, for the simple reason that, recalling Dobrokhotov, he recalled all that happy festive atmosphere amid which his youth had been flowing—the festive awareness of that youth, of the criminal, and therefore sweetly uncanny, participation in all the secret circles, the holiday atmosphere of gatherings, of songs, of "seditious" speeches, of dangerous plans and undertakings. . . .

That everlasting Russian need of holiday! How sensuous we are, how we crave to be intoxicated with life—not merely delighted, but really intoxicated—how we are allured by constant intoxication, by fits of drunkenness, how bored we are with everyday life and with regular work!

Russia in my time lived an extraordinarily ample and active life; the number of her sound, strong working people went on growing. Yet wasn't it the traditional dream of rivers flowing with milk, of unfettered freedom, of holiday, that was one of the main causes, for instance, of the Russian revolutionary spirit? And what, generally speaking, *is* a Russian protester, rebel, revolutionary, always ridiculously severed from reality and despising it, unwilling to submit himself in the slightest degree to reason, to calculation, to inconspicuous, unhurried, unobtrusive activity? What! to serve in the governor's office, to contribute one's miserable share to public affairs! No way— "A coach, give me a coach!"[18]

For my brother, both at school and in the university, a brilliant scholarly future was predicted. But did he then think of scholarship? He had, you see, to "renounce entirely all personal life, to devote himself to the suffering people." He was a kind, noble, bright, good-hearted youth, and yet in this he simply lied to himself, or rather tried to live—and actually lived—on fictitious emotions, as did thousands of others. What was the general reason for this "going to the people" on the part of youthful noblemen, for their revolt against their own set, for their circles, discussions, clandestine activity, their bloodthirsty words and deeds? In fact the children were flesh of the flesh, bone of the bone of their fathers, who had also been dissipating their lives in every way. Ideas were all very well; but in those youthful revolutionaries how much was there also of the mere longing for gay idleness under the cloak of hectic activity, of self-intoxication with meetings, noise, songs, all sorts of clandestine dangers—and this "arm in arm" with the pretty Subbotin girls—

with dreams of police searches and prisons, of sensational trials and companionable journeys to Siberia, to penal servitude, to the other side of the Arctic circle! What induced my brother, whose excellent achievements both at school and in the university were due entirely to his quite uncommon talent, to devote all the ardor of his youth to those "clandestine activities"? The bitter lot of Pila and Sysoyka?[19] No doubt, reading about it, he shed tears more than once. But why, then, like all his fellow revolutionaries, did he never notice either Pila or Sysoyka in real life, in Novoselki, in Baturino? In many ways he was a son of his father who would say, very appropriately, after a couple of glasses of vodka, "How splendid! I love drinking. It rejuvenates!"

"Rejuvenates"—the word had once upon a time been used at the distilleries, and the man who had drunk meant by it that something young and joyous entered into him, that there was going on within him a certain sweet fermentation, a release from reason, from the bonds and rules of everyday life. So the peasants say of vodka, "Why, then, it loosens a man up inside!" The famous dictum "Russia's joy is in drinking" is by no means so simple as it may seem.[20] Aren't the holy-foolery, and the tramping, the ritual orgies, the self-immolations, and all sorts of revolts akin to that "joy"—or even that amazing picturesqueness, that verbal sensuality for which Russian literature is so famous?

13

My brother was in hiding for a long time, changing residence, living under an assumed name. Then, when he decided that the danger was over, he came to take a rest in Baturino. But here, on the following day, he was arrested: his arrival had been reported by the estate agent of one of our neighbors.

It is remarkable that on the same morning as the police came to Baturino that agent was killed by a tree which was being felled in the park on his instructions. Thus in my mind has always dwelled the picture which I had then imagined: the vast trees already thinned by autumn, picturesquely defaced by autumn rainstorms and the first frost, bespattered with rotting leaves, their trunks and branches blackened and with motley remnants of their yellow and red garb; a fresh bright morning; the dazzling sunlight glittering on the lawns and descending in warm golden pillars among the distant trunks into the damp coolness and shadow of the ground, into the thin smoke of the still lingering morning mist shining ethereally blue; the crossing of two avenues, and there an old, splendid, spreading maple tree displaying the transparence of its huge open crown, the black pattern of its branches, with here and there large notched lemon-colored leaves hanging on them; its mighty trunk, petrified with age, was being cleft deeper and deeper by the axes of some shirt-clad peasants, their caps cocked backward, uttering cries of delight, while the agent, his hands deep in his pockets, was looking up at the tree's top, trembling in the sky. Maybe he was thinking of the cunning way in which he had hoodwinked the Socialist? And suddenly the tree cracked; its top jerked abruptly forward—and with a noise, gradually gaining speed, weight, and horror, it hurled itself at him through the branches of the neighboring trees. . . .

Later I was often at that estate. It once used to belong to our mother. My father, who had an insatiable passion for squandering everything, had long ago sold it and eaten up the proceeds. Upon the death of the new owner it passed to some grand lady living in Moscow and was forsaken: the land was leased out to the peasants, and the manor left to God's will. And often, passing by on the highway, from which it was only about a half-mile distant, I would turn off, ride down the broad oak alley that led to it, reach the spacious courtyard, leave the horse by the stables, and walk up to the house. . . . How many deserted manors and orchards there are in Russian literature, and how fondly have they always been described! Why does the Russian soul thus rejoice in waste, wilderness, ruin, decay? I would walk up to the house, pass the garden that rose behind it. . . . Stables, servants' cottages, granaries, and other outbuildings scattered about the desolate courtyard—all was huge, gray, all was going to rack and ruin and growing wild; and, overgrown with weeds and bushes, the kitchen gardens, the farmyards, which stretched beyond them and merged into the field, were going wild likewise. The wooden house covered with gray clapboard was of course rotting and dilapidated, growing more and more fascinating by the year, and I was especially fond of peeping through its windows, with their minutely grated frames. . . . How can one convey the sensation one feels at such moments, when one peeps stealthily—profanely, as it were—into an empty old house, into the speechless and mysterious sanctum of its remote, vanished life! And the park behind the house was of course half cut down, though in it still flaunted many age-old lindens, maples, silvery Italian poplars, birches and oaks, solitarily and silently whiling away in that forgotten garden their long life, their eternally youthful old age, the beauty of which seemed enhanced in that solitude and silence, in its blessed, divine purposelessness. The sky and the old trees, each of which always has its own expression, its own shape, its own soul, its own thoughts—can one contemplate them too long? I would wander for hours beneath them, not taking my eyes from their infinitely varied tops, branches, leaves, longing to understand, divine, and forever impress upon myself their images; I would sit thinking of them on the spacious slope below the park, among the huge oak stumps showing their coarse blackness amid high tender grass and flowers, over the shining ponds that still spread the full sheets of their waters at the foot of the hill in the valley. . . . How my soul would then sever itself from life, with what sad and kind wisdom, as if from some unearthly distance, would it look upon life, contemplating human

78

"things and deeds"! And unfailingly I would recall here both that unfortunate man killed by the old maple, which perished along with him, and the miserable lot of my brother unwittingly ruined by that man, and the far-off autumn day when he was driven away from Baturino to the town by two bearded policemen, to that very jail where once I had been so struck by the dismal prisoner gazing at the declining sun from behind the iron grating. . . .

That day my father and mother drove to the town in the wake of my brother's official carriage, quite beside themselves. Mother could not even cry; her dark eyes burned with a dry terrible flame. Father tried to look neither at her nor at me, smoked all the time, and kept on repeating, "Stuff and nonsense! Believe me—in a few days all this rubbish will be straightened out. . . . "

On the same night my brother was taken farther on, to Kharkov, the center of the clandestine group for belonging to which he had been arrested. We went to the station to see him off. I was chiefly struck, I think, by the fact that on arriving at the station we had to go to the third-class waiting room, where, watched over by the police, he was awaiting the departure of the train, no longer allowed to sit with ordinary, respectable, free people, already deprived of the liberty to make his own choices, of the possibility of drinking tea or eating pastries with them. And as soon as we entered that stinking, hideously disorderly, crowded, noisy room, I was literally heart-stricken by his look, by the sense of his being a prisoner, a man set apart and devoid of rights: he himself understood it well too, and was aware of all his humiliation; he smiled guiltily, ill at ease. He sat lonely in the farthest corner by the door leading to the platform, youthfully attractive and pathetic in his slenderness, his light gray suit, over which my father's raccoon fur coat was thrown. Around him there was an empty space,—the policemen now and again dispersed peasants and townsmen who thronged around and looked with fearful curiosity at this live Socialist—thank God, already caged! Particular curiosity was shown by a village priest, tall, in a high beaver cap and high dusty galoshes, who kept his wide-open eyes fixed on him and in a mysterious gibber poured out questions to the policemen, which they didn't answer. They looked upon my brother as a naughty boy whom, willy-nilly, they had to watch and to deliver where they were told, and one of them, with a kind, condescending smile, said to my mother: "Don't you be anxious, Madam; everything, please God, will be all right. . . . Come here and sit with us, it's still twenty minutes before the train leaves. . . . Now my assistant will go to fetch some boiling water and buy the gentleman anything you may order for him to eat on the way. . . . You did well to give the gentleman a fur coat—it'll be chilly at night in the carriage. . . . "

I remember that here my mother at last started to weep—she sat down on the bench next to my brother and suddenly began to sob, pressing her mouth with a handkerchief, while my father, making a sickened grimace, waved his hand and walked swiftly away. He could not bear sufferings and vexations, and he always, by way of instinctive self-defense, hastened to evade them somehow—he even avoided any partings if they were in the least painful, always suddenly cutting them short, hastily frowning and muttering that a drawn-out parting meant more tears. He went to the restaurant, drank several glasses of vodka, went to look for the colonel of the station police to ask permission for my brother to travel first class. . . .

14

That night I felt nothing beyond an embarrassed bewilderment. My brother had been driven away, my father and mother gone. . . . It took me some considerable time after this to live through my new mental distress.

My father and mother for some reason went away the very next morning. It was a sunny day, such as often happens in October, but even in the town one was chilled right through by the sharp north wind, and everything looked extraordinarily clean, bright, and spacious—the gaps of the streets, the vista of the empty surroundings seemingly quite devoid of air, the bright sky shining here and there with a sharp bluish-green between the swiftly sailing opaque white clouds. . . . I saw my parents as far as the monastery and the jail, between which the road, already frosted and hard as stone, multicolored by the sun and the shadows of the clouds, rushed away into the cold naked fields. Here the tarantass stopped. The sun, which, while we were getting ready and starting off, had risen somewhat higher, was now and again peeping from behind the clouds; but its dazzling light gave no warmth, and as soon as we got into the fields the wind began to blow so piercingly from the north that the coachman on the box had to duck his head; my father had on his fur coat and a winter cap, and his moustache waved in the wind and tears came to his eyes, dimmed by the wind. I got out, and my mother again began crying bitterly, pressing her warm gray hood to my face; as for my father, he merely crossed me hastily, put his cold hand to my lips, and shouted into the coachman's back, "Let's go!"

The tarantass, with its canopy half raised, began at once clattering off; the mighty chestnut haft-horse in the middle tossed up his head and shook the bell, which pealed out under the yoke; the bay trace-horses began to gallop harmoniously and freely, flinging up their croups, and for a long time I stood in the road, my eyes accompanying that canopy, watching the hind wheels racing away, the matted pasterns of the shaft-horse swiftly dancing between them under the chassis of the tarantass, the shoes of the trace-horses darting up high and lightly at its sides; for a long time I listened with anguish to the receding plaint of the bells. I stood in my light uniform coat, which the wind blew right through, resisting it with my shoulder, and remembered what my father had been saying the night before, during supper in our room in the Noblemen's Hotel, as he poured himself some beer.

"Stuff and nonsense!" he said firmly. "Pshaw! Fiddle-de-dee! Well, they've arrested him, taken him away, and maybe they'll banish him to Siberia—most surely they will—but then nowadays there are not a few of them so banished, and in what way, let me ask, is a town like Tobolsk worse than Elets, Voronezh? After all, everything's stuff and nonsense! The evil will pass, and the good will pass, as St. Tikhon Zadonsky has said—everything will pass!"[21]

I recalled these words, and far from feeling relieved, I was more pained by them. Perhaps everything really was nonsense, but that nonsense was my life; and why did I feel it to have been given to me, not at all for nonsense, and not just that everything should pass and vanish without a trace? Everything is nonsense—yet, because my brother had been taken away, the whole world seemed to me to have grown empty, become huge and senseless, and in this world I now felt as sad and lonely as if I were already outside it, whereas I had to be in it, loving and rejoicing in it! How could it be nonsense when it turned out that I loved—and had, evidently, always loved—that pleasant and pathetic "Socialist," who had sat the night before a prisoner at the station, in his gray coat and with a raccoon coat thrown over his shoulders—and he had been taken away somewhere, deprived of freedom and happiness, severed from us and from all ordinary life? Everything in the world seemed to be as before, just as usual, and everybody was free and happy and he alone was in chains and in misery. Here, propelled by that icy and unruly wind, is some plain ruddy-brown dog running along the road to the town, trotting sideways, absorbed in its own cares; and he is no longer there, he is somewhere in the unending, empty, shining southern distance, traveling in the locked compartment of a sunlit carriage, under the escort of two armed policemen who are taking him to somewhere called Kharkov. Here, its grated windows facing the monastery across the road, the yellow prison-house stands quietly against the sun, as uncanny, as different from everything else, as the one that awaits him in Kharkov, and yesterday he, too, spent several hours in that house and today he isn't there any longer—one feels only the sorrowful residue of his presence. Here, from behind the high crenellated monastery wall, the dull golden domes of the cathedral glitter marvelously, and the black branches of the old churchyard trees bend, and he can no longer see that beauty or share with me the joy of looking at them. . . . On the enormous locked monastery gate, on its pillars, were full-length paintings of two tall, sepulchrally emaciated saints in shrouds, with sad greenish countenances, holding long unfolded scrolls reaching to the ground: how long have they been standing thus, for how many centuries have they been not of this world? Everything will pass; everything passes; the time will come when we won't be of this world either—neither myself, nor my father, mother, and brother—and these ancient Russian saints with their holy and wise writings in their hands will still stand just as dispassionately and sadly on the gates. . . . And, taking off my cap, tears in my eyes, I began crossing myself before the gate, feeling ever more vividly with every minute my pity for myself and my brother grow—that is, feeling ever fonder of myself, of him, of my father and mother—and ardently imploring the saints to help us, for, however painful, however sad it may be in this world, it is nevertheless beautiful, and we still crave to be happy and love each other. . . .

I went back, frequently pausing and turning around. The wind seemed to blow still stronger and colder, but the sun was rising, shining, the day grew gayer, demanded life and joy, and over everything—over the town, over the deserted square, over the sacred, silent domain of the monastery with its high wall, churchyard grove, and golden cathedral cupolas, and over that boundless steppe across which, away, toward the pellucid green northern horizon, the road ran—there sailed, in the pale-blue, watery, bright autumnal sky, large and beautiful purplish clouds, and everything was bright and mottled, and over everything, light and picturesque, now and again alternating with the sun, ran airy opaque shadows. I would stand still and gaze, and then go farther. . . . Where did I not go on that day!

I walked all around the town. I traversed that black suburb which sloped down from the square to the tanneries, crossed the decrepit humpbacked stone bridge over the sweetly foul tributary of the river piled with rotting brown hides, and walked up the opposite hill to the convent—it shone against the sun with the chalky whiteness of its walls, and from its gate emerged a young nun in coarse boots and a rough black dress, but of such a fine, pure, old Russian iconographic beauty that I actually stopped short, taken aback. On the cliffs behind the cathedral I stood gazing at the rotten plank roofs of the townsmen's huts below, nestling among the mounds along the river, at the interiors of their dirty and miserable little courtyards—and all the time thought something about human life, thought that everything passes and repeats itself, that quite probably three hundred years ago those same plank roofs were there and all sorts of weeds that grow in the wild spaces, on the clayey mounds; then, in my mind, I saw my father and mother driving in a coach along the gleaming desolate fields; saw Baturino, where everything was so peaceful, familiar—now, of course, terribly sad, and yet unspeakably lovely and delightful; saw my brother Nicholas; the dark-eyed ten-year-old Olya, our very special fir tree in front of the hall windows, and the empty, bare, autumnal desolation of the garden, the unruly wind and the declining sun in it—I strove there with all my soul, but underlying all these thoughts and feelings I was incessantly aware of my brother. I looked at the river, which advanced in gray even ripples on the yellow cliffs, took a turn under them, and vanished in the distance; I thought again that, even in the days of the Pechenegs,[22] it had followed the same course—and tried not to look toward Riverside, toward the station reddening on its border, from which yesterday in the dusk my brother had been taken away, not to hear the melancholy, imperious sounds of the engines as they came through the wind in the icy evening air. . . . How agonizingly everything that I saw and lived through on that queer day became mixed up with my brother, and most of all, it seems, that sweet rapture with which I remembered the little nun coming out of the convent gate!

My mother at that time took a solemn vow of lifelong fasting for my brother's salvation, which she kept to very strictly all her life, to her dying day. And God not only spared but even rewarded her: in a year's time my brother was released and, to her great joy, was sent for three years to Baturino, to live under police supervision.

15

In a year's time I too obtained my freedom—I left school and also returned under my parents' roof, there to encounter days that were doubtless the most astonishing of all I have lived through.

It was already the beginning of youth, a period astonishing to everybody, and which, in my case, owing to certain peculiarities of mine, turned out to be particularly astonishing: for example, my vision was such that I could see all seven stars of the Pleiades; I could hear the whistle of a marmot from half a mile away, and I was capable of getting drunk on the smell of lily of the valley or an old book. . . .

Not only did my life at that time again undergo a sharp outward change, but it was marked by one more sudden and beneficent transition, a blossoming of all my being.

Astonishing is the spring burgeoning of a tree! And how astonishing it is when the spring is harmonious, happy! Then that invisible process which is incessantly going on within it shows itself, becomes manifest in a particularly marvelous way. Looking at the tree one morning, you are struck by the abundance of buds that have covered it during the night. And after a certain time the buds suddenly burst forth—and the black pattern of the twigs is at once strewn with countless bright-green flecks. Then the first cloud comes over, the first thunder roars, the first warm shower comes rushing down, and again a miracle happens: the tree has already become so dark, so splendid in comparison with its bare tracery of yesterday, has spread out its wide glossy greenery so thick and far, stands in such beauty and strength of young firm foliage, that you simply cannot believe your eyes. . . . Something of the kind happened also to me at the time. And now there came, for me too, not only the full and joyous life of spring, but also those magic days "When in mysterious valleys, in springtide, amid swans calling, near waters shining silently, the Muse began to visit me. . . ."[23]

Neither Lyceum gardens, nor lakes and swans of Tsarskoe Selo,[24] none of this had been bequeathed to me, a descendant of "ruined fathers."[25] But the great and divine novelty, the freshness and joy of "all the impressions of life,"[26] the valleys that are always and everywhere mysterious for a youthful soul, the waters shining silently, and the first, pitiful, unskillful yet unforgettable meetings with the Muse—all this I had, too. The setting in which, to use Pushkin's phrase, I was "blossoming out," was quite unlike the parks of Tsarskoe Selo. But how fascinating, how familiar Pushkin's lines about them sounded to me even then! How vividly they expressed the substance of what filled my soul—those secret swans' calls which sometimes resounded in it so fervently and appealingly. Does it matter what actually called them forth? Does it matter that I could not find a single word to render, to express them?

16

All human destinies shape themselves accidentally, depending on the destinies surrounding them. So also the destiny of my youth shaped itself, determining likewise my whole destiny. As in the old quatrain—

Restored to me the roof paternal
Bestowed the peace of lonely steppes
And wonted life and circle beloved
And ardor of enraptur'd soul. . . .

Why did I return to that roof? Why did I leave school? Would my youth have been as it was, and what shape would my whole life have taken if that, at first glance insignificant, event had not happened? My father used sometimes to say that I had left it for reasons quite inadmissibly unexpected and absurd, simply out of "lordly license," as he was fond of putting it; he called me a self-willed whippersnapper and reproached himself for his leniency toward my obstinacy. But he used to say something else—his opinions were always extremely contradictory—namely, that I had acted quite "logically"— he pronounced that word with great precision and refinement, that I had acted as my nature dictated to me.

"No," he would say, "Alexey's calling is neither the civil service, nor a uniform, nor the management of an estate, but the poetry of soul and life. Besides, thank God, there is nothing to manage any longer! And here—who knows?—he might prove to be a second Pushkin or Lermontov."

Indeed, there were many things that prevented my official education: that "license" which was so proper in olden times in Russia, and this not only in the nobility, and of which there was not a little in my blood; and the hereditary traits of my "daddy"; and my calling for the "poetry of soul and life," which had already clearly manifested itself by that time; and finally the accidental fact of my brother being exiled not to Siberia, but to Baturino.

I had grown at once physically stronger and more mature during my last year at school. Until then, I think, my mother's traits had predominated in me, but now my father's began to develop rapidly—his brisk liveliness, his resistance to circumstances, that sentimentality which was in him, too, but which he always instinctively hastened to nip in the bud, his unconscious perseverance in achieving his wishes, and his waywardness. That really very unimportant thing that happened to my brother, and which at the time had appeared to all our family as something dreadful, was not lived through by me all at once; nevertheless, it was, of course, lived through, and even contributed to my maturity and the revival of my forces. I felt that my father was right—"one cannot live like a weeping willow," life was "after all, an excellent thing," as he would sometimes say when drunk; and already I saw consciously that there really was something irresistibly wonderful in verbal creation. I made up my mind definitely to pass at all costs into the fifth grade and then get rid of school for good, return to Baturino, and become "a second Pushkin or Lermontov," a Zhukovsky, a Baratynsky,[27] my kinship with all of whom I seemed to feel so vividly from the first moment I learned of them, and on whose portraits I looked as upon family ones.

Throughout that winter I tried to lead a working, brisk life, and in the spring there was no need for me even to try. In the course of winter something, no doubt, had happened to me—in the sense, first of all, of bodily development—as happens unexpectedly to all adolescents on whose cheeks the down starts to grow, whose limbs become rough. Of roughness there was, thank God, no trace in me even at that time, but the down had already begun to grow golden, my eyes became a brighter and richer blue, and my face, its features becoming more clearly outlined, seemed to be coated with light and healthy sunburn. Accordingly, I passed my examinations in quite a different way from before. I crammed for whole days, delighting in my own tirelessness and trimness, feeling with joy all that young, healthy, pure something which sometimes makes examinations resemble the Passion Week, the fasting, the preparation for confession and communion. I would sleep for three or four hours, jump out of bed in the morning easily and quickly, wash and dress with particular care, say my prayers feeling assured that God would not fail to help me even with the aorists, leave the house with quiet firmness, tenaciously bearing in my mind and heart all that had been conquered the day before and which one now had to bring and hand over where it belonged, steadfastly and in full. And when the whole ordeal was happily over, another joy awaited me: neither father nor mother came from Baturino to fetch me this time, but they simply sent for me, as for a grown-up, a coach and pair driven by a young and giggling farmhand who, in the course of our drive, soon became my bosom friend. And in Baturino—it was a big and rather well-to-do village with three landowners' manors lost in parks, with several ponds and spacious commons—everything was already in blossom, turning green, enjoying the wonderful weather of late May, and suddenly I felt and realized that happy beauty, that splendor and brightness of foliage, the fullness of ponds, the mischievousness of the nightingales and frogs, as a youth, with sensuous fullness and force. . . .

That summer my brother Nicholas got married. He was actually the soberest of us, but he grew tired of doing nothing and married the daughter of a German steward of a government estate in Vasilievskoe. I think that this marriage, the holiday into which it turned the whole summer for us, and then the presence in the house of a young woman, also contributed a good deal toward my development.

Soon after that, unexpectedly, my brother George came to Baturino. It was a bright June evening; the radiant sun was peacefully and cheerfully vanishing behind the outbuildings of the manor; the courtyard already smelled of cooling grass; in its wistful evening beauty, as an old idyllic picture, rose our old house with its gray wooden pillars and steep roof; everybody was having tea on the garden veranda, and I was quietly walking down the courtyard to the stables to saddle my horse for a ride on the highway when suddenly in our rustic gate there appeared something quite unusual: a town cab! I remember to this day that peculiar prison pallor which struck me in my brother's familiar, and at the same time somehow quite new and strange, face. . . .

It was one of the happiest evenings in the life of our family, and the beginning of that peace and well-being which were for the last time to reign for three whole years before its end, its dispersion. . . .

17

It was already with the emotions of youth that I arrived in Baturino that spring. With the same youthful feeling I shared my brother Nicholas's drives to his sweetheart in Vasilievskoe, all their beauty: the free racing of the troika along the cart-tracks in the peaceful afternoon, amid the ever-thickening rye fields; the calls of the cuckoo in the remote birch copse still full of grass and flowers; the sight of the weird June clouds in the golden west, the blended evening odors of the village, its cottages, orchards, river, distillery, dishes being prepared for supper in the steward's house; the sharp, exhilarating sounds of the player piano played by his younger daughters, the Westphalian landscapes on the walls, the huge bunches of red-black peonies on small console tables—all that gay German hospitality which surrounded us in that house; and the increasingly intimate proximity of that tall, lean, plain, but somehow very nice, girl, who was on the point of becoming a member of our family and was already talking to me as to a relative. . . .

I could not as yet be best man; but the function of bride's page which I undertook did not suit me either when, dressed in a tight new glittering uniform and white gloves, with beaming eyes and pomaded hair, I fit a white silk shoe onto her foot in its slippery silky stocking and afterward drove with her in a coach, drawn by a mighty pair of grays, to Znamenie. It had been raining every day; the horses trotted, splattering about clods of blue-black mud; the full-eared, moist-laden rye fields bent their wet gray-green spikes toward the road; now and then the low sun shone through the heavy golden shower—it was said to be the sign of a happy marriage—the windows of the coach glittering diamondlike with teardrops of rain were pulled up; we felt squeezed inside its box, and, intoxicated, I breathed in the freshness of the bride's perfume and all that airy, snow-white something in which she was drowned, and I looked into her red happy eyes as I clumsily clasped the gold-cased icon with which she had been blessed. And during the wedding ceremony I felt for the first time, but profoundly, the wonderful Old Testament strain in that glad sacrament, which is particularly beautiful in a country church, under its poor but solemnly lighted chandelier, to the accompaniment of the harshly loud and exultant ejaculations of the rustic clergy, with the doors open to the green evening sky, a crowd of admiring shy country women and girls crowding through them. . . . And when this new and seemingly happy thing that entered our house with the young couple was crowned by the unexpected arrival of my brother, and our whole family proved after all to be reunited and flourishing, the idea of returning to school struck me as quite absurd.

I returned to town in the autumn and once more began attending classes, but I hardly looked at the lessons, and more and more often refused to answer the masters, who with polite, venomous calm would listen to my excuses of having a headache and, gleefully, in their fairest handwriting, write down an "F" against my name. I would spend all my time wandering about on the outskirts of the town; I would meet and see off the trains at the station amid the hurly-burly and bustle of incoming and outgoing passengers, envying those who hurriedly and excitedly took their seats, with lots of luggage, in the "long-distance" coaches; gasping when the bells rang and an enormous long-liveried porter, approaching the middle of the waiting room, sang out in a loud, solemn basso, announcing with a drawl, with stern and threatening sorrow, the departures and destinations of the trains. . . . Thus I lived till Christmas. As soon as the break arrived, I ran home at full speed, got ready in five minutes, hardly taking leave of the Rostovtsevs and Glebochka —he still had to wait for the coach from the country, while I was going by train, through Vasilievskoe—snatched my little suitcase, and jumping out into the street, flung myself with a crazy thought into the frozen, tattered sleigh of the first cabman I came across. Good-bye forever, school! His shaggy nag tore off, the sleigh whisked, bumping and clattering askew down the slopes, the freezing wind tore at the uplifted collar of my uniform overcoat, spattering my face with keen snow; the town was drowned in a gloomy snowstorm dusk, and I panted with joy. On account of snowdrifts I sat for two hours waiting at the station, until at last the train came in. . . . Oh! those snowdrifts, Russia, the night, the blizzard, and the railway! What bliss!—that train whitened all over, that snug, warm coziness of the carriage, the clatter of little hammers in the blazing stove, and outside the frost and the impenetrable snowstorm; then the bells, flames, and voices at some station hardly visible for snow just whirling up from the ground and down from the roofs, and then again the desperate cry of the engine hurtling somewhere into the darkness, into the stormy distance, into the unknown, and the first shock of the starting carriage, the vanishing light of the platform scintillating with diamonds passing across its frosted windowpanes—and again night, desolation, snowstorm, the howling of the wind in the ventilator, while one is surrounded by quiet warmth, the half-light of the lamp behind its blue curtain, and the ever-increasing, swinging, lulling motion sending you to sleep in the springy velvet seat, and the fur coat dangling ever more amply on its peg before one's sleepy eyes!

Our station was about six miles from Vasilievskoe, and it was already night when I arrived at the station. Outdoors raged such a storm that I had to spend the night in the cold station building, smelling of dim oil lamps, the doors of which banged in the void of night with a peculiarly hollow sound whenever the muffled, snow-covered conductors of freight trains, with red reeking lanterns in their hands, passed in or out. And yet this was lovely, too. I huddled on the narrow sofa in the ladies' waiting room, slept soundly, but woke up constantly with impatient expectancy of the morning, with the raging of the snowstorm and some distant rough voices coming from somewhere beyond the bubbling, boiling noise of the engine, which stood, its fire-belching ashpit open, under the windows—and I woke up, jumped to my feet in the rosy light of the quiet frosty morning with a purely animal briskness. . . .

An hour later I was already in Vasilievskoe, sitting at breakfast in the warm cheerful house of our new relative, Wiegand, not knowing where to look for happy confusion: coffee was being poured out by Annchen, his young niece from Reval. . . .

18

Beautiful—and especially that winter for me—was the manor of Baturino. The ancient stone pillars of the gateless drive to the courtyard, the powdery snow-covered courtyard, the snowdrifts crisscrossed by sleigh runners, silence, sun; in the pure frosty air the peaceful, sweet smell of wood-smoke

from the kitchens, that pleasing homelike something in the footprints trodden from the kitchen to the house, from the servants' quarters to the
dunghill, the stables, and other outbuildings surrounding the yard. . . .
Silence and glitter, the whiteness of the snow-laden roofs, the low wintry
park buried in deep snow, the bare branches showing reddish-black on both
sides of the house, our particular hundred-year-old fir tree lifting its pointed
black-green top into the bright blue sky from behind the roof of the house,
from behind its steep declivity resembling a snowy mountaintop, between
two quiet pennants of smoke. . . . On the sun-warmed fronts of the porches
sit nunlike jackdaws, cuddled up pleasantly, usually chattering but now very
quiet; and the ancient windows with the tiny squares of their frames look out
in friendly fashion, blinking because of the blinding bright light, and the icy
glitter of precious stones on the snow.

    . . . Creaking with frosted felt boots on the hard snow covering the steps,
one mounts the main porch, the one on the right, passes under its shed,
opens the heavy oak door black with age, passes through the long, dark,
gloomy vestibule. . . . In the footman's room with its big rough chest by the
window, it is still cool, bluish—the sun never comes here, its window looks
north—but the stove makes a booming noise, its brass door trembling. To
the right is a dismal corridor leading to the bedrooms, straight opposite—a
high door, also of blackened oak, opening into the big hall. In the hall there
is a fire; it is spacious and cold, and on its walls the portraits of some wood-
en, dark-faced grandfather in a curly peruke, and of the snub-nosed Emper-
or Paul, in a uniform with red lapels, look chilly, and the other old portraits
and chandeliers seem to be frozen right through, piled in a small long-
unused butler's pantry, to peep into which through its little door made half
of glass gave one, when a child, such mysterious delight. Yet in the hall everything is lapped in sunshine, and on the smooth and astonishingly wide floor-
boards the reflections of the upper colored windowpanes flame and melt
into a dappling of purple and garnet. Against the window on the left, at the
side, also looking north, are the black branches of a huge linden, and through
the sunny ones facing the door one sees the garden heaped up with snow.
The middle window, however, is entirely filled by an extremely tall fir, the
one that shows even between the house chimneys: behind that window, in
splendid rows, hang its snowy sleeves. . . . How unspeakably lovely it was on
frosty moonlit nights! One would enter—there is no light in the hall, only the
bright moon high up behind the windows. The hall is empty, magnificent,
full as it were of the finest vapor, and the dense fir, in its snowy mourning
garments, rises regally behind the panes, its pointed top vanishing in the
pure, translucent, unfathomable dome of blue where the wide-scattered
constellation of Orion shows white and silvery, and lower down, in the luminous void of the firmament, the splendor of Sirius glitters sharply, trembling
with azure diamonds—my mother's favorite star. . . . How often I wandered

around in that moonlit vapor across the long shadow of the window gratings lying on the floor, how many youthful thoughts did I ponder, how often I repeated Derzhavin's lordly proud lines: "Amid the dark-blue ether there swam the golden moon, through windows shining on my house, and with its pallid ray painted golden windowpanes upon my lacquered floor" . . .[28]

Lovely, too, were the new feelings I knew during my first winter in that house. It all passed in walks and endless talks with my brother George, which helped to develop me extraordinarily quickly; in drives to Vasilievskoe; and in reading the poets of Derzhavin's and Pushkin's time. In the Baturino house there were hardly any books. But now I began driving to Vasilievskoe, to the estate of our cousin, which crowned a hill opposite the government estate with a distillery of which Wiegand was the manager. Our cousin was married to a squire called Pisarev, and for many years we had not been to her house—old Pisarev, her father-in-law, was, in contrast to his son, a man of extremely serious disposition, with whom my father naturally very soon quarreled. In that year, the old man having died, relations between our houses were renewed, and I was given free access to the library that he had collected during his long life. That library proved to contain a multitude of marvelous little volumes in thick dark-golden leather bindings with golden stars on the back—Sumarokov, Anna Bunina, Derzhavin, Batyushkov, Zhukovsky, Venevitinov, Yazykov, Kozlov, Baratynsky. . . . [29] How admirable were their romantic vignettes—lyres, urns, helmets, wreaths,—their type, their rough, usually bluish paper, and, above all, the pure harmonious beauty, the nobility, the lofty style of every word printed on that paper! In their company I lived through all my first youthful dreams, the first enthusiastic transports of my spirit, my first real thirst for writing, my first attempts to satisfy it, the voluptuousness of imagination. That imagination was truly miraculous. When I read: "A young poet is flying into the battle,"[30] or "Roar, roar, from your steep heights, hush not, O white-haired torrent,"[31] or "Amid the green waves kissing Tauride, at morning dawn I saw a Nereid,"[32] I at once saw and felt that poet, and the torrent, and the green waves, and the sea morning, and the nude Nereid so clearly that I longed to sing, to shout, to laugh, to weep. . . . I marvel at the childishness, the inanity of everything that came at the same time from my own pen!

Blissful, too, was my first taste of being in love, which lasted peacefully and joyously throughout the winter. Annchen was a rather ordinary young girl, no more. But was it she who mattered? She was, besides, invariably happy, kindly, very good; she told me, sincerely and simplemindedly: "I like you very much, Aleshenka. You have 'pure and ardent feelings'!" Those feelings, of course, flared up instantly. I was inflamed at the first sight of her, as soon as she came out—in all the freshness of her German cleanness, her rather affected pink dress, her youthful prettiness— to meet me, chilled through with cold on the way from the station, in the Wiegands' dining room, and began pouring hot coffee for me. I had barely shaken her tiny fingers, still cold with water, when my heart gave a flutter and decided, "There it is!" And I left for Baturino completely happy. On the day after Christmas the Wiegands were coming to visit. And here they came, at once filling the whole house with their noisy German gaiety, unprovoked laughter, and that peculiar holiday spirit which guests bring with them in the country in winter, when, fresh from the frost, they throw off their fragrant cold coats, high galoshes, and felt boots. In the evening other guests came too, and we all, except the grown-ups, decided, naturally, to go around to the neighboring manors as mummers.[33] Noisily we disguised ourselves as best we could, mostly as peasants—my hair was curled tightly, my face rouged and powdered, a small black moustache painted with burnt cork—and we thronged out onto the porch, before which, in darkness, some sleighs were already standing; we took our seats, laughing and shouting to the accompaniment of the bells, and swiftly whisked off, cutting through the fresh snowdrifts. And, naturally, I turned out to be in the same sleigh with Annchen. . . . How can I forget that nocturnal, wintry ringing of the bells, that desolate winter night in the desolate snowy fields, the extraordinary, wintry, gray, soft mellowness with which, on such a night, the snow fuses with the low sky, while ahead one constantly fancies some uncanny little flames, the eyes as it were of some unknown creatures of the winter nights—how can I forget the snowy night air, the brisk chill penetrating under my raccoon coat and through my thin boots; the small, warm, girlish hand disengaged from a fur glove and, for the first time in life, held in one's young hot hands; and the girlish eyes already gleaming responsively, lovingly through the dusk!

19

And then came spring, the most extraordinary spring in all my life.

I remember as if it were now—I was sitting with Olga in her room, which looked into the courtyard. It was about five o'clock on a sunny March afternoon. Suddenly, buttoning up his fur-lined overcoat, my father entered with his usual briskness—his moustache was now already gray, but he still looked fit as a fiddle—and said, "A messenger from Vasilievskoe. Pisarev had some kind of a stroke. Going over there now—like to come with me?"

I rose, struck both by this news and by the unexpected lucky chance of going to Vasilievskoe and seeing Annchen, and we left at once. To our surprise, we found Pisarev looking as if nothing were the matter, healthy and cheerful, himself wondering and not understanding what had happened to him.

"Still, you ought to drink less," my father said to him next day when taking leave of him in the parlor.

"Rubbish!" replied Pisarev, laughing with his gray gypsy eyes, helping my father on with his overcoat—I see him as if it were now, well-built, dark-complexioned, black-bearded, in an open red silk Russian shirt, in light-black loose breeches and red, silver-embroidered Caucasian slippers. We returned home quietly; and soon the spring floods began, so swift and wild that our communications with Vasilievskoe were completely cut off for about two weeks. On Easter Sunday it became quite dry, the willows and the commons began to turn green. We all, with the exception of Olya and my mother, were proposing to go to Vasilievskoe and had already come out to take seats in the coach—when suddenly a horse appeared in the gateway, then a droshky, and in it our cousin Peter Petrovich Arseniev.

"Christ is risen," he greeted us, driving up to us, with an exaggerated calmness. "Going to Vasilievskoe? In the nick of time. Pisarev's kicked the bucket. Woke this morning, went in to his wife, then suddenly sat down in an armchair, and curtains. . . . "

Pisarev had just been washed and laid out when we entered the house. He lay, offering the usual sight of a dead man just laid out on a table—the sight which as yet merely struck me by its oddity—in that very hall where two weeks ago he was standing smiling on the threshold, screwing up his eyes against the light of the evening sun and his cigarette. He lay with eyes closed—I still can see their dark-purple bulge—but still quite like a living man, with hair and beard beautifully combed, still moist and jet-black, in a new frock coat and starched shirt with well-knotted black silk tie, covered to his waist by a sheet, under which one could discern his stiff bound feet. I gazed at him calmly and blankly, even touched his forehead and hands—they were almost warm. . . . By the evening, however, everything had changed. I had realized what had happened and, when we were called to the first requiem, entered the hall quite upset. Behind the hall windows the dark spring sunset still hung crimson over the distant fields, but the dusk rising from the dark river valley and the dark, dank fields—from all the dark cooling earth—was flooding it in ever-thickening waves from below; in the dark hall, crowded with people, one could only see dimly for incense, and through that darkness and dimness in everybody's hands were the golden flames of small wax candles, and from behind the tall church candles, which spread about the deathbed a red flame, there sounded ominously the ejaculations of the officiating priests, alternating oddly with the joyously and heedlessly persistent "Christ is risen from the dead." And I would now stare ahead where, in the smoky glitter and twilight, the dead man's face, somehow grown woefully crestfallen, gleamed dully and already horribly darkened in the course of the day; now feel overcome with warm tenderness, aware of it being the only salutary refuge, and seeking out in the crowd the tiny face of Annchen, who stood quiet and discreet, warmly and innocently lit up from below by the candle's flame.

In the night I had a painful, restless sleep, besieged by recurring, unnaturally bright, disorderly visions of some bustling throng, uncannily and mysteriously connected with all that had happened: everybody walked about hurriedly—and, what was most horrible, was silently guided, it seemed, by the deceased himself—from room to room, hastily giving each other advice, moving tables, armchairs, beds, chests of drawers. . . . In the morning I went out to the porch like a drunken man. The morning was quiet, warm and clear; the sun was warming up the dry porch, the courtyard with its bright, new, tender green, the garden, still bare of foliage yet gleaming tenderly and already turning soft gray in a springlike way. But suddenly I looked around— and saw with horror, close to me, standing upright against the wall, the long new, dark-violet lid of the coffin. I ran down the steps of the porch, went to the garden, walked for a long time in its bare, luminous and warm alleys, sat down on a bench in one of the walks bordered with low acacias. . . . The bullfinches were singing, the fluffy acacia was yellowing tenderly and gaily, the smell of the earth, of young grass, filled one's soul with a sweet and poignant feeling; monotonously, gravely and triumphantly, without disturbing the meek silence of the garden, the rooks shrieked far off in the lowland, on the old birch trees, where the young willows, as yet bare, looked like an olive-colored smoke of spring. . . . And in everything there was death, death intermingled with eternal, lovely, and futile life. Somehow I suddenly recalled the opening pages of *Wilhelm Tell*—I had been reading Schiller:[34] the mountains, the lake, a fisherman sailing and singing. . . . And there suddenly rang in my soul a sweet, joyous, free song of remote happy lands.

In a state, as it were, of ceaseless intoxication I passed that whole day, which kept me in continual tension: again there were requiems, again a throng, the coming and going of neighbors, and somewhere there, in the sunny nursery shut off on all sides, the carefree playing of the children, not yet understanding things, under the grieving and kindly inattentive supervision of the nurse, who now and again wept quietly to herself. . . .

And again dusk began to creep down, and again people began slowly gathering, waiting for another mass, thronging the hall, exchanging circumspect remarks. . . . The arrival of the priests and the ensuing silence, the lighting of the candles and the donning of vestments in that silence, all those mysteriously ecclesiastical preparations for the service, and then the first swing of the censer and the first exclamation—all this struck me now, on the dead man's last evening, as so full of significance that I could no longer raise my eyes toward what was in front, that pompous velvet coffin elevated upon tables placed together, and toward that mystical and terrible, picturesquely funereal thing which rose aslant in the coffin in all the sinister splendor of its golden covering, the small gold icon on the breast, and a new starchy-white pillow; in the gloomy darkness of the everlasting sepulchral sleep of the black-bearded face with its hollow, blackened eyelids, showing metallically lustrous through the warm, sultry smoke and the hot, trembling glitter. . . .

For this night also beds were put up for me and my brother George in his former study. The doors into the deserted hall, still full of incense, where a sexton was reading psalms in a low monotonous voice by the light of snuffed candles, were closed on all sides, the house at last hushed and calm. My brother, after a short talk with me, blew out the candle and soon fell asleep. But I could not even undress for anguish and fear, and lay down in my clothes; and barely had I also extinguished the candle and dozed off for a moment when I saw myself in the hall—and came to my senses in mad horror. I sat up and, with thumping heart, began peering into the darkness, taking in the slightest rustle of sound. Everything was extraordinarily, dreadfully quiet—one could hear only the remote indistinct psalmodizing in the hall. . . . I took myself in hand, flung my legs off the sofa, threw open the door of the study, ran across the dark corridor, and pressed my ear to the door from under which came the light from the hall: "The Lord reigneth; He is appareled with greatness; the Lord is appareled with strength . . ."—the sexton was saying in a low, wooden, and hurried voice behind the door.—"The floods have lifted up, O Lord, the floods have lifted up their voice; the floods lift up their waves. . . . Of old hast Thou laid the foundation of the earth; and the heavens are the work of Thy hands. . . . They shall perish but Thou shalt endure: yea, all of them shall wax old like a garment; as a vesture shalt Thou change them. . . . Let the glory of the Lord endure for ever; let the Lord rejoice in His works. . . . "

Seized by a spasm of rapturous sobbing, I walked quickly and clumsily away along the dark corridor and through the dark back parlor and vestibule. I walked around the house and stopped in the middle of the courtyard. It was dark and somehow peculiarly pure, fresh, and quiet. The ground was slightly frozen and stiff. Some very fine and pure vapor was just perceptible, silvery between the earth and the clear starlit sky. In the silence, from far off, came the even, muffled noise of the thawed river in the valley. I looked into the darkness beyond the valley, at the opposite hill—there, in Wiegand's house, a lonely belated light burned red.

"It is she not sleeping," thought I. "'The floods have lifted up their voice; the floods lift up their waves,'" I thought—and the light suddenly trembled, raylike, in my eyes with fresh tears—tears of happiness, of love, of hope, and of an almost hysterical, exultant tenderness.

Book Three

1

That terrible spring night in Vasilievskoe is even more memorable to me because it was on the eve of the funeral.

I fell asleep only when morning was drawing near. I was unable to return to the house at once—its outlines and the black coffin lid on the porch showed too ominously dark in the starlight; it was all too wildly in contradiction with what filled my heart to overflowing. I went into the fields; for a long time I walked in darkness blindly. . . . I came back when the east was already whitening and all over the village the cocks crowed; I slunk into the house by the same back door and fell asleep at once. Soon, however, through my sleep, the thought of some impending and particularly important moments began to torment me, and suddenly I started up again, having slept hardly three hours. The house was still divided into two quite distinct worlds; in one there was death, the hall with the coffin; in the other—that is, in all the remaining rooms, shut off from it on all sides by closed doors—our disorderly life was going on helter-skelter, impatiently awaiting the fatal climax of that disorder. I woke up with the acute sense of that climax having at last arrived, and was not a little surprised to see my brother, who shared the dead man's study with me, indifferently smoking a cigarette, sitting in his underwear on the sofa, from which a crumpled sheet trailed down to the floor, while in the corridor behind the door people were already walking hurriedly; one heard voices, curt questions and answers. In came Maria Petrovna, the head maid, bringing tea on a tray; she bowed silently without looking at us and, after placing the tray on the desk, went out, preoccupied. With trembling hands I began to dress. In the study, papered with oldish golden wallpaper, everything was simple, workaday, and even cheerful; fragrant cigarette smoke wafted about, telling of our masculine morning life. My brother was smoking and gazing absentmindedly at those same Caucasian slippers of Pisarev's in which I had seen him, in all his lively gypsy handsomeness, two weeks before, and which now sat peacefully under his desk. I, too, cast a glance at them, and everything became still more muddled in my head: yes, I thought, he is no longer here, yet here are his slippers still sitting there, and they can sit on for another hundred years! And where is he now, and where will he be to the end of time? And is it really true that somewhere there he has already met with all our long-departed, mythical grandmothers and grandfathers? And what is he now? Is it really he—that terrible something which is lying in the hall on joined tables, between those tilting edges of the coffin, unnaturally lit up in broad daylight by the dull flames of the candles reduced to short stumps that have thickly spotted and smeared the notched paper surrounding them on the tall silver candlesticks—he who only two days ago, on just such a morning as this, was entering, with newly combed black beard still fresh after washing, his wife's room next door, on the floor of which, a half-hour later, they were already washing his naked body, still almost alive, limply and helplessly flopping? And yet it is he, I reflected, and it is today that for him will befall that last, terrible, mystical thing which he seemed to have nothing to do with when alive, that most marvelous thing in the world in which for the first time in my young life I am going to take part—to live through the realization of those same remarkable words which at school, for some reason, I was supposed to learn by heart: "Three days after a Christian's death his body must be borne out to church. . . . As preparation for this serve, in the presence of the family, friends, and relatives of the deceased, intensive thurifications round his body and singing of chants about his laying at peace till the Last Judgment and the rising of all the dead. . . ." With great surprise I suddenly realized that at the moment Pisarev was that very Christian, and I felt horrified when I thought of the endless time which he had still to wait for that rising whereupon there is supposed to begin, and to last through eternity, something quite unimaginable, devoid both of sense and of purpose, and having no end. . . .

2

I watched avidly and with heart aflutter the bearing out of the body. The farmhands, looking festively sated and clean, were strong and young, yet it was with some awkward and fearsome tension, their heads averted, that they pushed their heavy load off the tables and raised it up on white lengths of cloth, when finally came the last moment of Pisarev's parting with his home and with the whole world. To me then, it seemed again that in that huge velvety violet box with its ghastly silvery paws there lay something sacred but at the same time obscenely earthly and foul. That something, with obediently crossed and petrified hands sticking out of the black frock-coat sleeves, woodenly swinging its dead head, floated low and obliquely, at the will of others, over the floor, amid the throng, the festive vestments, the incense, and discordant singing, its feet toward the wide-open door—and they will never again cross the threshold of that house!—first into the parlor, then to the porch, into the bright light and greenness of the spring courtyard, where, over the crowd, rose the crucifix, and two peasants were holding the lid of the coffin over their heads. Here the farmhands paused, straining their flushed necks with the lengths of cloth, and the singing became louder—"in token of the deceased passing over into the realm of disembodied spirits surrounding the throne of the Almighty and singing ceaselessly His thrice-blessed praise"—and from the top of the belfry, looking from behind the outbuildings right opposite the porch, which had hitherto been slowly dropping thin, pitiful sounds that grew ever louder and louder, there came a brief, sharp, intentionally absurd, tragic discord of the bass and alto, to which, in a simultaneous and discordant barking and howling, the frightened dogs filling the courtyard replied. So hideous was it that my cousin, in a long mourning dress, staggered and burst into sobs, the peasant women in the crowd started to cry, and my father, who was also clumsily holding the coffin, was distorted with disgust and pain. . . .

In the church I looked all the time at the cadaverous face of the deceased, who lay just in front of the Tsar's Gate, under the rotund closed cupola painted all over with stony blue-gray clouds amid which, from a rough blue triangle, oblong, cruel, and enigmatic, stared out the All-seeing Eye. The burial service was already proceeding, and that face, with its sharpened nose, its black transparent beard and moustache under which gleamed the flat sticky lips, was already sepulchrally crowned with the multicolored paper crown. I gazed thinking, "He now resembles an old-time grand prince; now he is forever ranked among the saints, among the host of all our forefathers and forebears. . . ." Already they were singing over him: "Blessed are those who are undefiled and walk in the law of the Lord," while I, full of torment and pain for him and of fond feelings for myself, thought thus: "Soon between his rigid fingers with blackened nails they will place the 'absolution,' anoint him with 'holy chrism,' sprinkle him crosswise with the 'earth,' cover him up with gauze, and put on the lid; they will take him out and bury him, and go away and forget, and years will pass, and my long and happy life will pass somewhere there, in my misty and bright future, and he, or rather his skull and bones, will still go on lying buried in the earth behind this church, amid the tall grass, under the little birch tree that will be planted today at the head of his grave and will one day grow into a big, fine, white-trunked tree, with its low gray-green crown rippling and sweetly quivering on a long summer day. . . ." Giving him "the last kiss," I touched the paper crown with my lips—and, Lord! what cold and stench blew up at me in that terrible moment, and how upset I was by the icy hardness of the dark-lemon frontal bone under that crown, in inconceivable contrast to all that living, springlike warmth that was wafting in so sweetly and simply through the grated windows of the church!

Afterward, standing behind the church among the old tombstones and monuments of various brigadiers and majors, I stared into the deep narrow pit, its hard and evenly cut flanks shining dully and desolately: rude and pitiless, the gray primeval earth flew there, hastily poured down upon the violet velvet, upon the white braided cross. I wanted to mortify myself profanely; I recalled the cold All-seeing Eye in the stone-cloudy sky of the church cupola, thought of the unutterable something which would be in that coffin in a week's time, even tried to persuade myself that, after all, on a certain appointed day the same thing would happen to me. . . . But I had no faith in it; the grave was already made flush with the ground; Annchen was wearing a new cambric dress; kindly and magnanimously, solving all things and encouraging all things, the last chant rang out, once more festive, once more Christ's, vanishing into the warm sunny air. . . . The world seemed to have grown still younger, freer, vaster and lovelier after someone had departed from it forever. . . .

3

On our way home from the churchyard our cousin stumbled along, pressing her handkerchief close to her eyes, heedless of anything in front of her. But my father held her firmly under the elbow and, trying to keep pace with her, continually told her all the empty, nice things one always says on such occasions: "It's no use, dear, to comfort you, but one thing I will say: remember that despair is a mortal sin, that you're not alone in the world, that you've got people who love you infinitely, that you've got children who give you a noble aim in life, and, most important of all, you are still so young, you have everything ahead of you."

Next to my father walked an old friend of his, a nobleman's peaked cap in his hand, a round and thick-set landowner, very sunburnt and of naturally dusky complexion into the bargain, who had some golden-brown spots on the yellowish whites of his brown eyes which had intrigued me ever since my childhood. He was hot because of the unaccustomed frock coat and starched shirt, because of his sturdy stoutness and the emotions which stirred him. And he, too, wheezing with haste and asthma, was saying the same things as my father: "Vera Petrovna, allow me to say this too: I was like a second father to the deceased after his father's death, it was I who baptized him, and brought him up, and gave him away when he married you—you realize my feelings. . . . Then, you know: I, too, became a widower early. . . . Yet Alexander is altogether right. You know what the peasants say? 'Death is like the sun, you can't look at it. . . .' No, you can't and you mustn't either, otherwise you can't live. . . . I am ashamed, you see, that he is no longer here while I still walk and wheeze, but does it depend on us?"

I looked at his large cropped silver-gray head with its broad nape, at the old worn wedding ring on his small dark hand. . . . I looked and realized that we all felt more or less ashamed, uneasy; and yet it was so infinitely sweet to return to life after that terrible burden which had been weighing us down for three days on end, and I caught myself thinking how fine it was to tread the soft spring earth, to walk bareheaded in the warm sun, to listen to the ceaseless, discordant cawing of the rooks, wrangling and bustling about with impetuous and agonizing ecstasy in all the neighboring gardens; to behold my cousin with new, almost amorous, eyes, her mourning, the beauty of her youth and sorrow; to think with a pang of the heart that on that day I had a tryst with Annchen at the edge of the garden. . . .

The house, too, seemed to have grown younger, having freed itself of its master. All its floors and windowpanes were washed, everything was tidied up, and the windows were thrown wide open to the sun and air. Over the threshold of the hall, where tables were placed and laid out for the funeral banquet, I was at once met by that dreadful smell unlike anything in the world which had been maddening me throughout the morning near the coffin. But that smell was in some peculiar stimulating way mixed up with the dampness of the floors, still dark with water, and with the spring freshness that wafted from everywhere into the house; and festively, destined for a feast of life not of death, the tables gleamed with tablecloths, knives and forks, glasses and decanters. . . . Yet how horrible that protracted and coarsely plentiful dinner was, interrupted every now and then by the already inharmonious, drunken voices of the choristers, who rose up and with feeling sang the eternal memory of the incomprehensible being whom they had just buried behind the church. My father was right when he said to me during dinner, "I know, I know, dear, how you feel now! We are already hardened, but you, on the threshold of life and with such an unmodern heart as yours into the bargain. . . . I can imagine your feelings!"

4

After the funeral I stayed in Vasilievskoe for a couple of weeks—still full of the intense and ambiguous sensation of that selfsame life whose incredible and dreadful end I had just contemplated with my own eyes.

It was the more agonizing for me in those days as I had to pass through another ordeal—the parting with Annchen, who was going home (though in that, too, I found some poignantly bitter delight).

My father and Petr Petrovich decided, for my cousin's sake, to remain for a time in Vasilievskoe. I also stayed behind with them—and not only for the sake of Annchen, for whom my passion increased every day: I wanted somehow to prolong the strange emotions that possessed me and made me hold on to *Faust,* which happened then, as if on purpose, to fall into my hands and fascinated me completely:

Now up, now down I speed,
In life-flow, stormy deed,
Rush hither or recede
A birth, a grave,
The tireless wave,
A change o'er rife,
A glowing life,
I make time's shuttle forward press,
And weave the Godhead's living dress.[1]

Ambiguous, too, was the life in Vasilievskoe. It was still veiled by great sadness, but it came back to order amazingly rapidly, acquiring something especially agreeable because of the changes that took and were taking place in it amid the blossoming and strengthening springtime beauty. Everybody felt it was high time to return to life with new and even redoubled forces. Special cleanliness was maintained in the rest of the house, where a good deal had been changed—some of the out-of-date furniture was taken to the attic, some things were shifted from one room to another, a new bedroom was arranged for my cousin next to the nursery, while their former bedroom, behind the little drawing room, was completely rearranged and turned into a spacious sitting room. Then nearly all the dead man's things were hidden somewhere—one day I saw his nobleman's gala uniform, his cap with red band, his plumed three-cornered hat being brushed on the back porch and put away into an old trunk. . . . New ways were introduced also into the management of the estate: it was now in the hands of my father and Petr Petrovich, and every one of the servants, as is usual between masters and workmen at the outset, was zealously obedient and wanted to hope that because of this new regime everything would now somehow go in a different way, properly. I was, I remember, greatly touched by it. Most touching, however, was the gradual return to life of my cousin, the way in which she was little by little coming to her senses, growing ever calmer and simpler, and already at times faintly smiling at table at the silly and charming questions of her children, while Petr Petrovich and my father were discreetly but invariably affectionate and attentive to her. . . .

And with astonishing swiftness those bittersweet days flitted by for me. After parting from Annchen late at night, sweetly tormented by the endless leave-taking with her, I would come home, go straight to the study, and fall dead asleep thinking of tomorrow's tryst. In the morning I hurriedly drank tea and sat impatiently, book in hand in the sunlit garden, awaiting the moment when it would again be possible to run across the river to take Annchen for a walk. During those hours the girls, Wiegand's younger daughters, always walked with us; but they usually ran ahead and did not disturb us. . . . At noon I came back for dinner, after dinner reread *Faust*, and waited for the evening tryst. . . . At night, in the remote part of the garden, the young moon would shine; mysteriously and cautiously the nightingales would sing. Forgetting her former bashfulness, Annchen would sit on my knees and embrace me, and I would hear the beating of her heart, for the first time in my life feel the blissful weight of a woman's body. . . .

At last she left. Never had I wept so fiercely and abundantly as on that day. But with what tenderness, with what poignancy of the sweetest love for the world, for life, for physical and moral human beauty, which, all unwittingly, Annchen had unveiled to me, did I weep! And at night when, already dulled by tears and hushed, I was again, goodness knows why, wandering to the other side of the river, the coach which had taken Annchen to the station overtook me, and the coachman, halting, handed me a copy of a Petersburg magazine to which, a month or so before, I had for the first time sent a poem. I unfolded it as I walked—and as if by lightning my eyes were struck and blinded by the magic letters of my own name. . . .

The next day, early in the morning, I walked to Baturino. I walked at first along the dry, already rutted cart track, amid the ploughed fields gleaming in the morning mist; then along a dewy boundary line toward the Pisarevs' wood; then through the wood—sunny, light-green, full of spring life and birdsong, of last year's rotting leaves and the first lilies of the valley. . . . When I came to Baturino, even my mother threw up her hands at the sight of my thinness and the expression in my chiseled eyes. And, after kissing her, I silently handed her the magazine and went to my room to wash and change, staggering with fatigue and not recognizing the familiar house, wondering at its having become so tiny and old. . . .

5

That spring I was in my sixteenth year. Yet, on coming back to Baturino, I was already quite confirmed in the belief that my entry into full-fledged adult life had been accomplished.

During the winter it had already seemed to me that I knew a great deal of what every grown-up man is supposed to know: I knew about how the universe was organized and about something called the Ice Age, and about the savages of the Stone Age, and about the life of the ancients, and the barbaric invasions of Rome, about Kievan Rus, and about the discovery of America, and the French Revolution, and Byronism, and Romanticism, and the men of the 1840s, and Zhelyabov and Pobedonostsev,[2] not to speak of a number of fictitious persons and lives which had insinuated themselves into me forever, with all their feelings and destinies—that is, all those Hamlets, Don Carloses, Childe Harolds, Onegins, Pechorins, Rudins, Bazarovs, whom no one could do without supposedly.[3]

. . . And now my life experience seemed to me enormous. I came home dead-tired but firmly resolved to begin living henceforth some already quite "full" life. What should that life comprise? I believed that it should consist of experiencing, among all its impressions and my favorite pastimes, as many as possible of certain lofty poetical delights to which I even believed myself to be somehow especially entitled. "We enter'd life with hopes so fine. . . ." With fine hopes, too, I was setting out now. Though what reason had I to expect them?

There was a sense of everything still lying ahead of me, a sense of my youthful forces, of bodily and mental health, of a certain handsomeness of face and great advantages of build, ease, and sureness of movement, of a light and swift gait, of courage and agility—how I rode, for instance! There was the consciousness of my youthful purity, my noble impulses, truthfulness, contempt for every meanness. There was an exalted state of mind, both inborn and acquired through reading poets who invariably spoke of a poet's lofty mission, of poetry being "God in the holy dreams of the earth,"[4] of art being "a step toward a better world." There was some soul-exulting delight even in that bitter passion with which, at moments, I also repeated something quite different—such as the caustic lines of Lermontov and Heine,[5] the complaints of Faust, turning toward the moon behind his Gothic window, his dying, disenchanted look, or the jovial, shameless sentences of Mephistopheles. . . . But then, did I not realize at times that all this did not suffice, that it was not enough to have wings in order to fly, that one's wings need training and air?

I could not help experiencing those quite peculiar feelings which are experienced by all very young writers who have already seen their name in print. But neither could I help knowing that one swallow does not make a summer. My father, in his moments of anger, called me a raw sprig of nobility; I found comfort in the thought that I was not the only one to have studied "this and that, at random";[6] yet I fully realized how dubious was that comfort.

Secretly (notwithstanding my being infected, thanks to reading and to my brother George, with a multitude of progressive opinions), I was still very proud of the fact that we were Arsenievs. But at the same time I could not help remembering our ever-growing impoverishment, and the fact that our disregard of this was positively abnormal in us. I grew up in the strange conviction that, despite all the merits of my brothers, George's especially, I was nevertheless the main heir to all those remarkable qualities which, granted all his shortcomings, made my father stand out so prominently, in my eyes, among all the people I knew. But my father was no longer the same as he had been; he seemed to have thrown in the towel, to be nearly always tipsy. What had I to feel then, at the constant sight of his permanently flushed face, his gray, stubbly chin, his grandly tousled head, his worn-out slippers and tattered dressing gown dating from the days of Sevastopol? And what pain it caused me at times to think of my aging mother, of Olya growing up! I also often felt a strong pity for myself, after having dined, for instance, on nothing but cold soup and returning to my room, my books and my sole riches—my grandfather's box of lacquered birchwood where I kept all my most private possessions—those sheets of gray paper smelling of mint tobacco, bought in our village shop with my last pennies and covered with "elegies" and "stanzas." . . .

I thought at times about my father's youth: what an enormous difference to mine! He had had virtually everything proper to a happy youth of his class, standing, and requirements; he grew up and lived in carelessness, which was natural considering the still great lordliness he so freely and quietly enjoyed; he knew no fetters to his youthful whims and desires; everywhere, with full right and cheerful haughtiness, he felt himself to be an Arseniev. And I had only a birchwood box, an old shotgun, my lean Kabardinka, a worn cossack saddle. . . . How I longed at times to be elegant and brilliant! Yet, on going to a party, I had to put on that same gray suit of my brother George in which he had been taken to the Kharkov prison and which secretly caused me torments of acute shame at the party. I was devoid of the sense of property, but how I dreamed sometimes of wealth, of fine luxury, of freedom of every sort, and of all the physical and moral joys connected with them! I dreamed of long voyages, of viewing the whole world, of extraordinary feminine beauty, of friendship with some fictitious, wonderful young men, my contemporaries and fellow dreamers, sharing my ardor and my tastes. . . . And was I not, at times, aware that I had never yet set foot beyond the district town, that my whole world was bound by the long-familiar fields and hillocks, that I saw only peasants and their womenfolk, that the circle of our acquaintance was confined to a couple of small estates along with Vasilievskoe, and the refuge of all my dreams was my old corner room with its dilapidated window-frames and the colored upper panes of the two windows facing the garden?

6

The garden had lost its blossom and put on its summer garb; all day long a nightingale sang there; all day long the lower frames of my windows were up, and I grew to be still fonder of my room because of the oldness of those windows consisting of minute squares, of the dark oak ceiling, oak armchairs, and the oak bed with its smooth and sloping flanks. . . . At first I did nothing but lie with a book, now reading absentmindedly, now listening to the nightingale's warbling, thinking of that "full" life which I had to live henceforth, and at times suddenly falling into a short and deep sleep, on recovering from which I invariably wondered afresh at the newness and loveliness of the things surrounding me, and felt so hungry that I would jump up and go and fetch either some jam in the pantry, that is, in the forlorn little closet whose glass door led to the big hall, or some black bread in the servants' cottage, which by daytime was always deserted. There, in the dark corner on the hot and dusty stove, lay Leonty, a long and incredibly lean old man, covered with thick yellow stubble and actually peeling with age, grandmother's former cook, who for many years now had been defending his incomprehensible cave-dweller's existence against infallible death. . . . Hopes for happiness, for a happy life about to begin! Yet often all that one needed for it was to recover like this from a sudden and short nap, and to run and fetch a crust of black bread, or to be called to tea on the veranda, and at the tea table to think that soon you would go and saddle a horse and ride at random along the darkening highway.

The nights were moonlit, and sometimes I would wake up in the dead of night, in its most desolate hour when even the nightingale was silent. The whole world was so quiet that I would seem to wake up because of the very excess of stillness. For a moment I would be seized with fear—suddenly I would remember Pisarev, fancy his tall shadow in the corner beside the living-room door. . . . But instantly that shadow vanished, I saw only a corner darkening through the thin twilight of the room, and behind the open windows gleamed the moonlit garden, calling one into its luminous, speechless realm. And I would rise, cautiously open the living-room door. In the twilight I saw Grandmother's portrait in a frilled bonnet looking at me from the wall; I peered into the hall where I had spent so many lovely hours on moonlit winter nights. . . . It seemed more mysterious now, and lower, because the moon, which was now passing to the right of the house, did not look into it and it had itself become gloomier: the linden behind its north windows, thickly covered with foliage, quite blocked up those windows with its huge dark canopy. . . . Going out to the veranda, I always wondered afresh, to the point of sheer bewilderment, even of some pain, at the beauty of the night: what is it, after all, and what must one do with it? Even now I still feel something of the kind on moonlit nights. What must it have been then, when it was all new, when one's sense of smell was such that one could pick out the scent of a dewy burdock from the odor of damp grass! The exceedingly tall, narrow triangle of the fir tree, moonlit on one side only, still raised its notched pointed top to the translucent night sky where a few sparse stars were glimmering, minute, peaceful, and so infinitely remote and wonderful, truly God's, that one felt an impulse to kneel and cross oneself before them.

The empty lawn before the house was flooded with a strange and powerful light. To the right, over the garden, a full moon shone in a clear and vacant sky with the hardly darkened reliefs of its deadly pale face filled from within with bright luminous whiteness. And both of us, now long-familiar to each other, looked long at each other, patiently and silently expecting something from each other. I only knew that we both missed something very much. . . .

Then I would walk, with my shadow beside me, along the dewy, iridescent grass of the lawn, enter the dappled twilight of the alley leading to the pond; and the moon followed me docilely. I walked, now and then turning round—it rolled, shining and breaking mirrorlike through the black and sometimes brightly brilliant pattern of the boughs and leaves. I stood on the dewy slope descending toward the brimming pond shining with its vast golden surface beside the dam on the right. I stood and gazed—and the moon stood and gazed. By the shore, below me, was the vacillating abyss, like a dark mirror, of the subaqueous sky, on which the ducks hung, sleeping their light sleep, hiding their heads under their wings, and deeply reflected in it; beyond the pond, to the left, darkly loomed Uvarov's manor, that same landowner whose illegitimate son was Glebochka; on the other side of the pond lay the clayey hillocks lit directly by the moon; and farther—a large nocturnally bright village pasture and a row of black cottages beyond. What silence! Only a living organism can be silent like this. The wildly anxious screaming of the suddenly awakened ducks, who stirred underneath them their vacillating mirrorlike sky, echoed as thunder might through the neighboring gardens. . . . And when I walked slowly farther on, along the pond to the right, the moon again rolled quietly alongside me over the dark tops of the trees, frozen in their nocturnal beauty. . . .

So we would make the tour of the whole garden. It was just as if we were also thinking together—and always about the same thing: about the puzzling, tormentingly amorous happiness of life, about my enigmatic future, which could not be but happy—and, of course, all the time about Annchen. The figure of Pisarev, living as well as dead, passed more and more into oblivion. What was left of my grandmother, beyond her portrait on the drawing-room wall? It was the same with Pisarev: thinking of him, I now usually saw mentally only his large photograph hanging in the sitting room of the Vasilievskoe house, a photograph dating from just after he had married (and probably expected to live forever!). There also came to my mind the old thought: where was that man now, what happened to him, what was the eternal life in which he supposedly was dwelling? But unanswered questions no longer caused me anxious bewilderment; there was even some solace in them: where he was—God alone knew, Whom I do not understand, but in Whom I must and do believe in order to live and be happy. . . .

Annchen tormented me for a longer time. Even in the daytime—whatever I looked at, whatever I felt, read, or thought, she was behind it all, my affection for her, the recollections linked up with her, the pain of there no longer being anyone to whom I could tell how I loved her and how many beautiful things there were in the world that we could have enjoyed together; of the night there is no need to speak—here she possessed me entirely. But time went on—and now Annchen, too, gradually began to be turned into a legend, to lose her living shape; somehow I no longer believed that she had ever been with me, and that she still lived somewhere in the present; already I had begun to think of her and feel her only poetically, with a yearning after love in general, after some universal, lovely, womanly image, confused with images from the poems of Pushkin, Lermontov, Byron. . . .

7

Once, at the beginning of summer, I read in *The Week*, to which I had subscribed that year, about the publication of the collected poems of Nadson.[7] What enthusiasm his name then aroused, in even the remotest parts of the country! I had already read some Nadson, and, try as I might, could not make myself respond. "Let the poison of pitiless doubts expire in the tormented breast" seemed to me mere rhetoric in bad taste: I could not feel special respect for poems in which cattails were said to grow on top of a pond, and even to bend their "green boughs" over it. But never mind—Nadson was a poet who died untimely, a young man with a beautiful and sad look in his eyes, of whom people wrote that he "expired amid roses and cypresses on the shores of the azure Southern sea." . . . When, during the winter, I read of his death and his metal coffin, "all drowned in flowers," being sent for solemn funeral to "frosty and foggy St. Petersburg," I came down to dinner so pale and excited that even my father looked anxiously at me and was reassured only when I explained the reason of my grief.

"Ah, is that all?" he asked with surprise, hearing that the reason was Nadson's death.

And added angrily, with relief, "What nonsense comes into your head!"

Now the item of news in *The Week* roused me enormously. In the course of the winter Nadson's fame had increased. The thought of that fame suddenly made me feel so giddy, called forth such longing for my own fame, after which I had to set out at once, without losing a single moment, that I decided to go the very next day to town to get Nadson's works in order to learn, properly this time, what he was like, what it was, besides his poetical death, which roused all Russia's admiration. There was no horse to ride: Kabardinka had gone lame, the work horses were too lean and ugly—I had to walk. And so I did, though the town was fully twenty miles away. I started early, striding along the hot and deserted highway without resting, and around three o'clock was already entering the library in the Commercial

Street. The young woman with curls on her forehead, who sat lonely and obviously very bored in the narrow room filled from top to bottom with books in battered bindings, looked at me, exhausted as I was by my walk and by the sun, with some curiosity.

"There is a line for Nadson," she said carelessly. "You won't get it for a month. . . ."

I was flabbergasted at first, disconcerted—to have walked twenty miles for nothing was no trifle!—but it turned out that she had merely wanted to tease me.

"But you're a poet too?" she added at once with a grin. "I know you, I saw you when you were still a schoolboy. I'll give you my own copy. . . ."

I launched into thanks and, blushing with confusion and pride, dashed out into the street with my precious book so joyously that I nearly knocked down a slim girl of about fifteen, in a gray gingham dress, who had just stepped out of a carriage standing by the pavement. The carriage was drawn by three strange horses—all piebald, all sturdy and small, all of exactly the same color, like birds of a feather. Still odder was the coachman, who sat bent over on the box: he was a red-haired Caucasian, extremely withered and lean, and extremely ragged, but a great swell, who wore a brown Caucasian fur cap cocked sideways and back. Inside the carriage sat a stout and majestic lady in a loose coat of Japanese silk. She looked at me rather severely and with surprise, while the girl jumped aside with real fear which flashed marvelously in her dark consumptive eyes and in the whole of her fine, pure face, with its slightly mauve-hued and touchingly unhealthy lips. I felt still more embarrassed, and shouted with undue fervor and refinement, "Oh, do forgive me—for God's sake!" and without turning ran down the street toward the market, with the sole thought of perusing the book as soon as possible and having some tea at an inn. Yet that meeting was not to end so simply.

I was definitely in luck that day. Some peasants from Baturino were sitting at the inn. On seeing me, with that glad surprise with which the inhabitants of the same village meet in town, they all shouted together: "There's our young master, isn't it? Welcome, sir! Don't be particular! Join us."

I joined them, also extremely glad, in the hope of getting home with them, and truly, they at once offered me a lift. It turned out that they had come to fetch bricks, that their carts were just outside at the brick kilns next to the Runaways' Quarter, and that they were proposing to start on the homeward journey in the evening. The whole evening, however, passed in loading bricks. I spent one, two, three hours at the brick kilns, gazing endlessly at the deserted evening fields stretching before me on the other side of the road, and meanwhile the peasants kept on loading their bricks. The vesper bells in town had died away, and the sun had sunk quite low over the reddened field—and still they were loading. I was simply exhausted with boredom and fatigue, when one of the peasants said jeeringly, struggling to the cart with a whole apronful of fresh pink bricks and jerking his head in the direction of the carriage drawn by three horses abreast raising dust on the track near the main road, "And there's the Bibikov lady driving. She is coming to our parts, to Uvarov. He told me the other day that he was expecting her for a stay, and he haggled over a sheep to slaughter. . . . Gentlemen they call themselves, too!"

Another took it up: "True, true, it's her. And that's her skinflint on the box. . . . "

Instantly I started up, staring more intently, and recognized the piebald horses that had been standing a bit earlier by the library—and suddenly understood what it really was that had been secretly bothering me since the moment I ran out: *she* had been bothering me—that slim girl. When I heard that she was going to our parts, to Baturino, I even jumped up from my place, inundated the peasants with hasty questions, and learned at once a good deal: that the Bibikov lady was the girl's mother, that she was a widow, that the girl was studying at an institute in Voronezh—the peasants called it "noblemen's establishment"—that they lived in their little manor near Zadonsk, in very poor circumstances, that they were related to Uvarov, that the horses had been given to them by another relative of theirs, their Zadonsk neighbor Markov, that his piebald horses were notorious all over the county, as was the skinflint Caucasian who had been in Markov's employ, at first, as usual, as a horse-breaker, then wormed his way in, became his bosom friend, bound to him by a terrible deed: once he whipped to death a horse thief who had wanted to steal the principal brood-mare from Markov's herd. . . .

We did not start till dusk, and dragged on the whole night at walking pace—as much as the two-ton load allowed the anemic horses to do. And what a night it was! At dusk, as soon as we had got out to the main road, a wind began to blow; it began to grow dark, somehow rapidly and uncertainly, disquietingly, because of the storm clouds coming from the east; it began to roar heavily, shaking the sky and booming more and more terrifyingly, lighting it up with red summer lightning flashes. . . . In half an hour pitch darkness set in, and a wind—now hot, now quite cool—tore about on all sides; pink and white lightning darted in all directions over the black fields; and every minute we were deafened by monstrous thunderclaps which, with an incredible roaring and a dry, sizzling crackling, burst out right over our heads. And a real hurricane swept along madly; the lightning tongues sparkled in the thunderclouds to their full height, like serrated white-heated serpents, with a fierce trembling and horror—and a downpour burst which lashed us with fierce booming to the sound of now ceaseless thunderclaps amid such apocalyptic flashing and flames that the infernal gloom of the heavens seemed to open up overhead to its uttermost depths; like some preternatural, timeless Himalayas, the mountains of clouds flashed, sparkling with copper. . . . Lying on cold bricks and covered with all the rags and coats which the peasants could give me, I was soaked through within five minutes. But what mattered that hell and flood to me! I was already under the full sway of my new love. . . .

8

At that time Pushkin was a genuine part of my life.[8]

When did he enter into me? I had heard of him since early childhood, and his name was always mentioned in our home with something like family intimacy, like the name of a man who was quite "one of ourselves," belonging, like us, to the same and very special set. He even seemed to me to write only our things, for us, and full of our feelings. The storm, which in his verses dimmed the sky with mist, "tossing up snowy whirlwinds," was the same that raged on winter nights around Kamenka. Mother would sometimes read to me (in an old-fashioned singsong and dreamy way, with a sad and tender smile), "Yesternight I sat with a hussar drinking a cup of grog"—and I would ask: "What hussar, mother? Our dead uncle?" She would recite, "A withered flower, odorless, I see forgotten in a book"—and I saw that flower in her own girlish album. . . . As to my youth, it all passed with Pushkin.

Lermontov was also inseparable from it: "Speechless lies the blue steppe, the Caucasus, like a silver ring, encircling it; over the sea, frowning, it sleeps quietly, like a giant bent over his shield, hearkening to the tales of wandering waves, and the Black Sea rumbles endlessly. . . ."

These lines responded to a truly marvelous youthful longing for distant wanderings awakening and forming my soul, to a passionate dream of things remote and beautiful, to a secret music of the soul! And yet most of all I communed with Pushkin. How many emotions he kindled in me! And how I made him accompany my own feelings and everything in which and by which I lived!

This life, of course, had plenty of prose, too; yet which prevailed—for me at least?

Here I wake up on a frosty sunny morning and feel doubly happy because I can exclaim with him, "There's frost and sun—a lovely day"—with him who described that morning so wonderfully and also gave me a wonderful image: "And still you doze, my lovely friend. . . ."

Or, waking up to see a blizzard, I recall that today we are to go out shooting, and again I begin my day as he did: ". . . Is it warm? Has the blizzard stopped? Fresh snow or not? Can one leave bed for saddle, or would it be better to while away the morning with one's neighbor's old magazines?"

Now there is spring twilight; Venus hangs golden over the trees; the windows into the garden are open; and again he is with me, voicing my secret dream: "Hasten my fair one: love's golden star has risen in the sky."

Now it is already quite dark, and a nightingale's song rings tormentingly all over the garden: "Did you hear, beyond the copse, the voice of the night, singing of love and sorrow?"

Now I am in bed, and a "sad candle" is burning beside me—really, a sad tallow candle, not an electric lamp—and who is this pouring out his youthful love, or rather the craving for it—he or I? "O Morpheus, give till morn a solace to my tormented love!"

And now again "the wood drops her crimson robe and the fields suffer from fierce sports"—the same to which I am so passionately addicted: "How swiftly my new-shod horse scours the fields that lie so wide and open! How his hoofs ring clanging on the frozen earth!"

At night a huge dim-red moon rises silently over our dead black garden—and again the marvelous words ring out: "Ghostly behind the pinewood rose a misty moon"—and my soul is filled with ineffable dreams of the unknown woman whom he has created, and who has captivated me forever, walking in this still hour, somewhere in another, far-off land—"by the shores washed by rumbling waves." . . .

9

My feelings for Lisa Bibikov were a result not only of my childishness but also of my fondness for our way of life, with which all Russian poetry was once so closely connected. I was in love with Lisa in an old-fashioned, poetical way, as with a being belonging entirely to our set of people. The spirit of that set, to which my imagination added a halo of romance, seemed to me the more beautiful as it was in the process of vanishing forever under my very eyes.

I saw our life growing poorer, but for that reason it became ever more precious; at times, oddly, I even rejoiced in that poverty . . . perhaps because here, too, I found a certain kinship with Pushkin, whose house, according to Yazykov's description, also presented a picture far from prosperous: "Walls miserably papered here and there; a battered floor; two windows; between them a door of glass; a sofa in a corner, under the icons; and a pair of chairs. . . ."[9]

At the time of Lisa's stay in Baturino, however, our poor life was enriched by hot June days, by the thick verdure of shadowy gardens, by the smell of passing jasmine and blooming roses, by swimming in the pond, which, on our bank, overshadowed by the garden and overgrown with thick cool grass, was picturesquely shaded by tall willows, their glistening foliage, their lustrous pliant branches. Thus Lisa became forever associated in my memory with those first days of swimming, with June pictures and odors—of jasmine, of roses, of strawberries at dinner, of those willows on the bank, whose elongated leaves have a strong smell and a bitter taste, of tepid water and the slime of the sun-warmed pond. . . .

I did not go to Uvarov's that summer—Glebochka was spending the summer near Kharkov in an agricultural school, to which he had been transferred on account of his meager achievements at school; nor did the Uvarovs come to see us, the relations between us being strained—the everlasting story of petty country quarrels; yet Mme Uvarov nevertheless asked my father's permission to swim in the pond on our side, and used to come with the Bibikovs nearly every day, and now and then I would meet them, as if by accident, on the shore and bow to them with studied politeness, and Mme Bibikov, who used to walk with an air of condescending gravity, her head up, dressed in a loose peignoir and with a beach towel on her shoulder, was soon answering me rather affably, and even smilingly, evidently remembering how the other day, in town, I had burst out of the library. Shyly at first, and then with increasing friendliness and eagerness, Lisa would answer too, already slightly sunburnt and with a sparkle in her large eyes. She now wore a white sailor dress with a blue collar, and a rather short blue skirt, and exposed to the sun her little dark head with a black, slightly curly pigtail tied with a large white bow. She did not swim, but merely sat on the shore while her mother and Mme Uvarov were swimming down where the willows grew especially thick; but sometimes she would take off her shoes to walk on the grass and enjoy its soft coolness, so that on several occasions I saw her barefoot. The whiteness of her small feet in the green grass was particularly charming. . . .

Once more came moonlit nights, and this time I took it into my head not to sleep at all at night—to go to bed only at dawn, and to sit in my room at night, in absolute solitude, with candles as my sole light, reading and writing verses, then to wander in the garden, gazing at Uvarov's manor from the side of the dam. . . .

In daytime on that dam peasant women and girls often stood, and, bending over a large flat smoothed-out stone lying in the water by the shore, their skirts tucked up above their knees—large, red and yet tender, womanly—talking in quick, brisk voices, they would beat wet gray shirts with rollers; sometimes they would stand erect, wipe away the sweat from their brows with tucked-up sleeves, and, with playful insolence, hinting at something, say to me whenever I happened to pass: "Lost something, kid?"—and then would bend down again and beat and whack still more vigorously, laughing at something, exchanging remarks, and I would hasten away: it was already difficult for me to look at them thus stooping, and to see their bare knees. . . .

Then another of our neighbors, the one whose estate was across the road from ours and whose son was in exile, old Alferov, had a visit from relatives, young ladies from St. Petersburg, and one of these, the youngest, Asya, was good-looking, agile and tall, merry and energetic, free-mannered in a way different from ours. She liked playing croquet, taking snapshots at random with her camera, riding; and imperceptibly I became rather a frequent visitor to that estate, concluded a sort of friendship with Asya in which she both maltreated me as a mere boy and at the same time obviously enjoyed my boyish company. Time and again she would take a snapshot of me; for whole hours we would knock about with croquet mallets, and it always turned out that I was making a mess of things, and she would pause every minute, and very cutely dropping her *l*'s, would shout at me in utter despair: "Oh, how si'y, goodness, how si'y!" But best of all we liked galloping late in the afternoon along the high road, and I could no longer listen quite tranquilly to her glad shouts on horseback, or view her colored cheeks and flying hair, or feel our solitude in the fields while I saw her figure, graceful as a lyre, posed superbly in the saddle; and her taut left foot, pressing the stirrup, kept flashing from under the floating skirt of her habit. . . .

But that was in the daytime or in the evening. And my nights I devoted to poetry.

Here it is already quite dark in the fields, the warm dusk thickens, and Asya and I are returning at a walking pace, passing through the village, with all its summer evening smells. After taking Asya as far as her house, I enter the courtyard of our manor, throw the bridle of the sweating Kabardinka to a farmhand, and hurry indoors to supper, where I am met with the gay banter of my brothers and sister-in-law. After supper, I go out for a walk with them, to the common behind the pond or again to the same highway, looking at the gloomily red moon rising beyond the black fields, from which soft even warmth wafts up. And after the walk I at last remain alone. Everything is hushed—the house, the manor, the village, the moonlit fields. I sit by the open window and read or write. The night wind, grown just a shade cooler, comes in puffs from the garden, here and there already lit up, and shakes the flames of guttering candles. The night moths flutter in swarms around them, crackling as they burn themselves with an agreeable smell; as they fall, they gradually strew the whole desk. An irresistible sleepiness makes me drop my head, but I do my best to overcome and defeat it. . . .

And by midnight, as a rule, sleep would be dispelled. I would rise, blow out the candles, and go into the garden. Now, in June, the moon followed its summer course, still lower. Round the corner of the house it stood, its broad shadow reaching far across the lawn; and from that shadow it was particularly pleasing to look up at a seven-colored star twinkling quietly in the east, far beyond the garden, beyond the village, beyond the summer fields, whence at times, hardly audible and therefore particularly charming, came the distant clucking of a partridge. The ancient linden near the house was in blossom, and smelled sweet; warm and golden was the moon. And again only the warmth was wafted up—as is usual before the dawn, the approach of which was already discernible yonder in the eastern sky, where the horizon was already faintly silvering. It was wafted up from that side, from beyond the pond, and quietly I walked down the garden to meet it, and went down to the dam. . . . The courtyard of the Uvarov manor merged into the village common, and the garden beyond the house into the field. And now, looking at it from the dam, I figured exactly where everyone was sleeping. I knew that Lisa slept in Glebochka's room, the one whose windows also looked into a garden, dark, thick, pressing close upon them. . . . And how can I express my feelings as I looked, imagining Lisa sleeping there in that room, to the accompaniment of leaves lisping like a quietly streaming rain, behind the open windows through which, now and again, that warm wind blew in from the fields, nursing that half-childish sleep of hers, than which nothing on earth seemed to me purer or more lovely!

10

This strange way of life lasted nearly the whole summer. And when it changed it did so unexpectedly and abruptly. One fine morning I suddenly learnt that the Bibikovs were no longer in Baturino—they had left the day before. I remember having spent the day very listlessly, not knowing what to do with myself; late in the afternoon I went to Asya—and what did I hear?

"And we are going to the Crimea tomorrow," she said as soon as she saw me, as blithely as if she meant to make me very happy. . . .

The world thereafter became so empty and boring that I took to going to the fields where they had already begun mowing our rye; I would sit for hours on end on the swaths in the field, gazing aimlessly at the mowers. There I sit, and around me is the drought, the glitter, the hot and motionless glow, the regular swish of the scythes; like a solid and high wall, against the blueness of the sky, gray in the heat, mounts a sea of dry, sandy-yellow rye, with full-eared, obediently bent stalks, and the ungirdled peasants advance upon it one after another, walking bandy-legged, moving slowly and evenly forward; their rustling scythes gleam in the sun as they leave one swath after another lying to the left of them, leaving behind them the yellow stubble looking like a prickly brush—wide, empty stripes; and gradually they bare the field ever more and more, make it look like something quite new, open up fresh outlooks and vistas.

"But why sit idle, sir?" one of the mowers, a tall, handsome, black-haired fellow, addressed me, somewhat unceremoniously but amicably. "Take my spare scythe and join us. . . ."

I rose, and without a word went to his cart. Then it began.

At first it was very painful. The speed, and every sort of clumsiness, so exhausted me that in the evening I could hardly get home—my back bent and broken, my arms aching below the shoulders and my hands smarting with bloody blisters, my face burnt, my hair clotted with dried sweat, feeling a great thirst and a wormwood bitterness in my mouth. But afterward I got so used to my voluntary punishment that I would even go to sleep with a blissful thought, "Mowing again tomorrow!"

After the mowing came the carting. This work is even harder. It is even worse—to thrust the pitchfork into a thick, dry, stiff sheaf, to lever up its slippery handle with one's knee and in one motion, making your stomach ache, fling up that magnificent rustling load, while it pours its sharp grains down on you, up onto the high cartload, growing bigger and bigger on the ever-dwindling cart, the rumps of sheafs sticking out on all sides . . . and then to encircle its top-heavy mountain, pricking on all sides and smelling stuffily of rye-warmth, with hard new ropes, to draw them tight with all one's might, to bind them fast to the cart . . . and then to walk slowly behind its swelling pile along the rutted and pitted cart track, ankle-deep in the hot thick dust, all the time watching the horse looking so insignificant under its cartload, and inwardly to strain all the time with it, to fear all the time that the miserable cart, everywhere creaking under its terrible load, might give way at some turning, that a wheel might catch too abruptly—and that the whole load would topple over hideously. . . . All this is no trifling matter, especially when one's bare head is exposed to the sun, one's hot, sweating chest smarts with chaff, one's legs tremble with overwork, and one's mouth is full of wormwood!

In September I spent all my days in the farmyard. There was a spell of grayish, miserable weather. In the yard, from early morning till late at night, a threshing machine would roar and boom, and pitch the straw about and raise thick clouds of chaff; some women and young girls were working briskly under it with their rakes, their dusty kerchiefs pulled low over their eyes, while others made the winnowing machine hum evenly in one of the dark corners, turning the handle of the fans that blew the grain inside, singing all the time with plaintive sweetness, and I would listen to them, now taking my place next to one of them so as to turn the handle, now helping them to gather the pure grain from beneath the winnowing machine into a measure, and afterward pour it with pleasure into an open sack standing near by. I felt ever closer to and friendlier toward those women and young girls, and goodness knows what it all would have come to—already one long-legged, red-haired wench, who used to sing the most dashingly and skillfully of all, and at the same time, notwithstanding all her apparent pertness and roughness, with a peculiar sad soulfulness, openly hinted that she would not refuse anything for, say, a pair of new scissors—had not a new event occurred in my life: unexpectedly, I found my way into one of the most important St. Petersburg monthlies, and I turned out to be in the company of the most renowned writers of the time, even receiving for it a money order for the goodly sum of fifteen rubles. "No," said I to myself, amazed by both these facts, "enough of that farmyard for me! I must take to my books and writings again." And I went at once to saddle Kabardinka. I intended to go to town, get the money—and set to work. . . . It was already nearly evening, but all the same I went to the stables, saddled the horse, and spurred it on through the village, along the high road. . . . Out in the fields it was sad, deserted, cold, inhospitable, yet how full of eagerness and freshness, of readiness for life and belief in it, was my youthful, lonely soul!

11

In the field it was growing gloomily dark; a sharp wind blew, and I breathed freely its late autumnal freshness, felt with delight its healthy chill on my hot young face, and spurred Kabardinka on and on. I had always loved to ride fast, and always loved the horses I rode; yet I was always terribly merciless to them. And here I rode especially fast. Was I thinking, dreaming of anything in particular? But whenever something important, or at least significant, occurs in one's life and one has to draw some conclusion from it or take some decision, one thinks little, but rather yields oneself to the secret workings of the soul. And I well remember that all the way into town my soul, roused into virile vigor, was working ceaselessly at some problem. What problem? I didn't know as yet; once more I felt a craving for some change in my life, for freedom from something, and a striving somewhere. . . .

I remember that near Stanovaya I halted for a moment. Night was falling, and the fields were still gloomier and sadder. There was not a soul, it seemed, not only on that desolate, quite forsaken road, but also for hundreds of miles around. Desolation, expanse, wilderness. . . . "Wonderful," I thought, giving the horse her head. Kabardinka stopped, heaving her flanks deeply and standing rigid. Feeling numb in the knees, I got off the warm slippery saddle, casting round me a vigilant and cautious glance, remembering the old stories of robbers around Stanovaya and secretly even longing for some terrible meeting, for an uncanny encounter with someone; I tightened the saddle girth and the leather belt round my coat, and adjusted the dagger hanging from it. The wind blew into my side, pressing it closely like cold water, striking and roaring in my ears, making something rustle stealthily out in the fields amid the dry weeds and the reaped grain. Kabardinka, the stirrups swinging at her sides and the saddle horn standing out, stood there looking wonderfully slender, her ears cocked as if also aware of all the evil repute of that spot, and also looking keenly and sternly down the road. Already she was quite dark with hot sweat, she had grown even thinner in the ribs and flanks; but I knew her power of endurance, knew that the single deep breath she took in when she stopped sufficed for her to head off again, though no longer young, to the full extent of her strength, knew her unfailing patience and affection for me. And, after nagging her with special affection and kissing her sensitive nose, I jumped into the saddle again and rode on faster than ever. . . .

Then came the night, dark and obscure, a real autumn night, and as in a dream one began thinking that there would be no end to this gloom, to the head wind, and to the harmonious beat of hooves in the dense darkness underfoot. . . . Then the distant lights of the town and suburbs opened up, for a long time seeming to stand still, seen with that particular sharpness and distinctness peculiar to autumn nights. At last they came nearer, grew larger, and the wooden roofs of the suburban houses showed black along the dark road, and beneath them the small shining windows looked out alluringly and cozily, showing the bright interiors of the cottages, their inhabitants having dinner there, in families. . . . And then it began to smell distinctly of all the complex odors of a populous town, numerous other lights and lighted windows began to flash past—and Kabardinka's shoes rang gaily and exhilaratingly on the cobbled streets. In the town it was stiller and warmer; it was still evening, not that black blind night which had long descended upon the open country, and I arrived at Nazarov's inn just in time for supper. . . .

How full was my soul that night! Not that I felt too excited, too happy, because I had found my way into a famous review, among famous writers—that, I recall, I took almost for granted. I merely felt somehow strongly and agreeably roused. I was fully in control of all my faculties, of all my mental and bodily sensibilities, and everything gave me a wonderful delight: that autumn evening in town; and the way in which, after trotting up to Nazarov's gate, I began pulling the ring of rusty wire hanging down from a hole in the post, sounding the bell loudly all over the courtyard; and the way in which, clattering on the cobbles, the limping steps of the caretaker came from behind the gate as he was opening the gate to me; and the coziness of the dung-covered stable yard where, in darkness, under the black sheds and the open, starlit, clearing sky, stood carts and loudly munching horses, forming a real camp; the peculiar, old, provincial foulness of the privy in the impenetrable darkness of that small outhouse where I mounted, my feet leaden with cold, up the rotten steps of the wooden porch, and where I fumbled long for the bolt of the house door; and the bright kitchen, warm and crowded, which then suddenly opened, with its thick smell of hot, greasy, salted meat and of dining peasants, and behind it the clean section where, at a big round table, brightly lit by a hanging lamp, presided over by the stout pockmarked hostess with a long upper lip, and the old host, a stern, morose man, a big bony fellow whose nondescript lank hair and Suzdal nose made him look like an Old Believer, there also sat at supper many sunburnt, weather-beaten people, in vests and high-collared shirts hanging loose from beneath the vests. . . . All except the innkeeper drank vodka, ate the overcooked cabbage soup,

116

with meat and bay leaves floating in it, from a huge common bowl. "O, wonderful!" I felt, O, how wonderful everything is—that wild inhospitable night in the fields, and this friendly, evening life in the town, those peasants and townsfolk drinking and eating, all that old provincial Russia with its coarseness, complexity, strength, domesticity, and my hazy dreams of some fairy St. Petersburg, of Moscow, of famous writers, and the fact that I, too, am about to have a good drink, and to set to with a wolf's appetite on the cabbage soup and the soft, white, city bread! Indeed, I ate and drank such a lot that afterward (when everybody at the inn had scattered after dinner and gone to bed wherever they chanced—in the courtyard, in the kitchen; had put out the lights and fallen sound asleep surrendering completely to bedbugs and cockroaches), I sat for a long time hatless on the porch steps, refreshing my slightly dizzy head with the air of the October night, listening in the nocturnal stillness, now to the watchman's rattle, cleverly executing a dance-tune somewhere away along the deserted street, now to the peaceful crunching of the horses under the sheds, sometimes interrupted by their brief scuffle and angry neighing, and all the time thinking out, deciding something with my blissfully tipsy mind. . . .

On that night I first conceived my plan of sooner or later leaving Baturino.

12

The innkeeper and his wife were the only ones to sleep apart, in a bedroom that looked like a chapel with its multitude of gold and silver icons in a case rising like a black upright tomb in the front corner, behind a large crimson icon-lamp, while we, that is, I and the five other guests, all had to sleep in the same room in which we had dined that evening. Three of us spent the night on the floor, on felt rugs, the other three, myself unfortunately among them, on sofas, hard as stone, of course, with upright wooden backs. And all night long, besides, I was of course devoured by bedbugs (small ones, particularly venomous, which darted boldly off the pillow as soon as I struck a match); and from the warm, odorous darkness around rose a loud snoring which made the night seem hopeless and unending, and sometimes that tireless rattle flaunted its terribly loud, voluptuous, bold, round, and hollow clatter right underneath the windows, and the door to the hosts' bedroom was left ajar so that the icon-lamp threw its red light right into my eyes, its black cross-shaped cork float, its dark radiant glimmer, and the oscillating shadows it sent forth resembling some fairy-tale spider in the midst of an enormous web. . . . I rose, however, as if nothing had been the matter as soon as I heard the innkeeper and his wife wake up, and those who slept on the floor started yawning, rising, lighting cigarettes, and pulling on their boots, and the cook ran in, treading on their feet and the felt rugs, dragging a huge smoking samovar smelling nicely of charcoal, and bumped it with one swing on the table, its thick steam at once fogging up the windowpanes and mirror.

An hour later I was already at the post office, where at last I received my first honorarium and that wonderful thick book, different from any other book in the world, in its virginally fresh yolk-colored wrapper, containing my poem, which at first glance seemed not to be mine even to me—it looked so pleasantly like some lovely real poem by a real poet. After that I had some business to do—to call, at my father's request, on a certain Ivan Andreevich Balavin, a grain dealer, in order to show some samples of our grain, inquire about their price, and if possible sign a sale contract. And now, from the post office, I made my way straight to his store, but I walked in such a way that the peasants and townsfolk whom I met looked with surprise at this young man in boots, in a blue cap and coat to match, who now and then slowed down in his walk and sometimes would even stop dead in the middle of the street, staring all the time at one and the same spot in a book which he held open before his eyes. . . .

Balavin received me at first dryly and even unfriendlily, with that groundless hostility which is often met with among Russian traders. His store in the grain row had its shutters flush with the pavement. The shop assistant led me through that store to the far end, to a little glass door curtained on the inside with a piece of scarlet material, and tapped hesitatingly.

"Come in!" shouted someone disagreeably from behind the door.

I entered, and to meet me rose from behind a large desk a man of undefinable age, dressed in quite a European fashion, with a very clean yellowish face that seemed almost transparent, with whitish hair neatly combed and parted in the middle, with a fine yellow moustache and a quick look in his light-green eyes.

"What is it?" he asked dryly and curtly.

I told him what it was, mentioned my name, drew out from my coat pocket, hurriedly and clumsily, the two little bags with grain, and laid them before him on the desk.

"Sit down," he said rather casually, again taking his seat at the desk; and without looking at me he began to undo the bags. Having done so, he took out a handful of one sort of grain, threw it up on his palm, rubbed it between his fingers and smelled, then repeated the same operation with the other sort.

"How much altogether?" he asked carelessly.

"How many bushels, you mean?" I asked.

"Well, not wagons I suppose," he said mockingly. "After all, your estate can't be so big. . . ."

I flushed, but he did not let me answer.

"That is of no consequence, however. Prices are weak at present: you know that yourself, I suppose."

And after mentioning his price, he proposed we bring the grain the very next day.

"I accept that price," I said, blushing. "Could I get an advance?"

He silently extracted his wallet from his side pocket, gave me a hundred-ruble note, and with a characteristically very accurate gesture replaced the wallet.

"Do you want a receipt?" I asked, blushing still more and feeling awkwardly pleased with my maturity and businesslike manner.

He grinned, replied that Alexander Sergeevich Arseniev was, thank God, well enough known to everybody, and, as if wishing to let me know that the business conversation was over, he opened a silver cigarette case that lay on his desk and handed it to me.

"Thanks, I don't smoke," I said.

He lit a cigarette and asked again in his casual manner, "Is it you who write poetry?"

I looked at him with great amazement, but again he did not let me answer.

"Don't be surprised at my taking an interest in such things, too," he said with a grin. "I am also, if I may say so, a poet. I even published a book once. Now I have naturally given up the lyre—no time, and my talent turned out to be minimal—I write only articles for newspapers, as you may have heard, but I still take an interest in literature, subscribe to many newspapers and reviews. This is, unless I am mistaken, your first appearance in a fat journal?[10] Let me heartily wish you success and advise you not to neglect yourself."

"How do you mean?" I asked, quite amazed now by the sudden turn our business talk was taking.

"I mean that you ought to think very seriously about your future. You'll forgive me for saying it, but for literary occupations one must possess some means and a sound education; and what have you got? Take myself. Without any false modesty I can say that I was not a dope; when still a small boy I had seen as much as I wish to God any tourist might see. Yet what did I write? It's embarrassing to remember.

"Here's an example:

I came to life amid the waste of steppes,
In an ordinary, stuffy cottage,
Where swinging sleeping boards
Replaced the carven furniture. . . .[11]

"I ask myself what imbecile wrote that? In the first place it is a lie. I was never born in a steppe cottage; I was born in town. Second, it is rather silly to compare sleeping boards to carved furniture. And third, sleeping boards never swing. And didn't I know all that? I knew it quite well, but I couldn't help writing this nonsense because I was uneducated, uncultivated, and too poor to receive an education. . . . Godspeed," he added, suddenly rising, holding out his hand, shaking mine firmly, and looking intently into my eyes.

"Let me serve as an occasion for serious reflection about yourself. To sit still in the country, to see nothing of life, to write and read at random is not a brilliant outlook. Yet one can see that you possess a real talent and, forgive my frankness, you give a very pleasant impression. . . ."

And suddenly he again became dry and earnest.

"Good-bye," he said, again somewhat casually, dismissing me with a nod and once more sitting down to his desk. "Remember me, please, to your father. . . ."

Thus unexpectedly my secret intention to leave Baturino received fresh confirmation.

13

That intention, however, was not realized soon.

My life again pursued its former course and became daily more carefree. I was being gradually turned—outwardly at least—into an ordinary country youth, already rather accustomed to sit in his estate, no longer estranged from its everyday existence. I went shooting, called on neighbors, on rainy or stormy days went to the village, to favorite cottages, whiled away my time in the family circle round the samovar, or else lay whole days long on the sofa with a book. And then something happened that had to happen sooner or later.

Our neighbor Alferov, who used to lead a lonely life, died. My brother Nicholas leased his vacated estate and lived there that winter instead of with us. Among his servants there was a maid called Tonka. She had just married, but immediately after the wedding had been forced by poverty and home-lessness to part with her husband: he was a saddler and after marrying went off again on his itinerant work, while she worked for my brother.

She was about twenty. In the village people called her "the jackdaw," "the savage," and because she was quiet thought her quite stupid. She had a very dark complexion, a gracefully and firmly built girl's body, small and strong limbs, dark nut-colored, narrow-slitted eyes. She resembled an Indi-an: the straight but rather rough features of a dark face, the coarse jet of lank hair. But in that, too, I found some charm.

I used to go nearly every day to my brother's; I admired her; I liked the firm, swift tread of her feet when she brought the samovar or soup tureen to table, the way in which she would meaninglessly look up: that stamping and that look, the coarse blackness of her hair parted in the middle and showing beneath an orange kerchief, the somewhat flat, bluish lips of her slightly elongated mouth, the slope of the dark youthful neck passing into shoulders—all this invariably roused in me a sweet and uneasy yearning. Sometimes, meeting her in the hall or the foyer, I would jestingly catch at her as she went by, and press her to the wall. Laughing silently, she would adroitly slip away—and there the matter ended. There was no amorous feeling between us.

But once, walking in soft winter dusk through the village, I turned absentmindedly to Alferov's manor, passed between the snowdrifts to the house, mounted the porch. In the dark foyer, especially dark at the top, a pile of red-hot embers in the freshly lighted stove showed red, gloomy and fantastic as in a black cave, and Tonka, bareheaded, straddling her bare legs, their tibias shining against the light with their smooth skin, was sitting on the floor against its mouth, illuminated by its dark flames, holding a poker in her hand, its white-hot end touching the embers; slightly averting from the glowing heat her dark flaming face, she was dreamily gazing at the embers, at their crimson peaks, frail and translucent, here already dying away under the fine lilac efflorescence and there still burning with blue-green gas. I banged the door as I entered—she did not even turn around.

"Why is it dark here? Is no one at home?" I asked, approaching her.

She threw her face farther back and, without looking at me, smiled somewhat uneasily and languidly.

"As if you don't know!" she said mockingly, and pushed the poker a little farther into the stove.

"Know what?"

"Come on, stop it. . . ."

"Stop what?"

"You must know where they are, as they've gone to you. . . ."

"I've been taking a walk, I haven't seen them."

"Tell me about walks. . . ."

I squatted on the floor, looking at her bare legs and her bare dark head, already full of inward tremors but laughing and pretending also to admire the embers and their hot dark-crimson glow. . . . Then suddenly I sat down beside her, embraced her, and threw her on the floor, catching her reluctant lips, hot because of the fire. The poker rattled, some sparks flew up from the stove. . . .

When afterward I rushed out to the porch, I looked like a man who had unexpectedly committed murder; I held my breath and quickly turned around to see whether someone was coming. But there was no one; to my surprise everything was ordinary and quiet; in the village, in the accustomed winter darkness, the lights burned in the cottages with an incredible calmness—as if nothing had happened. . . . I looked up, listened—and quickly walked away. I could not feel the ground beneath me, for two clashing emotions: the sense of a sudden, terrible, irremediable catastrophe in my life, and that of an exultant, victorious triumph. . . .

At night, through my anxious sleep, I was now and then seized by deadly anguish, by the sense of something terrible, criminal, and shameful that had suddenly caused my undoing. "Yes, everything is over," I would think, waking up, recovering my senses with difficulty. "Everything, everything is finished, destroyed, spoiled; obviously this must be so; it can no longer be fixed."

Waking up in the morning, I looked with quite new eyes around me, at that room so familiar to me, lit evenly by the fresh snow which had fallen in the night: there was no sun, but in the room it was quite light from the bright whiteness. My first thought on opening my eyes was, of course, about what had happened. But that thought no longer frightened me; anguish, despair, shame, feelings of guilt, had already left. On the contrary. But how can I go down to tea now?—I thought. And what should I do in general? Well, nothing, I thought; nobody knows anything, and nobody will ever know, and in the world everything is just as nice as before, and even more so than before: outside is my favorite, still, white weather; the garden, its bare branches covered with shaggy snow, is all piled over with white snowdrifts; in the room it is warm because of the stove lit by somebody while I slept and now roaring and crackling evenly, flutteringly drawing in the brass lid. . . . It smells bitter and fresh, through the warmth, from the frosted and thawing aspen kindling lying next to it on the floor. . . . And what happened is only that natural, necessary thing which had to happen—after all, I am already seventeen. I was once more overwhelmed with a feeling of triumph, masculine pride. How wonderful and terrible was what happened yesterday! And it will be repeated again, perhaps even today! O, how I do and will love her!

14

From that day on a dreadful time began for me.

It was a real madness which engrossed all my mental and physical forces, a life made up only of moments of passion, or of their expectation; and of torments of the cruellest jealousy, which really tore my heart asunder when Tonka's husband came to see her and she had to go away at night from the house where she usually slept, to sleep with him in the servants' quarters.

Did she love me? At first she did; she was secretly, but so completely, happy with that love that, try as she might, she could not hide her secret admiration for me or the glitter of her narrow drooped eyes, even when she saw me in the presence of my brother and his wife, as she waited on us. Afterward, she sometimes loved me and sometimes did not—at times she would be indifferent, cold, and even hostile—and those constant changes in feeling, always incomprehensible and unexpected, utterly exhausted me. At times I loathed her; yet even then the mere thought of her dark-silvery earrings, of that tender and lovely, still very youthful something in her lips, in the oval of the lower part of her face, and in the drooping narrow eyes, the mere recollection of the coarse smell of her hair mixed with the smell of her kerchief, made me quiver all over. I was ready then—and even with some greedy joy—for every humiliation before her, provided only that the first happy days of our intimacy would return, even if only for a moment.

I did my best to lead, at least outwardly, a life as respectable as I could, as like as possible to that which I had formerly led, but all my days had long ago been turned into a mere semblance of my former existence.

Winter passed; spring came. I paid heed to nothing. I remember that for some reason I was stubbornly learning English. . . .

God saved me unexpectedly.

It was a wonderful May day. I was sitting with an English textbook in my hand, by the open window in my room. Next to me, on the balcony, I could hear the voices of my brothers, my sister-in-law, and my mother. I listened absentmindedly, and, looking dully at the book, my head was full of desperate thoughts. I felt greatly tempted to dash for a moment to Alferov's manor; after all, my brother and his wife were with us and Tonka would probably be alone. At the same time my soul was weighed down by such a painful sense of my utter depravity, and I felt such bitterness and pain, such pity for myself, that thoughts of death came, as it were, gladly to my mind. The garden would now shine with hot sunlight and buzz with bees, now stand shrouded in a fine, blue shadow; in the infinitely remote blueness, still young and springlike, and at the same time bright and rich, an infinitely high large cloud would billow up and cover the sun, and the air would slowly grow dark-blue, the sky would seem still vaster, still higher, and in those heights, away in the happy springlike void of the universe, there would come suddenly the first faint sounds of thunder, as it were mercifully and magnificently, with gradually increasing sonority and resonance. . . . I picked up a pencil, and, still thinking of death, began to write in the textbook: "And again and again, above your head, between the clouds and the blue darkness of trees, the skies will be filled with blue, celestially pure and blissful, and again the billowy clouds will shine behind the trees, with heavenly snows, and a bumble-bee cling to a flower's crown, and the god of Spring shall roll forth his mighty thunders—and I, where will I be?"

"Are you there?" said my brother Nicholas, in a stern, unusual tone, approaching my window. "Come out for a moment, I have to tell you something. . . ."

I was conscious of growing pale, yet rose and hopped out through the window.

"Tell me what?" I asked with unnatural calm.

"Let's go for a stroll," he said dryly, walking in front of me toward the pond. "But, please, do take what I am going to say sensibly. . . ."

And pausing, he turned toward me, "Look here, my dear friend, you realize, of course, that the whole affair has been an open secret for some time?"

"What affair?" I asked, with difficulty.

"Oh, you know very well. . . . So I want to warn you: this morning I dismissed her. Otherwise the whole thing would probably have ended in murder. Yesterday he returned and came straight to me. 'Nicholas Alexandrovich, I've known everything for a long time. Let Antonina go at once, otherwise it will end badly. . . .' And, you see, he was white as chalk, and his lips so dry that he could hardly speak. . . . I earnestly advise you to be sensible and not try to see her any more. Besides, it is no use—today they are going away to stay somewhere near Livny. . . ."

I said not a word in reply, walked ahead of him, went to the pond, and sat on the grassy shore under the young glossy willow branches that arched down toward the silvery mirror of the water. Another magnificent roar came from somewhere in the fathomless voids on high, then something began to rustle heavily and rapidly, and round me rose a smell of the damp freshness of the spring verdure. . . . A straight, sparse rain sparkled out in long glassy threads from another big cloud raising its snowy pinions infinitely high, straight above me, and on the still, even surface of the glassy-white water began a leaping of countless nails. . . .

Book Four

1

My last days at Baturino were also the last of my family's former life.

We were all aware of the approaching end of the old order of things: "Our brood is flying off, darling," my father would remark to my mother. Nicholas indeed had already left the nest, and George was about to do likewise—the term of his surveillance was over. I alone remained; but my turn was near too.

And yet, as usual, none of us (except, of course, my mother) took the trouble to think matters out, and I least of all.

2

Once more, spring came round again. And again it seemed to me to be such as had never been before, the beginning of something quite unlike all my past.

In every convalescence there is one particular morning when, on waking up, you at last fully recover that simplicity, that everydayness, which simply means health, a return to the normal state, different though it may be from the one that preceded the illness—because of a certain new experience, wisdom. Thus it was, too, that I woke up one quiet and sunny May morning in my corner room, the windows of which, by right of youth, I had no need to curtain. I flung off the blanket, feeling a quiet satisfaction in all my young vigor and all that healthy, youthful warmth which during the night I had imparted to myself and to the bed. The sun was shining through the windows; blue and ruby spots from the colored windowpanes were burning on the floor. I lifted the lower window-frame—it was already like a summer morning, full of the peaceful simplicity proper to summer, of its soft pure morning air, the odors of the sunlit garden with all its herbs, flowers, butter-

125

flies. I washed, dressed, and began praying before the icons that hung in the southern corner of the room and always evoked in me, by their Arseniev antiquity, a sense of comfort, of submission to the unfailing and infinite flow of earthly days. On the balcony they were drinking tea and talking. Again my brother Nicholas was there—he often came to visit us in the morning. And he was talking—evidently about me: "Well, what else can be done? Naturally he must work; he must take up some job. . . . George, I think, after all will manage to find something for him as soon as he gets something himself. . . ."

Those words comforted me still more. Well, if you have to work, so much the better. Besides, there's time enough—George isn't going before autumn, and we still have ages till then. . . .

How remote those days are. It already requires an effort to recall them now as belonging to myself, notwithstanding their closeness when I think of them as I write this, trying continually to revive some distant youthful image. Whose image is it? It is, as it were, a likeness of my fictitious younger brother, who long ago vanished from the world, along with all his infinitely remote times.

I sometimes happened to pick up, in a strange house, an old photograph album. Strange and complex were the feelings evoked in me by the faces of those who looked at me from its faded pictures. First, a sense of extraordinary estrangement from all those faces, for there are moments when a man feels utterly estranged from his fellow beings. And then, coming from that sense, an acutely intense awareness of those men and of their epoch. Who were these creatures, these faces? All were human beings who had lived sometime and somewhere, each in his own way, with different destinies and in different epochs where everything bore its peculiar stamp; clothes, customs, temperaments, public opinion, and events. . . . Here was an austere-looking, old, important official, with the medal of an order under his tie, with a large high collar, with the broad, fleshy features of a clean-shaven face. Here was a society fop of Herzen's day, with curly hair and whiskers, a top hat in his hand, in a wide frock coat, and trousers no less wide, which made his feet look tiny. Here the head and shoulders of a sadly beautiful lady; a crazy hat set over a high chignon, a close-fitting flowered silk dress encircling her bust and slim waist, and with long earrings. . . . And here, a young man of the seventies: high shirt collar wide open and exposing the Adam's apple, the soft oval of the face barely touched with down, a youthful languor in his large enigmatic eyes, the long wavy hair. . . . A fairy tale, a legend—all those faces, their lives and epochs!

I feel just the same thing now, as I resuscitate my own image as I was once. Was I really thus? There was the youthful William the Second, there was a general called Boulanger,[1] there was Alexander the Third, the ponderous ruler of unfathomable Russia. . . . And there was, in those legendary times, in that vanished Russia, spring, and somebody, with a dark flush in his cheeks, with bright-blue eyes, who for no earthly reason tormented himself with English, and day and night concealed within himself a yearning for a future where all the loveliness and joy of this world seemed to lie in store for him. . . .

3

One day in early summer, I met Tonka's sister-in-law in the village. She stopped and said, "Somebody has asked me to remember her to you. . . . "

Back home, I saddled my Kabardinka and rode off wildly. I remember passing through Znamenskoe, through Malinovoe, going as far as the high road to Livny. . . . One of those serene early summer evenings was beginning, when the fields are full of a special richness of peace, beauty, and well-being. I paused by the roadside, wondering where else I should go, crossed it, and rode on across the fields. I rode toward the glow of the already dipping sun— and I reached a large wood, which began in a long dale with overgrown ravines and pits where flowers and grass, already cool and smelling toward evening of wood and meadow freshness, reached to the horse's belly. . . . All around, in every bush and copse, the nightingales sang and warbled sweetly; somewhere far off a cuckoo was ceaselessly calling, monotonous and persistent, as though convinced, amid all these vain nightingales' transports, of the sole rightness of its lonely, homeless sorrow, and its resonantly hollow voice seemed to be now near, now far, sadly and marvelously alternating with even more distant echoes of the evening woodlands. I rode on, listening, and then began instinctively to count how many more years of life it would foretell for me—how much was still left me of all this inconceivable thing called life— partings, losses, memories, hopes. . . . And the cuckoo went on calling, prophesying for me an infinity of days. But what lay hidden behind that infinity? In the mystery and heedlessness of the surroundings there was something quite terrifying. I looked at Kabardinka's neck, at her mane thrown to one side and swinging rhythmically with the motion, at the whole of that uplifted head which, once upon a time, in fairy days, would sometimes speak out in a prophetic voice; terrifying was its speechlessness, that silence never to be broken, the dumbness of a creature so near and so akin to me, living, sensible, feeling, thinking; and still more terrifying the fantastic possibility of it suddenly breaking that silence. . . . And with senseless, uncanny joy the nightingales sang, and with a magical perseverance the cuckoo went on calling in the distance, yearning continuously for some secret nest.

4

In summer I went to town to a fair, and there I ran across Balavin again. He was walking with a horse dealer. The latter was exceedingly dirty and shabby, while Balavin looked particularly neat and elegant—all his clothes were brand-new; he had a new straw hat and a glossy cane. The horse dealer, walking hurriedly by his side, was fiercely swearing something, every now and then glancing up savagely and inquisitively at Balavin—he walked on without listening, staring in front of him, cold and hard, with his light-green eyes. "All nonsense!" he dropped at last, carelessly, and greeting me as if we had met yesterday instead of two years ago, he took me by the arm and offered to go somewhere "to have tea and a little chat."

We went to one of the tearooms at the fair, and he began questioning me with a grin: "Well, how are you? What progress are you making?" and then to talk about the "distressing plight" of our affairs—somehow he knew them better than we did—and again about what I myself was to do. When I parted with him I was so dejected that I decided to go home at once. It was already drawing toward evening; the bells in the monastery rang for vespers; the fair, situated on a vast common next to it, was dispersing; the cows, led away behind the creaking carts, making for the high road, bellowed menacingly, choking; the cabs, returning empty, bumping into the dusty pits of the common, swept recklessly past. . . . I boarded the first that came my way and drove to the station—I was just in time to catch the evening train in our direction.

"Yes, what is to be done?" I thought, recalling Balavin's words and feeling more and more convinced that their meaning was actually hopeless. "I can't even imagine what is to be done in your case," he had told me. "Your fathers in similar circumstances used to go off to the Caucasus to serve in the army, or got attached to various Foreign Office departments, but where can you go or get attached to? I don't think you are capable of doing any work at all—you're made of different stuff. You spread yourself too far away, as the books of oracle put it. As regards Baturino, I can see only one way out: sell it as quickly as possible, before it has been auctioned off. In that case, something at least, however trifling, will stay in your father's pocket. And as for yourself, you ought to think it over. . . ." But what could I imagine? I asked myself. Go and work in his store?

The effect of that meeting was even to cool the ardor of my work on *Hamlet*. I had begun translating it for myself, in prose—it was by no means a play congenial to me. It simply chanced to fall under my eyes just at the time when I so longed to start a clean and laborious life. I immediately set to work, and was soon carried away by it, began to enjoy it, to stimulate my ability to work. Besides, I conceived at the time a childish notion of becoming a translator, of creating for myself an eventual source, not only of constant artistic delight, but of livelihood too. Now, back at home, I suddenly realized all the vanity of such hopes. I also understood that the days were going by and all my "dreams," which Balavin, without himself wishing it, had once more roused in me, were still only dreams. About our "distressing plight" I soon forgot; but "dreams" were another matter. . . . What actually did they consist of? Balavin chanced to mention, for example, the Caucasus—"Your fathers in such circumstances used to go off to the Caucasus"—and once more I thought that I would give half of my life to be in their place. . . . At the fair a young gypsy woman had told my fortune. How little novelty these gypsies have! And yet what feelings I had as she grasped my hand in her strong black fingers, and how much I thought about her afterward! She looked, of course, very motley in her bright-red-and-yellow rags, and all the time she gently swung her hips, telling me the usual silly stuff, throwing away the kerchief from her small jet-black head, and tormenting me, not only with her hips, with the dreamy sweetness of her lips and eyes, but also with her antiquity, redolent of distant lands, as well as with the fact that here too my "fathers" came in—was there a single one who had not had his fortune told by a gypsy?—the secret bond uniting me to them, the longing to feel it, for how could we really love the world as we do if it were quite new to us?

5

In those days I would often pause and, with the brusque surprise of youth, ask myself, "After all, what is my life in this incomprehensible, timeless, and gigantic world surrounding me, thrown into the boundlessness of past and future, and at the same time enclosed in a place called Baturino, within the limits of space and time allotted to me personally?" And I saw that life (my life or any other) was a succession of days and nights, of toil and rest, of meetings and talks, of pleasures and nuisances, sometimes called events; that it was a confused accumulation of impressions, pictures, and images, of which only the most insignificant part (and even that Heaven knows why and how) remained with us; that it was a ceaseless flow, never stopping for one moment, of incoherent feelings and thoughts, of confused recollections of the past and vague anticipations of the future; and still, there is something in it that seems to contain a certain kernel, a certain meaning and purpose, something extremely important which it is quite impossible to grasp and put into words, and, connected to that, an everlasting anticipation: anticipation not merely of happiness, of its peculiar fullness, but also of something else in which, once it came, that essence, that meaning, would at last suddenly reveal itself and be grasped. "You spread yourself too far away, as the oracle books put it. . . ." And indeed, secretly, I did so spread myself. What for? Perhaps, just in order to grasp that meaning?

6

My brother George left for Kharkov—and again, as once ages ago, when he was being taken to prison, it was a clear October day. I saw him off at the station. We drove fast along the well-trodden glistening roads, our hopeful talk about the future dispelling the sadness of the parting, that secret sorrow over a completed chapter of life which any parting sums up and therefore ends for ever. "Everything will be all right, by the grace of God," my brother said, selfishly loath as he was to distress himself and drive away his hopes about Kharkov life. "As soon as I see my way and can save some money, I'll send for you. And then we'll see what is to be done. . . . Want a cigarette?" he added, and was delighted to watch me light it clumsily for the first time in my life.

There was something particularly sad and odd in returning home alone. Somehow I could not believe that what we had secretly feared so long, had now happened, that my brother was gone, that I was returning alone and would wake up alone in Baturino the next day. Back at home, a still greater blow lay in store for me. I was driving home in icy purple dusk. As off-horse we had Kabardinka, who all the way from the station gave no respite to the shaft horse, running at a fast trot. On arriving, I didn't think about her, and she was given a drink without being taken out; still drenched in sweat, she caught a deadly cold, stood the whole night through without a cloth on, and died toward morning. At noon I went to the meadows behind the garden, where her body had been dragged. Oh, how cruel and clear was the emptiness in the world, what sepulchral sunlit silence, what transparence of air and cold, gleaming, barren fields! Kabardinka's dead carcass lay hideously black in the meadows, showing its high swollen flank and a slim long neck with head thrown far back. The dogs were already working away at her belly, tossing it about, tearing at it voluptuously; a swarm of old ravens loitered about expectantly, at times flashing fiercely up whenever the dogs, who growled anxiously even in the very midst of their hideous occupation, would suddenly fling their scowling and bloody muzzles at them. . . . And after lunch, as I lay dully on the sofa in my room, the autumn sky showing uniformly blue behind its minute square windowpanes, and black the bare trees, I heard some quick and heavy footsteps in the passage, and my father suddenly came in. He was holding his favorite Belgian double-barreled gun, the only treasure of his former luxury left.

"There," he said, putting it resolutely beside me. "I'm giving it to you. You're welcome to all I have. Perhaps it will bring you some comfort. . . ."

I jumped up, grasped his hand, but had no time to kiss it—he snatched it away and, bending rapidly, gave me a quick and awkward kiss on the temple.

"And in general don't distress yourself overmuch," he added, trying to speak with his usual briskness. "I don't mean, of course, the horse, but your position in general. . . . Do you imagine that I see nothing, that I don't think

130

about you? More than anyone! I feel guilty toward you all; I ruined you all. But the others have at least got something. Nicholas has at least some means, George has his education, and what have you got, except your beautiful soul? Besides, what does it matter to them? Nicholas is quite an average man; George will remain an eternal student, but you. . . . And, what is worse, you won't stay long with us, and what lies in store for you, God only knows! Yet, remember my saying: 'There is nothing worse than sadness. . . .'"

7

It was empty and quiet that autumn in our house. Never before had I seemed to feel such affection for my father and mother; but it was only my sister, Olya, who saved me in those days from the sense of loneliness that had seized me with peculiar force. It was with her that I now began to share my walks, to talk, to dream of the future; and it gave me pleasure and joy to find out, and to become more and more convinced, that she was much more grown up, riper both in soul and in mind, and much closer to me, than I could have expected. There was also in that new relationship between us a wonderful return to our remote, childish intimacy. . . .

Father had said about me, "What lies in store for you, God only knows." And what lay in store for her, with all the charm of her youth and all her poverty and loneliness in Baturino?

Still, at the time, I thought mostly about myself.

8

I gave up working and spent a lot of time in the village, at the cottages, went out hunting a good deal, sometimes with Nicholas, sometimes alone. We no longer had any greyhounds; only a couple of harriers were left. Great hunts, still preserved here and there in the district, would hunt down wolves and foxes, and go on distant and prolonged outings to outlying fields, to parts more promising than ours. We were glad to see even a single hare—or rather, we were glad to wander about, chasing the beasts across the autumn fields, in the autumn air. Thus I was wandering one day, late in November, in the neighborhood of Efremov. Early in the morning I had breakfasted in the servants' quarters on some hot potatoes, thrown the gun over my shoulder, mounted an old working gelding, called the dogs, and set off. My brother was busy winnowing, so I went alone. It was an exceptionally warm, sunny day, but the fields looked sad, and, as far as sport went, quite hopeless; sad because everything was so quiet and bare, and everything had that look of utter poverty and humbleness which is typical of the late autumn; and hopeless because of the recent rains: the ground was so muddy and sloppy, and not only the roads, but also the first winter crops, the first tillage and reaped fields, that the dogs and I had to make our way along the boundary lines. Quite soon I even stopped thinking of game, and the dogs did likewise—they ran quietly ahead, fully aware of the impossibility of chasing down anything in such a field, had there even been anything to chase, and getting a little livelier only whenever we reached some bare copse with a strong damp smell of rotting leaves, or crossed the reddish oak undergrowth, a ravine, a hillock. But there was nothing there either; everywhere was emptiness, stillness, a fluid, lifeless gleam, though clear and warm, amid which the clear country-side stretched away, autumnally bare, flat and neatly outlined—all those checkered plots of fields with alternating stubble, winter crops, and tillage, the russet hides of undergrowth, the islands of birches and aspens. . . .

It was from Lobanovo that I at last turned homeward. I passed through Shipovo, then came to that very Kroptovka where the family manor of the Lermontovs used to be. Here I rested with a peasant I knew, sitting with him on the porch, drinking kvass. Before us lay the common, behind it a small manor, long uninhabited, its aspect slightly improved by the garden raising its still black treetops in the pale-blue sky, behind a small old house. As I sat down I gazed and thought, as I always did whenever I happened to come to Kroptovka: was it really true that as a child Lermontov used to come to this very house, and that his father had spent nearly all his life here?

"They say it's going to be sold," said the peasant, also looking at the manor and screwing up his eyes. "They say Kamenev, from Efremov, is haggling over it. . . ."

And glancing at me he squinted still more.

"What about you? You aren't selling yet?"

"That's my father's business," I replied evasively.

"Of course, of course," he said, obviously thinking thoughts of his own. "I only meant to say that everybody's selling nowadays, bad days have come to the gentry. The people got spoiled; even their own work they do helter-skelter, not to speak of the gentry's; and the price of labor in the busy season is extravagant, and the nobleman's got no money to pay wages in advance—hardship, poverty. . . ."

I went on by a roundabout way, deciding, for fun, to pass through Vasilievskoe, to spend the night with the Pisarevs. And on my way I thought with particular intentness of the great poverty of our countryside in general. Everything around me was poor, miserable, and desolate. I rode along the highroad—marveling at its desolation and barrenness. I rode along the cart tracks, going through some hamlets and past some estates; what cottages, what manor houses, and what a miserable, meaningless life within them! Not a soul, either in the fields, or on the muddy roads, or in the equally muddy village streets and deserted manor courtyards. One even wondered where all

the people had gone, and how they were whiling away their autumn boredom and idleness, shut up in those cottages and manor houses. And then
once more I remembered the meaninglessness of my own life, too, amid all
this, and felt simply horrified at it, suddenly at the same time recalling Lermontov. Yes, here was Kroptovka, that forsaken house, which I could never
see without some infinitely sad and inexplicable emotions. . . . Here was his
poor cradle, our common cradle; here he had spent his early days, when his
child-soul pined, "with wondrous yearning filled," just as vaguely as mine
once; here he wrote his first poems, as inadequate as mine. . . . And what
came afterward? Afterward, all of a sudden: *The Demon, Mtsyri*, "Taman,"
"The oak leaf was severed from its native bough. . . ."[2]

"Where is the link between this Kroptovka and all that Lermontov
stands for? What is Lermontov?" I thought—and I saw first the two volumes
of his works; I saw his odd, youthful face with its staring dark eyes; then I
began to see one poem after another, not only their outward shape, but also
the scenes connected with them—in fact, I saw what I fancied to be Lermontov's earthly life: the snowy summit of Kazbek the Daryal ravine; that
clear valley of Georgia, unfamiliar to me, where the streams of Aragva and
Kura murmur, "clasped like two sisters"; the cloudy night and the seashore
hut in Taman; the vaporous sea blueness in which one can barely distinguish
a white sail; the young, bright-green plane tree beside something quite fantastic called the Black Sea. . . . What life, what destiny! Only twenty-seven
years, but how infinitely full and beautiful, up to the very last day, to that
dark evening on the desolate road at the foot of Mashuk when, as if from a
gun, the shot of a man called Martynov was fired from a huge old-fashioned
pistol, and Lermontov "was cut down.". . . All this I felt and imagined with
such vividness that my heart was suddenly filled to overflowing with rapture
and envy, and I even said aloud to myself that I had had enough of Baturino.

9

Next day, at home again, I still thought the same thoughts.

At night I sat in my room, thinking and reading at the same time—
rereading *War and Peace*.[3] The weather had changed completely overnight.
The night was cold and stormy. It was already late; the whole house was still
and dark. In my room the stove was lit; it blazed and roared the hotter, the
more angry and dismal were the inroads of the wind on the garden, the
stronger it shook the windows of the house. I sat reading and thinking about
myself, sadly and delightedly aware of that late hour, the night, the stove, and
the storm. Then I rose, dressed, went out through the drawing room, and
began pacing the lawn before the house on its already thin and frozen grass.
Around me the stormy garden rose black, and a pale light hung over the

lawn. The night was moonlit, but somehow tantalizingly Ossianic.[4] The icy northern wind roared intermittently, the tops of the old trees sighed dismally and in unison, the bushes gave out a sharp, dry noise and seemed to run ahead of me; over the sky, daubed with something whitish, over the small lunar patch in a large iridescent halo, some dark weird clouds rushed swiftly from the north, looking peculiarly sinister and dismal; they even seemed alien to our parts, belonging rather to some seascape the old painters of nocturnal shipwrecks used to paint. And I began to walk up and down, now against the wind, overcoming its icy chilliness, now driven forward by it and to think again—with the confusion and naivety so characteristic of one's innermost thoughts, especially in youth. This, I suppose, is how my thoughts ran: "No, I've never read anything as good as this! Yet, what about *The Cossacks*, what about Yeroshka, Maryanka? Or Pushkin's *Journey to Arzrum?*[5] Yes, how happy they had all been—Pushkin, Tolstoy, Lermontov.

"Yesterday, I heard that somebody's hunt rode by along the highroad to the outlying field, together with the hunt of the young Tolstoys.[6] Isn't it wonderful—I am *his* contemporary, and even his neighbor! After all, it is the same as if one were to live at the same time as and next to Pushkin. All this is his—these Rostovs, and Pierre, and the field of Austerlitz, and the dying Prince Andrey:[7] 'There is nothing in life, except the nothingness of all that I understand, and the greatness of something I don't understand, but which matters most. . . .' Someone told Pierre in his dream: 'Life means love. . . . To love life means to love God . . .' This is just what someone keeps on telling me; and how I love everything, even this wild night! Yet why am I so miserable? I should like to see and love the whole world, the whole earth, all the Natashas and Maryankas. I must at all costs get away from here."

In the ring around the milky, misty moon there was a kind of sinister, celestial omen. Its miserable, slightly tilted face was becoming sadder and mistier against the pale dimness of the sky; high up rushed smoky, leaden, even black clouds, mournfully veiling that face; from the north, from beyond the roaring garden, a black stormy cloud was rising, and the wind blew up the smell of snow. And I walked on and thought: "No, I can't go on living like this. I couldn't even if I had ten unmortgaged Baturinos. Isn't it terrible that Tolstoy himself, in his youth, dreamed chiefly of marriage, of family life, of running his estate! And now there is nothing but talk of 'working for the good of the people,' of 'repaying one's debt to the people.'[8] . . . But I don't feel, nor ever did, as if I owe anything to the people. I cannot, nor do I wish to, sacrifice myself for the people's sake, or 'serve' it, or play, as my father puts it, at political parties and problems at the county assemblies. . . . No, I must at last make some decision!"

I looked in vain for some decision to make, and returned indoors utterly bewildered with chaotic and fruitless thoughts. Meanwhile the stove had gone out, and the lamp had burnt out, reeking of oil and glimmering so faint-

ly that in the room one could perceive the uncertain light of that pale and dis-
quieting night. I sat for a while at the desk, then took my pen and suddenly
began to write a letter to my brother George, saying that I proposed to leave
shortly for Orel in order to look for some job on the staff of *The Voice*. . . .[9]

10

That letter decided my fate.

Of course, I did not leave "shortly"—first it was necessary to save up
some money for the journey—but nevertheless I went in the end.

I recall my last lunch at home. I remember that, as soon as it was over,
we heard a dull tinkle of bells under the windows, and behind them, quite
close to them, there arose a pair of shaggy, wintry, rustic horses—shaggy also
because of the snow that was falling ceaselessly that day in thick, milky flakes.
Heavens, how old it all is, all such departures, and how tantalizingly new it
was to me! Even the snow that fell that day seemed to me quite special, so
struck was I by its whiteness and coolness at the moment when, weighted
down by my father's heavy raccoon coat and escorted by the whole household, I went out to take my seat in the sleigh.

What happened next was like a dream—the long, silent drive, the steady
roll of the sleigh in that endless white realm of snowflakes where there was
neither earth nor sky, but only something white, streaming ceaselessly down,
and delicious winter road smells—of horse, of a wet raccoon collar, of sul-
phur matches and cheap tobacco when a cigarette was lit. . . . And then, in
that whiteness, there flashed the first telegraph pole, the wooden road mark-
ers came into sight, covered with snow, sticking out of snowdrifts by the
roadside—the beginnings of some new life, no longer of the steppes, that
something called "railway" which for a Russian has always a peculiar and
exciting appeal. . . .

When the train came in, I said good-bye to the farmhand, gave him the
coat, and asked him to remember me to everybody in Baturino. I entered a
crowded third-class car, feeling as if I were setting out on a journey that was
never to end. For a long time I even wondered at the indifference with which
some of the passengers drank tea or ate, others slept, and still others, with
nothing else to do, kept throwing logs into the iron stove, which was already
red-hot and breathing its flames all over the car. I rejoiced as I sat there in
that dry, metallic heat, in its smell of birch wood and cast iron, while behind
the window the gray-blue snow kept on falling and falling, and all the time
darkness was closing in. . . .

What followed was something very strange: my forebodings had been
right—ahead of me indeed lay a long and uncommon journey, whole years of
wandering, of homelessness, of reckless and unruly existence, sometimes

completely happy, sometimes utterly miserable—in a word, just what apparently suited me, and was perhaps only outwardly so fruitless and without meaning.

11

The vague thoughts with which I then set out were full of profound sadness and of fondness for everything from which I had just parted, all that I had abandoned to silence and solitude in Baturino; I even felt my absence from there and could see my deserted room which, in its almost pious stillness, seemed to retain something that was completed forever—my former self. But of course that sadness also held a great and secret joy, the happy awareness of the dream at last being somehow realized, of freedom, activity, movement (toward something the more alluring for its very vagueness). And these last feelings naturally heightened with each new station we passed, so that the preceding ones became ever fainter, until at last all my past, all I had left behind me, retreated into the distance as something dear but by now almost strange, and there remained only the present, which was gradually becoming more interesting and distinct. Already I was becoming partly used to the multitude of those strange, coarse lives and faces around me; I began somehow to discriminate among them and, alongside my own personal feelings, to live by my feelings toward them, to build up various conjectures about them, to distinguish different sorts of cheap tobacco, to differentiate the bundle on the knees of a peasant woman from the sham oak box on which a recruit opposite me was propping his elbow. I noticed already that the car was fairly new and clean, the yellow fluted planks of its walls warmed by an iron stove, and very stuffy because of those various tobacco smokes, on the whole rather pungent, even though giving one a pleasant homely sense of human life that somehow or other had barricaded itself against the snowy plains outside the window, where telegraph wires rise and fall as they flow endlessly past. And here, I already want to get out into the snow and wind, and unsteadily I walk toward the door. . . . The snowy cold coming from the fields blows into the platform of the car, all around me spreads the whiteness of fields now quite unfamiliar. The snow at last begins to fall more sparsely; it has grown brighter and still whiter around, while the train approaches somewhere and stops for a few moments: a desolate little station, stillness—only the engine ahead wheezes hotly—and everything is full of incomprehensible loveliness: that temporary torpor and silence, the wheezing expectancy of the engine, and even, it seems, the fact that the station itself is invisible behind a red wall of freight cars standing on the nearest track, on thawed rails between which a hen is walking, calm and homely, now and then pecking at something, somehow or other doomed to spend all her hen's life quietly at that very station and not caring in the least where and why you are going with all your dreams and sensations which, in their everlasting and lofty joy, are linked up with things outwardly so paltry and commonplace. . . .

As the evening drew closer all my feelings were fused into one: the expectation of the first big station. Long before it came I was again freezing on the platform, until at last I saw ahead, in the inhospitable twilight, many multicolored lights, tracks going in all directions, signal boxes, switches, spare engines, and then the station itself, its platform black with crowds. . . . You can easily imagine my haste as I dashed to the bright and odorous buffet and began burning my mouth with incredibly tasty cabbage soup.

All this ended rather unexpectedly—at least in appearance: as I sat after dinner contentedly smoking a cigarette by the dark window of the carriage, now rattling on again, in the smoky half-light of a thick candle supplied by the state and burning in a lantern in the corner, I reflected that here I was, strange though it may seem, nearing my destination, that same Orel which I could hardly imagine as yet but which was wonderful for the mere reason that there, past its station, ran the great highway across the whole map of Russia: north—to Moscow and beyond; south—to Kursk and Kharkov and, what was more, to Sevastopol itself, where my father's youth seemed to dwell forever. . . . And suddenly I found myself asking whether it was really true that I was going to join a paper called *The Voice* to take up a job. In this, too, of course, there was something terribly attractive—something called editorial offices and printers' shops. But Kursk, Kharkov, Sevastopol. . . . "No, this is all nonsense," I suddenly said to myself. "I will merely stop in Orel, get to know those people, see what they can offer me, tell them I must think it over and see my brother. Stop there—and then on to Kharkov."

But as it turned out I had no need even to stop at Orel. Everything turned out even better than I expected: it happened that our train was late getting to Orel, just in time for the train to Kharkov. And this other train happened to be a wonderful one, such as I had never seen before—a fast one, with an alarming American locomotive and composed of large, heavy cars (only first- and second-class) with woolen curtains on the windows, with lights showing faintly through the blue silk, with all the warmth and coziness of wealthy life, and to spend a night in that (and southward bound too) seemed to me the very acme of bliss. . . .

12

In Kharkov I tumbled at once into a world quite new to me.[10]

One of my characteristics has always been a peculiar sensitivity to light and air, and to the slightest variations in them. And the first thing that struck me in Kharkov was the softness of its air and that it seemed to be a little brighter than in our parts. I came out of the station, took a sleigh—I discovered that the cabmen drove with pairs here, with big bells—looked round me, and instantly felt that things were not quite as with us; it all seemed softer and brighter, even springlike. Here too it was snowy and white, but the whiteness was somehow different, pleasantly dazzling. There was no sun, but plenty of light, more in any case than one would expect in December, and its warm presence behind the clouds held out a promise of something very agreeable. And everything seemed softer in that light and air: the smell of coal from behind the station, the faces and the conversation of the cabmen, the jingling of the bells on horses harnessed in pairs, the gentle touting of the womenfolk selling bagels and seeds, gray bread and lard, in the station square. And beyond the square stood a row of exceedingly tall poplars, bare, but also looking truly southern, Ukrainian. And in the town there was a thaw in the streets. . . .

Yet this all was nothing compared to what lay in store for me later in the day! I had never before experienced so many new sensations, never in my life made so many new acquaintances. It sometimes happens that on the very first day after arriving somewhere one experiences a singular wealth of impressions and encounters. So it was with me on that day.

In my brother, who received me with glad surprise, there also proved to be something new—here in Kharkov he seemed different from what he used to be in Baturino—apparently less close to me, despite all the joy of our meeting. Besides, how strange his Kharkov life was! Granted that, as my father put it, he was an "eternal student," but, after all, he was an Arseniev. And where did I find him? In a steep narrow street, in a dirty stony courtyard reeking of coal and Jewish kitchens, in the overcrowded apartment of a tailor named Blumkin.

True, even this was all deliciously new to me, yet I was taken aback.

"Well, isn't it splendid that you've come on a Sunday and found me here!" he said, after kissing me. "Though why did you come, really?" he added at once, trying to speak in that tone of raillery so usual in our family.

I replied that I myself did not know why I had come . . . certainly in order to consult him at last, seriously, as to what I was to do with myself. But he was no longer listening. "We'll think up something!" he said with assurance, and instantly began to hurry me on to wash and tidy myself in order to go out with him to dinner to a small restaurant kept by a Pole called Lisovsky, where many of his fellow workers from the Zemstvo Statistical Bureau used to have meals. And so we went out and walked through one street after another, still talking at random, in the haphazard way one does at such times, while my eyes—I was already dressed in town fashion, and very much aware of it—strayed over those streets, which seemed to me quite gorgeous, and over the surroundings; the sun came out in the afternoon, the snow glittered and thawed, the poplars on Sumskaya Street raised their tops toward the puffy white clouds sailing in the moist blue sky, which seemed to be slightly steaming. . . .

Lisovsky's restaurant turned out to be a curious basement establishment, a bar with excellent and surprisingly cheap hors d'oeuvres—especially nice were the little blintzes, burning hot and strongly peppered, for a couple of kopecks. As soon as we sat down at a large separate table, some people approached and joined us, looking distinctly strange to me. I gazed at them the more eagerly as they were just those people (apparently set quite apart from the rest of the world) about whom I had heard so much from my brother when still in Baturino.

For some reason he introduced me to every one of them with cheerful haste and even, it seemed, with pride.

And soon my head turned giddy: because of that crowd of people, quite unusual to me, and so remarkable; and because of that crowded basement, through the windows of which the sunlight came springlike and gay from above, and all sorts of legs could be seen passing to and fro along the street; and because of the scalding borscht; and because the conversation at our table centered all the time around subjects strange to me, yet apparently exceedingly interesting—around the famous statistician Annensky, whose name was pronounced with invariable admiration; some governor on the Volga who was said to have flogged the starving peasants to prevent their spreading rumors of famine; the coming Pirogov Congress in Moscow, which, as usual, was to be a real event.[11] I can easily imagine how strikingly I stood out at that dinner party, with my youth, freshness, rustic suntan, health, simplicity, the ardent and eager attentiveness of my ears and eyes, which probably even looked like dull stupidity. My brother, too, was cast in quite a different mold. He also seemed to belong to quite a different world from the rest of them, in spite of his nearness to them; and he seemed younger, and somehow more naive, than any of them; he looked more distinguished, and even his manner of speaking was different.

Many among that company, as I was to realize in later years, were quite typical both in their outward appearance and in everything else. I already secretly disapproved of some of them in some respects: one, very tall and narrow-chested, was too short-sighted and stooped too much; he never took his hand out of his trouser pocket and all the time made slight vibrating movements with one leg over which his other leg was somehow miraculously screwed around; another, yellow-haired, with a transparently yellow and lean face, seemed to me to talk too much, with too much ardor and inspiration, while he would flick off his cigarette ash without looking at it, using the forefinger of the hand in which he held it; his neighbor was always grinning caustically at something and doing something which particularly annoyed me: with his two fingers he would roll a pellet of white bread over the long-soiled tablecloth. . . . But then there were others who were exceedingly nice: the Pole Hansky, with deep and sorrowful eyes and dry lips, who smoked continuously, inhaling the smoke and repeatedly lighting his already burning cigarette with a trembling hand; the large and picturesquely disheveled Krasnopolsky, who resembled Saint John the Baptist; the bearded Leontovich, who was older, and better known as a statistician than any of them, and who instantly charmed me with his kindly calm, his friendly reasonableness, and most of all with the extremely pleasant, purely Ukrainian timbre of his deep voice; then a certain Padalka, a small sharp-nosed fellow, bespectacled, completely absentminded, fiercely enthusiastic, always passionately resenting something, and at the same time so childishly pure and sincere that I instantly took to him even more than to Leontovich. I also felt a great liking for the statistician Vagin—such an obsessed statistician, as I was to learn afterward, that apart from statistics nothing seemed to exist for him in the world—a tall, strongly built fellow with dazzling teeth, handsome and cheerful in the peasant way—he was in fact of peasant extraction—who laughed uproariously and infectiously and spoke with broad northern inflections. . . . And two men roused in me a violent hostility: Bykov, a former worker, a sturdy fellow wearing a blouse, whose curly hair, thick neck, and bulging eyes really had something oxlike about them;[12] and another whose name was Melnik—he was scrubby, lean, rickety, of a sandy yellow color, bleary-eyed and snuffling, but extremely sharp-tongued and self-opinionated; many years later, to my complete surprise, he turned out to be a great personage under the Bolsheviks, some kind of "bread dictator." . . .

13

It was among such people that I spent my first Kharkov winter (and many years afterward).

Everyone knows what that class of people was like, how it evolved, what were its life and creed.[13] The most remarkable thing was that those who belonged to it, after passing when still in school through all that peculiar training which they were supposed to undergo at the outset—I mean, through some kind of "circle," then through participation in various student "movements" and in this or that "work," and afterward through exile, prison, or penal servitude—and continuing that "work" in one way or another, even afterward—that they led, on the whole, a life completely detached from the rest of the Russian nation, refusing even to regard as human beings people of various practical occupations, such as merchants, farmers, doctors, teachers (at least the ones who eschewed politics), government officials, priests, soldiers, and above all policemen , the slightest hobnobbing with whom was regarded as not only disgraceful but even criminal; they had everything for themselves, peculiar and impregnable: their own affairs, interests, happenings, celebrities, their own morals, their own rules of family life and friendship, and their own attitude toward Russia: the negation of her past and present and the dream of her future, the belief in that future for which they were in fact to "fight." There were, of course, among that set, people very different, not only in the degree of their revolutionary creed, of their "love" for the people and their hatred of its "enemies," but also in the whole of their outward and inward appearance. In general, however, they were all rather narrow-minded, downright intolerant, and their professed creed was rather simple: only we, and all sorts of "humiliated and insulted" people, are human beings; all the evil is on the Right, all the good on the Left; all bright things are in the people, in its "mainstays and aspirations," all the problems, in the government and in bad rulers (who were even regarded as a sort of a tribe apart), all salvation, in an upheaval, in Constitution or Republic. . . .

Such then was the set into which I was introduced in Kharkov. But what other set could I have joined? I had no "in" to any other sets and I did not seek one: the desire to penetrate them was already overshadowed by my conscious sense that, though much in my new surroundings did not suit me, there would be many things in other sets that would suit me still less—for, really, what had I in common with merchants or officials? And there was in my new environment a good deal that was simply pleasant. The range of my acquaintances grew quickly, and I liked the ease with which this could be done. I liked the studentlike modesty of life, the simplicity of ways, of mutual relations, in that atmosphere. Besides, life in that set was rather cheerful. In the morning—a gathering at the office, where there was a good deal of tea-drinking, smoking, and debating; then, a lively meal, for nearly all were in the habit of lunching in groups at small restaurants; in the evening—a fresh gathering, at a meeting, a soirée, or a private party. . . . That winter we used to go most often to Hansky, who was rather well off; then to Madame Shklyarevich, a rich and beautiful widow, where famous Ukrainian actors used to come quite often to sing songs about the "free cossacks," and even their own *Marseillaise*.

Of uncongenial things in that set there were plenty too. As I got used to it and began to see better, I came more and more to resent now one thing now another, and at times could not even hide my resentment, starting a heated and of course useless discussion on some subject; fortunately, the majority of these people took a fancy to me and forgave my resentments. I was aware of becoming permeated with a wholesale bias against all other classes of society; yet what did I find in mine? Here girls and boys were given books on political economy, while their parents themselves read only Korolenko or Zlatovratsky, despising Chekhov, for instance, because of his political indifference, blaming Tolstoy in a most violent way for his "most disgraceful and harmful propaganda of inactivity," for his "fussing about God like a child about its new toy," for sitting down to a "luxurious" table after playing at farmer or cobbler, while those peasants of Yasnaya Polyana whom he pretended to love so dearly were "bloated with hunger."[14] The way they spoke of literature in general was such that, despite my resentment, I gradually began to yield to a secret fear, thinking that perhaps such and such a work really ought not to have been written, or such other was unnecessary, whereas certain others (about some poor fellow called Makar or the life of the exiles) were just what was needed. They were always ready to do anything for Russia's good, yet strongly suspected all classes in Russia except the poorest and the most illiterate. The epoch of *Notes of the Fatherland* was regarded by them as the Golden Age, and its suppression as one of the greatest and most terrible events in Russian life;[15] and they called their own time "a time of muddle"—"there have been worse times, but never baser"[16]—asserting that all Russia was "suffocating" during it. They denounced as "renegade" anyone who would conceive the slightest doubt as to certain rules laid down by them and invariably scoffed at somebody's "moderation and punctiliousness"; they sincerely admired, for instance, Vagin's wife for her organization of Sunday slide lectures, and for herself preparing a lecture such as "On Volcanoes." At parties, even the bearded fellows would sing "hostile storms blow over our heads"[17]—and I felt so acutely the falsity of these "storms," the insincerity of emotions and thoughts readymade for life, that I did not know where to look and was asked, "And you, Alesha—are you pouting your poet's lips again?"

It was the wife of Bogdanov who asked me this, that same statistician who could twist his legs around in such an amazing way. The Bogdanovs were having a party; their small apartment was crowded and filled with tobacco smoke; the samovar was never off the table, and the corners were full of empty beer bottles. The gathering was in honor of a famous old "fighter" arrived incognito in Kharkov, famed for his widespread and indefatigable work, who had on countless occasions served terms of imprisonment in fortresses, had several times been beyond the Arctic circle, and had escaped from everywhere. The man looked like a troglodyte, shaggy and clumsy, with hair in his nostrils and ears, but his small eyes looked extremely clever and penetrating, and his conversation flowed volubly. Bogdanov himself was a nonentity, but his wife had long enjoyed a well-earned notoriety; in the course of her life she had met all kinds of celebrities and taken part in all kinds of undertakings. In the old days, she had been rather pretty, and had plenty of admirers; she was still merry and pert, sharp-tongued and quick-witted, and could turn the tables on anyone and display uncommon logical gifts; she was slim and youthful, and dressed for parties—curled her hair for them. She liked me, but took every occasion to scold me. At the moment I looked "pouty," because a group of people in a corner, having had their fill of the celebrity, of talking and drinking, were already singing, "We'll curse all the villains, we'll call all the fighters to battle."[18] I felt pained, uneasy, and my hostess, sitting next to me on the sofa with a cigarette in her fingers, noticed this and was annoyed. I did not know how to answer her and felt incapable of expressing my feelings, while she, without waiting for me to answer, started declaiming in her sonorous voice: "From those who rejoice, who prattle idly, who stain their hands in gore. . . ."[19] This seemed to me simply stupid—after all, I reflected, who *were* the people who thus rejoiced, prattled, and stained their hands! And then came something which I loathed still more for its studentlike bravado: "From a far-off, far-off land, from the wide mother Volga, for the sake of glorious labor, for the sake of merry freedom, have we gathered here. . . ."[20] I turned away from that "mother Volga" and "glorious labor" and noticed how Brailovskaya, a charming girl, silent and passionate, with the ardent and quizzical eyes of an archangel, glared at me from her corner with a challenging directness of hatred. . . .

On the whole my sympathies were no more with the political Right than theirs—that is, so far as my giddy-headed revolutionary sympathies were concerned, my sincere craving for goodness, humaneness, justice—but I simply could not bear to be reminded, even jokingly (and yet, of course, edifyingly), "You don't have to be a poet but you must be a citizen!"[21]—when I was being instructed, even indirectly, allegorically, that the whole meaning of life lies "in work for the good of the community"; in other words, for the peasants or workers, I felt beside myself. What! Must I sacrifice myself for the sake of some everlastingly drunken locksmith or a horseless Klim, and not a live Klim but a composite, whom in actual life they noticed as little as any cabman passing them in the street, while I had been truly fond of, and still was, wholeheartedly, of some of my Baturino Klims, and was ready to give my last kopeck to an itinerant sawyer timidly and awkwardly wandering around the town with a bag and a saw over his back, when he shyly asked me, a penniless youth, the naive and touchingly silly question, "Haven't you some work for me, young sir?" It was inconceivable to me how one could really talk of dying tranquilly after having honestly worked for the good of the community. I actually suffered now from those everlasting quotations from Shchedrin about "little Judases," about "Stupidville" and the mayors who entered it riding a white horse;[22] I would grind my teeth whenever I saw, on the walls of nearly every apartment I frequented, Chernyshevsky's spectacles and birdlike face, or Belinsky, lean as death, with enormous terrifying eyes, rising from his deathbed to meet the police entering his study.[23]

Besides, the Bykovs and the Melniks were in that milieu. One look at their faces made it difficult to get used to the idea that they, too, were working toward some beautiful future, and even regarded themselves as among the leading experts and dispensers of good to mankind.

Finally, there was a fellow known as Max, who occasionally appeared in Kharkov: tall, with crooked legs solid as oak roots, wearing thick Swiss hobnailed boots, very quiet and businesslike, very careful in his speech, with a tanned, rather rough face and a big potlike skull roundly and steeply expanding over it. He slept exceedingly little, ate frugally, and was forever and ever quite tirelessly on the move somewhere. . . .

14

So the winter passed.

In the morning, while my brother was at his office, I would sit reading in the public library. Then I would wander about, thinking of the books I had read, of the people walking or driving past, of their all probably being nearly happy and calm in their own way—every one of them engrossed in his or her own work and more or less secure, while I was only vaguely and vainly pining away with a desire to write something that I myself was unable to understand, something I had neither the daring to undertake nor the skill to cope with and was all the time putting off. At the same time, I was so hard up that I could not even afford to realize my poor secret dream of buying a nice notebook; this was the more bitter as a great deal seemed to depend on that book—my whole life, I felt, would somehow change its course, become livelier and more active—for what might I not write in that book? Spring was already starting; I had just read Dragomanov's collection of Ukrainian songs and was literally fascinated by the *Tale of Igor's Campaign,*[24] having chanced to read it for a second time and suddenly realized all its amazing beauty, and here I was again, drawn far-off, away from Kharkov, to the Donets sung by the poet of Igor, and there where the young Princess Euphrosinya seemed still to be standing on the town rampart, watching the same early dawn of the olden days, and to the Black Sea of cossack times, where some wonderful falcon sat on a white stone, and yet again toward my father's young days, toward Sevastopol.

Thus would I spend my morning, and then go to Lisovsky's, returning to reality, to those table talks and discussions which had already become a habit. Then my brother and I would rest, chatting and lounging on our beds in our tiny room, where after dinner a particularly heavy smell of a Jewish meal, of something warm, odorously alkaline, came through the door. Then we would do a little work—I, too, was sometimes given some calculations and précis from the office to do. And then once more we would go out to see people. . . .

Most of all I liked going to Hansky's. He was an excellent musician and would sometimes play for us for whole evenings. He opened up to me a strange world, hitherto quite unfamiliar, sweetly and poignantly exalted, a world that I would enter, at the sound of the very first notes, with an enraptured, uncanny delight, to acquire immediately that greatest of all illusions (of the would-be divine possibility of becoming all-blissful, all-powerful, and all-knowing) which only music and some moments of poetic inspiration can give. And it was strange to see Hansky himself, a man of such extreme revolutionary views—though he aired them less often and with more restraint than any of the others—sitting at the piano, his lips already made dark and sticky by that growing, tense, and ardent passion with which he always played. The sounds carried one off somewhere, racing, bar after bar, persistent, refined, fluent, and exultant, and so senselessly divine in their joy as to become almost terrible, and a wonderfully tragic image would arise in my mind: I kept on thinking that the time would come when Hansky would no doubt go mad, and then, in his narrow cell with grated window, his burning lips, his ecstatic eyes, dressed in a gray convict shirt, he would go on living, even without music, in the same senseless and joyful, illusory and exalted world. . . .

Once Hansky told us how he, when still young, had been to Mozart's house in Salzburg and seen there his old-fashioned narrow clavichord and, beside it, a glass case containing his skull. I thought: "When still young! And I?" And I felt so bitter, so mortified that I could hardly sit still, overpowered as I was with a sudden passionate desire to run instantly home and, without losing a moment, to set about writing some poem or story, to create something extraordinary, to become at once well known, famous, and then go to Salzburg to see with my own eyes that clavichord and that skull. . . .

Many years later I realized that dream which ever since had dwelt secretly in my heart, among so many other old and hidden dreams; I saw Salzburg, and the skull, and the clavichord. The keys were exactly the same color as the skull, and I longed to bend over and kiss them, to touch them with my lips. And the skull itself was incredibly small, like an infant's. . . .

15

Early in the spring I went to the Crimea. I was given a free ticket and had to travel under someone else's name, pretending to be a railwayman. . . . My youth passed in the throes of great privations!

I started off in a crammed and foul car of the night-mail train, terrifying simply in its length, such as I had never seen before. It came in already packed, and on the platform at Kharkov it was assailed by a fresh countless horde of people going south in search of work, with all their bags, bundles, bast shoes, and leg-wrappers tied to them, with kettles and stinking provisions: rusty kippers, baked eggs. . . . Besides, the hour was late, so that I had a sleepless night in store, then a long day, and another night without sleep. . . . But I was ready for anything—somewhere far-off my father's youth awaited me.

The vision of that youth had dwelt in my heart ever since my childhood. It was a late summer's day, infinitely remote and bright. There was something sorrowful in that day, but also great happiness. There was something associated with my hazy notion of the days of the Crimean War: some redoubts, some assaults, some soldiers of that peculiar epoch called "age of serfdom," and the death, on the Malakhov Mound,[25] of my uncle Nicholas Sergeevich, a handsome giant of a colonel, a rich and brilliant man, whose memory in our family had always been wrapped in legend. And above all, there was on that day a desolate and bright seaside hillock, and on that hillock, among stones, some white flowers like snowdrops, growing there for the sole reason, of course, that when still a child, one snowy and sunny winter day, I heard my father say, "And in the Crimea we used to pick flowers at this time of year in nothing but our tunics!"

And what did I actually find?

I remember that at daybreak after the first night, I woke up, squeezed in my corner, at some steppe station, already far from Kharkov. A candle in the corner was burning out; there was no sun yet, but the early morning was already quite clear and rosy. I gazed in surprise at the painful and hideous picture of people sleeping all over the place in that rosy light, and instantly I opened the window. And what a dawn it was! The far-off eastern sky was aglow with rosy flames, the air was full of that ecstatic freshness and clarity which can only be there in early spring at daybreak on the steppe; in the stillness, the larks, invisible in the sky, sing their fresh, sweet spring song; to right and left our train stretches like a motionless wall, and a couple of yards away a large grave-mound stands facing me in that steppe, smooth and boundless like a threshing floor. Even now I cannot understand what it was that so impressed me. It was unlike anything, both in its outline, so definite and yet so soft, and—what mattered most—in what it concealed. There was here, despite all its simplicity, something really extraordinary, something so ancient that it seemed infinitely alien to all living, modern things; and yet it was so familiar, so close, so intimate.

"Look, that's how people used to be buried long ago!" an old man said to me from a far-off corner. He alone was not asleep and sat bent over, puffing hotly at his pipe, his swollen, bleary eyes gleaming from beneath a ragged calfskin cap out of all that red, wrinkled something, overgrown with grayish stubble, which was his face. "In olden days people were buried so that their memory should be kept!" he said firmly. "Rich, they were." And after a pause he added: "Or maybe it is the Tatars who buried us so? All sorts of things happen in this world, young sir—bad and good alike. . . ."

And the second dawn was still more wonderful. Again I awoke suddenly at some station—and this time saw something heavenly: a white summer morning—here it was already summer—and something rather close-growing and all blooming, dewy and fragrant, a little white station all entwined with roses, a wooded cliff rising steeply above it, and thick flowering bushes in the ravine on the opposite side. . . . And the engine, before starting, called somehow in quite a different way, joyously and as though it were alarmed. And when once more it reached the free expanse of the plain, there suddenly appeared to me, from behind the wooded hills ahead, with all its vast desert rising skyward, something heavily blue, almost black, watery and misty, still gloomy, just on the point of breaking loose from the dark, moist, nocturnal womb—and I suddenly *recognized* it, with terror and joy. Yes, that's it—remembered, recognized!

As for Sevastopol, it struck me as almost tropical. What a luxurious station, warmed right through by soft air! How hot and shimmering were the tracks in front of it! The sky looked quite pale and gray with heat, but in this, too, was luxury, happiness, the South. The entire crowd of rustics whom we had been bringing with us had by now melted away. And here I was, almost alone at last, alighting from the train, my own name once more restored to me, and, staggering with weariness and hunger, I made my way to the first-class waiting room. It was noon; all was deserted; the vast buffet (the world of the rich, free, well-born people who arrived here by express trains!) looked clean and quiet, gleaming with the whiteness of its tables, the vases and sconces on them. . . . I could no longer restrain myself, miserly as I had been all the way—and ordered coffee and a loaf of white bread. They brought me this, looking at me askance—my appearance was rather suspicious. But never mind—I was once more myself, I delighted in the stillness, the cleanliness, the warm air drifting in through the windows and doors, and suddenly I saw something bright-colored like a little guinea-hen walk in unexpectedly, but quite simply, entering the waiting room through the door that stood open to the bright platform. . . . Ever since, the notion of southern stations has been linked up in my mind with that bright-colored creature.

But where was the thing which had seemed to be the object of my journey? In Sevastopol itself there proved to be no houses battered by guns, no silence, no wilderness—nothing dating from the days of my father and Nicholas Sergeevich, with their orderlies, their wine cellars, their billets. The town's life had long gone on without them; it had been rebuilt, dazzlingly white, elegant, and hot, with spacious white-canopied cabs, with its Karaim[26] and Greek crowd in the streets shaded by the bright verdure of southern acacias, with magnificent tobacco shops, with its monument of the stooping Nakhimov in the square by the steps leading to the Grafskaya pier, toward the green seawater and the battleships stationed outside it. There only, beyond that green expanse of water, was something that reminded me of my father—a place called Northside, the common graveyard; and from there alone the sadness and loveliness of the remote past, by now peaceful and immemorial, and even of something which seemed to be my own, now also long forgotten by everybody, drifted up toward me. . . .

And so I set out farther. I spent the night somewhere on the outskirts, at a cheap inn, and early in the morning left Sevastopol. By noon I was already beyond Balaklava. How strange was the mountainous world surrounding me! The endless white road; the bare gray valleys ahead; the bare gray loaves of the hilltops far and near, disappearing one after another and insistently calling me somewhere with their lilac and ashen-gray masses, their torrid and mysterious sleep. Where was that particular hill with white snowdrops? It vanished, drowned in some other unrecorded antiquity. I remember how I sat down and rested among some vast rocky valleys. A small Tatar herdsboy, a long crook in his hand, stood at some distance by a gray flock of sheep scattered like pebbles behind him. He was chewing something. I walked to him, saw that he was eating bread with goat cheese, and took out a silver coin. Still chewing and staring at me, he shook his head and handed me the whole bag hanging from his shoulder. I took it—he scowled fondly and gladly, his whole black-eyed face gleamed, his ears sticking out beneath his round cap twitched backward. . . . And along the white road a carriage with three horses abreast drove past us with a clatter of hooves and tinkling of bells; on the box sat a Tatar driver, in the carriage, an old man with black eyebrows and a peaked linen cap, and by his side, all wrapped up, looking all waxy and yellow, a young girl with dark, terrible eyes. . . . More than once, probably, many years later, in very different days, I saw her marble cross on the mountain above Yalta, among so many other crosses, under cypresses and roses, in the light fresh sea breeze of a bright southern day. . . .

At the Baidar Gate I spent the night on the porch of the post stage. The stage inspector refused to let me inside upon learning that I was not going to use any horses. Beyond the gate, in the fathomless dark abyss, the sea rumbled all night—timeless, slumbrous, full of incomprehensible, threatening majesty. Now and then I would enter under the gate: land's end and pitch darkness; a strong whiff of fragrant mist and cold waves; the rumbling would cease, then rise again, swelling like the rumbling of a wild dense forest. . . . The abyss and the night, something blind and unquiet, living a painful life, a life as of the womb, senseless and hostile. . . .

16

On returning from anywhere one always has a feeling that something must have happened during one's absence, some letter, some news must have arrived. Usually it turns out that nothing has happened, nothing has arrived. It was not so this time, however. My brother met me with great embarrassment: to begin with, my father had sold Baturino and sent us some money, writing an extremely sad and repentant letter. . . . For a moment I flashed with joy—this meant a fresh opportunity to go somewhere; but instantly this feeling gave way to acute distress—this meant that all our former life was irrevocably over!—and to a bitter pity for my father and mother and Olya: here we were, gay and carefree, we had springtime, plenty of people, the town; and they had to stay there, in the sticks, in solitude, in constant worry about us, and now about their own impending homelessness as well. . . . I had never been able to behold my father calmly in his sad moments or listen to his excuses for having beggared us all: at such moments I was always ready to run to him and even kiss his hands with what seemed to be warm gratitude for that very thing. And now, after Sevastopol, I could hardly hold back my tears. . . . Luckily, it turned out that he had sold only the land, not the house.

The second piece of news was still more startling. My brother felt utterly confused when he told me it. "Forgive me," he said, "for hiding it even from you; I didn't and still don't want our family to know about it. . . . The point is I am married. . . . Not legally, of course—she even goes on living with her husband, for the sake of the child—but you understand me. Now she's in Kharkov, she's leaving tomorrow. . . . Come and change, and we'll go to her; she knows and likes you in advance. . . ."

And he hastily told me his story. She came from a rich and aristocratic family, but had grown up full of passionate dreams about freedom and the good of the people, was married early in order to begin, "arm in arm with the man she loved," to live for the people only, to struggle for it. . . . Having through her become rich, the man she loved soon grew indifferent to his former aspirations, while to her they were something so holy and precious, and from her earliest youth had caused her, as one favored, such distress over her own good fortune among all the misfortunes of the people, and such shame even for her beauty, that once she had tried to disfigure herself, to burn with acid her hands too much admired by everybody. . . . She had met my brother in the South—he was then in hiding, living under an assumed name. . . . On realizing that she loved him, she flung herself in despair into the sea, only to be saved by chance by some fishermen. . . .

Changing obediently, I listened to this story with great surprise, feeling greatly excited and averting my eyes. For some reason I felt uneasy, annoyed at my brother; I felt a growing hostility toward his heroine—it all sounded much too romantic. Yet I was still more surprised when I crossed the threshold of her room in a large luxurious hotel where she was staying. How quickly she rose to meet me, how tenderly and familiarly she embraced me, how affectionately and wonderfully she smiled, how agreeably and easily she began to talk! The pleasant simplicity of her demeanor revealed the fine qualities of breeding, of upbringing, of a generous heart. She had a shy, womanly, yet amazingly untrammeled, charm; her gestures were soft and precise; in the timbre of her low-pitched, slightly singsong and delicately harmonious voice, as also in the purity and clarity of her gray, rather sadly smiling eyes with black eyelashes, there was an unaccountable charm. . . .

149

And yet I was wounded very much by this unexpected meeting, this sudden discovery that my brother had a life of his own, hidden from us all, an affection for someone other than ourselves. . . . Once more I felt lonely, with all my youthfulness, in that springlike atmosphere which surrounded me, and felt a bitter disappointment. But at the same time I seemed to have said to myself, "Well, so much the better for me—I'm quite free now in this wonderful country which has just revealed itself to me. . . ." And that country I fancied to myself as the boundless springtime expanse of all southern Russia, which fascinated me more and more, both in its old and its modern aspects. As for the modern, there was a vast and wealthy country with beautiful fields and steppes, cottages and villages, the Dnieper and Kiev, its strong and tenderhearted people, fine and neat down to the smallest details of its life—the heir to the real Slavs, those of the Danube, of the Carpathians. And as for the old, there was its cradle, the Svyatopolks and Igors, the Pechenegs and the Polovtsy—even those very words held a fascination for me—then the age of the cossacks' battles against Turks and Poles, Porogi and Khortitsa, the low islands and estuaries of Kherson. . . .

The *Tale of Igor's Campaign* drove me wild:[27] "'I wish,' he said, 'to break my spear on the border of the Polovtsian land, together with you, Russians. . . .' 'No storm is driving falcons across the wide fields—flocks of daws hasten to the great Don. . . .' 'Horses neigh beyond the Sula; glory resounds in Kiev; trumpets trump in Novgorod ; standards stand at Putivl. . . .' 'Then Prince Igor stepped into his golden stirrup and galloped into the open field. The sun barred his way with darkness; night, groaning with thunder, roused the birds; Div called from the top of a tree, bidding to hearken lands unknown, the Volga, the Sea-border, and the Sula country. . . .'"

". . . Carts creak at midnight, like swarms of swans let loose. Igor leads his hosts to the Don. . . . Eagles shriek and call the beasts to a feast of bones; foxes yelp at the crimson shields. O Russian land, thou art beyond the hills. . . ."

"Quite early the next morning, a bloodstained dawn announces the day; black clouds come from the sea . . . blue lightnings quiver through them; there will be a mighty thunder, and arrows shall rain down. . . .'"

And then:

"What noise is this, what rumor, I hear, early before the daybreak?"

"Svyatoslav dreamed a confused dream. 'In Kiev, on the mounts,' he said, 'they dressed me last night in a black shroud on a bed of yew. They poured out to me blue wine mixed with sorrow. . . .'"

"The sea spurted at midnight. . . . God shows Prince Igor the way out of the land of the Polovtsians into the Russian land, to his father's golden throne. The evening lights have gone out; Igor sleeps, Igor wakes, Igor in his mind measures the plains from the great Don to the little Donets. . . ."

And before long I again set out on my wanderings. I visited those very banks of the Donets where in the olden days the prince had fled from captivity, "like an ermine into the rushes, like a white goose onto the water"; then I went to the Dnieper, to the very spot where it "pierced the rocky mountains across the Polovtsian land"; I sailed past the white, springlike villages amid fathomless Dnieper plains blue with sun and air, upstream, toward Kiev—and how can I tell what singing echoes that spring and the tale of Igor awoke in me at the time: "The sun shines in heaven. Prince Igor is in the Russian land. Maidens sing on the Danube: their voices trail across the sea to Kiev. . . ."

And from Kiev I made my way to Kursk, to Putivl. "Saddle, brother, your swift steeds; mine are ready for you saddled outside Kursk. . . ." It was only many years later that the sense of Kostroma, Suzdal, Uglich, and Rostov the Great awoke in me:[28] in those days I lived under a different spell. What did it matter if Kursk turned out to be just a dreary county town, and the dusty Putivl still drearier? Hadn't there been the same wilderness, the same dust in the days when, early, as dawn broke over the steppe, on the wall planted with palisades, "Yaroslavna's lament" was heard?

"Yaroslavna, early in the morning, laments at Putivl town. 'I will fly,' she says, 'like a cuckoo along the Danube. I will wet my beaver sleeve in the Kayala river; I will wipe the Prince's bloody wounds. . . .'"

17

By that route I was already returning home. Now I was even in a hurry to get there: my nomadic passion was stilled for the time being; I longed for rest and work, and I looked forward to the summer awaiting me at Baturino as to something admirable, so full was I of the fairest hopes and plans, and of confidence in destiny. But, as everyone knows, there is nothing more dangerous than an excess of confidence in *that*. . . . In short, I stopped at Orel on my way.

Here I felt my wanderings to be nearly over: a few hours more and I should be in Baturino. It only remained for me to cast a glance at Orel itself—the town of Leskov[29] and Turgenev—and to find out at last what editorial and printing offices were like.

The energy I felt was something extraordinary. But I had grown dark and lean like a gypsy after five fairs: so far had I walked, so long sailed on the Dnieper, all the time on deck, in the joyous heat of the sun, in the glare of the water and the steamer's hot funnel, over which, all day long, hovered and melted something very fine, glassy, azure-fiery; in the stuffiness and dense warmth—of men, of the engine-room, of the kitchen. Thus I deserved, at last, some compensation. And so, alighting at Orel, I told a cabman to drive me to the best hotel. . . . It was a dusty lilac dusk; evening lights were scattered all over the place; a band was playing in the public garden, beyond the river. . . . Everyone knows the vague, sweetly disturbing feelings one has in the evening in an unfamiliar large town when one is completely alone. With such feelings I dined in the empty dining room of the old and respectable provincial hotel to which I had been taken, and afterward sat on the iron balcony of my room, above a tree, under which a streetlamp burned, giving a bright, elegant, dainty, though metallic, appearance to the translucent foliage. Below me people walked to and fro, talking, laughing, with lighted cigarettes; in the large houses opposite, windows were thrown open, and beyond them I saw lit-up rooms, people seated round a tea table or engaged in some work—a strange, alluring life which in those hours one watches with a particularly keen sense of observation. Later, in my endless wanderings about the world, I lived through many similar hours of solitary quiet and observation, and to many of them I owe a rather bitter wisdom. But on that warm night in Orel, with its regimental band blowing over to me from beyond the river, now its singsong languor, now the sadness or the rapture of its noise, I had no use for wisdom.

I had become quite unused to sleeping properly—and the large, comfortable, clean bed, the darkness, stillness, and spaciousness of my room, even struck me that night as strange. I even woke up as a traveler does—at daybreak. This accounts for my appearing at the offices of *The Voice* at an ungodly hour.

The morning was hot. The main street, white and bare, was still deserted. In order somehow to bring the moment nearer when, as I thought, it would be possible to appear at the editorial office without infringing the rules of decency, I walked first along that street, crossed a bridge, reached another street, large and lined with shops, all sorts of old warehouses and stores, ironmongers', chandlers', and grocers' shops, generally bearing witness to all that ponderous and plentiful well-being of which Russian towns were chock-full at the time. In harmony with that plenty and the rich morning sunlight, a dense and solemn kindly pealing of bells for mass came from the tall, heavy church by the bank of the Orlik. Accompanied by those booming bells—they even boomed right inside me—I crossed one more bridge, climbed the hill toward the government offices, huge buildings dating from the days of Nicholas I and Alexander II, in front of which a boulevard ran to the right and left, parallel with the long bright square, a wide avenue of lindens in their morning freshness, with a transparent shade. I knew the name of the street where the offices of *The Voice* were situated, and asked a passerby whether it was far.

"Over there, quite close to here," he said, and suddenly I felt my heart thump: soon I would be there!

The simplicity of that editorial office, however, was quite provincial. Beyond the square stretched garden after garden, quiet shady streets all drowned in gardens and overgrown with thick grass. In such a street, in a large garden, stood the long gray house containing the editorial offices. I approached, saw a door standing ajar right on the street, and pulled the handle of the bell. . . . It jangled somewhere in the distance, but with no effect whatsoever: the house seemed deserted, just like everything else around me: the stillness, the gardens, the lovely bright morning of a provincial steppe town. . . . I rang once more, waited for a while, and at last decided to walk in. The long corridor led somewhere into deep recesses. I went on and saw a large, low, extremely dirty room, encumbered all over with machinery, trampled, strewn with dirty greasy paper. All the machines were in motion and rumbled regularly, rolling some dark leaden boards forward and backward beneath their rollers, raising and lowering regularly some grates, laying aside, one after one, large sheets of paper, still white at the bottom, but on top already covered as if with grains of shiny black caviar; and from all these machines, their rumbling noise mingling sometimes with the voices of printers and compositors shouting to each other, came an odorous wind, a strong and pleasant smell of fresh printer's ink, of paper, lead, kerosene, and oil— things which instantly (and forever) became special for me.

"The editorial office?" somebody shouted angrily out of that wind, noise, and rumbling. "This is the printing office! Hey, take him to the editorial office!"

And, heaven knows from where, appeared a dirty boy, his round head covered in cropped lead-colored hair. "This way, please."

With hurried excitement I followed him back into the corridor, and a moment later was sitting in the vast reception room of the editor, who turned out to be a very pretty, small young lady; and in another five minutes I was already in the dining room, drinking coffee in quite a homelike fashion. Now and again I was plied with food and incessantly questioned; a few flattering remarks were made about my poems published in the St. Petersburg and Moscow monthlies, and I was asked to contribute to *The Voice*. . . . I blushed, thanked her, and smiled awkwardly, trying to hold down the almost rapturous delight which that unexpectedly wonderful acquaintance, that hospitality and attention had caused me to feel, and took with slightly trembling hands some homemade cakes that melted quickly and sweetly in my mouth. All this ended with my hostess suddenly pausing at the sound of animated voices behind the door, laughing and saying: "And here are my beauties who have overslept! I will now introduce you to two charming creatures, my cousin Lika and her friend Sashenka Obolenskaya. . . ."

And immediately two tall young girls in floridly embroidered Russian dresses, with colored beads and ribbons, with loose sleeves leaving their youthful rounded arms bare to the elbow, entered the dining room. . . .

Amazing were the rapidity and inertia, the somnambulism, with which I yielded to all that so accidentally befell me, beginning with such happy carelessness and ease, only to bring afterward so much pain and grief, to deprive me of so much mental and physical force.

Why did my choice fall on Lika?[30] Obolenskaya was in every way better than she. But when they entered, Lika looked at me with friendlier and more attentive eyes, talked to me in a simpler and livelier way than Obolenskaya. . . . And with whom did I so rapidly fall in love? With everything, of course: with that young female society to which I was so suddenly introduced; with my hostess's slipper, and with the embroidered frocks of these young girls, with all their ribbons and beads, their rounded arms and plump, elongated knees; with those spacious, low-ceilinged provincial rooms, their windows facing the sunlit garden; finally, even with the fact that the nanny brought to the dining room a flushed and slightly perspiring fair-haired boy, back from a walk, whose blue eyes gazed at me gravely and attentively while his mother kissed him and unbuttoned his coat. . . . Here, by the way, the table began to be cleared and laid for lunch, and it suddenly occurred to my hostess that I need not go away from lunch or leave Orel so soon as all that, and Lika snatched my cap, sat at the piano, and began hammering out some silly tune on it. . . . To cut a long story short, it was three o'clock when I left the editorial offices, surprised to think how quickly all had passed: I did not know yet that this quickness, this disappearance of time, is the first sign of the beginnings of what is called falling in love, the early stage of which is always senselessly gay, resembling an intoxication with ether.

19

Thus began for me another love which was destined to become a great event in my life. And that beginning was marked by a doubly marvelous episode.

I was leaving Orel as something already dear and familiar, with all the sorrow and tenderness of a first lover's parting and with ardent hopes for a new and early meeting. And why should it have happened that on that precise day there passed through Orel a certain funeral train of extreme importance? It was due at two o'clock sharp, only an hour before my train, and therefore my new friend, the owner of *The Voice*, who had to be present to meet it, offered to drive me to the station and thus give me an opportunity of seeing this rare sight. And now, just as unexpectedly as everything that happened to me in Orel, I found myself in a large but very select crowd, awaiting, in front of the rows of soldiers solemnly marshaled on the platform, the arrival of that majestic and uncanny something which somewhere was already rolling here, approaching us, in the company of various distinguished town and county representatives, of tailcoats, embroidered uniforms, three-cornered hats, heavy military epaulets, and a whole conclave of glistening cassocks and miters. Anyone who gets into such a solemnly high-strung company is at once infected with a certain numbness, so that, after standing still on the platform for about half an hour I came to my senses only at that unexpected moment when suddenly a huge engine decorated with mourning flags, with noise and clatter, swept toward us, and then a gorgeous, dark-blue something, with large clean windows and silk blinds, with golden eagles on the coats of arms flashed before our eyes. . . . At this point the whole crowd waiting at the station stepped back, and from the middle carriage of the train, which stopped softly and precisely immediately after, someone quickly appeared and stepped onto the red cloth spread out beforehand on the platform—a young giant with bright fair hair, in a red hussar's uniform, with sharp regular features and fine nostrils curved vigorously and as it were slightly contemptuously, with a rather too prominent chin; he struck me by his inhuman tallness, the length of his slender legs, the keenness of his regal eyes, but above all by his head, proudly and lightly thrown back, with short and waved bright fair hair, and a small pointed red beard curling firmly and beautifully. . . .[31]

Could I have thought, on that hot spring day, how and where I was to see him once more!

20

A whole life has passed since then.

Russia, Orel, spring. . . . And here, now, France, the South, Mediterranean winter days.[32]

Both of us have lived in a foreign country for a long time. This winter he is a close neighbor of mine, and seriously ill. One morning, unfolding a local French paper, I suddenly let it drop: the end. I have been long and anxiously following the course of his illness in the newspapers, time and again looking down from my mountain at that distant humpbacked promontory where his presence made itself felt all the time. Now there is an end to that presence.

It is sunny, bright, and cold. I come out from the house into the garden falling in its terraces to the small graveled square under the palms, from which one can see a whole country of valleys, sea, and mountains glittering in the sun and the blue air. A vast wooded lowland, its waves, hillocks, and cavities gradually rising, stretches from the sea to the foot of the Alps where I am. Below me, on a steep rocky ridge, one of the oldest villages of Provence nestles round the remains of its ancient fortress with the rude, primitive Saracen towers—itself also extremely rough, gray, stony, terraced, fused into a single whole, its crooked slating making it look as if it were covered on top with rusty scales. On the horizon ahead, the misty, nebulous white of the distant sea rises toward the luminously hazy sky. And that humpbacked promontory lies a little to the left, bathed in the morning sea-gleam that quivers around it. . . . I look long in that direction. The rising mistral flies up now and then as far as the garden stirs the hard, long leaves of the palms, makes a dry, cold rustle among them as if among graveyard wreaths. . . . Shall I go there? It is inconceivably strange to have met but twice, and both times in the company of death. But then, everything is inconceivable. . . . And this sun, glowing there so blindingly, plunging the sunny, hazy peaks yonder into their ancient, idly happy dreams of all the ages and races they have beheld— can that really be the same sun which once shone upon us both?

21

All day long there has been mistral, a sharp rustling and crackling of the palms, a restless wintry glitter. Toward evening it seems to subside.

At four o'clock I am already on the promontory, hurrying farther.

The road climbs through dense masses of southern gardens, following a long avenue. Here it is at last, that big old estate, that large white house at the foot of a vast and spacious garden, behind the wide-open gate at the end of a long avenue of old and gloomy palm trees. The late afternoon sun, all the light and glitter of the western sky is behind the house.

This is the first uncanny thing—those gates which death has opened wide and free to all, and a multitude of automobiles standing by.

But the avenue is deserted, everybody is already indoors. Rapidly I walk toward the house. The gravel crunches under my feet.

Before the porch, too, all is deserted. "This way?"

But I utter those words only because I feel suddenly bewildered: all of a sudden I notice on the porch a thing which I have not seen for a full ten years, and which strikes me as if the whole of my former life had suddenly and miraculously been resuscitated before my eyes: a Russian officer, clear-eyed and with ruddy moustache, wearing a tunic with shoulder-straps.

The high glass doors of the porch are wide open too. Beyond the doors is a half-dark vestibule and other similar doors, and still farther the half-light of a large French drawing room, something strange and beautiful: silk blinds lowered on the high semicircular windows and letting in the garnet-hued light of the sun they conceal, and a chandelier already lighted at this unusually early hour and sparkling with a yellowish-pink pearly light.

In the hall is a crowd of silent people. With a peculiar resignation I make my way toward the second set of doors, and then raise my eyes—and instantly notice the large yellow-gray countenance reposing in an inordinately long coffin, in a yellow oaken sarcophagus, the high Romanov brow, the whole of that dead old man's head, no longer fair but gray, yet still imperious and proud: the small beard, grown gray, juts slightly forward, the finely carved nostrils look slightly contemptuous. . . .

Then I notice and take in the details. Yes, a strange half-light; the lowered blinds letting through the red light of the late afternoon's sun; the lustre sparkling with pearls; the thin, pale, fluttering lights of the tall church candlesticks. Here there are people too, but only along the walls, and nearly all the space in the middle of the drawing-room is occupied by him. Against the wall on the left, a coffin lid of unusual shape—widened at the sides, tall and glistening with its yellow varnished oak, stands upright, leaning on the marble mantelpiece with its draped mirror. Right in the corner, behind the head of the coffin, an icon-lamp burns on a small table before an ancient silver icon, timid and tender as in a nursery.

Nearly all the rest of the room is occupied by the coffin. It is also strangely widened at the flanks, exceedingly long and deep, gleaming with its newness, varnish, beauty—and the terrifying thing is that within it is still another leaden casket, padded inside with white ribbed velvet. Around the coffin his last honor guard, consisting of officers and cossacks, stand in stiff, smart military attitudes, with drawn swords raised to the right shoulders, their caps on their bent left arms; their eyes, expressing with a sharp emphasis their absolute obedience and readiness, are fixed on him. He himself, lying full-length, revealing his extraordinary stature and half-covered by a tricolor flag, looks even more rigid. His head, once so striking and elegant, looks simple now, and democratic in an old man's way. The gray hair is soft and thin, the brow rather bald. This head now looks large—so childishly thin and narrow have his shoulders become. He wears an old, quite plain, ruddy-gray cossack uniform, with no decorations except the Cross of Saint George on his breast, with loose, much too short sleeves, exposing, above his long flat hands, his large yellowish arms, clumsily and heavily crossed; his hands are those of an old man, too, though still powerful, striking one by their woodenness and by the fact that in one of them he clasps in his fist, with menacing firmness, like a sword, an old cypress cross from Mount Athos, blackened with age. . . . I approach and take a place close to the foot of the coffin, by the palm branches and wreaths leaning against it.

Immediately the service begins. From the inner rooms come his relatives and friends; the old priest puts on his cassock; the lights of the wax candles in our hands burn warmly and tenderly. . . . How accustomed I am to all this by now—that low, harmonious chanting, the rhythmic tinkling of the censer, the sorrowfully submissive, dolefully affectionate invocations and supplications that have already sounded a million times on earth! Only the names change in these supplications, and for every name the turn comes in due time!

157

"Blessed is our God always, now, and forever, and unto ages of ages!"
"In peace let us pray to the Lord. . . ."
". . . for the ever memorable servant of God. . . ."
I still think of the man who once, on a hot sunny day, had been at the station in Orel. But only for a moment does that bright vision flash past in my mind. Sorrowfully and hesitatingly sound the supplications for the "godly Prince, the grand duke" who has just departed to join the host of all those who "yearn for Christ's solace" and now with them is humbly awaiting "peace, stillness, blissful memory," hoping "to present himself blameless before the dread throne of the Lord of Glory. . . ." His dead countenance, already turned to something beyond our reach, is still full of expression, but already quiet and still. His prominent eyelids are closed, his colorless lips are pressed tight, ashen under the moustache. . . . I notice the slightly swollen veins on his broad, aged temples and think—"tomorrow they will already be black." . . . I think of his past life, so vast and complex; and I think, too, of my own. . . .

"And further we pray for the peace of the soul of Thy departed servant . . . and that Thou wilt forgive him all his sins, whether voluntary or involuntary. . . ."

"God's mercy, the Kingdom of Heaven, and the remission of our sins we entreat of Christ, our King and God Immortal. . . ."

Then my eyes rest once more on the tricolor flag half-covering his legs, his cossack uniform; they see that petrified hand clasping the black cross, those rigid faces of the guards, so tense and alert, their peaked caps, blades, and epaulets, which I have not seen for ten years. . . .

"I am the image of Thy ineffable glory—be generous to Thy creature, O Lord, and grant unto me the home-country of my heart's desire. . . ."

When we all come out, it is already evening. The sun has just set; behind us, beyond the black palms, is a deep pink light in the sky. And ahead of us, far-off, is the vast picture of those eternal Mediterranean shores. In the background, against the dim, chill, rosy-blue eastern sky, everything is dominated by the dead mass of the snowy Alpine ridges, their flaming crimson already mournfully fading away, utterly alien to all living things, vanishing into their wild wintry darkness, their flanks already drowning in the dense gray-blue haze. As night draws on, the sea at their foot has taken on a stern, cold blue. . . .

22

During the night on my hilltop, the mistral sets everything booming, roaring, raging. Suddenly I wake up. In a dream I have just seen, or fancied, that during the leave-taking after the requiem, a tall slim girl was the last of those close to him to take leave of him. Dressed all in black, with a long mourning veil, she approached him so simply, bent over him with such womanly love, and for an instant, the fluttering end of her veil hid both the coffin's edge and the old, yet childlike, uniformed shoulder. . . . The mistral rushes on and on; the branches of the palm trees, rustling in stormy confusion, seem also to be rushing somewhere. . . . I rise and with difficulty push open the door onto the balcony. The cold strikes me in the face, and overhead a jet-black sky opens wide, covered with blazing stars, white and blue and red. Everything is rushing somewhere, on and on. . . .

Slowly I make the sign of the cross, gazing up at that baleful, terrible thing which blazes above my head.

Book Five

1

Those spring days of my first wanderings were the last days of my youthful monasticism. That first day in Orel, I woke up just as I had on the road—alone, free, tranquil, an alien in the hotel and the city—and I awoke at an unusual hour for the city: day had just broken. But the next day I woke up later, like everybody else. I dressed carefully, looking at myself in the mirror. . . . Yesterday, in the editorial office, I had been embarrassedly conscious of my gypsy tan, the weather-beaten leanness of my face, and my overgrown hair. I needed to look respectable, particularly since my circumstances had so unexpectedly improved yesterday. I received not only an offer to work for them but an advance as well, which I took—I blushed hotly, but I took it. And so I set off down the main street, stopped into a cigar store where I bought a pack of expensive cigarettes, and then on to the barbershop. I emerged with a beautifully shaped and fragrant head and with that particularly masculine energy one always gets on leaving the barber's. I felt like going back to the editorial office right away, the more quickly to continue the festival of new impressions that fate had so generously bestowed on me the day before. But to return immediately was out of the question. "What, he's come back again? And again at the crack of dawn?!" I walked around the city. First, just as yesterday, down Bolkhov Street, from there to Moscow Street, a long commercial road leading to the station, which I followed until, after some kind of dusty triumphal arch, it grew desolate and poor. Then I turned into a still poorer neighborhood, from which I turned back toward Moscow Street. Descending Moscow Street toward the river, I crossed an old wooden bridge that shook and buzzed with traffic. As I walked up toward the government offices all the church bells pealed, and along the boulevard approaching me, pulled by a pair of black steeds prancing quickly but evenly in fitting contrast to those peals, rolled the bishop in his carriage, blessing all he met with a serene wave of his hand, left and right.

Again, the editorial office was crowded, and little Avilova was cheerfully working behind her large desk. She smiled at me affectionately and then instantly turned back to her work. Lunch was again long and merry; after lunch I listened as Lika played the piano impetuously, and then I swung with her and Obolenskaya on the swings in the garden. After tea, Avilova showed me around the house, taking me through all the rooms. In the bedroom I noticed a portrait on the wall—a hirsute man with wide, bony shoulders and in glasses stared out discontentedly from the frame. "My late husband," Avilova said casually, and I was momentarily dumbfounded. I was struck by the absurdity of any kind of union between that consumptive man and the lively, pretty woman who had just unexpectedly called him her husband. Then she sat down to work again. Lika dolled herself up and said to us in that peculiar manner of speaking that had made me embarrassed for her when I noticed it earlier, "Well, guys, I'm out of here!" And she headed off somewhere.

Obolenskaya and I set out to take care of her errands. She invited me to go with her to Karachev Street, saying she needed to stop in at the seamstress's. I quite enjoyed the closeness that she had established between us with this intimate request, and I accompanied her around the city with that same feeling, listening to her precise speech. At the seamstress's, I stood and waited, taking particular pleasure in my patience, until she finished her negotiations and consultations. When we again came out onto Karachev Street it was already dusk.

"Do you like Turgenev?" she asked. I was tongue-tied. Because I was born and raised in the country people always ask that question, automatically imputing to me a love for Turgenev.

"Well, it doesn't matter," she said. "In any case, you will be interested. Not far from here is the estate that supposedly was described in *A Nest of Gentry*. Would you like to take a look?"[1] And we headed off to somewhere near the edge of the city, where on an isolated street collapsing into gardens, on a precipice above the river in an old garden sprinkled with new April verdure, was a long-abandoned, graying house with crumbling chimneys in which crows had begun to build their nests. We stood looking at it over a low fence past that sparse garden etched against the clear sunset sky . . . Liza, Lavretsky, Lemm . . . and I passionately yearned for love.

In the evening, we all went to the town park, to the summer theater—I sat in the semidarkness next to Lika, amicably enjoying all the noisy foolery that was taking place in the orchestra, on the stage, and in some kind of a square, illuminated from below, where, caught up in the thunderous, cavorting music, good-looking city girls and regal cuirassiers stomped on the floor and banged empty tin mugs. After the theater there was supper right there in the park, and I sat on the large, crowded terrace with the ladies and a chilled bottle of wine. Acquaintances came up to them from time to time. I was introduced to all of them, and they were all very amiable to me—except one who, having made a quick bow in my direction, ignored me completely thereafter. This was a man who later, without even noticing, caused me great spiritual torment: a very tall officer with an elongated, dull-swarthy face, unmoving dark eyes, and black sideburns, in a well-made frock coat reaching below his knees and tight stirrup pantaloons. She talked and laughed a great deal, showing off her spectacular teeth, knowing that everyone was admiring her. I could no longer look at them calmly, and I shivered when the officer briefly held her hand in his large hand upon leaving our table.

The first thunder roared on the day of my departure. I remember that thunder, the light carriage carrying me away to the station with Avilova, my feeling of pride in the carriage and the company, that strange feeling of first separation from the woman, for whom I had invented a love in which I already believed completely. And the one feeling that prevailed over all others—the feeling that I had made some kind of particularly lucky acquisition in Orel. On the platform, I was struck both by the size and the strength of all those festive, chosen people who expectantly milled around waiting for the train, and by the fact that, despite all the brilliance of their church attire, the priests who were standing in front of all the others with their crosses and censers in their hands seemed to be just simple folk. The grand prince's train finally rushed into the station with all its heavy force, and everyone was blinded by the red doloman worn by a bright ruddy giant who leaped from the train; but at that moment everything became somehow mixed up, confused—I don't remember anything else, except the sadly ominous solemn requiem. Then the oily steel bulk of the steam engine draped in coal-black flags started to rumble and with powerful, stuttering jerks of its pipes began to breathe anew, the joint of its drive shaft, long and smooth like a white ribbon of steel, reversed, and the blue mirrorlike walls of the wagon with their golden eagles started to move ahead. . . . . I gazed at the cast-iron wheels spinning faster and faster below them, at the brakes and the springs, and I saw only one thing: that they were all thickly covered with white dust, that magical dust of the long journey from the South, from the Crimea. The moaning train hid itself, continuing on its grand funereal run through Russia, en route to somewhere, to its goal, while I was already in the fairy-tale land of the Crimea, in the captivating Gurzuf days of the legendary Pushkin.[2]

My modest departing train was waiting for me on a distant side platform, and I was already glad of the solitude and rest that was in store for me there. Avilova stayed right until the train left, babbling cheerily the whole while, saying that she hoped to see me again soon in Orel, letting me know with her smile that she understood perfectly the amusing woe that had overcome me. At the last bell, I fell passionately on her hand; she brushed my cheek with her lips. I hopped into the compartment. It lurched and began moving forward while I, leaning out of the window, watched as she faded away, standing on the platform waving gently. . . .

After that, everything about the trip seemed poignant: the little train that would sometimes go along slowly and then suddenly speed up, rock crazily, and thunder. And those empty depots and way stations at which the train would stand endlessly for no apparent reason, and then soon I was surrounded again by what was my own, already familiar: the sloping hillocks of the fields drifting by the window, still bare and therefore particularly plain, the bare birch glades quietly awaiting spring, the barren horizon. . . . The evening was also barren, with a spring chill and a pale low sky.

2

I brought away one dream with me from Orel: somehow to continue, and as quickly as possible, everything that had begun there. But the farther away I rode, the less I remembered about it, as I gazed out the window over the fields, at the long April sunset. And already in the compartment it is twilight, twilight there through the windows in that sparse oak forest that passes by on the left of the train—bare, gnarled, strewn with last year's russet leaves now just peeking through from beneath the winter snows. And now I am standing, suitcase in hand, growing more and more excited: here is the Subbotin forest already, which comes just before the Pisarev station. The train sends a mournful warning cry somewhere into the emptiness. I stand out on the landing between the cars; the rain is drizzling down, somehow primevally raw, fresh, and a lone freight car sits in front of the station. The train goes around it, and while we're still moving I leap out. Then I run across the platform, pass through the weakly lit, hopelessly dreary and tramped-through station, and out through the dark lobby. In the circular yard in front of the station is a garden, now wretched and dirty from the winter, and a peasant cabby's nag is just visible through the murk.

This peasant, who sometimes waits weeks in vain for a fare, hurls himself toward me at full speed, enthusiastically agreeing with everything I say, ready to gallop off with me to the ends of the earth, and for whatever I please—"be worth my while, with luck"—and a moment later I'm calmly bouncing along in his small cart: at first through a wild and dark village, then, as it grows steadily more quiet, through the dark silent fields dead to the whole world, through a black sea of earth, beyond which something greenish glimmers in the infinite distance below the clouds to the northwest. An evening breeze comes to meet us over the field—a light, April, rainy wind— and somewhere in the distance a quail rustles, seemingly moving about at the whim of the wind. A few sparse stars flash through the clouds in the low Russian heavens. . . . Again, quails, spring, earth—and my former, poor, isolated youth! The road is excruciatingly long: seven miles across fields with a Russian peasant is no short trip. He has grown quiet and mysterious, and smells of his hut and the dry sheepskin of his threadbare coat. At my request to speed up, he is silent. Whenever we get to a rise, he hops down from the driver's seat, takes up the rope reins, and with measured steps, face turned aside, he walks beside his barely plodding little mare. As we approach the entrance to Vasilevskoe, it seems that it is already late night: not a light to be seen, nothing stirs. My eyes have adjusted to the darkness, and each hut, and each bare willow thicket in front of the huts, is clearly visible on the wide street that leads into the village. Then I see and sense the descent into the April dank of the low ground; on the left, the bridge across the river, on the right, the road leading up to the uninviting dark manor. Again, my emotions are acute: how terribly familiar everything is, and at the same time how new—that springtime rural darkness, squalor, and indifference! The peasant grows numb, dragging himself up the hill. Suddenly a light flashes in the window, there, from behind the evergreen hedge. Thank God! They're not asleep! Delight, impatience, and a tiny bit of boyish shame, when at last the cart stops at the porch and I have to alight, open the door to the foyer, go in, and see how they look me over with a smile. . . .

From Vasilevskoe I went for a ride the next day, in the quiet and bright morning showers, which would stop and then pick up again, through fields and fallow. Peasants plowed and sowed. The barefoot plowman was walking along behind the wooden plow, his white pigeon-toed feet stumbling in the soft furrows; his horse was churning up the earth, vigorously straining, arching, and behind the plow a blue-black crow hopped along the furrow, snatching crimson worms from time to time. And behind the crow, taking large even strides, strides an old man without a hat, a sowing sack over his shoulder, liberally and nobly rotating his right hand in perfect half-circles and showering the earth with seeds.

In Baturino, the love and joy that greeted me were almost painful. I was struck most of all not by the joy of my mother, but by the joy of my sister. I had not even dreamed of that charm of love and delight with which she threw herself at me on the porch after spying me through the window. And how charming she was in every way—her purity, her youth, the fresh innocence of her new dress, worn for the first time that day in my honor. Even the house entranced me with its wonderful old-fashioned plainness. In my room, everything was as if I had just left: everything was in exactly the same place, even that half-burnt tallow candle in the iron candlestick which had been standing on my desk the day of my departure in the winter. I walked in and looked around: the blackened icons in the corner; through the old windows with stained glass on top (lilac and scarlet) I could see the trees and the sky, and here and there the light-bluish rain sprinkled down on the green branches and twigs. In the room it is rather dim, spacious and deep . . . dark beamed ceiling, wooden and smooth walls of the same dark wood . . . the smooth heavy curved frame of an oak bed. . . .

3

It turned out that business was the excuse for another trip to Orel: someone had to bring the interest payment to the bank. I went, but I only deposited part of it and squandered the rest. This was no laughing matter, but something had happened to me and I did not give it much thought. The whole time I acted with a certain happy-go-lucky decisiveness. Going to Orel, I missed the passenger train, so I immediately hopped the locomotive of a freight train. I still remember how I climbed up the high iron steps into something crude and dirty, stood there and stared. The engineers were wearing something unbelievably greasy, shining like iron; their faces were just as greasy and shiny, the whites of their eyes expressively Negroid, and it seemed as if they had purposely painted their eyelids, like actors. The younger one smashed his iron shovel sharply into the soft coal piled on the floor and thunderously threw back the door to the boiler. Red hellfire poured out, and he vigorously damped that hell with a black shovelful of coal. The older one wiped his hands with a horrifyingly greasy rag and, tossing it aside, grabbed onto something and began to turn it. . . . An ear-splitting whistle sounded from somewhere, a blanket of blinding steam blasted forth, something thunderous deafened me, and we slowly inched forward. How savagely this thunder thundered then as our speed, our strength, grew and grew, as everything around us trembled, shook, and jumped. Time thickened and petrified, it was as if a fiery dragon was flashing past the hillocks—and how quickly each stretch of the rails came to an end! At each stop the nightingale's song beats, exalts, blesses from all the surrounding bushes in the peaceful quiet of the stations fragrant with woodland night air. . . . In Orel, I dressed ridiculously—in thin, foppish boots, a thin, long-waisted black vest, a red silk blouse, a black nobleman's cap with a red band. I bought an expensive cavalryman's saddle with such wonderful squeaky and aromatic leather that I was unable to sleep on the journey home from the joy of knowing it lay next to me. I went to Pisarev again, intent on buying a horse— for there happened to be a horse fair in the village just then. At the fair I made friends with several of my peers, long-time regulars at fairs, also wearing long-waisted vests and noblemen's caps, and with their help I bought a young thoroughbred mare (in spite of the gypsy who desperately foisted upon me a tired old gelding—"Buy Misha, sir, you'll love me forever for my Misha!").

After this, the summer turned into a continuous holiday for me, and I never spent more than three days in a row at Baturino. I was always visiting my new friends, and as soon as she got back from Orel I escaped completely to town. As soon as I would receive her short note, "I'm returned and hunger to see you," I would gallop off to the station, despite the unpleasantness of the note's foolish wit and the fact that it was already evening and the clouds were threatening. In the coach, as if drunk, I delighted in the speed of the train, which seemed even speedier because of the already raging storm, because the clatter of the train merged with the thunderclaps and the noise of the rain on the roof, and all that in the midst of the blue flame which periodically flooded the dark glass against which the fresh-smelling rainwater whipped and foamed.

It was as though nothing existed but the pleasure of merry meetings. But then—this was at the end of the summer already—one of my friends, who lived with his sister and his old father on a small estate on the steep bank of the river not far outside the city and who also spent time with her, invited a good-sized group over for his birthday party. He picked her up himself, and she rode back with him in his small gig, while I followed behind on horseback. I delighted in the sunny, dry expanse of the fields. The open, sandy-looking fields were everywhere covered with haystacks. Everything in me yearned to do something desperately suave. I grew shamelessly excited, reined in my horse, and then let her tear through the haystacks at a full gallop, her pastern bloodied by her sharp horseshoes. The birthday party on the dilapidated balcony lasted until evening, evening inconspicuously melted into night—lamps, wine, songs, and guitars. I sat beside her and held her hand in mine unabashedly, and she did not withdraw it. Late at night, as if we had planned it, we got up from our chairs at the same time and descended from the balcony into the darkness of the garden. She stopped in its warm blackness and, leaning her back against a tree, stretched her hands out to me. I couldn't quite see her, but I quickly divined her movements. . . . The sky soon turned gray, young roosters with husky and helplessly blissful voices began to crow on the estate, and a moment later the entire garden grew light from the great golden east, unveiling itself across the yellow fields and the river lowlands. . . . Then we stood on the cliff above those lowlands, and she, watching the sun flaring up on the horizon, forgetting all about me, sang Tchaikovsky's "Morning."[3] Breaking off on a note that was too high for her to reach, she caught up the smart flounces of her partridge-colored cambric skirt and darted toward the house. Confused, I stayed behind, already unable to stay on my feet, much less think through anything. I walked over to an old birch tree that stood on the slope of a ravine in the dry grass and lay down beneath it. It was already day, the sun had risen and, as always in late summer when the weather is fine, the dawn gave way suddenly to a bright hot morning. I lay my head down on the roots of the birch tree and instantly fell asleep. But the sun burned brighter and brighter, and I soon awoke in such heat and brilliance that I staggered off in search of shade.

The whole house was still asleep in that dry, blinding light. Only the old owner was awake. His cough could be heard through the open window of his study, under which grew dense, overgrown lilac bushes, and in his cough you could practically feel the old man's delight at his first morning pipe, his morning cup of strong tea with cream. Hearing my approaching steps and the sound of sparrows pouring out of the lilac bush that glittered in the sun, he glanced out the window and pulled his old robe made of patterned Turkish silk around his body. His face was frightful, with swollen eyes and an enormous gray beard, but he smiled with extraordinary kindliness. I bowed to him guiltily and went across the balcony through the open doors of the living room, which was perfectly lovely in its morning quiet and emptiness, with butterflies fluttering around and old blue wallpaper, armchairs, loveseats. I lay down on one of the incredibly uncomfortable crooked loveseats and again fell into a deep sleep.

But then—it seemed right away, although I had actually slept for some time—someone came up to me and, laughing, started to speak, ruffling my hair. I came to, and before me stood the children of the house, brother and sister, both dark fiery-eyed Tatar-looking beauties. He wore a yellow silk blouse, and she wore a jacket of the same material. I jumped up and sat down again. In a nice way they said that it was time to get up and eat breakfast, that she had left already—not alone, but with Kuzmin—and they gave me a note. I immediately recalled Kuzmin's eyes—sharp, impudent, somehow multicolored, the color of bees—snatched the note, and dashed into the old "maid's quarters." There, humbly waiting for me on a stool by a tub, was an old woman dressed in black who held a pitcher of water in her thin pigment-spotted hands. As I came in, I read, "Don't try to see me again," and started to wash my hands. The water was icy, sharp. "Ours is spring water, well water," said the old woman, as she handed me a long linen towel. I quickly passed through the foyer, grabbed my cap and whip, and ran out through the hot yard to the stable. . . . My horse began to whinny to me quietly and sadly through the dim light. She had been standing there all this time saddled, alongside empty mangers, with hunger-pinched sides. I grabbed the reins, jumped into the saddle, still somehow holding back my wild ecstasy, and darted out of the yard. Beyond the manor I abruptly turned into a field, dashing through the rustling stubble wherever my eyes took me. I reined in my horse at the first tumbling haystack and, tearing myself out of my saddle, sat down. My horse made noises, snatching with her teeth and pulling the sheaves overflowing from the cock by the ears of seemingly glassy grain: grasshoppers by the thousands, like pocket watches, ran through the stubble and the cut sheaves, as if a sandy desert were stretched around the sunny fields. I heard nothing, saw nothing, and mentally repeated only one thing: either she gives herself (those batiste skirts, the rustling of her fleeing feet in the dry grass) back to me tonight, this morning, or neither of us shall live!

With those insane feelings, with ridiculous conviction in them, I galloped off to the city.

4

I remained in the city for a long time after that, sitting for whole days with her in the dusty garden deep within the grounds of her widowed father's estate. Her father—a well-off gentleman, a liberal doctor—put no constraints on her. From the moment I galloped up to her, and when after seeing my face she pressed both hands to her chest, it was impossible to say whose love was stronger, happier, crazier—mine or hers (which also somehow suddenly appeared from nowhere). Finally, to give each other a little rest, we decided to part for a while. This was all the more necessary because I had run up an unpayable debt while living on credit at the Noblemen's Hotel. Along with that, the rains had begun. I put off the separation in every possible way—until, finally, I gathered all my strength and set out homeward in the midst of a rainstorm. At first all I did at home was sleep or quietly wander from one room to another, doing nothing, thinking nothing. Then I started to reflect: what was happening in me and how would it turn out? One day my brother Nicholas arrived. He came into my room, sat down without taking off his cap, and said: "So, my friend, your romantic existence continues along untroubled. No changes: 'A fox leads me through dark forests, over high mountains,' and who knows what is beyond these forests and mountains? I know all about it. I've heard a lot and guessed about the rest—these stories are all alike anyway. I realize that you've no desire now for rational discussion, but even so, what are your intentions for the future?"

I answered half-jokingly.

"Everyone is led on by some kind of fox. And where and why, of course, nobody knows. Even in the Gospels it is written: 'Go, young man, in your youth, where your heart takes you and where your eyes gaze!'"

My brother grew quiet, looking at the floor as if listening to the whisper of the rain in the pitiful autumn garden, then sadly said, "All right, go, go. . . ."

I kept asking myself: what should I do? It was perfectly clear. But the more persistently I tried to convince myself that tomorrow I should write a decisive farewell letter—it was still possible, we still had not reached the final stages of intimacy—the more I was seized by tenderness for her, delight in her, deep thankfulness for her love, the charm of her eyes, face, laugh, voice. . . . And then, several days later at dusk, a mounted messenger suddenly appeared on the grounds of the upper estate. Soaked from head to toe, he handed me a telegram: "Cannot bear any more, I wait." The frightening thought that I would see, hear her, in a few hours kept me awake until dawn. . . .

168

So thus I lived the whole autumn, sometimes at home, sometimes in the city. I sold the saddle and horse, and in the city I no longer lived in the Noblemen's Hotel, but at the boardinghouse of a certain Nikulina, on Shchepna Square. The city was different now, no longer the place where my adolescent years had passed. Everything was ordinary, routine—only sometimes, walking along Uspensky Street past the schoolyard and buildings, I caught something that seemed precious to me, some piece of my past. Long since, I had smoked habitually and got shaved habitually at the barber's where once upon a time I had sat with such childish obedience, looking out the corner of my eyes as my silky hair fell to the floor under the constantly clicking scissors. From morning until night we sat on the Turkish sofa in the dining room, almost always in solitude: the doctor left in the morning, and her brother, a schoolboy, left for school. After lunch the doctor slept and again went out somewhere, and the schoolboy busied himself with an energetic game, scurrying about with his ruddy Wolfy who, pretending to attack, barking, panting, raced up and down the wooden stairs to the second floor. At one point, those monotonous sittings, and perhaps my immoderate, unchanging sensitivity, started to bore her—she started to find excuses to leave the house, to visit friends or acquaintances. I began to sit on the sofa alone, listening to the shouts, raucous laughter, and clatter of the schoolboy and the theatrical barks of Wolfy playing crazily on the staircase, looking through tears out the half-curtained window at the even, gray sky, smoking cigarette after cigarette. . . . Then, again something happened to her: again she started to sit at home, and became so caressingly kind that I completely lost all understanding of what kind of person she was.

"So, my darling," she once said to me, "this is obviously the way it has to be." And joyfully puckering her face, she started to cry. That was after breakfast, when everyone in the house went around on tiptoe, allowing the doctor to rest.

"I just feel terribly sorry for Papa, there's no one in the world dearer to me!" she said, as always astonishing me with her immeasurable love for her father. And precisely a moment later, as if on cue, the schoolboy ran up and absentmindedly muttered that the doctor wished to see me. She grew pale. I kissed her hand and resolutely walked out.

The doctor, humming and smoking, met me with the gentle cheer of someone well rested and recently bathed after waking up from a good sleep.

"My young friend," he said, offering me a smoke, "I have long wanted to speak with you, you understand why. I am sure you are well aware that I am a man without prejudices. But my daughter's happiness is precious to me and I feel for you with all my heart, so let us speak frankly, man to man. Strange as it seems, I don't know you at all. Tell me, who are you actually?" he said with a smile.

Blushing and then becoming pale, I began to drag more deeply. Who was I actually? I wanted to answer with pride, like Goethe (I had just finished reading Eckerman at the time):[4] "I do not know myself, and may God spare me from knowing myself!" Instead, however, I said modestly, "You know that I write. . . . I plan to continue writing, to work on improving. . . ."

And unexpectedly I added, "Perhaps I will prepare and enroll at the university. . . ."

"The university! That would, of course, be excellent. But, after all, preparing for the university is not a trifling matter. And what field exactly would you be preparing for? Only for a literary occupation or for some public position?"

And again some nonsense popped into mind—again Goethe: "I live for the ages with the feeling of the unbearable inconstancy of everything earthly. . . . Politics can never be the concern of poetry. . . ."

"The public sphere is not the concern of the poet," I answered.

The doctor looked at me with slight amazement.

"So in your opinion Nekrasov, for example, is not a poet?[5] But after all you must follow the current trend of public life, at least to some extent. And you know what every worthy and cultured Russian lives for and worries over?"

I thought and recalled what I knew: everyone was talking about the reaction, about the leaders of the zemstvo, saying that "nothing was left standing of the progressive undertakings of the age of the great reforms" . . . that Tolstoy invited all to a "cell 'neath a spruce" . . . that we indeed are living in Chekhovian "Twilights." . . . I remembered a booklet of Marcus Aurelius's aphorisms distributed by the Tolstoyans: "A pediment taught me how callous are the souls of people reputed to be aristocrats. . . ."[6] I remembered a sad old Ukrainian, some kind of sectarian, with whom I had floated down the Dnieper in the spring, who constantly repeated in his own way the words of the apostle Paul: "Just as the Lord who seated Christ at His right hand is higher than any authority, power, strength, supremacy, or name named not only in this age but in the one to come, so our dispute is not against flesh and blood but against the authorities, the earthly leaders of the darkness of this age. . . ." I felt my longtime sympathy toward Tolstoyism—which liberated from all public ties and at the same time called on one to take up arms against "the earthly leaders of the darkness of this age," whom I hated too, and I launched into a Tolstoyan sermon.

"So, then, in your opinion, the sole salvation from all evil and wickedness is this notorious apathy and nonresistance?" asked the doctor with exaggerated indifference.

I hastened to answer that I was for action and resistance, "but only certain kinds." My Tolstoyism was constructed from those contradictory feelings that had been stirred in me by Pierre Bezukhov and Anatoly Kuragin, Prince Serpukhovsky from "Kholstomer," and Ivan Ilich, "So What Should

We Do, Then?" and "How Much Land Does a Man Need?" from the terrible pictures of urban filth and destitution described in the article on the Moscow census, and from poetic dreams of life amid nature and among the people created by *The Cossacks*, and my own impressions of Ukraine.[7] What happiness it would be to shake off the dust of our unrighteous life and trade it for an honest, hard-working life somewhere on a farm in the steppes, or in a whitewashed dirt hut on the banks of the Dnieper! I managed to express some of this to the doctor, omitting the part about the dirt hut. He listened attentively it seemed, but somehow quite condescendingly. There was a moment when his sleepy, heavy eyes grew dim and his compressed jaws began to tremble from a fit of yawning, but he controlled himself, yawned only through his nostrils, and said, "Yes, yes, I hear you. . . . So this means that you are not looking for any of the, how should I put it, normal blessings of 'this world' for yourself personally? But after all, there is more than just the personal of course. I, for example, am not thrilled by the peasants. I unfortunately know them well and very much doubt that they are the fount and source of all wisdom and that I am obliged to maintain with them that the earth rests on three whales, but does that mean that we are in no way obligated to them, is there nothing we must do? However, I don't dare lecture you in this vein. In any case, I am glad we had this chat. And now I will return to our starting point. I will speak briefly and, you will excuse me, quite firmly. Whatever the feelings are between you and my daughter and whatever stage of development they have now reached, I will say beforehand: she, of course, is completely free; but if she desires, for example, to establish any kind of solid tie with you and asks for, as it were, my blessing, she will receive from me a decisive refusal. I like you and I wish you all the best, but that is the way it must be. Why? It is quite a petit-bourgeois answer: I don't want to see you both unhappy, shivering in need, in an uncertain existence. And also allow me to say, quite frankly, what do you have in common? Glikeria is a pretty girl and, why hide it, rather fickle—today she is passionate for one thing, tomorrow another. She dreams, of course, not of a Tolstoyan cell 'neath a spruce—just look at how she dresses, even in our backwater. By no means do I mean to imply that she is spoiled, I simply think that she, as they say, is no match for you. . . ."

She was waiting for me, standing at the base of the stairs, and she met me with inquiring eyes that were ready for the worst. I quickly conveyed to her the final words of the doctor. She lowered her head.

"I could never go against his will," she said.

While living at Nikulina's rooming house, I sometimes went out and wandered aimlessly on Shchepna Square, then on to the fallow fields behind the monastery, where there was a large cemetery, surrounded by ancient walls. There only the wind blew—grief and grasses, the eternal peace of crosses and tombstones, forgotten by all, forsaken, somehow empty, like a solitary, vague thought of something. Above the gates of the cemetery a boundless blue-gray plain had been painted, pocked everywhere with yawning graves, gravestones fallen askew with skeletons rising forth from beneath them, toothy and bony, and with immemorially ancient monks and nuns in pale-green shrouds. And an enormous angel with a trumpet at his lips flew trumpeting over the plain, his pale-blue clothes flapping about behind in strips, his naked girlish legs bent at the knee, his long chalky feet streaming behind.

At the house a provincial autumnal peace reigned, it was empty—there were very few arrivals from the village. As I was returning, entering the yard, the cook, in peasants' boots, carried a rooster out from under the awnings opposite me.

"I'm taking him inside," she said, smiling for some unknown reason. "He's gone completely senile from old age, let him live with me now. . . ."

I climbed up on the wide stone porch, went through the dark entrance hall, then past the warm kitchen with its bunks, and on to the living room—the landlady's bedroom was there and the room with two large couches, on which the rare visitor from the petite bourgeoisie or clergy would sleep, but more usually just I alone. It was quiet—and within the quiet was the measured beat of the alarm clock in the landlady's bedroom. . . .

"You went for a walk?" asked the landlady affectionately, coming out with a smile of kind condescension. Such a charming, melodic voice! She was full-figured and round-faced. At times I couldn't look at her calmly—especially on those evenings when she returned from the bathhouse all red and drank tea for a long time, sitting with her hair still dark and damp, with a tranquil and languid shine in her eyes, in a white nightgown, resting her clean body freely and comfortably in a chair, and her beloved cat, silky white with pink eyes, purring on her plump, slightly separated knees. Outside, a sound: the cook was slamming the strong, solid shutters from the street, threading the iron kingpins of the elbow-shaped clamps from there into the room, through the round openings at the edges of the windows—somehow recalling ancient, dangerous times. Nikulina would get up, place the metal blades at the ends of the clamps into the locks, and then go back to her tea, whereupon the room seemed to become even more comfortable. . . . Wild feelings and ideas coursed through me then: to drop everything and stay here forever, in this house, to sleep in her warm bedroom to the measured beat of the alarm clock! A picture hung over one couch: an amazingly green forest, standing like a continuous wall, below it a log cabin, and alongside the cabin, a short bent old man laying his hand on the head of a brown bear, also short, tame, soft-pawed; over the other couch, something completely absurd for anybody who might have to sit or lie there: a photo-portrait of an old man in a coffin, important, white-faced, in a black frock coat—Nikulina's late husband. From the kitchen, in time with the long autumn evening, came a rhythmic tapping and an extended "A carriage was standing at the church, there was a magnificent wedding. . . ."—these were the hired day-laboring girls, singing and mincing fresh, tight heads of cabbage for the winter with sharp choppers. And there was a kind of bittersweet sadness in everything— in this vulgar song, in the measured household beat, in the old cheap picture, even in the deceased man, whose life somehow still dragged on in the pointlessly happy existence of the house. . . .

6

In November I headed home. On parting, we agreed to meet in Orel: she would go there on the first of December, and for propriety's sake I would go at least a week later. But on the first, a frozen moonlit night, I galloped to Pisarev to get on the overnight train she would be taking from the city. How I see, how I feel that long-ago fairy-tale night! I see myself halfway between Baturino and Vasilevskoe, on a level snowy field. The steam rises, the shaft-horse is shaking exactly one part of its harness as it breaks into a strong trot. The outrunner's rear end rises and falls, lumps of snow push upward from under the flashing white horseshoes. . . . Sometimes she suddenly tore herself from the path, collapsing into the deep snow, and then hurried anew, more intensely, getting tangled up in the snow and her fallen traces. Then she would take off strongly again, and again she'd carry on, forcefully tearing her reins. . . . Everything flies, rushes—and at the same time seems to stand and wait: in the distance the scaly crust of snow shines silver, while the low moon hangs white and motionless, turbid with frost, framed by a sadly mysterious, nebulously colored ring. And most motionless am I, frozen in this gallop and motionlessness, at its mercy for the moment, turned rigid and expectant, and at the same time quietly reliving a memory: the same kind of night and the same road to Vasilevskoe, only it was my first winter in Baturino, and I was still pure, innocent, happy—the happiness of my first days of youth, the first poetic ecstasies in the world of ancient tomes, brought from Vasilevskoe, their stanzas, epistles, elegies, ballads:

Galloping along. Emptiness all around:
The steppe before Svetlana's eyes. . . .[8]

"Where is all that now?" I thought, not forgetting, however, my primary state—numbed, waiting. "Galloping along. Emptiness all around," I told myself in time with this gallop (in the rhythm of a motion that has always had a hypnotic power over me), and I feel within me someone bold, ancient, heading somewhere in a shako and bearskin coat. The only intimations of reality are the driver in his heavy coat over a jacket standing on the front seat and the frozen oat straw covered with snowy dust stuffed, along with my feet, under the front seat. Beyond Vasilevskoe, on the descent, the shaft horse fell into a pothole and broke a shaft; while the workman was repairing it I was petrified with fear that I was going to be late for the train. As soon as I arrived I bought a first-class ticket with my last money—she traveled in first—and leaped onto the platform. I remember the moonlight, turbid through the frozen steam in which the yellow light of the platforms was lost, and the illuminated windows of the telegraph office. The train was already approaching; I looked in the turbid, snowy distance, feeling completely glassy from frost and icy internal shaking. A bell rang out unexpectedly and resonantly, the doors squeaked sharply and slammed, the quick steps of the people leaving the train station squeaked tightly and sharply—and there, in the distance, the dark and shaggy locomotive and its awesome triangle of dull-red flame seemed to move forward slowly in time with its heavy exhalations. The train approached with difficulty, covered with snow, frozen, screaming, squealing, whining. . . . I jumped onto the landing of the car and flung open the door— she was sitting in the darkness with a fur coat thrown over her shoulders under a lantern covered by a cherry-colored curtain, completely alone in the entire wagon, looking directly at me. . . .

The wagon was old, tall, with three axles; at full speed in the frost the whole thing shook and everything fell and collapsed somewhere, the doors and windows creaked, its frozen windows played like gray diamonds. . . . Everything happened by itself somehow, out of our control, our cognizance. . . . She got up with a hot unseeing face, straightened her hair, and, closing her eyes, sat down in a corner, inaccessible. . . .

7

That winter we lived in Orel.

How can I express our feelings as we got off the train in the morning and went to the editorial office, secretly united by our terrifying new intimacy?

I stayed at a small hotel and she, as before, with Avilova. We would spend virtually the entire day there, save for our precious hours at the hotel.

It was an uneasy happiness, exhausting both physically and spiritually.

I remember: she was at the skating rink one evening, I was sitting and working at the office—they had already started giving me some work, a way to make a living—and it was empty and quiet in the house. Avilova was off at some meeting, the evening seemed endless, the streetlight burning outside the window on the street, sad, useless. The approaching and receding footsteps of passersby, their crunch on the snow, seemed to carry or take something away from me; my heart was tortured with anguish, insult, jealousy: here I was, sitting alone over some absurd assignment unworthy of me, demeaning myself for her sake, and she was somewhere out there, on that icy pond surrounded by snowy-white embankments with black spruces, deafened by martial music, bathed in lilac gaslight and strewn with flying black figures—and she was happy there. Suddenly, a ring, and she quickly appeared. She was wearing a gray outfit, a gray squirrel cap, and she held a glistening pair of skates in her hands. Everything in the room was immediately suffused with her youthful, frozen freshness, the beauty of her face, rosy from frost and exercise.

"Whew, am I tired!" she said, and went to her room.

I went after her. She threw herself on the couch and lay back with a smile of exhaustion, still holding the skates in her hands. With an agonizing and by now familiar feeling, I looked at her long laced-up instep, at her leg wrapped in a gray stocking and visible underneath her short gray skirt—the heavy woolen material tormented me with desire all by itself—and I started to reproach her—after all, we hadn't seen each other all day! Then suddenly, with a pang of tenderness and compassion, I saw that she was asleep. . . . Coming to, she answered affectionately and sadly: "I heard almost everything. Don't get angry, I'm really very tired. I've just been through too much this year!"

8

In order to have an excuse to live in Orel, she began to study music. I also found an excuse: work at *The Voice*. At first, I even liked it: I liked that bit of regularity that had entered my existence, and I was calmed by a feeling of obligation that had entered a life otherwise devoid of obligations. Then, more and more frequently, something flickered in my mind: is this the kind of life I had dreamed of? There I was, perhaps in my prime; the whole world should be mine, and I didn't even own a pair of galoshes! Now, is all this just for the present? Well, what's in the future? It began to seem to me that not all was well, either in our intimacy or in the harmony of our feelings, thoughts, tastes, and, naturally, in her faithfulness. That winter I lived through the "eternal schism between dreams and reality," the eternal unrealizability of the fullness and integrity of love, with all the force of the first time, and it all seemed terribly unfair.

Most of all, I was tormented when I went with her to balls, or to visit people. Whenever she would dance with someone handsome, graceful, and whenever I saw her satisfaction, animation, and the quick swishing of her skirt and legs, the music beat painfully in my heart with its cheerful sonority, the waltzes brought me to tears. Everybody watched with pleasure when she danced with Turchaninov—that unnaturally tall officer with the black sideburns, the elongated, dull, and swarthy face and unmoving dark eyes. She was rather tall, but still, he was two heads taller than she. As he grasped her tightly and smoothly, protractedly twirling her, he somehow insistently looked down upon her from above, and in her upturned face I felt something joyous and unhappy, beautiful and at the same time endlessly hateful to me. How I entreated God then for something incredible to happen—for him suddenly to lean over and kiss her, and thereby immediately resolve and corroborate the heavy suspicions that were breaking my heart!

"You think only of yourself, you want everything your way," she once said. "You would, no doubt, gladly deprive me of any personal life, any society, and separate me from everyone the way you separate yourself. . . ."

And, indeed, as if corresponding to some secret law demanding that into any love, and especially love for a woman, a feeling of pity, of sympathetic tenderness must enter, I hated the moments of her happiness, animation, her desire to be popular, to shine, especially in the presence of others—and I passionately loved her simplicity, reticence, meekness, helplessness, and the tears that caused her lips to swell up at once, like a child's. It was true that in society I most often played the alienated, unkind observer, secretly reveling in my alienation and malevolence, keenly honing my impressionability, insight, and perspicacity toward every human inadequacy. But then, how I also wished for intimacy with her, and how I suffered at not attaining it!

I often read poetry to her.

"Listen, this is amazing!" I would exclaim. "To the plangent depths whisk my soul away, where sadness dwells like the moon o'er a glade."[9]

But she failed to experience any amazement.

"Yes, that's very nice," she said, lying comfortably on the sofa, both hands under her cheek, looking sideways, quietly and indifferently. But why 'like the moon o'er a glade'? Is that Fet? He basically has too many nature descriptions."

I was indignant: descriptions! I hastened to point out that nature is in no way separate from ourselves, that the slightest perturbation in the atmosphere means a perturbation in our own lives. She laughed, "Only spiders live that way, my sweet!"

I read:

How sad! The end of the path once more
This morning in powder disappeared
Once more the silvery serpents
Have crawled across the drifts. . . .[10]

She asked, "What kind of serpents?"

And I had to explain that these were snowstorms, blizzards.

And, growing pale, I read:

The frosty night glances dully
out from beneath the top of my carriage. . . .
Beyond the mountains and fields in a haze of clouds
Shines the frowning face of the moon.[11]

"But, my sweet," she said, "you know, I've never seen anything like that!"
I read on, but already with secret reproach:

The ray of sun through the clouds was hot and high,
And you drew in the shining sand by the bench. . . .[12]

She listened approvingly, but this was probably only because she imagined that she herself was sitting in the garden, drawing in the dirt with a cute parasol.

"That is truly charming," she said. "But enough of poetry, come closer . . . you're always cross with me!"

I often told her about my childhood, my early youth, about the poetic charm of our country estate, about my mother, my father, my sister: she listened with relentless indifference. Describing the poverty that had descended upon our family, I sought in her sympathy, tender emotion. For instance, I told her about how we once removed all the antique frames from our icons and took them to the city to pawn with Meshcherinova, a lonely old woman of terrible Eastern visage, hook-nosed and bewhiskered with bulging eyes, covered in silks, shawls, and signet rings, in an empty house crammed with all sorts of museum pieces, through which a parrot cried out all day long in a wild and dead voice. And what did I get instead of sympathy and tender emotion?

"Yes, that's quite horrible," she said inattentively.

The longer I lived in the city, the more I felt quite out of place in it; even Avilova changed toward me for some reason, and became dry and mocking. The more gloomy and boring my city life became, the more often I found myself wanting to be alone with her—to read something, talk, express my opinion. My hotel room was narrow, gray, and I felt terribly sorry for myself: for the little suitcase and few books that made up the whole of my wealth; for the lonely nights that were so barren and cold that I did not so much sleep through them as overcome them, in my sleep awaiting the dawn—the first frosty winter striking of the bell from the neighboring bell tower. Her room was also cramped; it was at the end of the hall, next to the stairs to the mezzanine, but it was peaceful, warm, and well-furnished, and her windows opened onto the garden. At twilight the little coal stove was lit; she could lie in the cushions of the sofa incredibly prettily, all curled up, with her uncommonly beautiful slippers tucked up beneath her. I said:

> The late-night storm howled
> In this empty, forested place.
> I sat down across from her
> As the firewood crackled. . . .[13]

But all these blizzards, forests, and fields, the poetically savage joy of comfort, home, and hearth were especially foreign to her.

For a long time it seemed to me that saying "Do you know those smooth autumn roads, stretched tight like lilac rubber bands, slashed by the thorns of horseshoes and shining beneath the low sun like a blinding golden ribbon?" should be enough to make her ecstatic. I told her how once my brother George and I had gone to buy birch logs in late autumn: the ceiling in our kitchen had suddenly collapsed, almost killing our cook, an old man who was always lying on top of the oven,[14] and so we had gone to the grove to buy this birch for a beam. It had been raining incessantly (small drops, falling quickly through the sun), and we rode at a trot in the cart with some peasants, first on the high road, and then through a grove that stood alone, rainy and glittering in the sun, surprisingly free, beautiful, and obedient, amid the clearings which were still green but already dead, and flooded by the high waters. . . . I told her how I pitied that spreading birch, covered from top to bottom with small rust-colored leaves, as the peasants clumsily and roughly gathered round, looked it over, and then, spitting into savage, creased palms, picked up their axes and happily struck at the black and white speckled trunk. . . . "You can't imagine how horribly wet everything was, how everything glistened and sprayed!" I said, and ended with the confession that I wanted to write a story about it all. She shrugged her shoulders.

"But darling, what is there to write about here? Why just describe nature?"

For me one of life's most complex and poignant delights was music. How I loved her when she played something beautiful! How my soul grew faint from rapturously selfless tenderness for her! How I wanted to live for a long, long time. Often as I listened I thought, "If we part someday, how will I listen to this without her! Indeed, how will I be able to love anything, take delight in anything, without her to share my love and delight!"

But the things I didn't like I judged so harshly that she was quite beside herself.

"Nadya!" she would shout to Avilova, leaving off the keys and turning sharply toward the neighboring room. "Nadya, listen to how he's carrying on!"

"And carry on I will!" I exclaimed. "Three-quarters of each of these sonatas is vulgarity, a mess, pure racket! Awk! now we hear the tapping of the graveyard spades! And here are fairies spinning in the meadow, and now a waterfall thunders! 'Fairy' is one of the words I hate most! It's even worse than the journalese 'fraught'!"

She convinced herself of her passionate love for the theater, and I hated it, growing more and more certain that the talent of most actors and actresses is only their relative skill at vulgarity—the best imitators of creators and artists according to the most vulgar models. All those eternal matchmakers in silk, onion-colored scarves and Turkish shawls, with obsequious grimaces and sugary accents bowing before the Tit Tityches who, with unwavering proud conviction, lean backward and hold an open left hand over their heart over the side pocket of a long frock coat; those porcine mayors and fidgety Khlestakovs, sadly, gutterally wheezing Osips, repellent Repetilovs, foppish indignant Chatskys, those Famusovs, twiddling their fingers and sticking out their plump plumlike actors' lips;[15] those Hamlets in torchbearers' raincoats, in hats with curly feathers, with dissolutely fake eyes, black-velvet thighs, and plebian flat feet—all of that just made me shudder. And opera! Rigoletto, bent in two with his legs forever spread apart and tied together at the knees against all the laws of nature. Susanin, lifelessly and blissfully rolling his eyes up to the sky and letting out a thunderous sound: "Ascend, thee, my sunrise!" The miller from *Rusalka* with twiglike, thin hands flung wide apart, shaking fiercely (but still wearing his wedding ring on his finger) and in such tatters, in such shredded, ragged pants, that it looked as if he had been attacked by a whole pack of rabid dogs.[16] In arguments about the theater she and I never even came close to agreeing: we lost all ability to compromise and reach any mutual understanding. Once a famous provincial actor on tour in Orel starred in *Diary of a Madman,* and everyone watched greedily, delighted by the way he sat in a bathrobe on his hospital bed, with his immoderately unshaven feminine face. For a long time, an insufferably long time, he was silent, frozen in some kind of idiotic gladness and ever-growing astonishment. Then he quietly raised his finger, and at last, unbelievably slowly, with unbearable expressiveness, twisting his jaw horribly, he began, syllable by syllable: "On th-is da-y . . ." Then, on the next day, he imitated Lyubim Tortsov even more magnificently; and on the third day, the purple-nosed, greasy Marmeladov: "May I venture, my dear sir, to engage you in pleasant conversation?" Then a famous actress penned a letter onstage: suddenly having decided to write something fateful and hurriedly sitting down at the table, she dipped the dry quill into the dry inkpot, and in one moment drew three long lines on the paper, stuffed it into an envelope, jingled the bell, and shortly, drily commanded the nice maid in the white apron who had just appeared, "Quick, dispatch this by messenger!"[17] After every such evening at the theater we would scream at each other until three o'clock in the morning, keeping Avilova awake, and I started cursing not only Gogol's Madman, Tortsov, and Marmeladov, but even Gogol, Ostrovsky, Dostoevsky. . . .

"Okay, say you're right," she would shout, her face pale and her eyes dark, and thus looking especially charming, "all the same, why do you need to fly into such a fury? Nadya, ask him!"

"Because," I would shout back in reply, "just for the way that actor pronounced the word 'aroma'—'a-ro-ma'! I could strangle him!"

And the same shouting always erupted after evenings spent with people from Orel high society. I passionately wanted to share with her the joy derived from my powers of observation. Steeled in observation, I wanted to infect her with my merciless attitude toward the world around us, but I despairingly saw that nothing came of trying to make her an accomplice to my thoughts and feelings except the exact opposite. I once said, "If only you knew how many enemies I have!"

"What enemies? Where?" she asked.

"All kinds, everywhere: in the hotel, in stores, on the street, in the station. . . ."

"And just who are these enemies?"

"Oh, everyone, everyone! What a collection of loathsome faces and bodies! Even the apostle Paul said, 'Not all flesh is flesh, for human flesh is different from animal. . . .' Some are simply horrific! How they place their feet when they walk, holding their bodies inclined as if they had gotten up from their hands and knees only yesterday! Yesterday I walked for a long time along Bolkhov Street behind a broad-shouldered, fleshy police officer, not taking my eyes off the overcoat covering his fat back, or off his calves encased in shiny, firmly bulging boots: ah, how I gobbled up those boots, their bootish smell, the smooth wool of that fine gray overcoat, the buttons on its waistband and that entire strong forty-year-old animal decked out in full military harness!"

"You should be ashamed of yourself!" she said, with squeamish reproach. "Can it really be true that you are so evil, so vile? I don't understand you at all. You're a mass of amazing contradictions!"

9

And all the same, arriving at the editorial office in the mornings, I greeted her gray coat in the cloakroom ever more joyfully and warmly. It was as if she herself were in it, some very feminine part of her, and beneath the hanger, her dear gray boots, the most touching of all. In my impatience to see her as soon as possible, I arrived earlier than everyone, sat down to my work—I looked over and corrected the local stories, read the big-city newspapers, compiled "exclusive bylines" from them, practically rewrote several stories by local belletrists, and all the while I listened, waited. Then, at last: quick steps, the rustle of a skirt! She ran up, looking completely new, with cool, fragrant hands, with a youthful sparkle in her eyes that shined even brighter after her deep sleep, hastily looked around, and kissed me. In just the same way, now and then she would drop into the hotel, smelling frostily of her fur coat and the wintry air. I would kiss her apple-cold face, and embrace all that warmth and tenderness beneath her coat, her body and dress. Laughing, she would dodge me: "Let go! I came on business!" She would call the valet, order him to clean the room, and she herself would help him. . . .

Once I accidentally overheard a conversation between her and Avilova. They were sitting one evening in the dining room and talking about me frankly, thinking that I was at the typographer's. Avilova asked, "Lika, dear, but what happens next? You know my attitude toward him; he is, of course, a dear, and I understand that you have fallen for him. . . . But what next?"

It was as if the ground had opened up beneath me. So, I'm "a dear"— nothing more! And she'd done nothing more than "fallen for me"!

The answer was even worse.

"But what can I do? I see no way out. . . ."

At those words such fury flared up in me that I was ready to charge into the dining room and shout that there was a way out, that within an hour's time there would be neither hide nor hair of me in Orel, when she suddenly said: "Nadya, how is it you don't see that I really love him! And furthermore, you simply don't know him—he's a thousand times better than he appears. . . ."

Yes, I could seem much worse than I was. I lived tensely, nervously, often treating people cruelly and arrogantly, and I easily slipped into despair, melancholy; however, I could easily change as soon I saw that nothing threatened our harmony, that no one was pursuing her. Then, my innate disposition to be good, lighthearted, and cheery would be immediately restored. If I knew that we were going to a party at which I would be neither insulted nor hurt, how gladly would I prepare! How I liked myself as I looked in the mirror, admiring my eyes, the dark circles of youthful flush on my cheeks, my snow-white shirt, whose starched folds opened, separated with an enchanting crackle! How balls delighted me, if I did not suffer from jealousy there. Before each ball I lived through cruel moments—I had to wear the tails that had belonged to Avilova's deceased husband—completely new, it is true, seemingly never worn, yet they cut me to the quick. But those minutes were easily forgotten—it was only necessary to leave the house, breathe in the frost, see the speckled starry sky, quickly climb into a hired sleigh. . . . God knows why they decorated the bright glittering entryways to ballrooms with red-striped awnings, why the policemen, directing traffic, danced around with such fury in front of them! But, so what; it was still a ball, a strange entryway, illuminated brightly and whitely by the hot light mixed with sugary snow, and all that play of quickness and harmony, the crisp cry of the police, policemen's whiskers frozen into a straight line, shiny boots trampling the snow, hands in white knitted gloves somehow peculiarly twisted out and hidden in pockets.

Practically every arriving gentleman was in uniform—there were many uniforms at that time in Russia—and everyone was defiantly excited by his rank, uniform—even then I had noticed that people, even those who have held various high positions and titles all their lives, never, throughout their whole lives, get accustomed to them. Those arriving men always excited me and immediately became the objects of my intense and hostile observation. But, on the other hand, the women were almost all pretty, desirable. In the vestibule, they charmingly divested themselves of furs and bonnets, turning into just the kind of people who should be walking along the red carpet up the wide staircase, in mirror-multiplied crowds. And then there was the magnificent emptiness of a hall just before a ball, its fresh coldness; the heavy grapelike cluster of the chandelier, playing with diamondlike radiance, the gigantic, bare windows, the sheen and fleetingly free open space of the parquet; the scent of fresh flowers, powders, perfumes, white kid gloves—and all that excitement of watching the arriving ball-goers, the anticipation of the resonance of the orchestra's first thunder, of the first pair, suddenly flying out into that expanse of still virginal hall, that pair always the most confident, the most graceful.

I always left for the ball earlier than they. When I got there, the arrivals would still be going on below; they were still piling strong-smelling coats, jackets, and overcoats onto the servants, and the air everywhere was too cold for a thin suit. In those strange tails, with a smooth coiffure, slender, as if I had grown still thinner, I stood easily, alien, alone—a strangely proud young man, playing some strange role at the editorial office—I felt at first so sober, clear, and so distant from everyone else that I imagined myself an icy mirror. Then everything became more peopled and noisy, the music thundered more familiarly, people were already crowding through the doors of the ballroom, the women had arrived, and the air turned thicker, warmer. As if tipsy, I started to look at the women more boldly and at the men more arrogantly, and I slipped through the crowd rhythmically, excusing myself, getting tangled up in some tails or uniform, ever more courteous and haughty. . . . Then suddenly I spied them—there they were, cautiously, with half-smiles, making their way through the crowd—and my heart stopped warmly, and somehow awkwardly and amazedly: they but not they; the same and yet not the same. Especially she—she was completely different! Each time at this moment I was astonished by her youthfulness, litheness: her figure constrained by her corset, the light and innocently festive dress, her arms bare from her gloves to her shoulders, freezing, stationary, adolescently lilac, the still uncertain expression on her face . . . only her hair was gathered high like that of the fashionable beauties. There was something especially attractive in that, but at the same time somehow already prepared to be free of me, to betray me, and even an inclination toward secret depravity. Soon someone would approach her and, with habitual ballroom haste, bow quickly. She would hand over her fan to Avilova, and with a certain absentmindedness she would graciously lay her hand on his shoulder, and circling, sliding on her toes, she would disappear, getting lost in the gyrating crowd, noise, music. And I, as if parting forever and with cold enmity, watched her go.

Small, lively, and always sturdily and cheerfully disposed, Avilova also surprised me at the ball with her youth and radiant good looks. Once, at a ball, I suddenly realized that she was all of twenty-six, and for the first time, not daring to believe it, I guessed the reason for her change toward me that winter—it could have been that she loved me and was jealous of me.

10

Then we parted for a long time.

It all started when the doctor arrived unexpectedly.

Entering the hallway at the editorial office one sunny frosty morning, I suddenly noticed the strong smell of some very familiar cigarettes and heard lively voices and laughter in the dining room. I stopped—what was going on? It turned out that it was the doctor who had smoked up the whole building, he who was talking loudly and with the liveliness of the kind of person who, having reached a certain age, remains there without any change whatsoever for years on end, enjoying his excellent condition, incessant smoking, and unending garrulousness. I was dumbfounded—what did this sudden arrival mean? Some kind of demands on her? And how should I enter, how should I behave? Nothing terrible happened, however, for the first few minutes. I quickly collected myself, went in, and was pleasantly astounded. . . . The doctor, in his kindness, was even a little embarrassed, and he hurried, laughing and almost apologizing, to declare that he had come "to get a break from the provinces for a week." I noticed at once that she was excited. For some reason, Avilova was also excited. All the same, one could hope that this was all due to the doctor, an unexpected guest who had just arrived on a trip to the big city from the provinces and was therefore drinking hot tea with special liveliness in someone else's dining room after a night on the train. I had already started to calm down. But then came the blow: from all the doctor said, I suddenly understood that he had not come alone, but with Bogomolov: a young, rich, well-known currier in our city, who had had his eye on her for some time; and then I heard the doctor's laughter: "He says he's insanely in love with you, Lika! He's come with the most definite intentions! And thus the fate of this unfortunate rests fully in your control. If you want him, he's spared; if you don't, you destroy him forever. . . ."

But Bogomolov was not only rich. He was smart, lively, and pleasant, had graduated from the university and lived abroad, spoke two foreign languages. His appearance could scare you at first: bright-red hair smoothly combed straight back and a tender round face, but he was enormously, inhumanly fat—either some kind of fantastically overfed baby grown to a wholly unnatural magnitude, or a young Yorkshire hog, huge, with fat and flesh positively luminous throughout. Still, everything about this Yorkshire hog was so splendid, clean, and healthy, that you were overjoyed by it: the blue eyes—a heavenly azure—the color of the face, ineffable in its purity; in all aspects, his laughter, the sound of his voice, the play of his eyes and lips, there was something bashful and endearing. His hands and feet were poignantly small, his clothes of English cloth: socks, shirt, tie—all silk. I glanced at her quickly, saw her uncomfortable smile. . . . And everything suddenly became alien to me, far away. I suddenly felt shamefully extraneous and unnecessary to the whole house. I was filled with hatred for her. . . .

After that we could never spend even an hour in private; her father or Bogomolov were always with her. A sly grin never left Avilova's face. She showed Bogomolov such courtesy and hospitality that from the first day he made himself completely at home, appearing in the morning and staying till the late evening, only spending nights at the hotel. In addition, the amateur drama club to which Lika belonged had started rehearsals. The club was preparing for a performance at Carnival and, through her, drew not only Bogomolov but the doctor himself into small roles. She said she accepted Bogomolov's wooing only for the sake of her father, in order not to insult him by being curt with Bogomolov, and I braced myself in every way, pretended I believed her, even forced myself to attend those rehearsals, trying in this way to hide my extreme jealousy and also the other torments I experienced at them: I didn't know what to do with myself, so embarrassed did I feel for her, for her pitiful attempts at "acting." And what a horrendous spectacle of human ungiftedness the whole thing was! The rehearsals were led by a professional, an unemployed actor who considered himself, naturally, a major talent, who reveled in his vile dramatic experience, a man of indeterminate age, with a face the color of putty and with such deep wrinkles that they looked like they had been made on purpose. He would repeatedly lose his temper, giving instructions as to how to play some role or other, would swear so crudely and rabidly that the sclerotic veins on his temples would pop out like cords, would himself play both male and female roles. Everybody struggled madly to imitate him, torturing me with each vocal expression, each bodily motion: no matter how unbearable that actor was, his imitators were worse. And why, to what end, did they act? Among them was a regimental woman of the kind found in every provincial city, bony, self-assured, impertinent; and there was a wildly costumed girl, always anxious, always waiting for something, who had mastered a manner of biting her lips. There were two sisters, known throughout the town for their inseparability and striking resemblance to one another: both tall scraggly brunettes, with black over-grown eyebrows, sternly silent—a genuine pair of black cart horses. There was a bureaucrat without portfolio for the governor: a blond with blue bug-eyes under red eyelids, very young but already balding, very tall, in a very tall collar, exhaustingly polite and delicate. There was a famous local lawyer, portly, enormous, barrel-chested, wide-shouldered, with large feet—when I spied him at balls in coat and tails I always took him to be the maitre d'. And there was a young artist: black velvet smock, long Hindu hair, a goatish profile replete with goatee, with the effeminate depravity of half-closed eyes and ten-der bright-red lips that were awkward to look at, the hips of a woman. . . .

Then came the performance itself. Before the curtain I wanted to poke around backstage: they were going mad, dressing, making themselves up, yelling, arguing, running out of the dressing rooms, bumping into each other and not recognizing each other, so strangely were they dressed (someone even had on a brown tailcoat with violet pants) and so dead were their wigs and beards, their immobile faces daubed with makeup and pink-plaster paste-ons attached to their lips and noses, with fake, sparkling eyes, with darkened, thick and heavy, winking eyelashes, as on mannequins. I ran into her and didn't recognize her either; I was amazed by her doll-likeness—her pink, gracefully outdated dress, thick blond wig, and the comic-strip attrac-tiveness and childishness of a treacly face. . . . Bogomolov played a yellow-haired janitor—they decked him out with special expressiveness to fit the picture of an "everyday type." The doctor played an old man, a retired gen-eral: he even began the performance, wearing a brand-new seersucker suit, sitting out in the country in a wicker chair under a green tree made of planks, which stood on the naked floor. He, too, was rouged, with enormous cotton-candy moustaches, and he leaned back in the chair, self-importantly looking at an unfurled newspaper. Despite the wonderful summer morning of the set, he was lit brightly from below by the footlights, astoundingly young-look-ing even with all his gray hair. He was supposed to say something deeply querulous after reading the paper, but he only stared, unable to say anything, not paying attention to the frantic hissing from the prompter's box: only when she sprung out from the wings at last (with childishly playful, charm-ingly sportive laughter), flung herself at him from behind, and covered his eyes with her hands, shouting, "Guess who?" only then did he yell too, artic-ulating each syllable: "Let go, let go, silly goat, I know perfectly well who!"

The auditorium was half-lit, the stage was bright, striking. Sitting in the first row, I glanced first at the stage and then around me: my row was made up of the very richest civilians smothered by their plentitude and the highest-ranking officials, as well as police and military figures. Everyone was com-pletely fixated by what was happening on stage—tense poses and unfinished smiles. . . . I couldn't even sit through the first act. As soon as something

185

tapped on the stage—a sign that the curtain would soon fall—I left. There, on the stage, they had let themselves go completely. In the well-lit and natural vestibule an old man used to everything helped me on with my coat, while the especially unnatural perky exclamations of the artists wafted out to us.

Finally I darted out onto the street. A feeling of destructive loneliness mounted within me to a kind of ecstasy. It was deserted, clean, and the streetlights shone motionlessly. I did not go home—for in my narrow room at the hotel it was already too terrible—but to the editorial office. I walked past the government offices and turned onto the empty square, in the middle of which rose the cathedral, its barely shining gold cupola lost in the starry heavens. . . . Even in the crunching of my feet on the snow there was something elevated, terrible. . . . It was quiet and peaceful in the warm house; the clock ticked slowly in the illuminated dining room. Avilova's little boy was asleep, and the nanny, having let me in, looked at me sleepily and left. I walked to that room beneath the stairs, already so familiar to me and so special, and sat in the darkness on the familiar and now somehow fateful divan. . . . And I waited, and was terrified of that moment when they would suddenly arrive, enter noisily, and, vying with one another, begin to talk, laugh, sit at the samovar, and share their impressions. More than anything I feared the instant when her laugh, her voice, would ring out. . . . The room was full of her; her absence and presence, all of her smells, she herself, her dresses, perfumes, and her soft housecoat, lying next to me on the pillows of the divan. . . . Through the window the winter night grew menacingly blue, and beyond the black branches of the trees in the garden the stars twinkled. . . .

During the first week of Lent she left with her father and Bogomolov (having turned him down). I had long since ceased even speaking to her. She got ready for the journey, crying all the while, always hoping that I would suddenly delay her, not let her go.

11

The days of Lent arrived in the provinces. Cabbies without a fare stood on the street corners, shivering, occasionally waving their crossed arms desperately and timidly hailing a passing officer: "Your honor! On the double?" Jackdaws, sensing that it would soon be spring, chattered nervously and with animation, but the crows continued to caw harshly and sharply.

Separation seemed especially horrible at night. Waking in the middle of the night, I was always stunned: how could I live now and what could I live for? Was it really I who was lying in the darkness of these meaningless nights for some reason, in some provincial capital, home to thousands of strangers, in this room with its narrow window, gray the whole night like some kind of tall, mute devil? In the whole city there was only one person I was close to—Avilova. But were we really close? It was an ambiguous and uncomfortable closeness. . . .

These days I arrived at the editorial office late. Avilova would smile joyfully when she saw me in the hall from the waiting room; she had again become sweet, affectionate, left off teasing me. Now I invariably saw her tranquil love toward me, her constant attention and thoughtfulness, and often spent whole evenings together with her. She would play to me for hours, and I would lie half-reclining on the divan, with eyes closed by the gathering tears of musical happiness and with the especially acute feelings of loving pain and all-forgiving tenderness that went with them. Entering the waiting room, I kissed her small firm hand and went to the room for regular employees. Our editorial writer was smoking there: a stupid, pensive man, exiled to Orel under the supervision of the police, rather strange-looking. He wore a peasant beard, a long, heavy brown coat, and blacked boots, which smelled quite strongly and pleasantly, and was left-handed besides: half of his right one was missing, and with the remainder of it, hidden in his sleeve, he would pin down a sheet of paper on the table while writing with his left. He would sit for a long time and think, smoke heavily, and suddenly pin the sheet down firmly and begin to scribble and scribble—strongly, quickly, and with simian agility. Next a short-legged old man in amazing glasses entered: the foreign columnist. In the hall he removed his long pleated coat of rabbit fur and his Finnish hat with earflaps; afterward, in his boots, wide trousers, and flannel shirt, belted with a small strap, he looked as small and frail as if he were ten years old. His thick dull-gray hair stuck out very far and sternly, and in various directions, which made him look like a porcupine; his glasses were also stern. He always carried two little boxes in his hands, a box of rolling papers and a box of tobacco, and at work he was always rolling cigarettes. Habitually looking at the metropolitan newspaper, he rolled and stuffed the light fibrous tobacco into a little machine, in its hinged copper tube, and absentmindedly groped for the papers; he pressed the arm of the machine against his chest, in the soft blouse, and deftly shot a cigarette out onto the table.

Then the layout editor and the copy editor stopped by. The layout editor came in calmly, independently; his politeness was amazing, as was his silence and his impenetrability. He was uncommonly thin and dry, with gypsy-black hair, an olive-green face, a dark moustache, and deathly, ash-gray lips. He always dressed with extreme care and cleanliness: black trousers, a light-blue shirt, a high starched collar perched above it: everything sparkled cleanly and newly. I sometimes spoke with him at the typographer's: then he would break his silence and look me in the eye evenly and intently with his dark eyes and would speak like a machine, without raising his voice and always on the same subject: the injustice that reigned in the world, always, everywhere, and in everything. The copy editor also stopped in by the by; there was always something he didn't understand or approve of in any given article he was editing, and he would ask the author of the article to change or explain: "I beg your pardon, but here it's not written quite felicitously." He was fat, clumsy, with tightly curled and somehow slightly wet hair, stooped from nervousness and fear that everyone would see that he was terribly drunk. He leaned toward the person from whom he had asked an explanation, holding his alcoholic breath, pointing from afar with a trembling and glistening, swollen hand to the line that was not quite clear or successful from his point of view. Sitting in this room I absentmindedly corrected various pieces written by other people, but more than anything else I stared out the window and thought: how and what should I myself write?

I now had one more secret suffering, one more bitter "unrealizable goal." Again I began to write things—now mostly prose—and again I began to publish what I wrote. But I didn't think about what I wrote and published. I was tormented by the desire to write something altogether different, something quite unlike what I was able to write and did write, something I was incapable of writing. To create in yourself something truly worth writing about from what life has given you—what rare happiness, and what psychological labor! And so my life turned more and more into this struggle with the "unrealizable goal," to the search for and capturing of this different but also ineffable happiness, to the pursuit of it, and to the incessant contemplation of it.

The mail came at noon. I went into the hallway and again saw the beautifully and carefully coiffed head of Avilova, invariably bent over her work. Everything about her was sweet, from the soft shine of her shagreen slippers under the desk to the fur wrap on her shoulders, which also shone with the lustre of the gray winter day and the winter window, beyond which was the raven-gray snowy sky. I took the new issue of a big-city journal from the mail and quickly tore it open. . . . A new Chekhov short story![18] There was something in the mere sight of that name that made me glance at the story—I could not even read through the beginning without feeling the envious pangs of delight it promised. Meanwhile, more people showed up in the waiting room, and they in turn gave way to others: those wanting to place advertisements came, as did a multitude of the most diverse people, all of whom were also possessed by the lust for writing. Among these was an old man with noble features in a downy scarf and down-filled mittens, holding a whole stack of cheap legal-sized paper on which stood the title "Songs and Thoughts," traced out with all the calligraphic brilliance of the age of goose quills; a young-looking officer, crimson with embarrassment, handed over his manuscript with the terse and politely firm request that it be looked over and, if accepted for publication, by all means without revealing the author's

188

real name—"Put down only the initials, if the editorial board deems that permissible"; behind the officer stood a middle-aged priest, perspiring from nervousness and his fur coat, who wanted to publish his "Village Sketches" under the pseudonym Spectateur; behind the clergyman was the district attorney. . . . This district attorney was a man of unusual fastidiousness; in the hall, with almost weird deliberation, he removed his new galoshes, his new fur-lined gloves, his new polecat jacket, his new fur hat. He turned out to be uncommonly tall, thin, toothy and clean, and he wiped his moustache with a snow-white handkerchief for nearly half an hour. All the while I greedily followed his every move, reveling in my writerly perspicacity.

"Yes, yes, he must certainly be clean, fastidious, unhurried, and thoughtful, since he is so rare-toothed and thickly moustached. . . . since his prominent brow already grows bald as an apple, his eyes sparkle clearly, consumptive spots burn on his cheeks, he has large and flat feet, and large and flat hands with big rounded nails!"

At lunchtime the nanny would return from her walk with the boy. Avilova would run into the hall, squat down agilely, remove his white lambskin cap, unfasten his long dark-blue and white lambskin coat, and kiss his fresh, flushed little face, while he absentmindedly stared into space, thinking something of his own, far away, indifferently allowing himself to be undressed and kissed. I caught myself envying it all: the boy's blissful vacancy, Avilova's maternal joy, the nanny's senile silence. I had begun to envy anyone whose life was filled with ready-made cares and worries, as opposed to expectation, the invention of things for what is in some ways the strangest of all human endeavors, the calling of the writer. I envied all who had simple, direct, definite duties that, when performed today, left them quite easy and free until tomorrow.

After lunch I went out. In the city the Lenten snow fell thickly in drowsy flakes, the kind of snow that, with its delicate, especially bright whiteness, fools you into thinking that spring is already quite near. A carefree cabby careened past me soundlessly through the snow—having just drunk a quick one somewhere, no doubt—looking ready for something good and fine. . . . What could have been more ordinary? But at that moment everything— almost every fleeting impression—struck me and, having struck, engendered an impulse not to let it, this impression, be wasted or vanish without a trace, to capture it immediately as my own with the lightning of useful aspiration, and to extract something from it. Here he flashed by, this cabby, and everything, how and why he flashed by, flashed sharply in my soul as well, and it left a kind of strange trace of what had just flashed there—how long and vainly it tormented my soul! Farther on was an opulent entranceway; near the sidewalk the black body of a lacquered carriage showed through the white flakes, and you seemed to see the black mark of the greasy tires of its rear wheels, which, partly submerged in the old snow, were being covered by the new. I walked by and looked at the towering spine of the thick-shouldered driver on the coach box, belted like a child under the armpits in a fat, pillowlike velvet jacket. And then I suddenly saw, behind the glass door of the carriage, inside that satin *bonbonnière*, an incredibly cute little dog, sitting, shaking, and staring intently as if it were just about to speak, with ears that looked like a bow. And again, just like lightning, that joy: ah, don't forget—like a real bow!

I stopped in at the library. It was an old library, unusually well endowed. But how depressing it was, how unnecessary! An old, neglected building, a gigantic bare foyer, the cold staircase to the second floor, the torn felt-upholstered oilcloth door; three rooms, filled from top to bottom with shaggy, frayed books; a long counter, a desk, the young, flat-chested, unfriendly quiet head librarian in a kind of black Lenten dress, with thin, pale hands and an inkstain on her index finger, and a neglected lad in a gray shirt, with soft, mousy, uncut hair who carried out her orders. . . . I went to the "reading room," a round room that smelled of soot with a round table in the middle on which lay *The Diocesan Gazette* and *The Russian Pilgrim.* . . . A single unchanging reader sat at the table; stooped over, and with an almost secretive manner, he leafed through the pages of a thick book. He was a skinny youth, a high-school student in a short shabby overcoat, constantly wiping his nose with a balled-up handkerchief. Who else would sit there besides us two, equally unusual because we were both alone in the entire city and because we both read? For a high-school student he was reading something quite unbelievable—Soshnye writings.[19] The librarian looked at me in amazement more than once as well: I asked for *The Northern Bee, Moscow Herald, The Polar Star, Northern Flowers,* Pushkin's *Contemporary.* . . . [20] At the same time I checked out all the new things, too—all the *Biographies of Famous People*—in order to find some sort of support for myself in them, to compare myself enviously with famous people. . . . *Famous People!* What a countless number of poets, novelists, and storytellers there had been in the world, and how many of them had lasted? The same names for all the ages! Homer, Horace, Virgil, Dante, Petrarch . . . Shakespeare, Byron, Shelley, Goethe . . . Racine, Molière . . . that same *Don Quixote,* that same *Manon Lescaut* . . . In that room, I remember, I read Radishchev for the first time with much delight. "I looked around—my soul began to sting from the sufferings of mankind!"[21]

Leaving the library in the evening, I walked quietly along the darkening street. Here and there, a slow peal hung in the air. Languishing with melancholy about myself and about her and about my distant home, I stopped into a church. This again was something unnecessary. Emptiness, semidarkness, the flames of sparse candles, several old men and women. At the counter, selling candles, stood a church elder, unmoving, sedate, with gray hair parted peasant-style, casting about his eyes with a merchant's severity. The guard barely dragged his worn-out legs from one place to another, straightening a leaning, overly hot melting candle here, blowing out one sputtering there, circulating the scent of wax and soot, and then squeezing it in his ancient fist along with other candle ends into a ball of wax. It was clear how deeply tired he was of our incomprehensible earthly existence and all its mysteries: the christenings, Eucharists, weddings, funerals, and all the holidays, all the fasts passing in eternal procession from year to year. The priest, in just a robe, unusually slim without a chasuble, domestically, femininely bareheaded, stood facing the closed holy gate, deeply genuflecting. His cross drooped and fell from his chest, and then, with a sigh, he raised his voice, sending it out into the sad, repentent dusk, into the melancholy emptiness: "God, sovereign of my life. . . ." Quietly leaving the church, I again inhaled the near-spring winter air, saw the bluish-gray twilight. Bowing his thick gray head low before me, with affected humility, was a beggar, holding his palm out like a scoop, ready to catch and grip a coin cast his way. He glanced at me and suddenly amazed me: the watery turquoise eyes of a chronic alcoholic and his giant strawberry nose, a triplet composed of three huge, bumpy, and porous strawberries. . . . ah! again how painfully joyful: a triple strawberry nose!

I went down Bolkhov Street under the darkening sky. The outlines of the rooftops of the old houses worry the sky, and there is an incomprehensible calming charm to these outlines. The old shelter of humanity—who wrote about that? The streetlamps were being lit, the windows of the stores warmly brightened, the passersby grew dark against the sidewalk, the evening turned blue, like bluing, and the city became sweet, cozy. . . . Like a detective, I followed one pedestrian after another, watching his back, his galoshes, trying to understand something, to catch it, to enter into him. . . . To write! Yes, I had to write about rooftops, about galoshes, about backs, and not at all in order to "fight tyranny and violence, to defend the oppressed and destitute, to create striking characters, to draw broad pictures of the public, of contemporary life, its mood and tendencies!" I quickened my steps and went down to the river. The evening was turning into night, the gas lamp on the bridge already burned brightly, and beneath the light he was bent over, thrusting his hands under his arms, doglike; looking at me, doglike, he kept shaking with a huge shake, and he dully muttered, "Your honor!" He stood barefoot right on the snow, with red paws, a golden mouth, in a ragged chintz shirt and short rose-colored underwear, with a swollen pimply face and turbidly icy eyes. Quickly, like a thief, I captured him, internalized him, and slipped him a silver coin. . . . Life is horrible!

But is it really "horrible"? Maybe it is something entirely different than a "horror"? The other day I had thrust a nickel toward just such a barefooted beggar and naively exclaimed, "All the same, it is horrible that you live this way!" and you should have seen the unexpected insolence, firmness, and anger with which he hoarsely cried out in reply to my foolishness, "There is absolutely nothing horrible about it, young man!" And past the bridge, on the first floor of a large house, the mirrored store window of a sausage shop shined dazzlingly, draped so richly and colorfully with sausages and hams that it was almost impossible to make out the white, bright interior of the store, festooned with meat from top to bottom. "Social contrasts!" I thought caustically, to spite someone while passing by the bright glow of the shop window. On Moscow Street I stopped into a cabbies' tearoom and sat in its hum of voices, crowdedness, and steamy warmth, watched the meaty, scarlet faces, the reddish beards, the peeling, rusty tray on which there were two white teapots with moist cords joining their tops to their handles . . . . an observation of the people's daily life? Not at all—it is just that tray, that moist cord!

12

From time to time I went to the railroad station. Past the triumphal arches the darkness began, a provincial nighttime no-man's-land. And so I pictured in my mind some kind of provincial town, unknown, unreal, existing solely in my imagination, but as if my whole life had taken place in it. I saw wide, snow-covered streets, shanties darkening in the snow, a red flame in one of them. . . . And I repeated to myself ecstatically: yes, yes, just write it like that . . . nothing more! Just three words: snow, hut, a lamp. A country winter breeze already carried the shrieks of the locomotives, their hissing and the sweet smell of coal, which evokes a deep soul-stirring sense of distance. Coming toward me were dark cabs with passengers—had the Moscow mail arrived already? And so it had—the buffet heated by the crowd, the lights, the smells of the kitchen and the samovar, Tatar waiters with spreading, blowing coattails, all bow-legged, dark-faced, high-cheekboned, and horsey-eyed, with round, close-trimmed, blue-gray heads like cannonballs. . . . At the common table sat a whole merchant community from the sect of eunuchs eating cold sturgeon with horseradish: large, effeminate, saffron-colored faces, narrow eyes, and fox-fur coats.[22] . . . The book stand at the station was always a great delight for me—like a hungry wolf, I circled round, attracted, studying the names on the yellow and gray spines of Suvorin's books.[23] But all of that so whet my eternal thirst for the road, for train cars, and turned into such yearning for her with whom I would have been inexpressibly happy to go anywhere, that I hurried off, scurrying into a cab and speeding along to the city, to the editorial office. What a wonderful combination—heartache and speed! Sitting in the sleigh, diving and bumping from pothole to pothole, I looked up—the night turned out to be moonlit. A pale face shines through the hazily passing winter clouds, flashes white. How high, how different from everything else! The clouds pass, uncovering it, and then again covering it over—it makes no difference, they mean nothing to it. I hold my head tilted back until it hurts, not taking my eyes off it and trying to guess when it will suddenly roll out from under the clouds, shining: what is it like? The white mask of a corpse? All the luminescence coming from within; but what is it like? Stearin? Yes, yes, stearin! I'll say that somewhere!

In the entryway, I ran into an amazed Avilova.

"Oh, just in time! We're going to a concert!"

She was wearing something black and lacy, very beautiful, that made her look even smaller, thinner, uncovering her shoulders, arms, and the tender top of her breasts. Her hair had been styled, and she was lightly powdered, which made her eyes seem even brighter, darker. I helped her on with her coat, restraining myself with great difficulty from not suddenly kissing that close naked body, curled fragrant hair. . . .

On a stage illuminated by all the chandeliers in the hall were some metropolitan celebrities: a beautiful woman and a gigantic dark man, both singers. Like all singers, he was strikingly robust, with the extraordinary crude strength of a young stallion. Glittering with lacquered shoes on huge feet, an amazingly sewn suit, a white chest and white tie, he defiantly and heroically thundered about courage, bravery, and fateful obligations. She, sometimes with him and sometimes separately, answered quickly, interrupting him with tender reproaches, complaints, passionate sadness, and ecstatic joy, hastily happy, laughing *fioritura*. . . .

13

I often got up at the crack of dawn. Looking at my watch, I saw that it wasn't even seven yet. I wanted passionately to wrap myself in the blanket again and to lie in the warmth a while longer; it was cold and gray in the room, in the darkness of the still sleeping hotel only the earliest sounds could be heard— the rustling of the valet's clothes brush somewhere at the end of the corridor, with a click at each button. But I was possessed by such a fear of spending another day in vain, possessed by such impatience to begin as quickly as possible—and today to do it right—to seat myself behind the desk, that I followed the sound, and urgently chased its jingling. How alien and repulsive everything was: the hotel, the filthy porter rustling his clothes brush somewhere, the squalid sheet-metal washbasin from which an icy stream hit the side of my face! How pitiful my youthful thinness in my gossamer nightshirt, how stiff the pigeon bunching itself into a ball beyond the glass on the granular snow of the windowsill! My soul was suddenly engulfed by a happy, audacious resolve: no! go back there this very day, to Baturino, to my wonderful, familiar house!

Nevertheless, having quickly drunk some tea and gathered up a few books that were lying on the junky table, which was propped up alongside the sink against the door to the next room, in which a faded sadly pretty woman lived with her eight-year-old son, I plunged headlong into my usual morning routine: preparing myself for writing, for the intense investigation of what was inside me, for the search within myself for something that, it seemed, would soon take shape, turn into something. . . . I awaited the moment, and was already terrified that again, again the episode would end only in expectation, growing agitation, cold hands, and then total despair and flight somewhere into town, to the editorial office. In my head, everything was muddled again. It was all excruciatingly arbitrary, disordered, a multitude of the most varied feelings, thoughts, ideas. . . . The most fundamental things were always my own, personal; did other people really concern me then, despite how much I observed them? So, I thought, maybe just start a story about myself? But how? Along the lines of *Childhood, Boyhood?*[24] Or still simpler? "I was born in a certain place at a certain time. . . ." But, lord, how dry, shallow—and fake! I didn't feel that at all! It was embarrassing and awkward to say, but that's how it was: I was born in the universe, in an infinitude of time and space where, supposedly, a solar system formed at some time, then something called the sun, then the earth. . . . But what is this really? What do I know about it except empty words? At first, the earth was a gaseous, luminescent mass. . . . Then, after millions of years, that gas became a liquid. Then the liquid solidified, and, supposedly, after that another two million years or so passed, then one-celled creatures appeared: algae, protozoa. . . . And then, the invertebrates: worms, mollusks. . . . And then amphibians. . . . And after the amphibians, giant reptiles. . . . And then some kind of cave man and the fire he discovered. . . . Later on, some Chaldea, Assyria, some Egypt, where it seemed that all they did was build pyramids and embalm mummies. Then some Xerxes, who ordered the conquest of Hellespont. . . . Pericles and Aspasia, the battle of Thermopylae, the battle of Marathon. . . . However, long before all that had been the legendary days when Abraham arose with his flocks and went to the Promised Land. . . . "In his faith, Abraham obeyed the call to go to the land promised him as his legacy, and he set forth, not knowing whither he went. . . ." Yes, not knowing! Just like me! "In his faith, obeyed the call. . . ." Faith in what? In the loving goodness of God's behest. "And set forth, not knowing whither. . . ." No, he knew: toward some happiness—that is, toward something that would be kind, good, would give happiness; that is, some feelings of love, life. . . . That is how I had always lived, only on that which induces love, happiness. . . .

On the other side of the door beyond the table, voices could already be heard, a woman's and a child's. She pumped the basin's treadle, water splashed, the tea boiled, the entreaties began: "Kostyenka, come on, eat your roll!" I got up and started to pace around the room. Kostyenka again. . . . Having given him tea, his mother would go off somewhere till noon. When she returned, she cooked something on the kerosene stove, fed him, and went off again. And what a torment it was to watch Kostyenka, who had become a kind of hotel brat. He spent the whole day wandering from room to room, looking in on one tenant, then another if he should be in, timidly saying something, at times trying to ingratiate himself by saying something obsequious; but no one listened to him, and some even chased him away, muttering, "Get along now sonny, don't bother me please!" In one room lived a small old lady, very serious, very proper, who considered herself above all the ordinary tenants and always passed through the halls not look-ing at anyone she came across, often, even too often, locking herself in the bathroom and then running the water full blast. This woman owned a large, broad-shouldered pug dog, so overfed that it had wrinkles in his neck, with glassy-gooseberry pop-eyes, a decadently twisted nose, a proud, contemptu-ously pronounced lower jaw, and a toad's tongue stuffed between two canine teeth. He usually had one and the same expression on his mug, expressing nothing except attentive impudence. He was, though, irritable in the extreme. And so, when Kostyenka was booted out of someone's room and encountered this pug dog in the hall, you could hear immediately how the dog's throat was seized with a growling, gurgling wheezing that soon gave way to indignant fury and finally resolved itself into loud and fierce barking, which would cause Kostyenka to burst into hysterical tears. . . .

Again seated at the table, I wallowed in the tedium of life and in its pen-etrating complexity, despite its ordinariness. Now I wanted to write about Kostyenka and about something else like that. For example, in Nikulina's house a seamstress had once stayed and worked for about a week. This mid-dle-aged petit-bourgeois woman had cut something out on top of a scrap-covered table, and then had put the tacked-together clothing into a sewing machine and began to whir, to stitch. . . . It was all worth watching: how she would distort her large dry mouth in every way possible while cutting out, following the motions and twists of the scissors; how she enjoyed tea from the samovar, all the while trying to say something nice to Nikulina; how she, while boring her with falsely animated talk—in pretend absentminded-ness—moved her large hand toward the basket with slices of white bread and cast a sidelong glance at the glass jar of preserves! And the crippled woman on crutches whom I met the other day on Karachaev Street? All cripples and hunchbacks walk defiantly, arrogantly. This one dived modestly toward me, holding the black handles of her crutches in both hands. While diving, she held herself up evenly on them and threw back her shoulders, under which black protuberances stuck out, and stared intently at me . . . a short coat, like a girl's, intelligent eyes, clear, clean, dark-brown and also like a girl's yet at the same time already knowing all about life, about its sorrows and myster-ies. . . . How wonderful some unhappy people are—their faces, eyes, in which you can see their souls laid bare!

Then I tried again to immerse myself in thinking about how to start a description of my own life. Yes, how! Of course, I had to discuss first of all, if not the universe in which I appeared at a specific moment, then at least Russia: to give the reader a sense of the country I belong to, as a summation of what life I appeared on earth. But what do I know about it, anyway? The life of the primitive Slavs, the quarrels of the Slavic tribes. . . . The Slavs were distinguished by their tall stature, red hair, bravery, and hospitality; they worshiped the sun, thunder and lightning, revered wood goblins, mermaids and water sprites, "the forces and phenomena of nature in general." . . . What else? The summoning of the princes, the ambassadors from Constantinople to Prince Vladimir, the toppling of Perun into the Dnieper amid the weeping of the masses. . . . Yaroslav the Wise, the squabbles among his sons and nephews . . . some Vsevolod Big Nest. . . .[25] And, worst of all—I knew next to nothing even about present-day Russia! Oh, certainly, the ruin of the landed gentry, starving peasants, zemstvo leaders, gendarmes, police, rural priests who, without fail, according to the writers, are burdened with enormous families. . . . And what else? There's Orel, the very picture of a Russian city— at least I could have learned about its life, its people. But what had I learned? Streets, cabbies, the driven snow, stores, signs—signs and more signs. . . . The archbishop, the governor . . . the gigantic, good-looking, and fierce cop Rashevsky. . . . And there was Palitsyn, the pride of Orel, one of its pillars, one of those bull-headed lunatics that Russia is so famous for: old, well-born—a friend of Aksakov, Leskov—lives in something like an ancient Russian palace, whose log walls are covered with rare ancient icons; wears a large caftan embroidered with multicolored threads; has a short haircut, heavy face, narrow eyes, a very sharp mind, is well-read—amazingly so, rumor has it. . . . What else do I know about this Palitsyn? Nothing at all!

Then I was seized by anger: why must I know things and people with complete perfection and not just write what I know and how I feel? I jumped up again and started to pace, enjoying my anger, embracing it like my salvation. . . . And, unexpectedly, I saw the Svyatogorsky monastery where I had been the previous spring, the motley camp of pilgrims along its walls on the banks of the Donets, the novice whom I chased all over the yard of the monastery, vainly insisting that he put me up somewhere for the night, how he shrugged his shoulders, ran from me, and seemed to flutter away—arms, legs, hair, flaps of his cassock—and what a narrow, flexible waist he had, a youthful, totally freckled face, frightened green eyes, and a completely unusual fluffiness, a whipping of light, thin, curly, pale-golden hair. . . . Then I saw the spring days when I, it seemed, sailed endlessly down the Dnieper. . . . Then the dawn somewhere on the steppes . . . how I woke up on a barren train bunk, completely stiff in the morning cold, and saw that nothing was visible through the windows, which were white with frost—no idea where the train was headed!—and I felt that it was magnificent, this lack of knowledge . . . with the morning keenness of feeling, I jumped up, opened the window, leaned out of it: white morning, white wet fog. It smelled of fog and spring mornings, and the fast pace of the train made it feel like my arms, my face were being beaten by wet laundry.

14

And it happened once that I overslept my wake-up time, for some reason. After waking, I stayed in bed. As I lay there, I looked out the window at the even white light of the winter day and felt an unusual tranquillity, a rare sobriety of mind and spirit, and the smallness, the simplicity of all that surrounded me. I lay there for a long time, feeling how weightless the room was, how much smaller it was than I, completely unconnected to me. Then I got up, washed and dressed, from habit crossed myself before the icon which hung at the head of my cheap iron bed—amazingly enough, the same one that hangs in my bedroom even today: a smooth, dark olive-colored board petrified with age in a crude silver frame whose outline surrounds the three angels sitting at Abraham's table, their wild Eastern brown-sooty faces staring out through the rounded holes. It was an heirloom from my mother's family, her blessing on my life's journey, on my exodus into the world from the near monasticism that had been my childhood, adolescence, the first years of my youth—that whole precious isolated span of my earthly existence, which now seems to me a completely unique period, a time so far away that it seems to have been transformed into some kind of separate existence, alien even to me. . . . Having crossed myself, I went to do some shopping that I had decided on while resting.

On the way, I remembered a dream I'd had that night. It was carnival time. I was living again with the Rostotsevs and I was at the circus with my father, looking at a whole small herd of black ponies running in the ring, six of them . . . they were fancily saddled with small copper saddles and little bells and were bridled most tightly—the red-velvet reins of the bridles were so taut on the saddles that their thick short necks, on which their short-cropped manes stuck out in black tufts, were bent into bows—and red plumes projected from their forelocks. They ran together, in an even row, at a jog-trot, with bells ringing and their black heads bent stubbornly, nastily; they were all matched in color, matched in height, all similarly barrel-chested, short-legged. And having run their fill, they suddenly stopped short, champed at their bits, and shook their plumes. The trainer, in tails, yelled for a long time and cracked his whip for a long time, until he finally forced them to drop to their knees and bow to the public. Then suddenly music started up, racing at a refreshed gallop, and it impelled them in a line around the ring, as if pushing them. I went to the stationery store and bought a thick notebook bound in black oilcloth. Upon returning I drank some tea, thinking: "Yes, that's enough. I'll do nothing but read and occasionally, without any preconceived notions, I will jot down various thoughts, feelings, observations. . . ." And, dipping my pen, I carefully and precisely inscribed: "Alexey Arseniev. Notes."

Then I sat for a long while, wondering what to write. I smoked up the whole room, but didn't torture myself. I was simply quiet and sad. Finally I began to write: "The well-known Tolstoyan, Prince N., came to the editorial office wanting to publish his report on the collections and disbursements for the starving population of Tula Province. Fairly small, rather fat. Some kind of soft Caucasian-style boots, lamb's-wool cap, a coat with a lamb's-wool collar—everything old, worn, but expensive and clean—a soft gray shirt belted with a small strap under which his round belly protruded, and a gold pince-nez. He behaved very modestly, but I found his good-looking, sleek, milky face and cold eyes very unpleasant. I immediately detested him. I, of course, am no Tolstoyan. But, then again, I'm not at all what everyone thinks. I want life and people to be sublime, loving, uplifting, and I just can't stand anything that interferes with this."

"A little while ago I was walking up Bolkhov Street, and this was the scene: sunset; a freezing western sky was clearing, and from this green transparent and cold sky the whole town was illuminated in a bright evening light, the incomprehensible anguish of which it is impossible to describe; and on the sidewalk stood a broken-down old organ-grinder, blue from the cold. He filled the frozen evening with the sounds of his decrepit barrel organ, with its flutelike whistling, modulations, and wheezing. A romantic melody broke through the whistling and wheezing—somehow distant, foreign, ancient—which also tormented the soul with its dreams and regrets over something. . . ."

"Everywhere I experience depression or fear. An image I saw two weeks ago is still before my eyes. It had been evening then, too, only dark and overcast. I had stopped by chance into a certain small church. I noticed some candles burning in the darkness near the iconostasis, very low to the floor. I approached and froze: three wax candles stuck to the head of a child's coffin sadly and faintly illuminated the pink coffin with its paper-lace trim and the swarthy high-browed child that lay within. It would almost have seemed that he was simply sleeping, had it not been for something porcelain about his little face, something lilac around his swollen closed eyelids and triangular mouth, if it hadn't been for the infinite peace, the eternal estrangement from everything worldly in which he was lying!"

"I have written and published two stories, but everything about them is false and unpleasant: one is about starving peasants, whom I've never seen and don't actually care about; the other is on the commonplace theme of the ruin of a country estate, and it, too, is all made up. In the meantime, all I

198

want to write about is the immense silver poplar that grows in front of the home of the poor landowner R., and about the immobile stuffed hawk that stands atop the cabinet in his study and stares down eternally, eternally, with shining eyes of yellow glass and outstretched brown wings. If I write of ruin, I want only to express its poetic nature. Destitute fields, the destitute remains of some manor house, its gardens, servants, horses, hunting dogs, the old men and old women (that is, the 'old masters'), who huddle together in the back rooms, having ceded the main section to the young—everything tragic and touching. And moving on, to describe what these 'young masters' are like: ignoramuses, loafers, impoverished but still believing that they are blue bloods, the highest, noble estate. Aristocratic peaked caps, Russian shirts, wide trousers, boots. . . . As soon as they get together there is drinking, smoking, and boasting. They drink vodka from antique goblets meant for champagne. Guffawing, they load blank charges into guns and fire at burning candles, blowing them out with their shots. One of these 'young gentlemen,' a certain P., moved from his ravaged estate to the water mill which, of course, has long been out of commission. He lives there with his peasant mistress, who has a barely noticeable nose. He sleeps with her on a bunk, in the hay, or 'in the garden,' meaning beneath the apple tree next to the hut. On the bough of the apple tree hangs a broken piece of mirror that reflects the white clouds. Out of boredom he sits and throws stones at the peasants' ducks swimming in the backwater near the mill, and with each stone the ducks all at once, all together, with squawks and a horrible noise, cast about the water."

"Our former house serf, the blind old man Gerasim, walked, like all blind men, with his face uplifted as if he were listening, groping his way instinctively with a stick. He lived in a hut on the outskirts of the village, a bachelor, with only a quail that sat in a linden-bark cage and always banged against it: it jumped up against the linen top and grew bald from hitting the cage day after day. Despite his blindness, Gerasim went to the field every summer morning at dawn to catch quail, to delight in their calls, which were wafted over the field by the warm wind that blew in his blind face. He said that nothing on earth is sweeter than that moment when your heart stops as the quail comes closer and closer to the net, its wings beating all the harder, all the louder, and all the more terribly for the hunter. He was a true, selfless poet!"

15

I did not want to go to the editorial office for lunch, so I went to the inn on Moscow Street. There I drank several shots of vodka and ate a bit of a herring: its cracked head lay on the plate; I looked and thought, "I should write this down, too—the herring has mother-of-pearl cheeks." Next I ate stew straight from the pan. The place was uncrowded, it smelled of pancakes and fried smelt, the low-ceilinged room was full of fumes, the white-coated waiters ran by, dancing, curving their spines and throwing back their heads, while amidst it all the owner looked the very model of the Russian spirit. He stood in a picturesque pose at the bar, attentively followed each of them with an unfavorable eye, playing his long since mastered role of strictness and piety. Little black nuns looking like jackdaws in crude lace-up shoes quietly made their way between the tables jammed with petit-bourgeois, quietly bowing low and holding out black books with silver cloth crosses on the bindings, and the petit-bourgeois, frowning, drew from their purses their most battered pennies. . . . It all seemed a continuation of my dream. I was somewhat tipsy from the vodka, the stew, and remembrances of childhood, and I felt close to tears. . . . Returning home, I lay down and fell asleep.

I awoke at twilight with a feeling of grief and remorse for something. I looked in the mirror, and while combing my long hair I noticed without pleasure its excessive theatricality and went to the barber. At the barber's a shortish man with a bare skull and ears jutting out—like a bat—sat beneath a white sheet, while the barber spread an amazingly thick and luxuriant layer of foam over his upper lip and cheeks. Dexterously scraping all this milkiness off with a razor, the barber again spread some on, and again scraped it off, this time from underneath, carelessly, with short jerks. The bat half stood on bowed legs, pulling the sheet with him, stooped down, blushed crimson, and began to hold it to his chest with one hand and to wash himself with the other.

"Shall I spritz you?" asked the barber.

"By all means," said the bat.

And the barber began to spritz the bat with the fragrant atomizer and slapped his moist cheeks lightly with a washcloth.

"There you are," he said clearly, pulling off the sheet. The bat rose, and he looked quite terrifying: large, big-eared skull, lean and wide face, morocco red, his eyes shining childlike after the shave, his mouth a black hole, and he himself broad-shouldered, short-trunked, spidery, with thick legs curved like a Tatar's. Thrusting a tip at the barber, he donned a wonderful black overcoat and bowler, lit a cigar, and left. The barber turned to me: "Do you know who that is? An incredibly rich man, the merchant Ermakov. Guess how much he tips me, always the same? Take a look. . . ." He opened his palm and, smiling merrily, showed me. "Two whole cents!"

Then, as was my wont, I went out to wander the streets. Coming upon the gates to a churchyard, I walked through and entered the building—out of my solitude and sadness I had developed a habit of going into churches. It was warm and sadly festive from the glow of the candles, burning brightly in big clumps on the high candleholders circling the altar. On the altar lay a copper cross set with fake rubies, and before it stood the priests, passionately, sadly singing, "We bow to your cross, Christ, our lord. . . ." In the twilight by the entrance stood an enormous old man, coarse and strong, in a long coat and leather galoshes, like an old horse, sternly humming (for somebody's edification), singing along. And in the crowd by the altar stood a pilgrim, warmly front-lit by the waxy golden light. He was cavernously thin, bent over, and his face, dark and thin like an icon's, was barely visible through the strands of his long dark hair, which hung primitively monklike and feminine-ly over his cheeks. He held a tall wooden staff, rubbed to a shine from long years of use, firmly in his left hand. Over his shoulders was slung a leather sack, and he stood alone, unmoving, separate from all the rest. I looked, and again tears welled up in my eyes, as sweet, sorrowful feelings of my home-land, of Russia, of all her dark antiquity irrepressibly rose up in my heart. Someone behind me gently tapped my shoulder from below with a candle; I turned around and there was a bent old woman in a light coat and a large shawl, with one good tooth jutting out: "To the cross, sir." With joyful obedi-ence I took the candle from her cold, deathly hand with the bluish nails, strode to the blinding candleholders, and awkwardly, ashamed of my awk-wardness, somehow stood the candle by the others, suddenly thinking, "I will leave!" Stepping back and bowing, I quickly and carefully withdrew into the dimness toward the exit, leaving behind me the dear and cozy light and warmth of the church. On the church portico, the cheerless dark met me, and the wind, droning somewhere high above. . . . "I go!" I said to myself, putting on my hat, having decided to go to Smolensk.

Why Smolensk? In my dreams were the Bryansk, "Brynsk" forests, "brynsk" robbers. . . . In some kind of alleyway I stopped into a tavern. In the tavern, sitting at a table, shouting, lowering his head, pretending to be drunk, playing the old Russian favorite—bemoaning one's own ruin—was some sort of dis-gusting fellow. "A mistake, a dreadful one, led me to hard labor!" Someone with dark sparse whiskers, his head cocked back, looked at him squeamishly from another table, and judging from his long neck, his sharp, large, shifting Adam's apple moving beneath the thin skin of his throat, he was a thief. By the bar tottered a tall, intoxicated woman, apparently a laundress, in a thin dress that clung to her emaciated legs. She beat the counter with her glassily shiny, thin, overworked hands, trying to prove someone's caddishness to her neigh-bor. A crystal shot glass with vodka stood on the bar in front of her, and from time to time she would take it, hold it, and still not drink, replace it again, and again rant, tapping her fingers. I wanted to drink some beer, but the fetid air in the tavern was too putrid, the lamp burned too wretchedly, and something oozed from the rags rotting on the sill below the frozen windows. . . .

Unfortunately, Avilova had guests over, sitting in the dining room. "Ah!" she said. "Our dear poet! Do you know each other?" I greeted her and bowed to the guests. Beside Avilova sat an old, wrinkled gentleman with clipped whiskers dyed brown, with a brown hairpiece on his brow, wearing a white silk vest and a black smoking jacket; quickly rising, he acknowledged me with an extraordinarily polite bow that exhibited astonishing flexibility for a man of his age. The lapels of his jacket were covered with the kind of black embroidery that I had always admired and that always stirred in me envy and longing for just such a jacket. The center seat was occupied by a lady, talking incessantly and very skillfully. She offered me a sculptured hand like a seal's flipper, and on the glossy cushion of her palm you could still see the crenelated stripes left from the stitches of her gloves. She spoke gracefully, quickly, panting a bit; she had absolutely no neck and was quite corpulent, especially at the back, around the armpits, stonily round and firm at the corseted waist. A smoke-colored fur lay around her shoulders, the fragrance of which, mixed with the scent of sweet perfume, woolen dress, and warm body, was exceedingly stuffy.

At ten o'clock the guests rose, said their sweet nothings, and left.

Avilova broke into laugher.

"Ah, at last!" she said. "Come, let's sit together in my room. I must open the window in here. . . . Well, my darling, what's going on with you?" she said with a caressing reproach, extending her hands toward me.

I squeezed them and answered, "I'm leaving tomorrow. . . ."

She stared at me fearfully.

"Where?"

"To Smolensk."

"What for?"

"I can't live like this any longer. . . ."

"And what's in Smolensk? But, let's sit down . . . I don't understand any of this. . . ."

We sat on the sofa, covered with a summer slipcover of striped ticking.

"There, do you see that ticking?" I asked. "It's railroadlike. I can't even look at that ticking without feeling pulled to leave."

She settled down deeper, stretching her legs out before me.

"But why Smolensk?" she asked, looking at me with bewildered eyes.

"Then to Vitebsk . . . to Polotsk. . . ."

"What for?"

"I don't know. First of all, I really like the words: Smolensk, Vitebsk, Polotsk . . ."

"No. You're kidding?"

"I'm not kidding. Don't you know how wonderful some words can be? Smolensk was eternally burning in the past, eternally being besieged . . . I feel somehow intimately related to her—there, once upon a time, in a terrible fire, some ancient documents of our family burned completely, and we lost some great inherited rights and ancestral privileges. . . ."

"It gets worse and worse! Are you really so depressed? She doesn't write you?"

"No. But it isn't that. Life in Orel isn't for me. 'The migrating caribou knows her own pastures. . . .' And my literary work is going absolutely nowhere. I sit all morning and my head is completely filled with nonsense, as if I were a madman. What am I living for? In Baturino there is a shopkeeper's daughter and she has already lost all hope of getting married. Now she lives only on her acute, nasty nosiness. I too live on that."

"What a little baby you are still!" she said tenderly, smoothing my hair.

"Only the lowest organisms develop quickly," I answered. "And who is not a baby? Once I came to Orel and on the train beside me sat a member of the Eletsk district court, a venerable serious man who looked like the king of spades. . . .He sat for a long time, reading *The New Times,* and then got up, left, and disappeared. I even got worried, so I went out of the compartment and opened the door to the landing. In the din of the train, he could neither hear nor see me, and what did I find? He was dancing with wild abandon, performing the most reckless tricks with his legs, in time with the rhythm of the wheels."

Raising her eyes to me, suddenly quiet, she asked with great gravity, "If you like we could go to Moscow together."

Something shuddered inside me horribly . . . I blushed, and muttered, declining, thank you, no. . . . To this day I remember that moment with the pain of a great loss.

16

I spent the next night on the train, in a bare, third-class coach. I was completely alone, and even a bit frightened. The weak light of the wall lamp quivered sadly, swinging across the wooden benches. I stood next to the dark window, a cold draft blew sharply through invisible holes, and, covering my face with my hands to block the light, I tensely gazed out into the night, into the woods. Thousands of red bees flew by, whirled around, and sometimes, together with the winter freshness, the wood burning in the locomotive smelled like incense. . . . Oh, how magical, melancholy, severe, stately was that forest night! The unending, narrow, and deep swathe through the forest, the great, dark apparitions of the age-old pines crowded tightly and densely along it. The brightened squares of windows sped obliquely along the white snowdrifts at the edge of the forest. Occasionally a telegraph pole passed by—reaching higher and deeper into the dark and the mystery.

The morning was a sudden, jaunty awakening: everything was bright, calm, and the train was already in Smolensk, at the main station.[26] I jumped off, greedily swallowing the clean air. . . . At the doors of the station people crowded around something. I ran up, and there lay a wild boar, killed in a hunt—dirty, gigantic, mighty, paralyzed and frozen, a horribly cruel sight.

The long, gray needles of his dense bristles stuck out everywhere, interspersed with dry snow; he had swinish eyes, and two huge white incisor fangs. "Stay here?" I thought to myself. "No—on to Vitebsk!"

I arrived in Vitebsk toward dusk.[27] The evening was frosty, bright. Everywhere it was snowy, muffled and clean, virginal. The city seemed to me ancient and not Russian: high, connected buildings with pitched roofs, small windows, and deep, semicircular gates on the first floor. You would constantly meet old Jews, in long coats, in boots and white stockings, with forelocks—resembling the tubular, curling horns of a ram—pallid, with sadly imploring, completely dark eyes. On the main street there was a promenade: a dense crowd of heavy young women, dressed with provincial Jewish sumptuousness in thick velvet coats—lavender, blue, and garnet—was slowly moving along the sidewalk. Following them humbly, at a distance, were the young men, all in derbies, also in forelocks, with the maidenly tenderness and roundness of Eastern candylike faces, with silken youthful down trimming the cheek and languid, antelope glances. . . . I walked through the crowd as if under a spell in this city that I imagined so ancient, while feeling all the miraculous newness of my experience.

It grew dark, and I arrived at some kind of square, where a golden Roman Catholic church with two bell towers rose up. Upon entering, I found dim light, rows of benches, and an altar in the front surrounded by a half-circle of flames. And just then, sluggishly and pensively, an organ started to sing out somewhere above me, flowing softly and fluently, then starting to expand, to grow—harshly, metallically . . . starting to tremble roundly, to grind as if breaking out from something muffling it, and then, suddenly escaping, it overflowed plangently with heavenly singing. . . . In the front, amid the candle flames, here and there, sounding nasally, Latin phrases rose and fell. In the dim light, along both sides of the thick stone colonnade that ran forward toward the front of the church, disappearing into the darkness like dark ghosts, some suits of iron armor stood against the walls. In the heights above the altar, a huge, multichrome window faded dimly. . . .

17

That same night I left for Petersburg. Leaving the church, I went back to the station, to the train for Polotsk. I wanted to stay there in some old hotel, to live in complete solitude, for no apparent reason. The train for Polotsk left very late. In the station it was empty and dark. The buffet was lit only by a sleepy lamp on the counter, the wall clocks ticked so slowly that it seemed time itself was running down. I sat alone for a whole eternity, in the deathly quiet. Then at last the fragrance of a samovar rose from somewhere, and the station started to come alive, brighten; and hastily, without understanding myself what I was doing, I bought a ticket for Petersburg.

There, at the Vitebsk station, in endless expectation of the train to Polotsk, I experienced the feeling of my own terrible alienation from all that surrounded me. I was astonished and uncomprehending. What is all this that stretches before me, and what am I doing, why am I in the middle of it all? A quiet, semidark buffet with a sleepily burning lamp at the bar, a twilit expanse of station hall, long and high, and a table standing in the center, decorated with the standard ornament of public stations: a drowsy old manservant with a bent back and hanging, immovable coattails, who sank onto his legs and dragged himself out from behind the table when the buffet filled with the spicy smell of a nighttime station samovar. With unhappy, senile awkwardness, he climbed up on the chairs alongside the wall and lit the wall lamps in their translucent spheres with a trembling hand . . . then the strapping gendarme, who shook his spurs disdainfully, walked through the buffet to the platform in a full-length overcoat, its slit in the back calling to mind the tail of a priceless stallion . . . what is all this? What is it for? Why? And how dissimilar to everything else was the freshness of the winter night, the snow, which the gendarme carried in with him from outside, going out to the platform! It was at that very moment that I awakened from my torpor and suddenly decided, for some reason, to go to Petersburg.

A winter rain was falling on Polotsk, the streets were wet, wretched.[28] I only glanced at it between trains, and I was gladdened by my disillusionment. For the rest of the trip I jotted: "Endless day. Endless snowy and wooded expanses. Always through the windows a wilted paleness of sky and snow. The train either enters a forest, looking dark against its thickets, or leaves it, coming again into a mournful expanse of snowy plains, where along the far horizon, above the blackness of the forests, a dull leaden something hangs in the low sky. The stations are all wooden. . . . The North, the North!"

Petersburg seemed to me the most extreme North. The cabby whisked me in the twilight blizzard through the unfamiliarly regular, high, and uniform streets toward Ligovka, toward the Nicholas Station. It was just a bit after two, but the round clocks on the public hulk of the station were already illuminated through the blizzard. I stayed a few feet away from it, on the side of Ligovka next to the canal. It was horrible there—firewood storage sheds, cabstands, teahouses, taverns, beer halls. In my rooms, which the cabby had recommended to me, I sat for a long time, not undressing, looking out from the height of the sixth floor through the endlessly sad window, into the snowy afternoon murk, floating from my weariness and the tossing of the train . . . Petersburg! I felt it strongly: I was in it, entirely surrounded by its dark and complex, sinister greatness. It was warm and stuffy in the room from the smell of old woolen curtains and the same sort of sofa, from the strong stench of something reddish that is used to scrub the floors in the cheapest hotels. I went out, running down the steep stairs. In the street, the fresh coldness of the impenetrable blizzard struck me. I hailed a passing cabby and flew off to the Finland Station, to experience the feeling of foreign climes. There, I quickly got drunk, and suddenly sent her a telegram: "I'll be there the day after tomorrow."

Enormous, overpopulated, and ancient Moscow met me with a glistening, sunny thaw, melting snowdrifts, slush and puddles; a rumble and jingle of horsecars, a noisy confusion of pedestrians and riders, an amazing number of dray sleds, heavily laden with goods; muddy, crowded streets, and the postcard picturesqueness of the Kremlin walls, palaces, courts, and the golden cathedral cupolas that gleam crowdedly among them. I marveled at St. Basil's, walked among the cathedrals in the Kremlin, had lunch at Egorov's famous pub on Hunter's Row. It was splendid there: downstairs, rather gray and noisy from the mass of tradesmen, but upstairs, in contrast, the two low-ceilinged chambers were clean, quiet, decorous—they didn't even allow smoking—and cozy, with the sunlight streaming through the small, warm windows from somewhere in the yard and the canary singing in a cage; in the corner the white light of an icon-lamp flickered, and on one wall, taking up its entire upper half, glimmered the somber-toned varnish of a dark painting: a tiled upturned roof and a long terrace on which inharmoniously large yellow-faced Chinese figures in golden robes and in green caps were drinking tea, just like on cheap lampshades. . . . On the evening of the very same day I left Moscow. . . .

In our city, sleds had already given way to wheels and the wild winds blew from the Sea of Azov. She was waiting for me on the dry light platform. The wind was pummeling her spring hat, preventing her from seeing. I spotted her from far off as she searched for me among the passing cars confusedly, squinting against the wind. There was in her something touching and pitiable that always strikes us when we see a loved one after a long separation. She had grown thin and was modestly dressed. When I jumped from the train, she wanted to lift her veil from her lips, but she couldn't, and so she kissed me awkwardly through it, seeming deathly pale.

In the cab she quietly tilted her head toward the wind, just repeating several times bitterly and dryly, "What have you done to me, what have you done to me!"

And then she said, just as seriously, "You're going to the Noblemen's Hotel? I'll go with you."

Entering the room, which was on the second floor, large, with a foyer, she seated herself on the sofa, observing the bellboy who was ungracefully putting my suitcase down on the carpet in the middle of the room. When he finished, he asked if there was anything else.

"Nothing more, thanks," she answered in my stead. "You may go. . . ."

And she started to take off her hat.

"You're being awfully quiet. Aren't you going to say anything?" she said indifferently, restraining her trembling lips.

I got down on my knees and embraced her legs, kissing them through her skirt and crying. She lifted up my head, and I again saw and felt those indescribably delightful lips and the fatefully blissful trembling of our hearts. I jumped up, turned the key in the lock, and closed the translucent curtains with icy hands—outside the window the wind shook a black spring tree on which a rook was dangling and worriedly bawling, like a drunk. . . .

"My father asks one thing," she said quietly a bit later, lying still. "That we wait at least half a year before getting married. Wait for me. You are my entire life anyway, do with me what you will."

Unlit candles stood on the dressing table; the motionless curtains hung dully, while various strange figures stared down from the stucco molding of the chalky white ceiling.

18

We left for the Ukrainian town to which my brother George had moved from Kharkov.[29] We were both supposed to work for the agricultural statistics bureau, which he was directing there. We spent Holy Week and Easter in Baturino. My mother and sister took an immediate shine to her; my father addressed her tenderly and most informally, offering his hand every morning for a kiss; only brother Nicholas was reserved, coolly polite. She was quiet and a little lost in the happiness that came from the novelty of her belonging to my family, my home, the estate, the room where I had spent my youth, which seemed wonderful and touching to her now, my books, which she examined with shy joy. . . . Then we left.

Overnight to Orel. A transfer at dawn to the Kharkov train.

In the sunny morning we stood in the corridor of the sleeper alongside a hot window.

"How strange that I've never been anywhere except Orel and Lipetsk!" she said. "We're in Kursk now? That's already the South for me."

"Yes. For me, too."

"We'll have lunch in Kursk? You know, I've never had lunch in a train station in my life. . . ."

After Kursk, the farther we went, the warmer and happier it got. On the embankments along the rails there were already thick grass, flowers, white butterflies, and the butterflies had summer in them.

"It's going to be hot there in the summer!" she said with a smile.

"My brother writes that the whole city is filled with gardens."

"Ah, Ukraine. I never could have imagined. . . . Look, look, what enormous poplars! And already completely green! Why are there so many mills?"

"Windmills, not mills. You'll see the chalk mountains soon, then Belgorod."

"Now I understand you. I wouldn't be able to live in the North either, without this abundance of light."

I lowered the window. The sunny wind blew warm, the engine's smoke smelled southernly of coal. She shaded her eyes from the sun, which played in hot stripes over her face, over the young dark hair dancing on her forehead, and over her simple sundress, blindingly illuminating and warming it.

In the valleys below Belgorod, the modesty of the blossoming cherry gardens was lovely, the huts were whitened with lime—in the station in Belgorod the delicate quick talk of the peasant women selling bagels.

She went out to buy and bargain, satisfied with her business sense and her use of Ukrainian words.

In the evening in Kharkov, we changed trains again.

At dawn we arrived.

She was sleeping. The candles in the car were burning down. It was still night on the steppes, a dark dawn, but behind it in the distance the low and enigmatically greening east. How different the land here is from ours, this naked unbounded plain with heavy silvery-green burial mounds! A sleepy way station blinked by, not a single bush or tree by it, and it was made of stone, bare, light-blue in this secret birth of sunrise. . . . How lonely the stations are here!

Finally day was breaking inside the car. Only dawn below, along the floor, but above it, daybreak already. Still asleep, she hid her head under the pillow, drew her legs up. I carefully covered her with an antique silk shawl my mother had given her.

19

The station was far from the city, in the wide valleys. The building itself was small and pleasant, full of affable lackeys, affectionate porters, and gracious cabbies atop the coach boxes of homemade tarantasses, harnessed with pairs of horses.

The city was filled with verdant parks. From the Hetman's cathedral on the edge of a mountain it looked out to the east and the south. In the eastern valley a steep hill stood apart with an ancient monastery on its summit, and beyond it all was green and empty as the valley gave way to the rolling steppe. To the south, beyond the river and its merry meadows, the glare of the sun obscured the view.

Many of the streets seemed crowded because of the parks and poplars that stretched in rows along the planks of the "boardwalk," where one frequently met proud, big-bosomed women in tight-fitting dresses, with heavy water yokes on their strong shoulders. It was May, so there were many thunderstorms and showers. The poplars were remarkable for their height and girth, and they delighted us; how green their firm leaves glistened, and how fresh and resinously sweet they smelled! The spring here was always bright and joyous, the summer sultry, the fall long and serene, the winter mild, with wet winds: the cabbies' sleighs were decked out with bells, with their delightful muffled murmuring.

Kovanko, the old man we settled in with on one of these streets, was large and tan, with a round-cropped head of gray hair and an entire estate in his possession: courtyard, cottage, house, and garden behind it. He himself took the cottage, while we rented the whitewashed house, shaded by the garden behind and with a big glass gallery along the facade. He worked somewhere or other and, once home from work, he would eat a big dinner, relax, and then, half-dressed, would sit under an open window and sing, smoking his pipe, "Oh, they're mowing on the hill. . . ."

The rooms of the house were low-ceilinged and simple; an ancient chest covered with a plain cloth with colored embroidery sat in the hall. Our servant was a young cossack girl, whose beauty had a touch of Tatar in it.

My brother had become even more sweet and dear. My hopes were fulfilled—between them there arose a close and friendly intimacy; in all my disagreements, either with her or with him, each always took the other's side.

Our circle of coworkers and acquaintances (doctors, lawyers, politicians) was similar to my brother's circle in Kharkov. I got on with them easily and was happy to see Leontovich and Vagin, who had also moved from Kharkov. The only difference between this group and the one in Kharkov was the fact that it consisted of people who were more moderate, who lived in the prosperous style of this city, and they amicably socialized, not only with people from all other city groups, but even with the chief of police.

We gathered most often at the home of one of the members of the local government: he was the owner of five thousand acres of land and a flock of ten thousand sheep; his home was kept rich and worldly—for his family— while he himself, small, modest, poorly dressed (once upon a time he had even been exiled to Yakutsk), seemed a pitiful guest there.

20

In the courtyard there was an old stone well, two white acacias grew in front of the cottage, and near the porch of the house, shading the right wall of the glass gallery, towered the dark heights of a chestnut tree. That summer everything was hot, sultry, and sunny, even before seven, and the hens would fill the air with their monotonous, inquiringly confused cackling from the henhouse. But the house, especially the back rooms that looked out over the garden, remained cool. In the bedroom, where she would splash herself, standing in her little Tatar slippers, her breast heaving from the cold, it smelled freshly of water and perfumed soap: embarrassed, she'd turn toward me with her wet face covered from hair to neck with soap, and stamp her heel, "Get out!" Then from the rooms where the windows opened out onto the gallery would come the smell of brewing tea—the cossack girl walked there, clattering around in her heavy boots. She wore shoes on bare feet; her bare ankles, thin as a thoroughbred mare's, glowed Middle-Easternly beneath her skirt; her round neck in an amber necklace also glowed; her dark little head was lively and delicate, her slanting eyes sparkled, and her seat wagged with every movement.

My brother would come to tea, cigarette in hand, with the smile and mannerisms of our father: he was not large, was growing stouter, and did not look like him; but something of the older man's baronial manner showed through. He had begun to dress well; his way of crossing his legs, sitting, and taking a drag on his cigarette revealed a certain noblesse oblige; at one point everyone had been convinced that he would have a brilliant future, and he himself had been convinced of it, but now he was content with the role he played in this remote Ukrainian town, and he came to tea with a twinkle in his eyes. He felt full of strength and health; we made up his family, very dear to him, and to go with us to work, which, like in Kharkov, half consisted of smoking and conversation, was a daily pleasure. When at last she would appear, finally quite ready and dressed with summer merriment, he'd just beam, kissing her hand.

We'd walk past the marvelous poplars, whose oily leaves shone in the sun, over the planks of the boardwalk, beneath the hot walls of the houses and warm gardens, the blue silk of her open parasol etched roundly against the azure. Next we would cross the sultry square and enter the yellow government building. There below it smelled like the boots of the watchmen and the cheap tobacco they smoked. All sorts of clerks and officials in black lustrine coats would be mounting the stairs to the second floor anxiously, papers in hand, heads bent in the Ukrainian manner, a cunning breed and highly experienced, for all their seeming simplicity. We'd cross beneath the stairs into the depths of the first floor, into the narrow rooms of our department, very pleasant due to the boisterous slovenly intellectuals who filled them. . . . It was strange for me to see her in these rooms, behind all the questionnaires that she stuffed into envelopes for distribution.

At noon the watchmen would bring us tea in cheap glasses and cheap saucers with slices of lemon, and at first the government-issueness of it all even gave me a kind of pleasure. Now all of our friends from other departments would converge on us to chat and smoke. Sulima, the government secretary, would come. He was a handsome, somewhat stooped man with gold glasses and wonderfully shiny velvet-black hair and beard. He had an ingratiating tread, an ingratiating smile, and the same manner of speaking; he smiled constantly and constantly played up his gentility, his refinement: he was quite an aesthete, and dubbed the monastery that stood on the hill in the valley "the frozen chord." He came often and gazed upon her ever more blissfully and mysteriously: approaching her desk, he would bow low to her hand, lift his glasses, and sweetly, quietly smile, "And what are you distributing today?" At this she'd pull her hand away and try to answer as nicely but simply as possible. I was completely calm, I was no longer jealous of anyone.

At work, just as at the editorial office of Orel's *Voice,* I came to occupy a special position: as a worker people looked on me with affectionate derision. I sat and unhurriedly calculated and compiled statistics: how much tobacco had been sown in such and such a region and such and such a district, how many sugar beets, and what kinds of measures were being taken "in the struggle" with the beetles that damaged those sugar beets. Sometimes I simply read something, paying no heed to the conversations going on around me. I was happy just to have my desk and the opportunity to order brand-new quills, pencils, and good writing paper from the supply room in any quantity.

At two o'clock work ended. My brother would rise, smiling, "Home with the lot of you!" Everyone would grab their summer coats and hats with animation. The crowd would spill out onto the sunny square, shaking hands with one another, and go their separate ways, silk and canes shining.

21

In the hours before five o'clock the city was empty, the parks scorching hot beneath the sun. My brother slept, while we simply lounged on her wide bed. The sunlight, having circled the house, already shone through the windows of the bedroom, looking in on us from the garden, and the mirror above the washstand reflected the garden and its sunny green leaves. Gogol had studied in this city, and all the surrounding areas were his, too—Mirgorod, Yanovshchina, Shishaki, Yareski—we often recalled, laughing, "How ravishing and how sumptuous is a summer day in Ukraine!"[30]

"Boy, is it hot!" she said, sighing happily and lying on her back. "And how many flies there are! How does it go from there, about the vegetable gardens?"

"'Like emeralds, topaz, and sapphires, ethereal insects scatter above the vegetable gardens. . . .'"

"There is something magically wonderful about that. How terribly I would like to go to Mirgorod! We must certainly go somehow. All right? Please let's go somehow! Only, how strange and unpleasant he was in real life. He was never in love with anyone, not even when he was young."

211

"Yes, there was only one senseless action in the whole of his youth—a trip to Lübeck."

"Like yours to Petersburg. . . . Why do you like to travel so much?"

"And why do you like to receive letters so much?"

"Who would send them to me now?"

"All the same, you love it. People are always waiting for something happy and interesting, they dream of some joy, some kind of event. This is what makes the road so attractive. Then there is freedom, space . . . the novelty that is like a holiday, that enhances our sense of life; that's all we want, after all, and we search for it in any strong emotion."

"Yes, yes, you're quite right."

"You said 'Petersburg.' If only you knew how horrible it was and how I immediately and forever understood there that I am a southerner to the depths of my soul. Gogol wrote from Italy: 'Petersburg, snow, scum, offices—I dreamed about this all: I awoke again in my native land.'[31] And I too awoke only here. I cannot hear the words Chigirin, Cherkasy, Khorol, Lubny, Chertomlyk, and Dikoe Pole calmly; I cannot see thatched roofs, cropped peasant heads, peasant women in red and yellow boots, even the bark baskets full of cherries and plums they carry on a yoke, without excitement. 'A seagull soars, and groans as if crying over her young; the sun shines warmly and the wind blows over the Cossack steppes. . . .' That's Shevchenko, a truly brilliant poet![32] There is no country in the world more beautiful than Ukraine. And the most important thing is that she has no history now—her historical life ended long ago, and once and for all. There is only the past, songs and legends of it, a kind of timelessness. This is what delights me most of all."

"You're always saying that—it delights, it's a delight."

"Life must be delightful. . . ."

The sun began to set, pouring in generously through the open windows onto the varnished floor, and a mirrorlike reflection played on the ceiling. The windowsills burned even hotter, and the flies seethed joyfully there, in small clumps. They stung her cool, bare shoulders. A sparrow suddenly landed on the sill, looked around with vigilance and animation and, taking wing, disappeared again into the sunny green garden, already transparent in the late afternoon sunlight.

"Tell me something else," she said. "Tell me, will we go to the Crimea sometime? If you only knew how I dream about it! You could write some kind of story—I'm sure you'd write it wonderfully—and then we'd have money and could take a vacation. . . . Why did you give up writing? You waste and squander your talents!"

"Once there were cossacks who were called 'ramblers' from the verb 'to ramble.' You see, I am a rambler. 'To one God gives hearth and home; to another he gives the will to roam.' The best thing in Gogol is his notebook: 'A

212

steppe gull with a tuft raised like a parenthesis takes off from the road . . . the boundary of the road, green, with thistles growing along it, and nothing beyond except the endless plain. . . . Sunflowers above the fences and ditches, and the straw awning of a freshly plastered hut, and the pretty red border trimming the window. . . . Ye ancient roots of Russia, where feelings are truer, and the Slavic nature is more tender!'"[33]

She listened attentively. Then she suddenly asked, "And tell me, why did you read me that passage of Goethe's? You know, the part about how he left Fredricka and suddenly imagined a rider traveling somewhere in a gray, sleeveless jacket, trimmed in gold lace. How did it go?"

"'I myself was that rider. I was wearing a gray, sleeveless jacket, trimmed with gold lace, such as I had never worn.'"[34]

"Yes, it's somehow so wonderful, and horrible. And then you said that every man in his youth longs for this jacket in his dreams. . . . Why did he leave her?"

"He said that his 'demon' forced him to."

"Uh-huh, and you too will stop loving me soon. But, tell me the truth, what do you long for most of all?"

"What do I long for? To be a kind of ancient Crimean khan, to live with you in the palace of Bakhchiseray. . . . Bakhchisaray is in a stony, terribly hot ravine, but in the palace itself there is eternal shade, coolness, with fountains, and mulberry trees outside the windows. . . ."[35]

"You're not serious?"

"Yes, I'm serious. After all, I'm always living on some kind of horrible nonsense. Take that steppe gull, the union of the steppes and the sea that it represents. . . . My brother Nicholas used to make fun of me, saying that I was congenitally a bit of an idiot. I suffered deeply until once I happened to read that Descartes himself said that in his inner life clear and reasonable thoughts always occupied the most insignificant place."

"And so, would there be a harem in this palace? I am also quite serious. You yourself pointed out to me—remember?—that many different kinds of emotion are mingled in masculine love, that you experienced it toward Nikulina and then Nadya. . . . You are, after all, awfully frank with me sometimes! You even said something of this sort not long ago about our little cossack."

"I only said that when I looked at her I longed to go somewhere on the salty steppes and live in a yurt."

"See, you said it yourself, you want to live with her in a yurt."

"I didn't say with *her*."

"Then with whom? Oh, another sparrow. It scares me so when they fly in and bang into the mirror!"

And, leaping up, she quickly and clumsily clapped her hands. I caught hold of her and kissed her bare shoulders, her legs. The difference between the hot and cool parts of her body astounded me most of all.

Toward evening the intense heat abated. The sun was already behind the house, and we drank tea in the glass gallery by the windows opening out onto the courtyard. She read quite a bit these days, and at this time she would always question my brother about something, and he would instruct her with pleasure. The evening was endlessly quiet, motionless—only the swallows darted about the courtyard and, soaring up, became lost in the deep heavens. They talked and I listened: "Oh, they're reaping on the hill. . . ." The song told about how the laborers were reaping. It flowed along evenly, slowly, with the sadness of separation, then it gained momentum and rang out strongly—with freedom, distance, courage—to a martial beat:

> And from beyond the hill,
> Beyond the high one,
> The cossacks are coming.

The song drawlingly and sadly admired how a cossack army flowed through the valley, how the famous Doroshenko took the lead, going in front of the rest. And behind him, it said, left behind him was Sagaidachnyi: "He'd traded his wife / For tobacco and pipe." She lingered, proudly marveling at so strange a man. But then she followed the beat of a drum with especially joyful abandon:

> I can't waste my time
> With a woman!
> But tobacco and pipe
> For the road are
> What a Cossack needs.

I listened, sadly and sweetly envying something.

We strolled in the sunset, sometimes walking to the city, sometimes to the square on the cliffs behind the cathedral, sometimes out of the city, into the fields. There were several paved streets in the city lined with all kinds of Jewish businesses, with an incomprehensible number of watch repairers, pharmacies, and tobacco stores. The streets were lined with white stone and exhaled the warmth of the day's heat. Passersby drank sparkling water with many-colored syrups at kiosks on the corners, and everything bespoke the South, and pulled you somewhere even farther south; I remember that for some reason I often thought about Kerch at that time. Gazing out from the cathedral into the valley, I would travel in my mind to Kremenchug, to Niko-laev. In the field outside the city, we walked through the completely rural western outskirts. The huts, cherry orchards, and gardens stretched out into the plain, straight as an arrow, along the Mirgorod road. In the far distance, by the telegraph poles, a Ukrainian wagon slowly dragged along, pulled by two oxen staggering in their yoke, bowing their heads toward the ground. It dragged along and disappeared, along with the poles, as though vanishing into the sea. The last poles just barely rose in the distance, like matchsticks. This was the road to Yanovshchina, Yareski, Shishaki. . . .

We often spent evenings at the city park. Music played, and from a distance the illuminated terrace of the restaurant stood out against the surrounding darkness like a theater stage. My brother went straight to the restaurant, while we would sometimes wander out to the side of the garden that ended by the cliff. The nights were dark, thick, warm. In the darkness somewhere below, flames flickered and chantlike songs rose and fell, sung by the boys of the outskirts. The songs mingled with the darkness and silence. The luminous links of a train thundered by, and it was then that you could sense the depth and blackness of the valley. The train gradually grew quiet, faded, as if it had disappeared underground. And again songs could be heard, and all around the circle of the horizon the valley reverberated with the incessant warbling of toads, enchanting the quiet and dark, toppling the valley into a seemingly endless stupor.

When we came back up to the crowded terrace of the restaurant after the darkness, she was blinded and pleasantly embarrassed. My brother, already tipsy and deeply emotional, instantly waved to us from his table, where he sat with Bakin, Leontovich, Sulima. They seated us noisily, ordering another bottle of white wine, glasses, and ice. Eventually the music would stop; the park beyond the terrace would become dark, empty; and from somewhere now and then a puff of wind would blow the candles in the hurricane lamps covered with nighttime insects; but they would keep saying the night was still young until at last they agreed that it was time to go. And all the same, we would not break up right away. We would walk home in a pack, talking loudly, stamping on the boardwalks. The gardens slept, mysteriously dark and warmly lit by the low glow of a late moon. By the time we would enter our yard, now alone, the moon was gazing in, shining on the dark windows of the glass gallery; crickets hummed quietly; each acacia leaf along the wing of the house, each twig, was silhouetted against the white wall with amazing precision and elegance.

The minutes before sleep were the sweetest of all. A candle burned simply on the nightstand. Coolness entered the room through the open window with the delight of freshness, youth, and health. Sitting on the edge of her bed in her bathrobe, she would stare at the lamp with dark eyes and plait her softly shining braids.

"You're amazed at how I've changed," she said. "But if only you knew how you've changed! Only you've started to pay less attention to me, especially when we're not alone. I'm afraid that I'm just like the air for you: it's impossible to live without it, but you don't even notice it. Aren't I right? You claim that this is precisely the greatest love. But it seems to me that I'm not enough for you."

"Not enough, not enough," I answered, laughing. "Nothing is enough for me now."

"That's what I'm saying: you're being pulled somewhere. George already told me that you've asked to go on the road with the traveling statisticians. What for? To shake along in the heat and dust in a light carriage, then to sit in the hot government offices and endlessly survey the locals about the same questions that I send out?"

She raised her eyes, tossing her braid over her shoulder.

"What is pulling you away?"

"Only that I'm happy. It really seems to me that nothing is enough."

She took my hand. "Are you truly happy?"

23

The first time I left, I went exactly where she had wanted to go together— along the Mirgorod road. Vagin took me with him to Shishaki, where he had been sent for some reason.

I remember how scared we were that I would oversleep, for we needed to leave as early as possible, before the heat—and how tenderly she woke me. She had arisen before dawn and made me tea, suppressing her sorrow that I was going alone. It was gray and cool, and she kept looking through the window: could it really be that rain might spoil my trip? Even now I can feel the tender and nervous excitement with which we jumped up when we heard the sound of the bell at the gate, impetuously saying farewell and running out to the fence to the impatiently waiting carriage, where Vagin sat in a long sailcloth shirt and a gray summer cap.

Soon the bells died away into the giant windy expanse, the day cleared, became dry and hot, the carriage rolled smoothly in the deep road dust, and everything around was so monotonous that soon I didn't have the strength to stare into the distance of the sleepily bright horizon and tensely wait for something to come out of it. At noon in that burning desert of grain we passed something totally nomadic: the endless sheepfolds of Kochubei. "Noon, sheepfolds," I wrote between bumps of the carriage. "The sky is gray from the intense heat, hawks and gray crows . . . I am perfectly happy!" In Yanovshchina I wrote about the tavern: "Yanovshchina, an old tavern, its dark interior and cool semidarkness; the Jew said he had no beer for sale, 'only an ade.'—'What kind of ade?'—'Oy, an ade! A violet ade.' The Jew was gaunt, in a long coat, but the ade was brought out from the back room by his son, a schoolboy, an unusually plump adolescent wearing a new belt high around his light-gray coat, very handsome in a Persian sort of way." Beyond Shishaki I immediately recalled Gogol's notebook: "And suddenly a declivity in the middle of the flat road—a precipice down into a valley and below, forest depths and beyond the forests—more forests, past the near and green ones they are remote, blue, and beyond them the stripes of silvery straw-colored sand. . . . Above the rapids and the steep slopes a squeaky windmill flapped its wings. . . ."[36] Below the precipice, in the depths of the valley, the river Psel meandered, and one could see the verdant gardens of a large village. For a long time we searched for a certain Vasilenko with whom Vagin had business, and after discovering he wasn't home, we went outside and sat under the linden tree beside his hut, surrounded by the dampness of the meadow willows and the croaking of frogs. We sat that way with Vasilenko all evening, eating and drinking fruit liqueur. A lamp illuminated the green leaves from below, while we were enveloped by the impenetrable darkness of the summer night. Then in that darkness the gate suddenly banged and beside our table a well-dressed young lady appeared. She was an acquaintance of Vasilenko, the local public medical assistant, palely powdered to a leaden pallor. Of course she discovered immediately that he had some kind of city guests visiting. At first she was embarrassed, did not know what to do with herself, and said anything that came to mind. Then she started to drink with us, shot for shot, cackling more and more at all my wisecracks. She was terribly nervous, broad cheekboned, sharply dark-eyed. She had sinewy hands, strongly smelling of carbolic, a bony collarbone, and beneath her thin blue blouse lay firm breasts. Her waist was thin, and her hips wide. Late at night I walked her home. We walked in the black darkness, along the dried-up ruts of some kind of sidestreet. Somewhere beside a wicker fence she stopped and laid her head on my chest. It was only with difficulty that I did not let myself go. . . .

Vagin and I arrived home late on the second day. She was already lying in bed reading; seeing me, she jumped up with joy and surprise: "What, back already?" When, rapidly describing my entire trip, I began to make fun of the medical assistant, she interrupted, "Why are you telling me this?" And her eyes filled with tears. "You're so cruel to me!" she said, hurriedly looking for her handkerchief under the pillow. "It's not enough that you leave me all alone. . . ."

How many times in my life have I recalled those tears! I even recall how I recalled that evening once twenty years later. It was at a seaside dacha in Bessarabia. I had come back from swimming and was lying in the study. It was a hot and windy midday, strong and silkily hot: the sounds of the garden by the house were now calming, now crazily increasing. The lightly bending tree branches swayed to and fro in the shadow and sparkle. . . . When the wind strengthened, blowing noisily, it suddenly pushed away all of the forest green surrounding the windows of the shady study, revealing a sultry enamel sky and simultaneously exposing a shadow on the white ceiling. The ceiling, growing brighter, became violet. Then it quieted down again, the wind rushed away, lost itself somewhere deep in the garden over the precipice overlooking the shore. I looked at all this, listened, and suddenly thought: once upon a time, twenty years ago, in those long-forgotten Ukrainian provinces where we had just started our life together, there was a similar midday; I woke up late—she had already gone to work—the windows to the garden were also open, and outside there was noise, shaking and colorful sparkling, just like now. And there was that kind of happy wind that agitatedly invades a room, wafting a promise of breakfast on the scent of fried onions. Having opened my eyes and inhaling that wind, I propped my elbows on my pillow and started to look at the other one, lying alongside, in which there still remained a slight hint of the violet scent of her dark, marvelous hair and the handkerchief which she had clutched in her hand for a long time after making up with me; and, recalling all that, I recall that since then I have lived half a lifetime without her, have seen the whole world and still live and see, while she has been gone from the world for an eternity already. Cooling off a bit, I flung myself off the couch, went out as if floating on air along the alley of acidic-scented trees toward the precipice, and looked through the tunnel of trees at a vitriolic blue-green piece of the sea, which suddenly seemed frightening and miraculous, newly created. . . .

That night I swore to her that I would never go anywhere again. In a few days I left once more.

24

When we were in Baturino, brother Nicholas had said: "I pity you from the bottom of my heart! You dug your grave early!"

But I didn't sense a grave.

As before, I considered my work a matter of accident. I couldn't imagine myself married. The mere thought of life without her terrified me, but the prospect of our eternal inseparability also seemed unlikely: had we really united forever and would we live so until old age? Would we, like everybody else, have a house, children? The last part—children, a home—seemed to me especially unbearable.

"So we'll get married," she said, dreaming about the future. "I would really like that, and anyway, what could be better than a wedding? Maybe we'll have a child. . . . Oh, would you really not want that?"

Something sweet and mysterious tugged at my heart. But I laughed it off.

"Immortals create; mortals produce copies of themselves."

"And I?" she asked. "How will I live when our love and youth have passed and you no longer need me?"

That was very sad to hear, and I answered passionately, "Nothing is ever going to pass. I'll always need you!"

Now it was I (not she, as it had been in Orel) who wanted to love and be loved while remaining free and preeminent in everything.

She touched me most deeply when, having put her hair up for the night, she would come to kiss me goodnight and I noticed how much taller I was than she when she had no heels on, and how she looked up into my eyes from below.

I felt my love for her most strongly in the moments when she expressed the greatest devotion to me, self-renunciation, and a belief in my right to special feelings and actions.

We often reminisced about our winter in Orel, how we had parted there, how I left for Vitebsk, and I said, "Yes, Polotsk, whatever attracted me there?"

With that word—Polotsk or, in the old form, Polot'sk—I had long connected the legend of the ancient Kievan Prince Vseslav, which I had read long ago in my adolescence. He was deposed by his brother, fled to "the dark regions of the Polochani," and lived out his days in "abject poverty" in a hermitage, at prayers, at labor, and in "the charms of memory." It is said he invariably woke up in the predawn hours with "bittersweet tears," in a delusionary dream that he was again in Kiev, "lord and master of his principality," and that the bells were summoning to midnight mass not in Polotsk, but at the Kiev Cathedral.[37] Since then the Polotsk of that day always seemed to me to be perfectly marvelous in its antiquity and coarseness: dark-gray winter days, some kind of log citadel with wooden churches and black peasant huts, snowdrifts trampled down by horses and passersby in sheepskins and bark shoes. . . . When I finally made it to the real Polotsk, I found, of course, not the slightest similarity to what I had dreamed. Nevertheless, to this day there are still two cities for me: the imagined Polotsk and the real one.

And now I see the real one poetically, too: it is dull, wet, cold, dark, but the train station has a large, warm hall with enormous semicircular windows. The chandeliers are already lit, even though it's just dusk outside. In the hall there is a large mass of people, both civilian and military, hurriedly finishing meals before the arrival of the train for Petersburg. Everywhere there is conversation, the click of knives on plates, the smell of sauces, soup wafted by flying waiters, back and forth. . . .

As always at times like this, she listened to me with a special, intense interest and, having taken it all in, agreed with conviction, "Yes, yes, I understand you!" And I took advantage of this, suggesting to her, "Goethe said: 'We are dependent on the creatures of our making.' There are feelings which I can not resist at all: sometimes my mental perception of something evokes in me such an intense striving toward it, that is, toward whatever lies beyond this perception—understand: beyond!—that I can't even express it to you!"

Once I went with Vagin to Cossack Fords, an ancient village south of the Dnieper. We were accompanying settlers heading for the Far East. We returned in the morning by train. When I arrived from the train station, she and my brother were already at the office. With a manly tan and energetic, pleased with myself and excited by the desire to tell her and my brother right away what rare sights I had managed to see—a whole horde had passed before my eyes going to that fabled region, ten thousand kilometers from Cossack Fords—I quickly walked through the whole empty tidy house, went into the bedroom to change and wash up and, with a kind of painful pleasure, looked at all her things on the dressing table, at her embroidered throw pillow—it all seemed infinitely dear and lonely, and it evoked in my soul the happiness of my guilt. Then I saw an open book on the night table and stopped for a minute: it was Tolstoy's "Family Happiness," and on the opened page a section was underlined: "All my thoughts at that time, all my feelings were not mine but his thoughts and feelings, which suddenly had become mine. . . ." I looked a few pages further and saw more marks: "That summer I often went into my bedroom and, instead of my former anguish of desires and hopes for the future, I was engulfed by the worry of current happiness. . . . The summer passed and I began to feel lonely. He was always away on trips and neither regretted nor feared leaving me alone. . . ."[38]

I stood for several minutes, motionless. It seemed that it had never occurred to me that she might (and did) keep from me secret, and most importantly, unhappy thoughts and feelings, and already in the past tense! "All my thoughts and feelings *at that time*." "That summer I often *went*." Most unexpected was the last part: "The summer passed and I began to feel lonely. . . ." So her tears that night when I arrived from Shishaki were not merely coincidental?

I went into the office with special cheer, kissed her and my brother joyfully, talked and joked unceasingly. Having patiently waited in quiet torment for us to be alone, I said sharply, "So, you've been reading 'Family Happiness' without me?"

She flushed red.

"Yes. And what of it?"

"Well, I'm stunned by your marks in it!"

"Why?"

"Because it's completely obvious from them that you're tired of living with me, that you're lonely and disappointed."

"How you always exaggerate!" she replied. "What disappointment? It's just that I was a little sad and spotted, it's true, a few similarities . . . I assure you it's not at all like what you imagine."

Whom was she reassuring? Me or herself? I was very glad to hear all that. I wanted very much to believe her, and it was best for me to do so . "A seagull with a tuft took off from the road. . . . She ran, her waist wrapped in a light-blue apron, and her breasts bounced about under her linen dress. Bereft of shoes, her legs were bare to the knees, and health and strength played. . . ." How much did it have going for it? And could I refuse? Besides, I thought it could be totally combined with her! At every opportunity I tried to instill one thing in her: live only for me and through me, don't deprive me of my freedom or will—I love you, and this will make me love you even more. It seemed to me that I loved her so much that I could do anything to her, that anything was forgivable.

25

"You've really changed," she said. "You've become more steadfast, gentler, nicer. You've started to enjoy life."

"Yes, and my brother Nicholas and your father predicted that we would be very unhappy."

"That's because Nicholas didn't like me. You can't imagine what his cold politeness at Baturino did to me."

"On the contrary, he spoke of you with great affection. He said he felt sorry for you, too. Just a girl, and think what awaits you in the future: in what way will your existence differ in a few years from the existence of any petty provincial bureaucrat? Do you remember how I used to picture my future jokingly? A three-room apartment, fifty rubles a month salary. . . ."

"He only felt sorry for you."

"He was wrong. He said that his entire hope lay in our being saved by my 'recklessness,' that I would turn out to be unfit even for such a career, and that we would soon part, 'or you'll drop her pitilessly,' he said, 'or she you, having spent some time in good old statistics and having understood the fate you've prepared for her.'"

"He relied on me in vain—I will never drop you. I would drop you only if I saw that you no longer needed me, that I was hindering you, your freedom, your calling. . . ."

Whenever a person goes through something bad, he continually returns to one and the same tortuous and useless thought: how and when did it begin? How did it all come to be, and how could I have ignored the signs that should have warned me? "I would drop you only if. . . ." How could it be that I didn't pay attention to words like that—to the fact that there was, after all, some "if"?

I overvalued my "calling," took advantage of my freedom more and more recklessly—my brother Nicholas was right. It became harder and harder to stay at home: as soon as there was a day off, I left immediately, went someplace.

"Where did you ever get such a tan?" asked my brother before dinner. "Where have you been?"

"I was at the monastery, by the river, at the station. . . ."

"And always alone," she said by way of reproach. "How many times have you promised that we'd go together to the monastery, and I've been there all of once the whole time. And it's so nice there, such enormous walls, swallows, monks. . . ."

I was ashamed, and it was painful to meet her gaze. But, fearing for my freedom, I only shrugged my shoulders.

"And what are monks to you?"

"And what are they to you?"

I tried to change the subject.

"I saw something very strange there today at the cemetery: an empty but fully prepared grave. One of the brothers had one dug for himself in advance, complete with a cross at its head: the cross was already engraved with the name of the person who would be buried there, when he was born. Even the word 'died' was already engraved, with a blank space remaining only for the date of his future demise. It was clean everywhere, orderly, nice paths, flowers—and suddenly this waiting grave."

"There, you see. . . ."

"What am I supposed to see?"

"You're trying not to understand me. But do what you want, Turgenev says it best. . . ."

I interrupted, "It seems that you read nowadays only to find something related to you and me. But then, all women read like that."

"Fine, then I'm a woman, but I'm not as selfish. . . ."

My brother stopped us tenderly:

"That's enough, guys!"

26

By the end of the summer, my position with the government office was further regularized: before I had merely been "attached" to the department, but now I was put on the staff and assigned to a new job that could not have suited me better. I became the "curator" of the governmental library—various publications that had accumulated in the office's cellar. This job, which Sulima had dreamt up for me, required the sorting and organization of these publications, their shelving in a space specially furnished for this purpose in a long vaulted room in the semibasement, providing the required quantity of shelves and cabinets, and, finally, watching over them and distributing those which proved necessary to one department or another from time to time. I sorted, shelved, and proceeded to watch in expectation of imminent distribution. But, as it turned out, I didn't have to distribute anything—the departments only needed these publications in the fall, before the zemstvo meeting. And so I became simply a watchman, sitting in this semibasement room, delighting in the uncommon fortresslike thickness of its walls and vaults, its deep silence—not a sound was to be heard from anywhere—and its small window set high above the floor with the sun shining through the top and the roots of all the wild bushes and grasses that grew in the vacant lot behind the government building visible from below. From this time on, my life became even more free: I sat for whole days in this crypt in complete solitude, I wrote, read, and, when I wanted, could lock the low oak door, leave, and go wherever my thoughts took me, without having to check back in for an entire week.

For some reason I would go to Nikolaev, and often I walked to a farmstead on the outskirts of town where two brothers, Tolstoyans, had made their home for religious reasons. At one time I went to the large Ukrainian village, one station from the city, every Sunday evening, returning home by the late-night train. . . . Why did I leave and go there? She sensed that secret thing which, in addition to everything else, was the reason for my wanderlust. My story about the medical assistant in Shishaki had affected her far more than I had thought. From that time on, feelings of jealousy had begun to develop in her, which she tried to conceal, not always successfully. Thus, two weeks after the story about Shishaki, going completely against the grain of her dear, noble, and still maidenly character, she suddenly acted like a most commonplace "housewife"; she found some pretext and harshly and firmly dismissed the cossack girl who served us.

"I know well that this grieves you," she said to me unpleasantly. "How could it not, when her little boots 'pattered' around this room so wonderfully like, as you say, 'a young filly,' when she has such shapely ankles and such slanting sparkling eyes! But you forget how insolent and capricious that little filly is, and that my patience has limits, after all. . . ."

I answered with my whole heart, in complete sincerity, "How can you be jealous of me? I look at your incomparable hand here and think: for this single hand I would give all the beauties on earth! But I am a poet, an artist, and any art, in the words of Goethe, is sensual."

27

One August evening I went to the farmstead to see the Tolstoyans.[39] The city was empty at this still sultry hour, particularly as it was a Saturday. I walked past the shuttered Jewish stores, the rows of old commercial stalls. The bells rang slowly, announcing vespers, and the streets were already covered with long shadows from the parks and houses, but everything still floated in that special late-afternoon heat that you get in southern cities at the end of summer, when everything has been burned brown in the parks and gardens that bake beneath the sun day in and day out, when everything and everywhere—the city, the steppes, and the cultivated plots alike—is sweetly fatigued by the long summer.

In the square at the city well, a big Ukrainian woman stood like a goddess in fitted boots on bare legs; she had brown eyes and that open, wide brow that is typical of Ukrainians and Poles. The late-afternoon distance of the southern horizon with the hills of the steppes barely visible gazed down the street, which ran from the square beneath the mountain into the valley. Having gone down this street, I turned onto a narrow alley between the petit bourgeois estates of the city's outskirts and crossed the meadow in order to climb the hill that rose behind it and then pass out onto the steppe. On the meadow, in the barns amid the blue and white cottages, flails flashed through the air: the very men who sang or chanted church-style in the summer nights so wildly and wonderfully were threshing here. The entire steppe, wherever the eye could see, was golden from the thick stubble. There was such a deep, soft dust lying on the wide path up that it seemed as if you were walking in velvet boots. And everything around—the steppe and the air—glimmered unbearably in the low sun. To the left of the path, on a cliff above the valley, stood a hut with peeling, whitewashed walls—the Tolstoyans' farmstead. I left the path and went there straight through the stubble. The farmstead itself turned out to be empty, both in and around the hut. I glanced in through an open window: a black mass of innumerable flies buzzed thickly on the walls, on the ceiling, and on the pots on the shelf. I looked through the gate to the barnyard—just the evening sun reddening against the dry dung. I went to the vegetable patch and discovered the wife of the younger Tolstoyan; she was sitting on the edge of the patch. I approached, and she didn't notice me, or pretended not to notice; she sat sideways, motionless, small, lonely, her bare legs stretched out, with one hand resting on the ground, the other holding a straw in her mouth.

"Good evening," I said, approaching. "Why are you so sad?"

"Stop a bit and sit down," she answered with a laugh and, tossing aside the straw, offered me a sunburnt hand.

I sat and stared: she was like a little girl guarding the vegetables! Hair bleached from the sun, a peasant shirt with a low-cut neck, an old black frock covering her femininely developed hips. Her small bare feet were dusty and, like her hands, dark and dry from sunburn. How can it be, I thought, that she goes barefoot on the manure and sharp grass! Since she was from our circle, where bare feet are never shown, her feet made me uncomfortable, and yet they attracted my gaze. Feeling my eyes, she tucked them underneath herself.

"And where are your menfolk?"

Again she laughed.

"Our men have both gone. One holy brother went down to the meadow to thresh. He is helping some poor widow. The other took a letter to the city for the great teacher: the standard weekly account of all our sins, temptations, and carnal struggles. In addition, the standard 'harassments,' which he's also obliged to report: in Kharkov 'Brother' Pavlovsk was arrested for the dissemination of pamphlets—against military service, of course."[40]

"You seem quite out of sorts for some reason."

"I'm sick and tired of it all," she said, shaking her head and throwing it back. "I can't do it anymore," she added quietly.

"Can't do what?"

"Can't do anything. Give me a cigarette."[41]

"A cigarette?"

"Yes, yes, a cigarette!"

I gave her one and lit a match; she quickly and clumsily began to smoke. Abruptly inhaling and exhaling the smoke from her mouth like a woman, she became quiet, gazing into the distance beyond the valley. The low sun still warmed our shoulders, and the long firm watermelons that lay beside us pressed their sides into the dry earth among the burning stakes, jumbled up, like snakes. . . . Suddenly she hurled the cigarette away and, putting her head on my knees, began to sob greedily. And as I comforted her, kissed her hair, which smelled of the sun, squeezed her shoulders, and gazed at her feet, I well understood why I had been coming to the Tolstoyans'.

And Nikolaev? Why did I need to go to Nikolaev? On my way, I wrote a little something: "Just left Kremenchug, evening. At the station at Kremenchug, on the platform, in the buffet, a multitude of people, southern swelter, southern crush of the crowd. In the compartments, too. Mostly Ukrainian women, all young, tan, fiesty, aroused by the road and the heat—heading somewhere 'down south,' to work. The blazing fragrance of bodies and village clothing, the way they chirp, drink, eat, and play with their quick, almond eyes, so excites me that it is even difficult to. . . ."

"A long, long bridge across the Dnieper, the red, dazzling sun through the window to the right, below and far into the distance the swell of turbid yellow water. On the sandbar, a multitude of women completely freely taking off all their clothes and swimming. There one throws off her shirt, sprints away, and awkwardly falls chest-first into the water, fiercely beating it with her legs. . . ."

"Already far beyond the Dnieper. The evening shadow on the empty hills, covered with mowed hay and stubble. For some reason, I thought of Svyatopolk the Accursed:[42] on the same sort of evening he rode on horseback along this valley at the head of a small regiment—where, what was he thinking about? That was a thousand years ago, and everything was as splendid on earth as it is now. No, that is not Svyatopolk there, that is some wild peasant, striding along on his sweaty horse in the shadows of the mountains, and behind him sits a woman with her hands tied behind her back, with disheveled hair and bare young knees, gritting her teeth, looking at the back of his head as he stares watchfully ahead. . . ."

"A moonlit, moist night. Through the windows the flat steppe, the black mud of the roads. The whole compartment sleeps, semidarkness, the butt of a thick candle in a dusty lantern. The dampness of the field blows in through the lowered window and mingles strangely with the thick, rank air in the compartment. Several women are sleeping on their backs, limbs akimbo. Lips wide apart, breasts underneath their nightshirts, firm hips in dresses and skirts. . . . One just now awoke and stared directly at me for a long time. . . . Everyone was sleeping, and it seemed that she was just about to call to me in a mysterious whisper. . . ."

The village where I went every Sunday lay close to the station, in a spacious and flat valley. One day I rode aimlessly all the way to this station, climbed down, and walked off. It was twilight. Ahead of me the huts whitened in their gardens, and closer by, a decrepit windmill darkened the pasture. A crowd stood by it, and beyond the crowd a violin wailed stirringly and dancing feet stomped. . . . . Later I spent several Sunday evenings standing in that crowd, listening to the violin and the stomping, and those long, choral songs until midnight; I would stand next to a buxom, red-haired girl with large lips and strangely bright yellow eyes. And taking advantage of the closeness, we immediately secretly held hands. We stood quietly, trying not to look at each other, knowing the terrible consequences if the locals noticed why some kind of city slicker had started to frequent the old windmill. The first time, we wound up next to each other by accident. Then, later, as soon as I drew near, she would turn to me right away, and feeling me beside her, she would take my hand for the whole evening. The darker it got, the firmer she held it and the closer she pressed to my shoulder. At night, when the crowd began to thin out, she hid behind the windmill. I quietly walked along the road toward the station, waited until nobody was left by the windmill, and ran back. We agreed on this without uttering a single word, standing silently below the windmill, silently, blissfully tortured. One night she walked me to the station. A half an hour remained until the train left, and in the station it was dark and quiet. Only the crickets chirped tranquilly in the distance, where a crimson moon rose above the dark gardens of the village. A freight car stood on the side tracks, its doors open. Horrified myself at what I was doing, I automatically pulled her toward the open compartment and climbed up. She jumped in after me and firmly embraced me. But I struck a match to look around, and jumped back in horror: the match illuminated a long, cheap coffin in the middle of the compartment. She skittered away goatlike, and I followed her. . . . Underneath the train she kept falling over and choking with laughter, kissing me with wild delight, and I couldn't figure out how to escape. After that, I never again appeared in the village.

In the fall we experienced that festive time which happened in the city at the end of each year—the meeting of all the zemstvo delegates of the district at the district congress. The winter also passed festively for us: there were performances of the touring Ukrainian theater with Zankovetskaya and Saksagansky, concerts of celebrities like Chernov, Yakovlev, Mravina, there were lots of balls, masquerades, parties by invitation only.[43] After the zemstvo congress, I left for Moscow to visit Tolstoy, and upon returning I gave myself over with particular pleasure to worldly temptations.[44] And they, those temptations, seriously changed our external life—it seems we didn't spend a single night at home. And our relationship also changed imperceptibly, worsened.

"Once again, you're becoming a different person," she said one day. "A real man. For some reason, you've started to wear that French-style beard."

"You don't like it?"

"No, it's all right. How everything changes, though!"

"Yes. And you've started to look like a young woman. You've lost weight and grown even prettier."

"And you're growing jealous of me again. There, I'm even afraid to admit something to you."

"What?"

"That I want to go to the next masquerade in costume. Something inexpensive and completely simple. A black mask and something black, thin, long. . . ."

"And what would that stand for?"

"Night."

"So we're getting Orel all over again? Night! That's pretty vulgar."

"I don't see anything vulgar or Orel-like in it," she answered dryly and independently, and I was frightened to sense that there really was something of the past in that dryness and independence. "You have simply started to be jealous again."

"Why have I become jealous again?"

"I don't know."

"No, you do know. Because you have started to drift away from me again. Because you want to be desired, to be showered with masculine ecstasies."

She smiled nastily.

"You shouldn't talk. You haven't parted from Cherkasova all winter."

I blushed.

"Come off it! So I'm guilty if she happens to go to the same places we go? It hurts me most that you've stopped being open with me, as if you have some secret. Tell me straight: what is it? What are you hiding?"

"What am I hiding?" she answered. "Sadness—sadness that we no longer have our former love. But why speak about that. . . ."

And, growing silent, she added, "And as for the masquerade, I'm ready not to go, if you don't like it. It's just that you are so strict with me, you call all of my dreams vulgar, deprive me of everything, and deny yourself nothing. . . ."

Again during the spring and summer I wandered a lot. At the beginning of autumn, I once again saw Cherkasova (with whom, until then, there really hadn't been anything) and discovered that she was moving to Kiev.

"I am abandoning you forever, my dear friend," she said, looking at me with her hawklike eyes. "My husband is waiting for me there. Would you like to accompany me to Kremenchug? In complete secrecy, of course. I have to spend a whole night there before I catch the boat. . . ."

29

That was in November, and even now I can still see and feel those immobile, dark weekdays in that remote Ukrainian city, its unpeopled streets, narrow wooden sidewalks, black gardens behind fences, and the naked height of the poplars along the boulevards, the empty city park and the boarded-up windows of the summer restaurant, the wet air of those days, the graveyard odor of decaying leaves—and my obtuse, aimless wanderings along those streets, in that park, and the same thoughts and recollections over and over again, always the same. . . . Recollections, they are so weighty, so horrible that there is even a special prayer appealing for salvation from them.

Then one fateful day her secret torments, about which she had only spoken once in a while, drove her mad. That day, my brother George returned from work late, and I even later. She knew that we would be getting home late, for the council was again preparing for the annual zemstvo congress. She remained home alone, not going out for several days as she did each month, and, as always at that time, she did not act like herself. She probably lay for hours on the sofa in our bedroom, feet tucked beneath her, as was her habit, smoking heavily; she had started to smoke some time earlier, ignoring my requests and demands for her to quit a habit so unbecoming to her. Most likely she kept staring straight ahead, and then she suddenly stood up and without crossing out anything wrote me several lines on a scrap of paper that my brother found on the commode in that deserted bedroom when he returned. Then she rushed to pack some of her things, casting the rest aside, strewing them about. For a long time, I couldn't bring myself to pick up and put away all those other things. By nightfall she was already far away, heading home, to her father. . . . Why didn't I go after her immediately? Maybe out of shame, and maybe because I knew very well her intransigence at certain moments of life. And in answer to my telegrams and letters I received at last only a couple of words: "My daughter has left and she has forbidden me to disclose her whereabouts to anybody."

I don't know what would have become of me at that point if my brother had not been with me (despite his helplessness and absentmindedness). He did not give me the note she had written right away, but prepared me first—very awkwardly. Finally he made up his mind, cried a little, and handed it to me. The note was written in a firm hand: "I can no longer stand watching you move farther and farther from me. I cannot continue to bear the insults which you relentlessly and ever more frequently hurl at my love. I cannot kill it within me, but at the same time I cannot but realize that I have stooped to the lowest limits of humiliation and disillusionment with all my stupid hopes and dreams. I pray to God that he may give you the strength to survive our separation, to forget me, and to be happy in your new, completely free life. . . ."

I read through the note in a glance and, feeling the earth was collapsing beneath my feet and the skin on my face turning to ice, growing taut, said quite insolently: "What else could I have expected? It's the usual story, these 'disillusionments'!"

After that, I had the courage to go into the bedroom and lie down on the sofa with an entirely indifferent countenance. At twilight, my brother cautiously looked in on me, but I pretended to be asleep. At a loss in the face of unhappiness of any kind and, just like our father, unable to endure it, he was quick to believe I was really asleep. Taking advantage of his obligation to return to the council meeting that evening, he dressed quietly and left. . . . I think I did not shoot myself that night only because I firmly decided that it didn't matter whether I did it then or the next day. When the room started to grow light from the moonlight milkiness shining through the window to the garden, I went out to the dining room, lit the lamp, and at the sideboard I drank one teacupful of vodka, then another. . . . Leaving the house, I walked along the streets. They were horrifying: silent, warm, moist, and all around, in the bare gardens and among the poplars of the boulevard, a white haze stood thickly, mixing with the moonlight. . . . But to return home was even more horrifying: to light a candle in the bedroom and to see by its light those discarded stockings, shoes, summer dresses, and that colorful robe that she wore when I would embrace her before bed, kissing her uplifted, submissive face, feeling her warm breath. Only being with her, by her, could have saved me from that horror of frenzied tears, and she was nowhere near.

Then came another night. The same meager candlelight in the still silence of the bedroom. A late-autumn nighttime rain seethed insistently beyond the black windows. I lay and stared into the front corner. In its recess hung an old icon, at which she used to pray before going to sleep: an old board, like cast bronze, the facing side painted vermilion, and on the red lacquered background the Mother of God in gold raiment, stern and humble, with large, black eyes outlined by a dark band. That awful band! And an awful, sacrilegious combination of thoughts: the Mother of God and she, that icon and all those articles of femininity she had tossed aside in her senseless haste to leave.

Then a week passed; another; a month. I had left work long ago, and avoided all contact with people. I worked through recollection after recollection, day after day, night after night—and for some reason I thought: in this way, at some time, in some place, some Slavic peasants dragged themselves "draggingly" along the forest roads from pothole to pothole, burdened with their heavy load of boats.

30

For another month or so I was tormented by her ubiquitous presence at home and in town. Finally I began to feel that I didn't have any more strength to endure this torture, and I decided to go to Baturino to spend some time there without worrying about the future.

It was very strange getting on that moving car, hurriedly embracing my brother one last time—to get on and tell myself that I was free as a bird again! It was a dark winter night without any snow, the wagon rumbled in the dry air. I planted myself and my bags in the corner by the door, sat, and recalled how I had loved to repeat to her a Polish proverb, "Man is created for happiness, like birds for flight," and I doggedly looked out the black window of the rumbling car so that no one would see my tears. Overnight to Kharkov. . . . And that other night, from Kharkov, two years before: spring, dawn, her deep sleep in the twilit car. . . . I sat tensely in the half-light under the lamp amid the heavy and crude crush of car, and awaited one thing—the morning: the people, their motion, a cup of hot coffee at the Kharkov station. . . .

Then there was Kursk, also evocative: a spring midday, lunch with her in the station, her joy: "For the first time in my life I'm having lunch in a train station!" Now, toward the evening of a gray and harsh frozen day, our immeasurably long and unusually ordinary passenger train stood in front of this station. An endless wall of third-class wagons, heavy and large, which set the Kursk-Kharkov-Azov railway line apart. I stepped out and looked around. The dark locomotive was so far out in front that it was scarcely visible. People were hopping down from the steps of the train with teapots in their hands—they were all equally repulsive—and rushing to the buffet for boiling water. . . . The others in my car also stepped out: a merchant, indifferent and exhausted by his unhealthy corpulence, and a terribly animated and infinitely curious guy whose common dry face and lips had revolted me the entire day. He cast a suspicious glance at me—I had also attracted his attention the entire day: "like, the young lord, just sits silent all day, must think he's God's gift!" But he still advised me in a friendly patter, "Bear in mind, they always got roast goose here incredibly cheap!"

I stood, thinking about the buffet where I could not go—the table at which we had once sat was there. The harsh Russian winter was already in the air even though there was still no snow. What sort of grave awaited me there in Baturino! The old age of my father and mother, the decay of my unhappy sister, a decrepit estate, a decrepit house, a barren, flat garden in which an icy wind blew, the winter barking of the dogs—in the winter, when that wind blows, their barking is somehow peculiar, unnecessary, empty. . . . The tail of the train was also endless. On the opposite side, behind the barrier of the platform, the barren poplars loomed like brooms, and behind the poplars, on the frozen cobblestone roadway, local cabbies awaited fares, their appearance speaking wordlessly of melancholia, of the ennui of this place called Kursk. Beneath the poplars on the platform women stood, muffled and girded with the ends of shawls, their faces blue from the severe cold. They called out obsequiously, invitingly—they were selling those same incredible geese: enormous, frozen, with purple skin. Those who had already gotten water cheerfully ran back from the station into the warm cars, happily suffering the cold, haggling like thieves with the women along the way. . . . With a hellish unhappiness the locomotive finally growled, threatening me with the continuation of the long trip. . . . Worst of all was that I didn't know where she had gone. If it hadn't been for that I would have overcome all shame long ago, caught up with her somewhere and made her come back to me, whatever the cost—her wild deed was no doubt a fit of insanity, and only shame prevented her, too, from repenting.

My new return to the paternal roof was unlike the one three years before. I looked at everything now through different eyes. And everything in Baturino seemed even worse to me than I had imagined on the way there: the wretched peasant huts, the coarse shaggy dogs, and the coarse iced-over gutters by the thresholds, covered with ferrous mud, clumps of this mud on the path to the garden, the empty yard in front of the gloomy house with sad windows, an absurdly high and heavy roof dating back to the days of my grandfathers and great-grandfathers, and two porches, darkened by awnings, whose wood had turned blue-gray from sheer age—everything was old, somehow neglected and pointless—and the pointless cold wind bent the tops of the ancient spruce that rose from behind the roof of the house, in the garden, pitiful in its winter nakedness. . . . In the daily life of the house I also found a transformation toward crude poverty—the cracks in the stove were smeared over with clay, the floors had been covered with horse blankets for warmth. . . . My father alone tried to counterbalance all this: thinner and smaller, completely gray, he was now always clean-shaven and smoothly combed, not dressed with his former carelessness—it was torture to see this austerity of old age and poverty—apparently for my sake, fearing my shame and unhappiness, he acted more cheerful and happier than everyone. Once, holding a cigarette in a trembling wizened hand and looking at me with tender sadness, he said, "Well, my friend, everything is fitting—both the anxiety and the sorrows, the joys of youth and the peace and tranquillity of old age. . . . What about those 'worldly blandishments'?" he said, his eyes laughing. "The devil take them all:

> In this empty hermitage
> Breathing the freedom of the fields
> In our tranquil cottage
> We taste the worldly blandishments. . . ."

Whenever I recall my father I always feel remorse—it always seems that I never appreciated or loved him enough. I always feel guilty that I knew so little about his life, especially his youth—I didn't bother to find out more when I had the chance! I still try to and cannot fully comprehend what kind of person he was—a person of a very specific age and a specific generation. The whole nature of his talent was useless, but of an incredibly wonderful lightness and variety. He possessed a lively heart and a quick mind. He understood everything, grasping it all at the slightest hint. Combined in him was a rare spiritual openness and spiritual secrecy, a character externally simple and internally complex, a sober, penetrating worldview and a singing, romantic heart. That winter I was twenty years old, and he was sixty. It is somehow hard to believe: I was once twenty years old, and my youthful strength, in spite of everything, was only just beginning to blossom! And his whole life was already behind him. Yet no one that winter understood like he did what was happening in my heart, no one else sensed that combination of sorrow and youth I carried inside.

That day we were sitting in his study. Snow already covered the ground, the sunny day was quiet and unassuming; illuminated by it, the snowy courtyard looked in affectionately through the low window of the study. The study was warm, smoky, and neglected; this neglect, coziness, and the permanence of the simple furniture had been dear to me since I was a child, and it was inseparable from all the habits and tastes of my father, from all my childhood memories of them and of him. After having spoken about "worldly blandishments," he set aside his cigarette, took down the old guitar from the wall, and began to play one of his favorite folk songs. His gaze became firm and merry, while something melted in him at the same time. In accord with the tender merriment of the guitar, with a sorrowful laugh he murmured of something dear and lost, how everything in life passes no matter what we do, and tears are of no use. . . .

Soon after my arrival I could bear it no longer and one day raced away, rushed headlong to the city. I returned that same day having accomplished nothing— at the doctor's house I was simply turned away. With the courage of despair I jumped down from the cabby's sleigh onto the familiar, now terrible porch. In horror I looked through the half-covered window of the dining room, where we had passed so many days sitting on the sofa—those first autumn days of ours!—and pulled the bell. . . . The door opened and I found myself face to face with her brother, who blanched and said in a clear voice, "Father does not wish to see you. And she, as you know, is not here."

This was the same high-school student who had carried on so furiously with Wolfy that autumn up and down the stairs. Now before me stood a gloomy, very swarthy young man in a white shirt of an officer's cut, in high boots, with the beginnings of a black moustache and an adamantly angry gaze in his small dark eyes, pale malachite because of his swarthiness.

"Please go," he added quietly, and it was evident how his heart was beating beneath his shirt.

And all the same I stubbornly waited every day that winter for a letter from her—I couldn't believe that she could be so stonily cruel.

31

In the spring of that same year I learned that she had come home with pneumonia and had died within a week.[45] I also learned that it had been her wish that her death be kept from me as long as possible.

❋ ❋ ❋

I still have to this day the brown morocco notebook that she bought for me as a gift with her first month's salary: that day, perhaps, was the most touching of her whole life. . . . On the first page of this notebook you can still read the few words that she wrote in giving it to me, with two mistakes, made in anxiety, haste, bashfulness. . . .

❋ ❋ ❋

Not long ago I saw her in my dreams, the only time in my whole long life without her. She was the same age as she was when we had our lives and youth in common, but in her face there was already the sublimity of faded beauty. She was thin, and it looked as though she was wearing mourning. I saw her dimly, but felt such a surge of love and joy, and such a physical and spiritual closeness as I have never felt for anyone.

Alpes-Maritimes
1927–1929, 1933

Notes

1. Stephanie Sandler, *Distant Pleasures: Alexander Pushkin and the Writing of Exile* (Stanford, 1989), p. 1.

2. Quoted in Julian Connally, *Ivan Bunin* (Boston, 1982), pp. 11–12.

3. For a full discussion of this tradition in Russian culture, see Andrew Baruch Wachtel, *The Battle for Childhood: Creation of a Russian Myth* (Stanford, 1991).

4. Philippe Lejeune, *Le Pacte autobiographique* (Paris, 1975), p. 14. Translation mine.

5. Janet Gunn provides an excellent definition of the bond that forms between reader and writer of an autobiographical text: "the reader experiences the autobiographical text as an occasion of discovery: of seeing in the text the heretofore unexpressed or unrecognized depth of the reader's self—not as a mirror image, nor even as a particular manifestation of some shared idea of selfhood, but as an instance of interpretive activity that *risks* display. . . . In a word, the reader discovers the *possibility* of selfhood through interpretation." *Autobiography: Towards a Poetics of Experience* (Philadelphia, 1982), p. 19.

6. Georges Gusdorf, "Conditions et limites de l'autobiographie," in *Formen der Selbstdarstellung* (Berlin, 1956), p. 115.

7. Quoted in A. I. Baboreko, *I. A. Bunin: Materialy dlia biografii* (Moscow, 1967), p. 48. For information regarding the substantial autobiographical subtext of *The Life of Arseniev*, see the notes to this edition.

8. In fact, according to a scholar who has had access to the manuscripts of the novel, Bunin took great pains to make the final version less autobiographical than the drafts: "while working on the novel (even including the final correction of the manuscript), Bunin strove to avoid excess autobiographicalism . . . Bunin made approximately a quarter of all the cuts in the manuscript at the expense of biographical detail." B. V. Averin, "Iz tvorch-

eskoi istorii romana I. A. Bunina 'Zhizn' Arsen'eva,'" in *Buninskii sbornik* (Orel, 1974), p. 68.

9. Vladimir Nabokov, *Speak, Memory* (New York, 1947), pp. 40–41.

10. There is only one other work of Russian émigré literature that can compete with Bunin's in this regard: Vladimir Nabokov's novel *The Gift*. In the first chapter of the novel, Fyodor Godunov-Cherdyntsev, the work's sometime first-person narrator and the displaced scion of a Russian gentry family, reads a review (actually, the review is a figment of his hopeful imagination) of his first book of poetry: a collection devoted to childhood. The putative reviewer describes the collection in terms that precisely define the peculiar mix of the general and the specific so characteristic of the pseudo-autobiography: "the author sought, on the one hand, to generalize reminiscences by selecting elements typical of any successful childhood—hence their seeming obviousness; and on the other hand he has allowed only his genuine quiddity to penetrate into his poems—hence their fastidiousness." Vladimir Nabokov, *The Gift* (New York, 1963), p. 21.

11. I. A. Bunin, "Kniga moei zhizni," *Literaturnoe nasledstvo*, vol. 84, bk 1, pp. 383, 384.

12. There are a number of possible sources for the name Arseniev. It is well known, of course, that this was Lermontov's mother's family name. Her estate was in Tula Province, not far from where Bunin grew up. I suspect, however, that the choice may have had more to do with a book published in Tula in 1903. Called *Rod Dvorian Arsenievykh 1389–1901*, it goes back into the "mists of time" to search for the origins of the real Arseniev family. It begins with a note from the editor that sounds not unlike the statement of Bunin's narrator: "The Arseniev clan is glorious, both due to the antiquity of its extraction and because of its loyal service to the Tsars and the Fatherland" (p. 1).

13. The theme of physical exile as a stimulus to childhood memories is also of crucial importance to the narrator of *The Gift*. In the first chapter, Godunov-Cherdyntsev wonders what it would be like to return someday to his family estate in the Russian countryside. Having considered this, he concludes: "But there is one thing I shall definitively not find there awaiting me—*the thing which, indeed, made the whole business of exile worth cultivating:* my childhood and the fruits of my childhood. Its fruits—here they are, today, already ripe; while my childhood itself has disappeared into a distance even more remote than that of our Russian North" (pp. 37–38; italics mine). The phrase "the fruits of childhood" refers to the book of poetry that Godunov-Cherdyntsev has produced.

14. I. A. Bunin, "K vospominaniiam o Tolstom," *Literaturnoe nasledstvo*, vol. 84, bk. 1, pp. 396–97.

15. Bunin quotes from Pushkin's 1829 lyric "A Winter Morning."

16. I. A. Bunin, "Rech' na iubilee 'Russkikh Vedomostei,'" *Literaturnoe nasledstvo*, vol. 84, bk. 1, p. 318.

Notes

In preparing these notes, the editor borrowed much from previous Russian commentaries on Bunin's novel, particularly those of L. Kotlyar and A. Baboreko.

1. Arseniev's creator, Ivan Alexeevich Bunin, was born on October 10, 1870 (old style), in the Central Russian city of Voronezh. He did not live permanently in the country until the family moved to his father's estate, Butyrki, in 1874.

2. Like the Arsenievs, Bunin's family was indeed an ancient one. Among his ancestors were men who had served under Russia's tsars from the fifteenth century. Also among his ancestors were the early-nineteenth-century Russian poets Vasily Zhukovsky and Anna Bunina.

3. Agni: the god of fire for the Vedic religion of India and Ceylon. Bunin traveled to Ceylon in 1911 and subsequently studied both Buddhist and Hindu religious practices.

4. The Bunins' estate, Butyrki, was situated in the Elets district of Orel Province, approximately 260 miles south of Moscow, the very center of the so-called black-earth district, Russia's traditional breadbasket. Like many other noble Russian families, Bunin's was quite impoverished by the 1870s.

5. Bunin's father, Alexey Nikolaevich Bunin, was born in 1824 and died in 1906. Arseniev's portrait seems to be quite close to the actual life and personality of Bunin's father.

6. Bunin's mother, Lyudmila Alexandrovna Chubarova, lived from 1835 to 1910.

7. The Day of the Forty Martyrs falls on March 22 according to the Russian church (Gregorian) calendar, which in the nineteenth century was twelve days behind the Western (Julian) calendar.

8. The day of St. Flor and St. Laurus falls on August 31 according to the Russian church calendar.

9. Vasilisa the Wise is the main character in one of the most popular of Russian fairy tales.

10. The Archpriest Avvakum (1620–82) was the leader of the Russian Old Believer movement. Avvakum and his followers objected to changes in church liturgical practice made in the 1650s during the reign of Tsar Alexey Mikhailovich. Avvakum was imprisoned and eventually burned at the stake for his dissident religious beliefs. During his imprisonment he wrote his most famous work, *The Life of the Archpriest Avvakum*. In this brilliant work, Avvakum reveals a great deal about himself and his views in the context of a vitriolic attack on the new church practices. The passage quoted by Arseniev comes toward the very beginning of the text, and is cited by Avvakum as one of the insights that led him to become a priest.

11. Alexey Konstantinovich Tolstoy (1817–75), historical novelist and

playwright, best known for his dramatic trilogy *The Death of Ivan the Terrible* (1866), *Tsar Fedor* (1868), and *Tsar Boris* (1870). This quotation, slightly mangled, as are most of Arseniev's, is from a letter to S. A. Tolstaya of September 27, 1867.

12. Baalbek is a ruin from the Hellenized culture of Syria dating from the second and third centuries A.D. It is located in present-day Lebanon. Paestum is in southern Italy, not far from Salerno, and is noted for its three Greek temples of the fifth and sixth century B.C. Although most English speakers associate "Kremlin" with the Moscow Kremlin, the word simply means a fortified citadel in a city. All Muscovite cities were built around a kremlin, within which a city's most important churches and palaces were grouped for protection.

13. "My little Antoinette had a large quantity of things from the colonies: a parrot, birds of all different colors in a cage, collections of shells and insects. In her mother's dressing table I saw amazing necklaces made of aromatic berries. In the attic, which we sometimes climbed up to, there were animal skins, strange bags and suitcases on which you could still read the addresses of cities in the Antilles." (The quotation is given in French in Bunin's text.) Pierre Loti was the pseudonym of the French writer Julien Viaud (1850–1923). Loti was an extremely popular writer around the turn of the century. This citation is from his novel *Le Roman d'un enfant* (1890).

14. Alexander Sergeevich Pushkin (1799–1837): Russia's most famous lyric poet and, to Russians, the greatest Russian writer. Arseniev quotes frequently from the works of Pushkin in the course of the novel. Here, he is referring to Pushkin's long mock-epic fairy tale in verse, *Ruslan and Lyudmila* (1820). This was Pushkin's first long work, and it catapulted him to fame. It remains popular among readers of all ages. All the quoted lines come from the prologue to the tale.

15. Nikolay Vasilievich Gogol (1809–52): Gogol, who came from Ukraine, was the leading prose writer in Russia in the first half of the nineteenth century. The works Arseniev recalls here are from Gogol's early collections, *Evenings on a Farm Near Dikanka* (1831–32), and *Mirgorod* (1835). "Old-World Landowners," the first story in the latter collection, is, on the surface at least, a sentimental idyll describing the life of a husband and wife on a provincial estate. On closer examination, however, it is not clear whether Gogol is idealizing or mocking the landowners. "A Terrible Vengeance" (from the second part of the former collection) is a gothic horror story set in Ukraine at some undefined past time and filled with apparitions, ancient curses, blood, and gore.

16. The ecclesiastical language of the Russian Orthodox church is not Russian (an East Slavic language) but Old Church Slavic, which is based on a medieval South Slavic dialect. To a Russian, particularly to one who goes to church frequently, the language of the mass is more or less comprehensible but not without difficulty.

17. Petr Lavrov (1823–1900): The leading theoretician of Russian populism. His most famous work was *Historical Letters*, an influential compilation and development of Western social and historical, mostly positivist, theory drawn from such figures as Proudhon, Comte, and Spencer. Under the influence of his theories, many young men and women from the educated classes attempted in the 1870s and 1880s to "go to the people" in order to repay what they saw as their debt to the masses of peasants. The peasants, however, generally proved unreceptive to these earnest attempts to improve their position in life and frequently turned the young idealists over to the police.

Nikolay Gavrilovich Chernyshevsky (1828–89): Chernyshevsky started his career as an aesthetician, literary critic, and radical theorist. He was best known, however, for his utopian novel *What Is To Be Done?* (1863), which was meant to provide a blueprint for radical change in Russian society. This novel became the bible of the Russian radical movement, and its leading characters were admired and emulated by generations of left-leaning Russians.

18. Bunin's youngest sister, Alexandra, was the model for Nadya.

19. Kiev catacombs: Kiev's Monastery of the Caves (Kievo-Pecherskaia lavra) is perhaps Russia's most celebrated monastery. It was founded in the eleventh century and got its name from the extensive system of underground catacombs in which some of its monks lived and prayed. The lives of its most famous monks were recorded in one of the earliest surviving works of old Russian literature, the so-called *Paterikon*.

20. Bunin attended the boys' school or "gymnasium" in Elets for a bit over four years. As opposed to the so-called practical schools (*real'nye uchilishcha*), the gymnasia were schools that provided the nineteenth-century version of a liberal education. The first Russian gymnasium was founded as early as 1726. In Arseniev's day, according to the new, more conservative rules introduced in 1871, the major emphasis was on Latin and Greek. The gymnasium consisted of eight grades, and boys usually began to study at the age of ten. In the early 1880s there were approximately 55,000 male gymnasium students in Russia. Female gymnasia were introduced only in 1862, but by the early 1890s, there were approximately the same number of male and female gymnasia in the country. Graduation from the gymnasium conferred the right of automatic admission to one of the universities and was considered necessary for most government and private-sector white-collar jobs.

21. After the death of Bunin's grandmother, the family moved from Butyrki (which was sold in 1883 to pay debts) to her nearby estate, Ozerki.

22. Upon graduation from the gymnasium, the class valedictorian received a gold medal. Bunin's eldest brother, Yuli, had graduated not from the Elets gymnasium but from the one in Voronezh. In 1881 he was expelled from the mathematics department of Moscow University for his involvement with the populist movement.

23. It is a Russian custom when anyone is departing on a long journey for all those present at the parting to sit in silence for a moment.

24. "The rosy dawn colored the east" is the first line of "The Cherry," an amazingly vulgar pastoral that, in contemporary editions, is marked "attributed to Pushkin." The first few stanzas of this dactylic dimeter are innocent enough and were evidently often included in anthologies for children. Presumably, the poem was cut off before the section in which the shepherd and shepherdess consummate their love and the title fruit's full potential is realized.

25. Bunin passed the examinations for entry into the Elets gymnasium in August, 1881.

26. The tailor and his wife are speaking Yiddish, the native language of the vast majority of the Jews in nineteenth-century Russia. Most Jews in the Russian Empire were required by law to live in the so-called Pale of Settlement, in what is today Ukraine, Poland, Lithuania, and Belorus. Elets lies well outside this area and so would have had very few Jewish inhabitants. Indeed, Arseniev is probably seeing Jews for the first time in his life.

BOOK TWO

1. Mamay was a military leader of the Tatars in the second half of the fourteenth century. He was defeated by the Russian forces led by Dmitry Donskoy at the Battle of Kulikovo in 1380, but he did inflict serious damage to the central cities of Russia.

2. Arseniev's gymnasium was in the town of Elets, which in 1889 had a population of approximately 36,000. Elets is an ancient city, first mentioned in the chronicles in 1146 as a border post of the dukedom of Ryazan. It was sacked first in 1395 by Tamerlane, and then by other Tatar armies in 1415 and 1450. Elets was an important and prosperous market town for the agricultural products of the Central Russian "black earth" region.

3. Unlike in Western Europe and America, in Russia the merchants belonged to a class entirely set apart from the rest of society. Their patriarchal, traditional Russian ways distinguished them from the westernized gentry class to which Arseniev belonged, while their relatively good education and affluence set them apart from the peasants. Merchants and their ways were the favorite subject for the Russian dramatist Alexander Nikolaevich Ostrovsky (1823–86), whose plays would likely have been the sole source of information young Arseniev might have had about the merchant class before moving in with the Rostovtsevs. In Elets, Bunin lived with a merchant family named Biakin.

4. "The sky in the hour of watch" is from the poem "The Hut" (*Izba*) by Nikolay Platonovich Ogarev (1813–77).

5. "Come ye O suffering" is from the poem "The Vagabond" by the well-known Slavophile Ivan Sergeevich Aksakov (1823–86).

6. "Under the vast tent" is from the poem "Russia" (*Rus'*) by Ivan Savvich Nikitin. Nikitin came from a background quite similar to Rostovtsev's, which may explain the merchant's fondness for this rather conventional poem.

7. Mikhail Dmitrievich Skobelev (1843–82) and Mikhail Grigorevich Chernyaev (1828–98) were two of the most famous and popular military heroes of Russia's military expansion during the 1870s and 1880s in the south and east. Skobelev was one of the heroes of the Russo-Turkish War of 1877–78, while Chernyaev was the leader of the Russian volunteers in Serbia in 1876, and then, from 1882–84, the military governor of Turkestan. The Tsar-Emancipator was Alexander II, who received this unofficial title for having liberated the serfs. Alexander Alexandrovich was Tsar Alexander III. He ascended the throne in 1881 after the assassination of his father and ruled until his death in 1894.

8. Aorists are a type of past tense in ancient Greek and Old Russian used to denote finished actions.

9. In Russian Orthodox churches, the altar is located behind a screen of icons called the iconostasis. The priests pass from the hidden area around the altar to the public area in front of the iconostasis through doors in the middle of it called *tsarskie vorota* ("the Tsar's gate" or "holy gate"). The iconostasis itself is a complicated construction rising from floor to ceiling and comprising rows of icons arranged in hierarchical order.

10. Prince Alexander Nevsky (1220–63), a warrior-king, was canonized for his efforts to defend the Russian lands militarily against the Swedes and diplomatically against the worst depredations of the Tatars.

11. In Book 6 of the Odyssey, Nausicaa rescues Odysseus after he has been washed ashore in her father's kingdom.

12. Arkhipovs and Zausailovs—these family names clearly do not belong to members of the gentry class.

13. Bunin's brother Yuli was arrested in 1884.

14. St. Peter and Paul Fortress was the first structure to be built after the founding of St. Petersburg in 1703. Initially it was meant as a fortification to protect the city from attack, but by the nineteenth century it fulfilled only ceremonial roles. The fortress itself was converted into a prison, and at various times in the nineteenth century many of Russia's most famous political prisoners were incarcerated there.

15. Nicholas I ruled from 1825 until his death in 1855. He was generally disliked by the Russian gentry, both for the severity with which he suppressed the gentry-led Decembrist revolt that took place after the death of his brother, Tsar Alexander I, and for the dour, bureaucratic cast of his reign.

16. These qualities are all derived from the attributes of Rakhmetov, one

of the characters in Chernyshevsky's novel *What Is to Be Done?* Rakhmetov is the incarnation of revolutionary sainthood and became a kind of idol for Russia's revolutionary youth.

17. Alexander Nikolaevich Radishchev (1749–1802) was the author of *A Journey from Petersburg to Moscow*. This book, in parts openly critical of the established order of things although by no means a call to revolution, aroused the ire of Catherine the Great after Radishchev published it in 1790. He was arrested soon after and sentenced to death, a sentence that was eventually commuted to ten years in Siberia. Radishchev later came to be seen as the first Russian revolutionary to have suffered for his beliefs. Chatsky is a character in Alexander Sergeevich Griboedov's (1785–1829) play *Woe from Wit* (1824). Chatsky is an angry young man who returns from abroad to find Russian society dominated by cretins, apple-polishers, and toadies. He roundly criticizes all around him—without, however, taking any kind of positive steps. Rudin is the main character of Turgenev's eponymous novel of 1856. Rudin is a stirring talker who sees many of the problems with Russian society; but, like so many male characters in Russian literature, he is unable to take any kind of action. After having disgraced himself at home, he dies futilely on the barricades during the Paris uprising of 1848. Alexander Ivanovich Herzen (1812–70), one of Russia's leading Westernizers and socialists, lived in exile after 1847, publishing his most influential journalism in his paper, *The Bell*, between 1857 and 1867. Ogarev was a leading "civic" poet and a friend and colleague of Herzen's.

18. "A coach, give me a coach": Chatsky's final words in *Woe from Wit*. These words are generally interpreted as a statement of his justified disgust with the established order of things and with Russia, and a sign of his desire to turn his back on it.

19. Pila and Sysoyka are characters in a novella called *The People of Podlipnoe* by the "raznochinets" writer Feodor Mikhailovich Reshetnikov (1841–71). The hard lot of these downtrodden characters of peasant origin brought tears to the eyes of populists like George Arseniev. The "raznochintsy" were people of lower-class background (often from priestly families) who made up the bulk of the Russian intelligentsia in the nineteenth century.

20. "Russia's joy is in drinking": the first recorded use of this dictum is in the oldest of the Russian chronicles, *The Tale of Bygone Years*. When the representatives of Islam try to convince Prince Vladimir to convert to their religion, they tell him that adherents of Islam are circumsized, eat no pork, and drink no alcohol. Vladimir answers that such a religion would not answer, for "Russia's joy is in drinking; we can't exist without it" (under the year 986 A.D.).

21. Saint Tikhon Zadonsky (1724–83).

22. The Pechenegs were a nomadic tribe of Turkic origin that lived

along the borders of the Kievan Russian kingdom. In the tenth and eleventh centuries they and the Russians fought constantly. By the thirteenth century this tribe had more or less disappeared.

23. "When in mysterious valleys": here, as elsewhere in the novel, Arseniev perceives his life through a filter of Pushkin's poetry. He cites the autobiographical lines provided by Pushkin's narrator (also called Pushkin) in *Eugene Onegin*, chapter 8, stanza 1. As usual, citing from memory as Russians almost invariably do, Arseniev makes a few mistakes. The lines should read: "In those days, in mysterious valleys, / In springtime, to the calls of swans, / Near waters radiant in the stillness, / To me the Muse began appearing." *Eugene Onegin*, trans. V. Nabokov (Princeton, N.J.: Princeton University Press, 1964), 1:281.

24. The Lyceum was the boarding school that Pushkin attended. Founded by Alexander I, it was housed on the grounds of the royal palace in Tsarskoe Selo, some twenty miles outside of St. Petersburg.

25. Here Arseniev characterizes his position through a borrowed line from the poetry of Mikhail Yurevich Lermontov (1814–41). In the 1838 lyric "Duma" (Cogitation), Lermontov characterizes his as a lost generation, unable to accomplish any important or necessary tasks. He ends with a prediction of how his generation will be seen by its descendants: "And with the severity of a judge and citizen, our descendant / Will insult our ashes with a sneering verse, / The mockery of a betrayed son / Over his ruined father."

26. "All the impressions of life" is a phrase from Pushkin's lyric of 1823, "The Demon."

27. Vasily Andreevich Zhukovsky (1783–1852): poet and translator best known for his ballads, elegies, and translations of English and German romantic poetry and the *Odyssey*. Evgeny Abramovich Baratynsky (1800–1844): one of the greatest of Russia's lyric poets who also wrote important narrative poems.

28. These lines are quoted from the poetry of Russia's greatest eighteenth-century poet, Gavrila Romanovich Derzhavin (1743–1816). They come from the beginning of his poem "Videnie Murzy" (The Vision of a Murza, 1783). As usual, they are slighly misquoted: in this case, Arseniev skips lines three and four of the poem and substitutes "shining" for a synonymous verb.

29. Sumarokov, Anna Bunina, etc. The list includes many of Russia's leading eighteenth- and early nineteenth-century poets. Alexander Petrovich Sumarokov (1718–77) was best known as the first writer of verse tragedy in Russia, but also as a moderately talented lyric poet. Anna Bunina (1774–1829), the first Russian woman poet of note, was allied for most of her career with the neoclassicist school. She is the least well-known of the poets in this list, and may well have been included because of her family connection with Bunin. Konstantin Nikolaevich Batyushkov (1787–1855) was the

leading Russian lyric poet of the first decades of the nineteenth century, known primarily for his elegant elegies. Dmitry Vladimirovich Venevitinov (1805–27) was one of the founders of the "wisdom lovers," a group of Russian metaphysical poets. Nikolay Mikhailovich Yazykov (1803–47) was a poet known primarily for his anacreontic verse. Ivan Ivanovich Kozlov (1779–1840) was a poet known for his elegies, translations, and his Byronic long poem, "The Monk."

30. The first line (slightly reordered) of Kozlov's poem "The Young Poet."

31. The first lines of an untitled 1821 verse of Baratynsky.

32. From Pushkin's 1820 lyric "The Nereid." Tauride was the ancient name for the Crimea.

33. Around Christmastime it was a Russian custom to go mumming. A similar scene is described by Tolstoy in *War and Peace*.

34. Friedrich Schiller's (1759–1805) dramas were extraordinarily popular in Russia throughout the nineteenth century. With their note of rebellion and their high emotion, his plays appealed to something in the Russian spirit. "Wilhelm Tell," which recounts the story of the liberation of Switzerland, appeared in 1804. The play became even more famous in Rossini's operatic version (1829).

BOOK THREE

1. *Faust,* the long poem by Johann Wolfgang von Goethe (1749–1832), was published in two parts, the first in 1808, the second in 1832.

2. Andrey Ivanovich Zhelyabov (1850–81) was a Russian revolutionary, one of the leaders and organizers of the "People's Will" party. He was executed for his part in the assasination of Alexander II. Konstantin Petrovich Pobedonostsev (1827–1907) was, after 1880, the Ober-Procurator of the Holy Synod. A leading advisor of Alexander III and Nicholas II, Pobedonostsev was considered the main architect of the reactionary policies of the government after the assassination of Alexander II and through the end of the century.

3. Hamlets, Don-Carloses, Childe Harolds, etc.–a whole string of more or less romantic, protesting heroes: Don Carlos, the hero of Schiller's eponymous play of 1787; Childe Harold, the hero of Byron's (1788–1824) first major long poem, "Childe Harold's Pilgrimage," published at intervals during the 1810s; Onegin, hero of Pushkin's novel in verse, *Eugene Onegin,* published at intervals in the 1820s; Pechorin, hero of Lermontov's novel *A Hero of our Time* (1840); and Bazarov, the main character in Turgenev's novel *Fathers and Sons* (1862).

4. From Zhukovsky's lyric "Neither happiness, nor glory here. . . ."

5. Heinrich Heine (1797–1856), major German lyric poet, quite popular in Russia.

6. Pushkin's description of the education of his hero (and his contemporaries) in chapter 1, stanza 5 of *Eugene Onegin*.

7. Semen Yakovlovich Nadson (1862–87): for a few years just before and after his poetic death from consumption, Nadson was by far the most popular lyric poet in Russia. His slick, dreamy, and sometimes angry poetry remained amazingly popular into the first decade of the twentieth century. "Let the poison of pitiless doubts expire in the tormented breast" is from an 1878 verse that begins "The shadows of night lay all around."

8. This entire section was composed by stringing together excerpts from Pushkin's and Lermontov's lyric verse. "Tossing up snowy whirlwinds": from Pushkin's 1825 lyric "A Winter Evening," which begins: "The snowstorm covers the sky with fog, / Tossing up snowy whirlwinds." "Yesterday I sat with a hussar . . . ": first lines of Pushkin's lyric "A Tear" (1815). "A withered flower, odorless . . . ": first lines of Pushkin's lyric "The Flower" (1828). "Speechless lies the blue steppe . . . ": from the concluding lines of the sixth and final stanza of Lermontov's poem "To the Memory of A. I. Odoevsky" (1839). "There's frost and sun—a lovely day / And still you doze, my lovely friend": first lines of Pushkin's lyric "A Winter Morning" (1829). "Is it warm? Has the blizzard stopped? . . . ": from the first section of Pushkin's lyric "It's winter. What can we do in the country?" (1829). "Hasten my fair one . . . ": from Pushkin's very early lyric (ca. 1814) "To Deliya." "Did you hear, beyond the copse . . . ": first lines of Pushkin's early lyric "The Singer" (1817). "A sad candle is burning beside me": from Pushkin's 1823 lyric "Night." "O Morpheus, give till morn a solace . . . ": first lines of Pushkin's 1816 lyric "To Morpheus." "The wood drops her crimson robe . . . ": first lines of Pushkin's 1825 lyric "19th of October." "How swiftly my new-shod horse": first lines of an untitled Pushkin lyric of 1828. "Ghostly behind the pinewood rose a misty moon": from an untitled lyric of Pushkin's that begins "The overcast day's gone dark" (1824). "By the shores washed by rumbling waves": from the same poem as the previous line.

9. "Walls miserably papered here and there . . . ": from a poem by N. M. Yazykov, "On the Death of A. S. Pushkin's Nanny."

10. The most prestigious venue for publication in nineteenth-century Russia was the so-called fat journal. These publications were, as a rule, monthlies that included sections of belles-lettres and criticism, as well as foreign and domestic cultural and political coverage.

11. "I came to life amid the waste of steppes . . .": first lines of a poem called "Recollections" by the self-taught Elets poet E. I. Nazarov, who served as the prototype for Bunin's character Balavin.

BOOK FOUR

1. General Boulanger (1837–91), French royalist general and political figure.

2. "With wondrous yearning filled" is from the last stanza of Lermontov's poem "Angel" (1831). Lermontov's early verse was indeed derivative, and this poem is quite conventional. *The Demon, Mtsyri,* "Taman," "The Oak Leaf" all date from Lermontov's short but intense mature period. In the paragraph that follows, Arseniev reviews Lermontov's life through his works, noting such milestones as his trips to the Caucasus, his long poem *Mtsyri* (from which the quotation "clasped like two sisters" is taken), and the novel *A Hero of Our Time* (which contains the story "Taman"). He ends with an evocation of Lermontov's fatal duel, fought in the shadow of Mount Mashuk in the northern Caucasus town of Pyatigorsk.

3. Novel by Lev Nikolaevich Tolstoy (1828–1910), published between 1863 and 1866.

4. Ossian was the invention of the Scottish poet James Macpherson (1736–96). Macpherson claimed to have discovered ancient Gaelic epics written by Ossian. Their romantic imagery captivated all of Europe, even after it was discovered that Macpherson himself had been the author.

5. Tolstoy published his novella *The Cossacks* in 1863. Yeroshka and Maryanka are both from the cossack village, and they personify the healthy, uncorrupted nature of the cossack "noble savages" in contrast to the Europeanized and spoiled Olenin. *Journey to Arzrum* is a liberally reworked travelogue in which Pushkin describes his journeys through the Caucasus with the Russian armies during the campaign of 1829. It was written and published in 1836.

6. Tolstoy's estate at Yasnaya Polyana was within striking distance of Bunin's family's estate, Ozerki.

7. These are all characters from *War and Peace*.

8. By the 1880s, Tolstoy had for the most part renounced writing fiction and had begun to develop his own version of Christianity, which would come to be called Tolstoyism. Bunin himself flirted with becoming a Tolstoyan in the 1890s, and his later interest in Buddhism may also have been influenced by the Buddhistic strain in Tolstoy's teaching. As late as 1937, Bunin wrote an investigation of Tolstoy's personality and beliefs entitled "The Liberation of Tolstoy" ("Osvobozhdeniia Tolstogo").

9. In 1889 and 1890, Bunin worked on the staff of the *Orel Messenger*. Orel itself is a pleasant provincial city, then the capital of Orel Province. At that time it had a population of roughly 70,000.

10. Kharkov is the major city of eastern Ukraine. Bunin spent approximately two months in Kharkov with his brother Yuli in 1889.

11. Nicholas Pirogov (1810–81) was a famous Russian physician. After

his death "progressive" doctors organized conferences in his name.

12. The word *byk* in Russian means "ox."

13. In this chapter Bunin attacks the Russian intelligentsia. An "intelligent," in one historian's definition, is "someone not wholly preoccupied with his personal well-being but at least as much and preferably much more concerned with that of society at large . . . one's level of education and class status are of secondary importance . . . by the 1890s [to be an intelligent meant] to stand in staunch opposition to the entire political and economic system of the old regime" (Richard Pipes, *Russia under the Old Regime* [New York: Scribners, 1974], pp. 252–53). The intelligentsia's narrow-minded attitude and general intolerance naturally caused it to be roundly disliked not only by many Russian writers of a conservative point of view (like the mature Dostoevsky and Tolstoy), but also by more tolerant writers like Chekhov and, following Chekhov, Bunin.

14. Vladimir Galaktionovich Korolenko (1853–1921) was a beloved writer in Russian "progressive" circles for his optimistic stories showing the triumph of the human spirit, particularly among the lower classes. Makar is the main character in Korolenko's story "Makar's Dream" (1885). Nikolay Nikolaevich Zlatovratsky (1845–1911) was a populist fiction writer who concerned himself with the life of Russia's peasants. Later in life he became influenced by Tolstoyism. Presumably, George Arseniev's friends read his earlier realistic stories about peasant life. Anton Pavlovich Chekhov (1860–1904) was vilified by the "progressive" Russian intelligentsia of the 1890s because his stories did not contain an overtly "progressive" message. Tolstoy came under attack in the same circles for his religious searchings (the intelligentsia were all, of course, atheists) and for his doctrine of nonresistance to evil.

15. *Notes of the Fatherland* was one of the leading Russian fat journals from its inception in 1818 until its suppression in 1884. It went through many editorial changes, but the period described here is that between 1868 and 1884, when the journal was controlled by the left-leaning poet Nikolay Alexeevich Nekrasov (1821–78) and the satirist Mikhail Evgrafovich Saltikov-Shchedrin (1826–89).

16. From a poem by N. A. Nekrasov, "Contemporaries."

17. A quotation from the famous revolutionary poem and song "Woman of Warsaw" (1897) by G. M. Krzhizhanovsky (1872–1959).

18. From a song entitled "The Workers' Marseillaise" by the populist P. L. Lavrov.

19. From N. A. Nekrasov's poem "Knight for an Hour."

20. The opening lines of a poem by N.M. Yazykov entitled "Song" (1827).

21. From Nekrasov's poem "Poet and Citizen."

22. "Little Judas" is a character in Saltykov-Shchedrin's dark satirical

novel *The Golovlev Family* (late 1870s), while "Stupidville" is the name of the city that symbolizes Russia in his *History of a Town* (1869).

23. Vissarion Grigorievich Belinsky (1811–48) was Russia's first influential literary critic. He was revered in leftist circles both for his embracing of realist writing and for having been perhaps the first true Russian intelligent, the forebear of Chernyshevsky, Dobroliubov, and so on.

24. *The Tale of Igor's Campaign* is the greatest work of Old Russian literature. Probably composed in the late twelfth century, it was discovered only in the late eighteenth century. It describes a disastrous campaign against the Polovtsians undertaken by Igor of Novgorod-Seversk in 1185.

25. The Malakhov Mound was a Russian fortified position on the southern side of the city of Sevastopol. It was taken by French troops after a furious assault in August 1855. Its capture weakened the city, which fell soon afterward.

26. The Karaim are a small fundamentalist Jewish sect that lived from unknown times on the Crimean peninsula.

27. In the section that follows, Arseniev travels through Ukraine under the sign of *The Tale of Igor's Campaign,* which is the source of all of the quotations in this chapter.

28. Kostroma, Suzdal, Uglich, and Rostov the Great: after the destruction of the Kievan kingdom by the Tatars in the thirteenth century, the only more or less independent Russian principalities were those in the North, along the upper reaches of the Volga River. The greatest flowering of civilization in these areas occurred after the time described in *The Tale of Igor's Campaign,* and the style of their civilization was quite different.

29. Nikolay Semenovich Leskov (1831–95) was another of the brilliant writers who hailed from the Orel area. Overshadowed during his lifetime by Tolstoy, Turgenev, and Dostoevsky, Leskov came to be appreciated in the twentieth century for his brilliant style.

30. The prototype for Lika was Varvara Vladimirovna Pashchenko, with whom Bunin fell in love while working for the *Orel Messenger.*

31. The young hussar was Prince Nikolay Nikolaevich Romanov (1856–1929). From 1915 to 1917 he was the commander-in-chief of the Russian army. After the Revolution he emigrated to France. He was accompanying the body of his father, also Nikolay Nikolaevich Romanov (1831–91), the younger brother of Tsar Alexander II.

32. Bunin wrote the majority of *The Life of Arseniev* in a villa near Grasse in the south of France.

BOOK FIVE

1. Ivan Sergeevich Turgenev (1818–83), one of the leading Russian novelists of the nineteenth century, was brought up and lived for many years on his estate not far from Orel. His novel *A Nest of the Gentry* was written in 1859. It centers on the unconsummated love of Liza and Lavretsky (both mentioned later in the paragraph). Lemm is also a character in the novel. Arseniev's professed indifference to Turgenev is ironic, since of all nineteenth-century Russian writers Turgenev's prose style is closest to his own.

2. During Pushkin's exile from St. Petersburg (1820–26) he visited the Crimean seaside resort town of Gurzuf. This town is only about twenty miles from the Romanov palace, Livadiya.

3. Petr Ilich Tchaikovsky (1840–93) composed more than fifty art songs (*romansy* in Russian). According to the complete edition of his songs, however, none is entitled "Morning."

4. Johann Peter Eckerman (1792–1854) was Goethe's secretary toward the end of the great writer's life. His "Conversations with Goethe During the Final Years of His Life" remains a major, although by no means entirely reliable, source of information about Goethe's worldview.

5. Nikolay Alekseevich Nekrasov (1821–78) was by far the most renowned Russian poet of the mid-nineteenth century. His prosaic verse was imbued with the type of progressive civic spirit that was expected from Russian literature in that period.

6. Arseniev's catalog represents a cross-section of oppositional views to official policies of the reign of Alexander III. After the assassination of the relatively liberal Alexander II in 1881, a period of reaction set in. The liberal intelligentsia, to whose camp the doctor certainly would have belonged, decried this tendency. Simultaneously, Tolstoy and his followers were propagating a religion that called for nonresistance to evil and disengagement with society. Certain aphorisms by the stoic Roman emperor/philosopher Marcus Aurelius (A.D. 121–80) were looked upon favorably by the Tolstoyans.

7. As is usually the case throughout the novel, Arseniev's views are shaped not by reading and thought, but by intuitive revelations provided by his reading. Here he provides a jumbled catalog of characters from Tolstoy's novels and short stories, including *War and Peace* (Pierre Bezukhov and Anatoly Kuragin), "Kholstomer or the Story of a Horse," "The Death of Ivan Ilich," etc., as well as from some of Tolstoy's nonfictional work.

8. Arseniev is here misquoting a couple of lines from the ballad "Svetlana" by Vasily Zhukovsky (1783–1852).

9. These lines of poetry are a slight misquotation from a lyric by the Russian poet Afanasii Fet (1820–92) entitled "To a Songstress." (1857) Fet, a good friend of Tolstoy's, was one of the few Russian poets of the second

half of the nineteenth century to continue the lyric tradition that had been characteristic of the first third of the century. By quoting from Fet, as opposed to one of the more civic-minded Russian poets, the young Arseniev is indicating his alignment with the pure Russian lyric tradition, which was on the brink of a major comeback in the 1890s. Bunin's own poetry (on which his initial reputation was based) was noticeably influenced by Fet.

10. Arseniev quotes the first stanza of another poem by Fet, an untitled lyric of 1862.

11. These lines are taken from a poem by Yakov Polonsky (1819–98) entitled "Winter Journey." Polonsky was another of the rare "aesthetic" poets of mid-nineteenth-century Russia. In his preference for Fet and Polonsky, Arseniev is making a strong statement about his literary taste.

12. This couplet is taken from another poem of Fet's, an untitled lyric of 1885. As usual, Arseniev misquotes the poem, whose first line should read: "The ray of sun through the lindens was hot and high."

13. This is the first stanza of an untitled lyric of 1842 by Fet. The rest of the poem goes on to describe the lyric subject's feeling of alienation from his beloved. Arseniev's use of a poetic subtext to make his feelings known is typical of his tendency to experience the world through literature, but the hint is clearly not one that Lika is capable of understanding.

14. Russian kitchen ovens were built in such a way that there was a large platform above the oven itself. This was always the warmest place in the house, a favorite sleeping spot.

15. Arseniev provides a catalog description of some of the most famous roles from commonly performed plays in Russia in the late nineteenth century. Tit Titych Bruskov is a character in the comedy "Your Party—My Headache" (1856) by Alexander Ostrovsky (1823–86). Ostrovsky was Russia's leading dramatic writer of the nineteenth century, producing serious drama as well as comedies. His comedies dealt with the Russian merchant milieu, and Tit Titych is one in a long line of self-important Russian merchants who appear in his plays. Khlestakov is the main character in Nikolay Gogol's (1809–52) play "The Inspector General"; his servant is named Osip; the mayor is that of the town in which the action of the play takes place. Repetilov, Famusov, and Chatsky are all characters in the verse comedy "Woe from Wit," by Alexander Griboedov (1795–1829).

16. Here Arseniev lists the most famous and overperformed operas on the Russian provincial stage in the late nineteenth century: *Rigoletto* by Giuseppe Verdi (1831–1901); *A Life for the Tsar* by Mikhail Glinka (1804–57; the main character in the opera is Ivan Susanin); and *Rusalka* by Alexander Dargomyzhsky (1813–69).

17. In the nineteenth century it was common to revise various Russian novels as one-person vehicles for famous actors or to excerpt sections of larger plays. Arseniev here notes a stage version of Gogol's short story "Diary of

a Madman," an extract from Ostrovsky's *Poverty's No Vice* (in which Lyubim Tortsov is a main character), and a version of Marmeladov's monogue drawn from Dostoevsky's *Crime and Punishment*. It is not clear which play or novel the actress's scene is derived from.

18. At the time this novel is set Chekhov was unquestionably the leading Russian prose writer. The fortunate Arseniev would have been reading such masterful stories as "The Man in the Case," "Gooseberries," "About Love" (all from 1898) or "The Darling" or "The Lady with the Little Dog" (1899). It is also likely that he read "The Peasants" (1897), a story whose brutal naturalistic pictures of life in the Russian village would later be echoed in Bunin's own novella "The Village" (1909–10).

19. Soshnye writings were accounts of landholdings prepared for the purposes of taxation in Muscovy from the fifteenth through the seventeenth centuries.

20. As we already know, Arseniev's reading tastes run to the poetry of the so-called Golden Age, the 1820s and 1830s. The titles mentioned here are among the most famous journals and almanacs of that period.

21. A. N. Radishchev's *Journey from Petersburg to Moscow* (from which the citation is taken) is a strange work to have caught Arseniev's fancy. It is written in a heavy, highly archaic style, and was known for its "progressive" politics, an excessive veneration of which Arseniev has castigated before. The quotation comes from the first page of the work.

22. The *skoptsy* (castrates) was a religious sect that had broken off from the heretical sects called *khlysty* (from *khlyst*: whip) in the late eighteenth century. They believed that the carnal desires of the flesh are the cause of all the world's evil and castrated themselves to avoid them. They and other sects were frequently persecuted by the government. But at the same time the sects, with their closed communities and work ethic, made up a disproportionate percentage of Russia's merchant community.

23. Aleksey Sergeevich Suvorin (1834–1912) was the most famous and successful Russian book publisher from the late 1870s to the turn of the century. His firm published cheap editions of Russian classics, and it held a monopoly on the sale of books in Russia's railroad stations.

24. Lev Tolstoy's trilogy *Childhood* (1852), *Boyhood* (1854), and *Youth* (1857) marks the first example of a Russian pseudo-autobiography devoted to childhood and is, to a great extent, the model for Arseniev's work (see the Introduction to this edition for more details).

25. Arseniev mentions here a random collection of important events in old Russian history from the 980s to the mid-eleventh century. According to the "Primary Chronicle," the Kagan Vladimir, having decided to convert to a monotheistic religion, sent emissaries from his court to the representatives of Judaism, Islam, and Eastern and Western Christianity in the early 980s. In 988 he and his court converted to Byzantine Christianity and threw the idol

of Perun (the Slavic god of thunder) into the Dnieper. Yaroslav the Wise was one of Vladimir's sons, and ruled as Grand Prince of Kiev from 1019 to 1054. His reign is generally considered to be the highpoint of the Kievan Russian kingdom. After his death, the kingdom fell into a constantly squabbling mass of princedoms ruled by Yaroslav's descendents. Although they theoretically owed allegiance to the Grand Prince of Kiev, they frequently failed to come together, even when outside pressures should have forced them to do so. Vsevolod Big Nest was prince of Novgorod from 1177 to 1212.

26. Smolensk was the capital of Smolensk Province in Western Russia. This ancient city is located some 350 miles from Moscow and in the period described had a population of approximately 40,000.

27. Vitebsk was the capital of Vitebsk Province and lies some five hundred miles west of Moscow. The city is an ancient one, dating back to at least the eleventh century, when it was an important center of the Polotsk Principality. In the late nineteenth century, Vitebsk was a city of approximately 60,000, almost half of whom were Jewish.

28. Polotsk was the former capital of the Polotsk Principality, a major city in the eleventh to thirteenth centuries. By the end of the nineteenth century, however, it had fallen on hard times, and its population was approximately 20,000.

29. In 1892, Bunin moved with V. V. Pashchenko to Poltava in central Ukraine, where his brother found him a job with the statistics bureau. Bunin spent the next two years in this pleasant provincial city.

30. Gogol lived in Poltava from 1818 to 1820. He was born and raised not far from the city, and his early stories are all set in this area. The line cited here is from the beginning of the story "The Sorochinsk Fair," the first story in Gogol's first collection, *Evenings on a Farm Near Dikanka*.

31. Letter (slightly misquoted) from Gogol to Zhukovsky dated October 30, 1837.

32. Taras Shevchenko (1814–61) is considered the greatest Ukrainian poet, the creator of the modern idea of Ukraine, and the national prophet. The quoted lines are from a short poem entitled "To Osnov'ianenko" (1840).

33. Notebook entry from Gogol, *Polnoe sobranie sochinenie*, vol. 7 (Moscow, 1951).

34. Goethe, from *Dichtung und Wahrheit*.

35. Bakhchiseray was the capital of the Crimean Khanate until the destruction of the khanate by the armies of Catherine the Great in 1783. The palace was constructed in the early sixteenth century. Arseniev probably got most of his information about Bakhchiseray from Pushkin's Byronic poem "The Fountain of Bakhchiseray" (1822).

36. Gogol notebooks, *Polnoe sobranie sochinenie*, vol. 7 (Moscow, 1951), p. 377.

37. Vseslav was one of the sons of Yaroslav the Wise. He appears in many

entries in the Chronicle from the mid-eleventh century, constantly fighting wars with his brother princes as they jockeyed for control of the Russian kingdom.

38. Tolstoy's story "Family Happiness" was published in 1859. It tells of Masha, a young orphaned noblewoman who is brought out of the depression she falls into after her mother's death by Sergey, an older neighbor and friend of the family. Eventually, she realizes that she loves Sergey, and they marry. However, their love is destined to undergo many trials as Masha grows and develops. Ultimately, the story ends with their having achieved the happiness promised by the title. Lika may very well have been reading the story precisely in search of such happiness, but the passages she chose come from a part of the story in which Masha is expressing grave doubts as to the future of her relationship with Sergey.

39. By the 1890s, many young Russians decided to heed the teachings of Tolstoy and go to the people. They did not, however, do what the populists of the 1870s and 1880s had done. Instead of trying to educate the peasants, they strove to emulate them (or at least an idealized image of them); they moved to the countryside, set up communal subsistence farms, and preached pacifism and civil disobedience. At around the turn of the century, Tolstoy was one of the most famous people in the world; Tolstoyan communities were founded in many countries, and adherents continually sent the "sage of Yasnaya Polyana" detailed descriptions of their activities.

40. Most of Tolstoy's religious writings could not be published in Russia due to the strict ecclesiastical censorship. Instead, they were published abroad, smuggled back into Russia, and distributed by Tolstoy's followers.

41. Among the tenets of Tolstoyism was asceticism, including the eschewal of alcohol, tobacco, and meat. This is why Arseniev seems so shocked by the woman's request for a cigarette.

42. Svyatopolk the Accursed was one of the sons of Vladimir, the first Russian prince to convert to Christianity. After the death of his father, Svyatopolk conspired to seize the throne for himself. In his drive for the throne, he killed three of his brothers (Boris, Gleb, and Svyatoslav), only to lose out to another brother, Yaroslav the Wise. According to the Chronicle (which was, of course, written at the behest of the winning brother), Svyatopolk suffered untold privations and eternal damnation for his fratricidal behavior.

43. M. K. Zankovetskaya (1860–1934) was a leading Ukrainian actress, one of the founders of the first Ukrainian theater in Kiev. P. K. Saksagansky (1859–1940) was a popular actor who frequently toured the provinces both as actor and director. E. E. Chernov (1842–1904) was also a famous actor, while L. G. Yakovlev (1858–1919) and E. K. Mravina (1864–1914) were leading opera singers.

44. As noted earlier, Bunin himself flirted with Tolstoyism in the early 1890s, although he seems never to have been a full-fledged believer.

45. Varvara Pashchenko, the prototype of Lika, left Bunin in 1894. She did not die, however, but married an acquaintance of Bunin's. The former lovers remained friends for years afterward. This is just one example of Bunin's willingness to play with autobiographical facts in order to create a more effective narrative for his fictional hero.